TALL, SILENT AND LETHAL

TALL, SILENT AND LETHAL

R.L. MATHEWSON

This is a work of fiction. All of the characters, organizations and events described in this novel are either products of the author's imagination or are used fictitiously.

Edited by R.L. Mathewson, Jessica Atchison and Jodi Negri

Cover designed by Rochelle McGrath

e-book ISBN: 9781310833557
ISBN: 1505436907
ISBN 13: 9781505436907

OTHER TITLES BY R.L. MATHEWSON:

The Cursed Hearts Series:
Black Heart

Nonfiction Titles:
How to Write, Publish and All That Good Stuff...

This book like every book that I have ever written or ever will is dedicated to my children, Kayley and Shane who have been with me through this journey from day one.

This book is also dedicated to the readers for their support, kind words and making me believe that anything is possible. Thank you.

Pytes live in a world where their immortality, strength, speed and ability to withstand the sun should make them gods. Instead, they are forced to live in fear. Their ability to create a stronger, more powerful army of vampires has Masters all over the world waging wars to find them and Sentinels determined to stop them.

Even as they fight for their freedom they know that one day they'll have to choose a side....

PROLOGUE

Herrmann Manor
Mainz, Germany
1941

"Your sister tells me that you've been fighting again."

Christofer's hand stilled in mid-slash over the back-side of the parchment that he'd been forced to reuse, the fresh charcoal lines blurred by the stains seeping through the thin material from the other side. After a slight hesitation, he continued making the line, duplicating it from the image seared in his mind, only making the jawline longer than befitted a six year old girl's face.

"There's nothing much to tell, Father," he said, shifting slightly closer to the fireplace so that he could see better, but far enough away so that the heat wouldn't curl the parchment in his hands.

"I see," his father mused as Christofer registered the sounds of one of the crystal decanters on the side table being picked up. "Did you at least win?" his father asked, sounding thoughtful as he poured whiskey into a crystal glass.

"No, Father," Christofer answered, not bothering to look up as he reached for the glass that he knew was waiting for him.

"But you didn't run," his father clarified as he lowered himself to sit by Christofer in front of the fire.

Chuckling, Christofer looked up as he took a sip of whiskey, welcoming the soothing amber fire down his throat as he studied his father, still in his well-tailored suit, sitting by him on the unforgiving stone floor of the great hall. In any other castle it would have been an unusual sight to see the lord of the manor sitting in his finest on the cold stone floor, but not here.

His earliest memory was of his father with an indulgent smile, sitting down by his side late one night after he'd sneaked out of the nursery to draw horrible chalk figures on the smooth gray stones that made up the great hall's floor. Since that night, his father and he had created a tradition of sorts. He would sneak out of his room when the need to rip the images that haunted his thoughts out of his head and place them onto parchment became too much. For his part, his father would sit by him, quietly watching him work while he pretended that the most taxing responsibility in his life was to sit by his son and watch him make the images inside his head come to life.

"No, Father, I certainly didn't run," he said, shifting a bit and trying not to wince when the movement tugged at his sore ribs.

"Good," was all his father said as he took a small, satisfying sip from his glass.

Christofer didn't bother to tell his father that the boys had all been younger than him by a good five years, or that they'd taken great pleasure in tormenting the great Lord's son, the village freak as they liked to call him when his father wasn't around to hear them, and he never would. His father liked to pretend that he was a normal sixteen-year old boy on the cusp of manhood and Christofer cherished that feeling too much to give it up even if it meant that his father would put an end to his daily torment.

Moments like this, late at night when the only sounds came from the crackling fire, the parchment shifting on his lap, and the occasional sounds of a servant making his way through the halls lighting candles and adding wood to the fires that burned low throughout the house, they could pretend that Christofer had his entire future waiting for him. They could pretend that he would be leaving for University soon and that it would be time to talk to him about all those things that young men needed to know before they started to make their way into the world, but that time would never come for them.

Christofer was a sixteen-year-old man stuck in the body of a ten-year-old boy, a weak ten-year-old boy. There would be no discussions of which University to send him to, what he should study so that he could ensure the continued survival of his family's wealth. There would be no talks about women, serious or teasing, because no woman in her right mind would have anything to do with a man that was destined to remain a boy for the rest of his life, no matter how rich and powerful his family was.

He was nothing more than a burden to his family. His birthright passed down to him from his mother would be the only thing that would remain in his grasp. Everything else would go to the babe in his stepmother's womb, God willing this one was a boy. Otherwise all their hopes to carry on his father's line would rest with six-year-old Marta and the man that she would one day marry.

It was a humiliating existence for a first son, for any son for that matter. He honestly couldn't imagine anything more humiliating than knowing that one day he would be able to pass for his younger sister's child. He would never be a man and they all knew it....

"Is this Marta?" his father asked, undoubtedly knowing where his self-pitying thoughts were taking him.

"Yes," Christofer said, placing his glass carefully on the stone floor before he continued drawing, needing an escape more than ever even if it only came from drawing on a piece of used parchment.

"She's going to be beautiful," his father said with a fond smile as he shifted slightly to the side so that he could get a better look.

"Yes, she is," Christofer agreed with a bittersweet smile as he gazed down at the woman with kind eyes and a sweet smile, relieved that this curse, whatever it was, had passed his sister over completely.

One day she would have the life that she deserved, be the woman that she was meant to be, and not stuck frozen in time like him. He was sure of it. She was growing at a normal rate, appearing to be a healthy six year old girl that loved to follow her older brother everywhere and bug him at every opportunity for stories, drawings and tea time with dolls. She was, much to his relief and to the relief of his father, normal.

"What's on the other side?" his father asked, making everything in him go still and making him wish that he'd chosen any other parchment than the one on his lap.

"It's nothing," Christofer answered, but it was too late. His father, always curious about his work, was already reaching out and taking the parchment out of his trembling fingers and turning it over.

For a moment his father didn't say anything. He didn't have to, the resemblance to Christofer's mother and her father was unmistakable. Unwilling to look at the man that he would never be, Christofer picked up his glass and finished off his drink, wishing that his body wasn't so damn small so that he could handle more than one glass of whiskey.

"This will be you one day," his father said, his tone firm as though he truly believed it.

"No," Christofer said, shaking his head as he looked at the fire, "it won't."

"The doctors could be wrong," his father quickly explained, repeating an old argument that was better left off dead. "Once the war is over we could bring you to Berlin, Austria, London and maybe to America to-"

"To what, Father?" Christofer asked, wishing that his father would finally give up the dream that he would one day wake up and be normal like everyone else. "To spend a fortune? To get poked and prodded and called a freak in a dozen new languages before they finally turn us away with the news that there is nothing that they can do?" he asked, hating the bitter edge to his voice.

"They could-" his father pushed, his tone as desperate as Christofer's was bitter.

"They can make me grow?" he asked, chuckling coldly as he reached over and took the parchment from his father's hands and flipped the image over so that he didn't have to see what should have been and continued to work on Marta's image.

"Maybe," his father said softly although they both knew that he wasn't bringing up traveling because of his deformity.

His father wanted to send him away with his sister and stepmother before Hitler's men finally came knocking on their door. It was only a matter of time now before that knock came and when it did, they could only hope that his father had managed to get enough of the women and children from the village sent off before it was too late.

They'd all heard the rumors and even though they prayed that was all they were, rumors, they couldn't behave as though they were blind to the truth. They'd seen the soldiers marching past their village, seen the arm bands marking Jews, communists and traitors. They knew something was going on and they knew that it was only a matter of time before this war and Hitler's cause plowed through their town, leaving it in shambles.

For the past year, his father had been carefully, and as quietly as possible, sending villagers out of Germany. It was a slow process, but by the end of the year they should have the village deserted and when that time came, they would leave under the guise of visiting relatives in

London. Only they most likely would never be coming back, not while a tyrant like Hitler ruled them.

"I think it would be best if I sent you and your sister to stay in London," his father said quietly.

The charcoal in Christofer's hand stilled once again. "It's not necessary," he said, dreading leaving his father behind as much as he dreaded being called a freak somewhere new.

"I believe it is very necessary, Christofer," his father said with a sad smile marking his tone.

"But, Father-" he started to argue even though he knew that it was pointless. His father might be tolerant of him and his condition, but he was still his father and his word would be obeyed.

"I'm off to bed," his father said, carefully getting to his feet. "Try not to fall asleep in front of the fire," his father said with a forced smile.

"I'm almost done," he lied, knowing that he'd rather work until exhaustion took over instead of lying in his bed, forced to think about all the things that were out of his control.

"Just promise me one thing," his father said quietly as he stood over him, forcing Christofer to look up and meet the eyes that once held a great deal of humor and now only held sorrow.

"Anything, Father," he swore without a moment's hesitation.

"Promise me that you'll always watch over your sister."

Christofer forced a smile, because he knew that his father wouldn't be asking this of him unless he'd already settled the plans to send them away.

"Even when she's being a brat and in desperate need of a spanking," he promised, earning a chuckle from his father, the last sound of amusement that his father would ever make as it turned out.

ONE

New York
Williams Mansion
Present Day…..

"Izzy, he's going to find out," Kale said, sighing as the woman in the bed next to him pulled the sheet off her head so that she could give him what she probably thought was a murderous glare, but really, the woman was just too damn cute to pull it off.

"Are you planning on telling him?" she demanded as she took a big bite out of a chocolate caramel candy bar that actually looked pretty tasty so he snatched it away from her.

When she opened her mouth, no doubt to demand that he give it back to her, he took a huge bite out of the candy bar as he glared right back at her, silently reminding her of their agreement. She could either share or go find herself a new hiding spot. In the end, she simply muttered as she pulled the sheet back over her head and continued getting her sugar fix.

"I knew you'd see it my way," Kale mumbled smugly as he settled back against the extra firm pillows that he'd demanded the women in this family buy for him.

At first they'd simply rolled their eyes at him and told him to get his own goddamn pillows. So, that's exactly what he did. Since he didn't like to shop or spend his own money if he didn't have to, he decided to save some time and money and just grab a pillow or two from one of the other rooms.

Once he'd helped himself to the pillows on Ephraim and Madison's bed, he couldn't help but notice just how big and comfortable their bed was, so of course he took that. He would have taken their comforter and sheets too, but they just didn't do anything for him so he helped himself to the comforter on Caine and Danni's bed and the sheets from Izzy and Chris' bed. After his bed was all set up, he couldn't help but notice that the rest of his room looked pretty bare.

It took him a good five hours of ransacking the rest of the mansion before he had his room the way that he liked it. Not even an hour after he'd finished, the banging on his door started right along with the demands to return their stuff. He ignored them until the women of the house got pissed, gave up and offered to shop for whatever he wanted as long as he returned their stuff. Since that deal worked in his favor, he allowed the women the privilege of shopping for his needs. It really was the least that he could do.

"I want a Coke," Izzy mumbled pathetically from beneath the sheet, which reminded him that he needed to ask her something.

"Why exactly are you hiding under that sheet?"

The sounds of candy wrappers crinkling was accompanied by the large mound that was Izzy shifting beneath the sheet as she explained, "Because this is the last place that he'd look for me."

Well, that was probably true, Kale had to admit. The large Sentinel male probably wouldn't expect his adorable pregnant mate to be hiding out in another man's bed, especially a shifter's bed. He was supposed to be the enemy since he didn't work for the Sentinel Council. Technically, he shouldn't even be allowed in this house since it was under the Council's protection. If it wasn't for the small woman devouring a shit load of junk food in his bed he'd probably be holed up in some hotel room, planning his next job instead of checking in to make sure that everything was okay.

"Does the sheet provide you with added protection?" he asked distractedly as a fresh wave of exhaustion hit him.

He was so fucking tired. That wasn't anything new. He was always tired, but over the past couple of months it seemed as though exhaustion was hitting him harder than ever before. He needed a break, some rest, but he'd come too far to stop now. He was so close, so damn close, to his goal.

One more year and everything that he'd worked so hard for would be his. He could go back home, buy a cottage out in the middle of nowhere, and live out the rest of his existence without worrying about anything other than resting, eating and enjoying his well-earned solitude. He was going to forget that anything else existed in the world for a while.

Except for her maybe, he thought as he watched the mound beneath the sheet shift again. He wasn't sure how it happened, but this small Sentinel female somehow became his best friend, his only friend, and his family. Thanks to her, he had to adjust his goal to include her, her mate and their children. That wasn't something that he was entirely happy about.

He liked the way his life used to be, the way it should be. He hated complications and there was no doubt in his mind that Izzy was a huge complication. She was his one and only weakness and he fucking hated that.

He hated the fact that he thought about her a little too much and worried about her whenever he was away from her. His focus should be on his goal and not the woman devouring a year's supply of junk food in his bed. He shouldn't care if she was okay never mind happy. The woman was a Sentinel and therefore his enemy, he reminded himself with a glare as he caught a whiff of peanut butter and chocolate.

"Hey!" Izzy snapped as he snaked his hand beneath the sheet and stole the bag of miniature peanut butter cups that she'd tried to hide from him.

"Mine."

"But-"

"*Mine.*"

"Well, let me just have-"

"Mine!" he snapped, allowing his voice to deepen, becoming more animal than man and giving her the only warning that she was going to get if she-

"Yeah, cause that really scares me," she said dryly as she raised the sheet off her head just long enough for her to search for the bag of peanut butter cups and steal them.

"I'm seconds from shifting and tearing this bed apart, woman!"

"Uh huh," she said around what sounded like a mouthful of peanut butter cups, *his* peanut butter cups.

He crossed his arms over his chest as he narrowed his eyes dangerously on the lump beneath the sheet. Any other woman would have given up the peanut butter cups as she cowered, begged and pleaded for his mercy, but not this woman. No, this woman knew that he would never hurt her. Screw her over for dessert? In a heartbeat, but he would never cause her any harm and that knowledge pissed him off.

"I want a Coke," Izzy mumbled again, earning a tired sigh from him as he settled more comfortably back against the pillows and closed his eyes.

"You can't have Coke," he reminded her.

"I know," she said, not sounding happy about it and he couldn't really say that he blamed her. The woman's Coke addiction was almost as bad as his.

He couldn't imagine going an hour, never mind a day without his caffeine fix. It was the only thing that gave him the energy to move most days and kept him from killing everything in sight, he thought as he reached over, not bothering to open his eyes, and grabbed the can of Coke that he'd forgotten about and took a long, deep satisfying sip.

"That better not be what I think it is," Izzy bit out, sounding close to committing violence.

"It is," he said, pausing only to rub it in her face with a loud satisfied sigh before he finished it off and tossed the empty can aside.

"I hate you," Izzy sighed heavily, sounding miserable as she shifted beneath the sheet until she was curled up against his side. She buried her face against him as her small hands found his bicep and squeezed, nails digging in as she did her best to bite back a whimper, but he heard it.

He always did.

He didn't need to ask what was bothering her. He knew exactly how much pain she was in no matter how hard she tried to hide it. He hated this, hated feeling this helpless and he fucking hated the little bastard that had done this to her.

One day.......

He would catch up with Joshua and when that day came he would pay the man back for every ounce of pain that he'd caused Izzy with interest. Izzy's family wanted to save Joshua and they probably thought that he was onboard with their game plan. He wasn't. But, as long as they kept him informed of what they'd learned about the little bastard he would keep letting them think that. They really didn't need to know about the excruciating death that awaited Joshua and if he had his way, they never would.

Not that he really cared if his plans for the little prick upset the misfits of Pytes, Sentinels and humans that made up this family. He didn't give a damn if his plans upset them. The woman curled up beside him, clutching onto him almost desperately was the only one that he really cared about.

"What's wrong?" he asked, pretending that he wasn't aware that agonizing pain was shooting through the hip that Joshua had callously destroyed. Izzy hated the reminder of what her one time best friend had done to her, but he suspected that she hated the fact that her injury reminded everyone else of the monster that Joshua had turned into, more.

"Nothing," she bit out through clenched teeth as her grip on him tightened to the point that he knew he'd be sporting some rather nasty bruises for a few hours. He could have pulled away from her, but he wouldn't do that since this was the only thing that he could do to help ease some of her pain.

"Then why are you clinging to me?" he asked softly, giving her the opportunity to stop trying to be brave all the time and allow someone to take care of her.

"I missed you," she said, her voice breaking on a sob as her nails dug into his skin.

"Well, that went without saying," he said, pushing the sheet off her so that he could pull her into his arms.

As soon as she was in his arms, she turned her face against his chest, grabbed a fistful of his shirt and released a heart-wrenching scream of pain that had him biting back a curse and wishing that the little bastard was around so that he could kill the son of a bitch. Since that wasn't an option, he settled for holding her tightly against him and placing his hand on the large swell of her belly where his godchildren kicked and squirmed, frightened for their mother.

They laid like that for hours, Izzy crying and Kane doing what he could to comfort her and her unborn babies. Several times he begged her to let him go get

Chris, but she wouldn't allow it. She didn't want her mate to see how bad her injury was, which was fucking ridiculous since everyone in the goddamn mansion knew how bad it was.

It wasn't something that Izzy could hide, not with the way that she walked, the strain of pain around her eyes or the muffled cries that she tried to hide from all of them. Izzy wasn't fooling any of them with the brave façade that she put on everyday. This pain was killing her and Kale honestly didn't know how she was going to survive the next one hundred and seventy years left in her life like this. Hell, he didn't know how he was going to survive seeing her like this for another minute.

"Don't tell anyone," Izzy said softly, speaking for the first time in hours.

After a slight hesitation, he decided that arguing with her would be pointless. She wanted to keep pretending that no one knew and for now he would allow her that delusion. "I won't."

"What in the hell is going on here?" the voice laced with murderous rage demanded, taking them both by surprise, which was saying a lot since he was an Alpha and nothing should be able to get by him.

As one they looked up and found Chris standing at the foot of the bed. The muscles in his arms and neck bulged as he glared their way, but a little to the right. Unable to help himself, Kale shot a look over to the right just as Izzy did, and took in the large pile of junk food and empty wrappers and knew that Izzy was in deep shit.

"It's not what it looks like!" Izzy said, almost desperately as she tried to shift away from the evidence of her binge, but there was nowhere to go.

"Tell me that you didn't feed my precious babies all that sugar," Chris demanded as he crossed his massive arms over his chest, his glare shifting to Izzy, whom Kale suspected was trying to climb out of the bed and make a run for it, but her damaged hip and the twins she carried hindered her efforts to escape.

"I didn't!" the little junk food addict lied.

"Then why are you in his bed?" Chris drawled, his glare never wavering from his panicked mate.

"For sex?" Izzy said, sounding hopeful as both men rolled their eyes.

"I cannot believe that you went behind my back and did this," Chris said, sounding truly pissed as he moved around the bed and carefully scooped her up in his arms, throwing an accusing glare towards the massive pile of wrappers and junk food as he did it.

"B-but, I didn't!" Izzy protested even as she wrapped her arms around her mate's neck. "It was all Kale! He needed the energy for our marathon of sex!"

"Uh huh," Chris said, clearly not believing her as he focused his attention on him.

"House meeting after patrol," Chris simply said, obviously expecting to be obeyed, which was really fucking sad.

"Can't," Kale said, leaning over to pick through the remains of Izzy's junk fest.

"Oh, I think that you can," Chris drawled lazily.

"And why is that?" Kale asked, already planning on leaving in an hour for the job in Ontario that would bring him one step closer to his goal.

"Because we need your help hunting down the other Pytes."

TWO

C loe couldn't help feeling a little disappointed as she parked in front of the pharmacy and took in her surroundings. When she'd accepted this job she'd pictured this quiet southeastern Massachusetts town a little bit differently. Something along the lines of the colonial era came to mind, maybe a pilgrim or two roaming the streets, but alas, there was nothing special to set this town apart from the dozen or so other towns that she'd called home over the years.

With a disappointed sigh, she climbed out of her small SUV. Fighting a yawn, she opened the door and walked inside and headed straight to the back of the pharmacy. After waiting in line for ten minutes she handed over her prescription and information. Once she'd played twenty questions with the pharmacist and he felt that she wasn't a drug lord hellbent on turning his quiet little town into her own personal drug empire, she was gestured to the waiting area that consisted of three long park style benches lined up against the back wall.

A young couple sat on the first bench. The woman, who was obviously pregnant, was quietly reading a gossip magazine while the man next to her openly checked Cloe out. Okay, that was just creepy and made her want to slap him upside the head. Ignoring him, she shifted her gaze to the next bench where two, grumpy, old men sat looking less than welcoming.

Finally, on the last bench she spotted just one man, a large man, well over six feet tall if she had to guess, sitting at the far end of the bench. The hood of his grey sweatshirt was pulled over his head, effectively shielding his face. He was leaning to the side, using his fist as a pillow and leaving a large portion of the bench empty. With an inward sigh, she walked over and sat down. She was aware of the shocked expressions from everyone around them, but ignored them as well, too tired to really care.

Their eyes shot from her to the guy sitting next to her as if they couldn't quite believe that she'd sat there or that he'd let her. Whatever their problem was, she didn't care. She wasn't here to get involved in small town drama. She had a job to do and as soon as she had her prescription she would go start it.

—

This young woman was......odd.

He watched as she stepped in line, noting the way that the rest of the customers stopped what they were doing to watch her every move and listen to every word that she spoke as though they had every right in the world to do it. She seemed completely oblivious of their welcoming glares as she sat down next to him. This town had a knack for scaring young women away.

They'd been going out of their way to do it since they'd decided over thirty years ago that he was no longer welcome in their town. Thanks to their drama he no longer had to worry about women approaching him. It was the only part of the small town bullshit that he actually appreciated. Well, that and the fact that he never had to wait in line since no one in town had the balls to come within ten feet of him.

After a minute, she raised a challenging brow in his direction. He ignored it as he looked her over out of the corner of his eye. Her flannel shirt was open, revealing a tight gray tee shirt that ended right above her belly button and a rather shapely athletic stomach. Her chest was good size too, he realized, reminding him of just how much of an asshole he truly was. A surge of guilt had him looking away from her chest to take in the rest of her. His gaze shifted to the thick, black watchband on her wrist and then up to her face.

She was a natural beauty with chestnut hair and intelligent grey eyes. Her lips were full and somewhat pouty looking. This girl could easily blend in with the other women in this town and be beautiful by their standards, but that wasn't her. He could tell that she wasn't the type of woman who'd be happy merely blending in. She had the look of a woman who would beat the shit out of a man and then roll her eyes when he whimpered.

"I know you're awake," she suddenly announced on a bored sigh.

He had to smile, a rare feat for him, but one that he couldn't help at the moment. "Never said that I wasn't."

She glanced over at him and looked pointedly at his hooded head. "Oh?"

"It's not my fault if everyone assumes that I'm asleep," he explained, deciding that it couldn't hurt to kill some time talking with this odd woman.

She arched a perfectly shaped brow at that. "Yes, you're right. I often wear a hooded sweatshirt to the drugstore and pretend to be asleep just to play mind games with the populace."

"Do you really?" he asked, a small chuckle that sounded a bit rusty and unpracticed escaping him and making him realize that it had been too damn long since anyone had made him laugh.

She ran a hand through her hair. Mesmerized, he watched as her hair fell back in place. "All the time," she murmured as she looked around the store.

The two gossiping men and the young woman, who'd been reading, looked over and scowled in their direction. If the young woman sitting next to him was bothered by the attention it didn't show.

"I don't think they like you," he said in a conspiratorial whisper, knowing that their glares were solely meant for him. When they heard him, they glared harder, sending the silent message that played like a broken record at this point, the one that told him to get the hell out of their town.

"Oh no, I shall have to end it all tonight at the stroke of midnight after professing my undying love for my favorite boy band in my pink lacey diary," she said in such a slow and toneless manner that he couldn't help but chuckle.

"Is there a problem? Is he bothering you?" one of the elderly men barked in demand.

"Everything's fine," she said, shrugging off the elderly man's concerns.

"Christofer, your prescriptions are almost done," the pharmacist announced, shooting the woman beside him a nervous glance and leaving no doubt in his mind whatsoever that his order had been rushed to get him out of the store and away from the young woman who'd made the mistake of sitting next to him.

"Thank you," Christofer said as he leaned back against the bench, not really caring if he was making anyone nervous. He was enjoying himself, probably for the first time in years. It also didn't hurt that the woman sitting next to him was giving off a mouthwatering aroma.

"So, you're a Christofer, huh?" she asked in an amused tone.

"Yes, and you are….," he prompted.

She looked thoughtful for a minute. "Sorry, I don't go around telling strange hooded men my name anymore."

"Was there a time when you did?"

"Oh definitely, it was about a week ago." She cocked her head to the side as she studied his cloaked figure. "You have really bad timing."

He chuckled. "Damn, I guess I do," he said on a heavy sigh. He sat up and pushed the hood off his head, expecting her to act like every other mindless hormonal woman and fawn over him. It was too bad since he was actually enjoying her company.

She didn't bat an eye as she said, "Nice hair," and went back to looking around the store.

Self-consciously, he ran a hand over his hair only to discover that it was sticking up in places thanks to his hood. This was an unexpected pleasure. Not that he was shallow or anything, but women in his experience generally took one look at him and acted like lovesick fools. He rather liked her indifferent attitude.

———

"Your name?" he asked again. "You can tell me now since I'm no longer a cloaked stranger, but a man with a serious case of hat hair. Surely I'm harmless enough."

"Oh, I don't know about that," she mused, trying to ignore the impulse to stare at him. He was far too handsome for his own good with short, golden blonde hair that reminded her of a perfect sunrise, bright laughing blue eyes and a chiseled face that made him hotter than any man that she'd ever seen or probably ever would.

His eyebrows came together over that comment. "Why would you say that?"

She looked pointedly around the suddenly quiet pharmacy. "Because you just gave every woman in this store heart failure." After a short pause she added, "Except for one of course."

He looked around the store only to realize that every woman had stopped talking, shopping, and apparently breathing, just to stare at him. Great, just what he needed. He normally kept his head covered to avoid this kind of aggravation.

"It's really not funny," he muttered when she laughed, a low, rich laugh that had him wishing that she'd do it again just so that he could savor the sound.

"Oh, I beg to differ. It's rather entertaining."

He shook his head in disbelief. Who was this woman?

"I know that I've earned your name now."

She sat back and glanced at the women, who quickly pretended to go back to shopping. "I guess I do owe you something for the entertainment even if it was only for a moment."

"I rather think that you do."

"Cloe."

"Cloe?"

"That's my name. Do you prefer Christofer or can I call you Hoodie?" she teased with a sexy little smile that grabbed his attention and held it.

He ran a hand through his hair again, trying to make it behave. "As much as I would love a nickname like that, I'm afraid that you'll have to settle for Christofer."

She sighed theatrically. "Well, I guess I can't get everything that I want in life. Damn shame too. I was really looking forward to knowing a man named Hoodie. Now the dream is over."

"You're an unusual woman, did you know that?"

"Wow, a charmer, too? Be still my beating heart I may perish."

He chuckled, earning more curious stares from their audience.

"All set, Christofer," Joe said, holding up two small white bags.

"Well, that's me," he said, reluctantly getting up.

He really hated leaving her like this. He discreetly scented the air and swallowed a groan. His knees nearly buckled in ecstasy. She smelled so damn good. Type B positive blood, but not like any B positive that he'd ever scented. She smelled mouthwatering. The only downside, she wasn't a virgin. Virgin blood was like fillet mignon to him and would have made a rather welcomed treat today.

There was still something about her blood that drew him.....

He inhaled again. Her scent was far more inviting than any virgin's. Damn, as he forced himself to go up to the counter he actually contemplated breaking the promise that he'd made to his sister by taking this woman out back and draining her.

It had been forty years since he'd promised not to feed from the source and he'd never come closer to breaking his word than today. He looked back at Cloe who was now reading a pamphlet on Alzheimer's. If he drained this young woman his sister would never know.

Cloe didn't live in town. Otherwise he would have definitely noticed her by now. Maybe she was visiting someone? Or maybe just passing through town and stopping to fill a prescription? If that were the case then Marta would never know that he took her.

Shit.

He felt his eyes start to burn and his gums throb as his fangs slid down. Casually, he pulled up his hood as he signed for his sister's medication. He could do this. Marta would never know. If she did find out he would simply explain about the draw this woman's blood had on him and hope that she didn't go after him with that damn cane of hers. His stomach growled as her scent grew stronger.

He didn't need to turn his head to know that she was now standing next to him. Joe must have waved her over.

Out of the corner of his eye he saw the pharmacist push a small white paper bag towards her.

"Thank you," Cloe said as she signed for her medication.

It was on the tip of his tongue to ask her out for coffee, lunch, anything to get her out of this store and away from human eyes when she said, "See you around, Hoodie. I mean, Christofer," she added with a wink.

He froze.

She was staying in town?

Shit!

His stomach roared in protest, demanding a taste of the blood that was starting to drive him out of his fucking mind. Cloe playfully patted his stomach, sending a new awareness through his system and making his cock twitch in pleasure. It took him by surprise, robbing him of the ability to breathe as he struggled to get his body under control. He hadn't allowed himself to react to a woman in nearly fifty years and he didn't want to now, but it looked as though what he wanted no longer mattered.

"You might want to feed him," Cloe said with a wink as she stepped past him. He watched as she bent over to pick up a red shopping basket and nearly growled. Did she know how delectable that little round ass of hers was?

Without a backwards glance, she headed down an aisle. Damn it! If he stayed here any longer he'd follow her down that aisle and drain her. He wouldn't be able to help himself. For a moment he stood there, struggling with the need to go after her. A not-so-discreet cough reminded him of the reason why he couldn't. With one last glance in the direction that she'd disappeared, he grabbed his sister's prescriptions and practically stormed out of the store. He jumped into his car and drove the usual five minute ride home in two.

He slammed the car door shut, rocking the car, and headed for the back door of the large white farmhouse that could really use a paint job. Once inside, he dropped the medication on the kitchen table and headed for the basement. He hesitated at the door for a moment as he contemplated going out back and getting back to work, but the loud yawn that escaped him reminded him that he'd spent the better part of the last week working and could really use some sleep.

"Christofer, is that you?" Marta's scratchy voice called out from the living room.

"Yes, it's me. I'll be downstairs if you need anything," he said as he closed the door behind him. Not that it mattered since he could still hear everything Marta said or did perfectly and she knew it. Well, as long as he was paying attention, which he did at least forty percent of the time.

"I forgot to tell you that-"

"Tell me later, I'm going to get some sleep!" he yelled loud enough so that she could hear him as he walked across the large finished basement to the refrigerator. He yanked the door open and grabbed two bags of blood and headed over to his bed where he flopped down on his back. He closed his eyes as he drank, imagining that it was Cloe's blood, but it didn't work.

His stomach knew that it was getting a cold substitution. Disgusted, he tossed the empty bags aside and picked up a book, hoping that a little distraction would get his thoughts away from where they didn't belong. When reading didn't help he tossed the book aside and closed his eyes, hoping that a nap would help ease the tension in his body.

As he drifted off, he couldn't help but wonder what he'd done to deserve such a fucked up existence.

THREE

Twenty minutes later Cloe was pulling into the wide driveway of what appeared to be an old farm. It was actually very pretty even if the large white farmhouse looked like it could use some work. She looked around, noting the dirt road that continued ahead of her, winding past an old shed for a few hundred yards until it ended in front of a large white barn. The property was large and had a homey look to it that put a smile on her face. She'd always loved old houses.

After taking a moment to check to make sure that her hair and clothes looked decent, she made her way up to the front door and knocked. A moment later an old woman with a slight curve to her back opened the door and greeted her with a welcoming smile.

"Hello, Ms. Petersen?" Cloe asked, returning the smile.

"You must be Cloe. Please, come in," Ms. Petersen said as she slowly moved to the side. With a murmured, "Thank you," Cloe stepped inside.

"Let's have a seat in the living room," Ms. Petersen suggested as she slowly walked towards a small sitting room.

All of the furniture was small, elegant with small patches of worn brown leather covering the barely-there padding on the back of the chairs and seats. In short, none of it looked comfortable. No wonder Ms. Petersen was hunched over. She would be too if she had to sit on this rigid furniture every day. Lace doilies covered all the tables as well as the backs of each chair, making the room look very old fashioned.

Upon further inspection, she noted the layer of dust, stacks of newspapers, junk mail and dull floors. If the rest of the house was anything like this then it was going to need a good cleaning, which of course was one of the reasons that she was here.

"Have a seat, dear," Ms. Petersen said, smiling warmly. Cloe picked up a slight accent, but couldn't quite place it. She sat down, but only after Ms. Petersen had.

"I was hoping that my brother would join us for this, but it seems that he needed a nap," Ms. Petersen said with an amused smile.

If the man was as old as the woman sitting in front of her then Cloe could understand his need for a nap. Heck, she was only twenty-eight and she really could use a nap after driving up from Florida on only two hours of sleep.

Ms. Petersen looked her over before giving her an approving nod. "You'll do just fine," she said softly.

"Ah, thank you," Cloe said, not really sure what the correct response to being perused over like a car for sale was.

Ms. Petersen clasped her hands together. "Now let's see, your room is on the second floor. You may have whichever room you want. My brother turned the dining room into my room several years ago, because I have such a difficult time climbing stairs," Ms. Peterson explained as Cloe nodded in understanding.

"My brother has the basement as his bedroom. That is the first rule actually now that I think of it. Please do not go down there. My brother likes his privacy and if he discovered that anyone was down there he would become very upset."

"I understand. I won't intrude on his privacy," she quickly agreed since she had no desire to walk in on a ninety-year-old man in his birthday suit. Not her thing. Seriously.

"I should probably also mention that he would be very upset if anyone went in the barn," Ms. Petersen added with an apologetic smile. "That's where he keeps all his artwork."

"I understand," Cloe said with a reassuring smile and a nod.

"Let's see," Ms. Petersen said as she took out a folded piece of paper. "My friend Gladyce told me that I should write down the rules and what I expect so that there won't be any misunderstandings."

'That sounds like a good idea," Cloe said encouragingly. The other woman nodded and smiled again, pleased that Cloe was so agreeable. From her experience as a live-in caregiver, Cloe knew all too well that a great deal of the elderly were treated little better than children and their opinions were often ignored. It was something that always bothered her and something that she strove not to do.

"Hmm, where to start...oh! Okay, no smoking or drinking in the house." She looked up to gage Cloe's response. When Cloe simply nodded, she continued. "No men in your room." That rule was more than fine with Cloe since men were the last thing she felt like dealing with at the moment.

"Anything else?" Cloe asked encouragingly.

Ms. Petersen frowned at her list. "That seems to be it for rules. Do you have a problem with any of them?"

"Absolutely none."

"Good, good, okay now the chores.....the house needs a deep cleaning and then daily cleaning. Then there's the lawn and you put down on your resume that you can do work as a handyman?" she asked, looking up at Cloe.

"Yes," Cloe hesitantly answered.

She almost lied, knowing exactly where this conversation was headed. More times than she could count, her employers or their family tried to squeeze as much work out of her for her base salary as they possibly could. That sucked, because if that happened she was out of here. She was done with being used.

"Good! There's plenty of things around here that could use some attention. Oh, especially the house. It needs to be scraped and painted," Ms. Petersen rambled on about all of the things that could use some attention, oblivious to Cloe's lack of enthusiasm.

Somehow Cloe stopped herself from groaning her frustration. Well, it looked like she was going to have to accept that live-in position in Pennsylvania after all. "Ms. Petersen-"

"Now, according to Bernice, that's my friend, handy-men make about fifteen to twenty dollars an hour. So, let's just say twenty dollars an hour for every hour that you work as a handyman. Is that sufficient?"

Cloe blinked. Then blinked again. "You want to pay me extra for doing handyman work?"

Ms. Petersen's smile slipped as her expression turned confused. "Of course, why would I expect you to do that for free when I hired you to be my helper? No," she shook her head firmly, "if you're going to do extra work then you'll get paid for it. My brother will be more than happy to pay you for it, especially since he was supposed to do it himself for the past ten years."

Cloe felt her eyes widen at that announcement. "No, that's fine. I'll do it when the rest of my chores are done." No way was she about to sit around while an old man climbed a ladder and fell, then had a massive heart attack and died. Yeah, she could live without the added guilt.

Ms. Petersen looked back at her list for a moment before putting it away. "Let's see, there's also cooking, shopping, and running errands," she said, worry taking over her features as she finished her small list with a distressed, "Oh, no!"

She threw her arms up and tried to get to her feet. It took several tries and one of Cloe's hands before she managed to stand up. "There's nothing in the house to eat!" she announced as she grabbed her cane and headed towards an oversized black purse. "I'm afraid my brother forgot to do the shopping again," she said with a weary sigh. "It's one of the reasons why I finally decided to get a helper."

Cloe nodded, wondering just how much this woman expected of her brother. If he was anything like his sister he probably had enough problems with just taking care of himself.

Ms. Petersen pulled out another list. "Would you mind terribly going grocery shopping? You can add whatever you want to the list for snacks."

Cloe took the list and placed it in her pocket. "That's very kind, but it wouldn't be right. Meals are one thing, but I wouldn't feel right about having you pay for my snacks. I'll pay for them and if I have something you like then we'll share."

"Oh!" Ms. Petersen looked absolutely delighted. Then she frowned. "I'm afraid I wouldn't know what kind of snacks they have nowadays. It's been so long since I've been to the grocery store. Usually my brother takes the list and storms off."

Cloe's heart broke at Marta's wistful expression. She had no doubt that Ms. Petersen would prefer to go shopping for herself and get out of the house. Cloe didn't know much about her brother, but the least he could do was take his sister out for a ride.

"Why don't you join me? That way if you see something that you like you can get it," Cloe suggested.

"Well, I don't know," she said, looking down at her cane. "I wouldn't want to slow you down. That's why my brother doesn't take me."

Unless her brother was the Road Runner he had no business talking. No doubt he was just as slow.

"That's fine. I'm sure they have an electric scooter at the store that you can use."

"Really?" Ms. Petersen smiled, looking excited.

"Really. Do you want to go…..," Cloe's voice trailed off as she watched Ms. Petersen grab her oversized bag and hurry to the front door as though she was afraid that Cloe was going to change her mind.

Poor thing, Cloe thought, following after her.

———

With a pained sigh, Christofer climbed the stairs, slowly. It was time to make Marta's dinner. Actually, it was past time to make her dinner, he realized after a quick glance down at his watch.

Shit.

He must have been more exhausted than he'd thought. He'd slept for a good five hours. Feeling like an asshole for making her wait, he moved his ass faster.

Trying not to cringe when he saw the dirty counters, floor and stove, he made his way to the refrigerator. He couldn't remember the last time that he'd scrubbed down the kitchen, but it definitely needed it. After he finished this next project he'd focus on getting the house cleaned up for his sister.

"Shit," he muttered as he opened the refrigerator door and then the cabinets to find them empty. Looked like he forgot to go shopping, again, he realized with a wince.

"I guess it's pizza tonight," he mumbled, unable to help but feel a little relieved that he didn't have to cook tonight. He grabbed the portable phone and headed into Marta's part of the house. "Marta, what do you want on your pizza?" he yelled.

No answer.

"Marta?"

When she didn't answer, he closed his eyes and listened for her heartbeat. Nothing. Dread filled him. As much as he hated living in this town, he loved her and couldn't imagine his life without her.

He ran to her room and damn near fell to his knees with relief when he didn't find her body. Then he went to the living room and when he didn't find her there, he searched the rest of the house, but there was no sign of her. He closed his eyes and inhaled again only to shake his head in disgust when he picked up Cloe's lingering scent on his clothes.

He ran outside and searched the backyard and adjoining woods, but there wasn't any sign of her. This wasn't like Marta. She never left the house to visit one of her friends without telling him first. More to the point, she *couldn't* leave the house if he didn't give her a ride.

An old memory of watching her being dragged from their childhood home tried to take over, but he pushed it aside before he lost control. Not knowing what else to do, he headed back into the house to find his cellphone. He called all her friends, who yelled at him for calling at the ungodly hour of seven o'clock until he explained to them that Marta was missing. Then they panicked and began reminiscing about past events that had terrified them, like when Evelyn's poodle went missing for nearly a half hour. Before he did something like snap at the old women, he politely got off the phone, knowing Marta would hit him upside his head with her cane if he upset any of her friends.

He called the police next only to learn that he needed to wait twenty-four hours before he could file a missing person's report. Why in the hell was he paying taxes if they weren't going to do their job? He asked them that only to have them hang up on him.

Finally, he walked out onto the front porch and waited and wondered what the hell he should do next. This wasn't like Marta. She hadn't stepped out of the house without him in almost four decades.

No, something was wrong here. Someone had taken his sister. He slowly got to his feet, allowing the anger to build inside him. He was going to kill whoever dared lay a finger on her. His fangs shot out of his gums as his eyes burned and for the first time in nearly fifty years he welcomed them. He would never allow anyone to hurt his sister, not again.

Just as he was about to tear the town apart to find her, a small black SUV pulled into the driveway and parked next to his truck.

His jaw dropped as he watched....no, it couldn't be. It was! *Shit.* Hunger slammed into him as he watched Cloe climb out of the vehicle. He squeezed his eyes shut and forced them to shift back to normal. It took a few swipes of his tongue before his fangs receded. When he felt like he had a good grip on his control, he opened his eyes to watch her every move. She didn't even glance his way as she walked quickly around the car and helped someone out.

Marta.

He watched through narrowed slits as his sister grabbed her cane with a polite "thank you" and a big smile. She walked around the vehicle, grinning hugely as if he hadn't just spent the last two and a half hours worrying about her.

"Oh! There you are!" Marta said when she spotted him standing on the front steps. "Oh, I had such a wonderful time! First we went to the buffet that I've wanted to go to for years! Oh, it was so delicious! They cut the meat right there for you!"

She continued rambling on, oblivious to his seething anger. "I had a salad, and then some pasta, ham, turkey, fried chicken. Oh, it was so delicious! Then we went and tried the soft serve ice cream over on Wilmington." He stood there waiting for her to realize that she was in trouble. He had no idea where that woman got off taking his sister, but he was going to find out. Then he was going to drain her dry for taking his sister without his permission and scaring the ever-living hell out of him!

"Did you know that they had electric scooters at the grocer's?" she asked in an accusing tone, cutting into his murderous thoughts.

Shit.

He had known. He just hadn't told her because he didn't want to chance even that slowing him down. He hated going out in public and having her along would just prolong the experience.

"It was so nice to pick out my own fruits and vegetables. The produce and meat departments are so much larger than I remembered. Cloe was so nice. She never once complained about how slow I was going," she said casually, but he didn't miss the reproachful tone in her voice.

He watched the woman in question open the hatch of her SUV. Something whacked him on the thigh, rather hard. He glared down at his sister who made no move to hide the fact that she'd just hit him with her cane.

"Don't just stand there. Go help her bring in the groceries," Marta said with a huff before she continued making her way inside the house.

Oh, if she was about forty years younger he'd actually consider pulling her over his knee and spanking her like their father had when they were children. She sent him a look that told him if he didn't move his ass soon that she would come back down the stairs to give the other leg a good thump. Damn it, when had she gotten so bossy? He grumbled about annoying little sisters as he walked over to Cloe.

Cloe had three bags in her arms when she finally turned around and spotted him. Her warm smile appeared genuine, making him instantly cautious. No one looked at him that way except for Marta. Everyone else looked at him as if he was a freeloading freak. No, this woman was up to something. She'd already kidnapped Marta. Granted, she'd returned her, but from what he'd heard she was already spending Marta's money like there was no tomorrow. Correction, she was spending *his* money like there was no tomorrow.

"Hey, Hoodie, I'm surprised to see you here," she said as she somehow managed to pick up another bag.

"It's Christofer," he said evenly, making her smile falter a little.

"Yes, of course. I'm sorry," she said sheepishly as she moved to step past him. He moved to the right, cutting her off.

"As much as I'd love to stand here and chat with you, Christofer, these bags are kind of heavy," she said as she tried to adjust her grip on the bags.

"What are you doing here, Cloe?" he asked softly as he fought the urge to lean in and inhale her scent more deeply into his lungs.

"At the moment? Probably developing a hernia," she groaned.

His lips twitched, despite his mood.

"Christofer, you help her!" Marta yelled from the front steps.

Grinding his teeth so that he didn't say something that would upset his sister, he reached out and relieved Cloe of the bags. She took a deep breath and nodded. "Thank you," she murmured with a grateful smile.

He expected her to go inside and leave the bags to him, but instead, she turned around and grabbed three more bags and easily stepped around him and headed for the house, leaving him to follow after her or stand there looking like an idiot.

"So, are you Marta's grandson?" she asked in a conversational tone as they walked towards the house

"No, I'm her brother," he answered, stepping to the side so that Cloe could walk on the path.

Cloe's back became ramrod straight, causing her to stumble before she righted herself. Without a look back, she hurried inside the house, leaving him to wonder what the hell that reaction was about.

FOUR

"What the hell do you mean you hired her? She's not staying here!" Christofer shouted from the living room. Whatever Marta's response was, it was quiet.

Cloe sighed as she headed back out to her car to grab the rest of the grocery bags. It had been a while since she had to buy this much food for one of her employers, but Marta had insisted that there wasn't anything in the house. After a quick inspection of the kitchen before heading back outside, Cloe quickly agreed that they hadn't overdone it.

After grabbing her iPod, she grabbed the last of the bags, locked her car, and headed back inside. Once she was back in the kitchen, she could hear him yelling again. With a sigh, she cranked up the volume on her iPod.

Whatever his problem was about her being here she had no doubt that Marta would win. Normally she wouldn't care one way or the other about losing a job, but Marta was a very nice, feisty, if somewhat shy woman who needed more help than her spoiled brat brother was giving her.

At first she'd been a little unnerved at the discovery, but she'd been working with the older generation for a long time now and Christofer was not the first very young sibling that she'd encountered. That didn't bother her. No, what bothered her was the fact that the nice guy she'd thought she'd met in the pharmacy was really a toad who treated his sister, his *elderly* sister, like an unwanted dog.

The man didn't want to take his sister anywhere when she clearly wanted to go out and live her life. Marta damn near broke her heart when she got all excited about driving to the grocery store. Then she began pointing out all the places she'd heard about, heard not been to, to Cloe and told her how she was just dying to try this or that. Finally, Cloe hadn't been able to take it any longer and took her to the buffet. Marta seemed so excited to be there. It was obvious to Cloe that she hadn't been out to eat in a very long time. Marta acted the same way at the store.

When she'd thought the brother was an old man she'd been fine with the situation, realizing that there wasn't much that an elderly man could do to help his sister. She'd decided that she would try helping them both out, but when she'd discovered the brother was much younger, healthy and lazy she got a bit pissed. This was classic elderly neglect. For God sakes there wasn't so much as a box of baking soda in the house.

After she put the last of the groceries away and no one came to tell her that she had to leave, she decided to make herself useful. She grabbed the new cleaning supplies they'd bought and started cleaning.

The counters, stove, table, refrigerator and cabinets probably took a half hour to clean. She swept up the floor and was about to get the mop, but decided she would just have to get on her hands and knees and scrub the damn floor. It was clear that the floor hadn't been mopped in years. Well, at least not properly, she amended a moment later when she spotted the telltale signs of a mop having been moved over the floor at some point. With a resigned sigh, she filled up the bucket with hot soapy water, grabbed the brush and got to work.

As she worked, her mind kept going back to the playful banter she had with Christofer at the pharmacy. It really was a pity that he'd turned out to be such a spoiled little ingrate. Oh well. Marta said he stayed in his basement room most of the time and only came up to check on her or make her a meal so she probably wouldn't run into him very often if she stayed.

Even though she'd just met Marta, she wanted to stay and help her. She seemed so nice and clearly she needed someone to take care of her. Her brother certainly wasn't doing it, she thought with a snort of disgust. No wonder the townspeople seemed to hate him, she was certainly starting to.

———

"Woman," Christofer said in warning, "if you hit me with that damn cane again I'm going to take it!"

She didn't even hesitate when she whacked him on the ass. He glared at her as he smartly jumped out of the way of the next swing. She matched his glare with one of her own.

"You do not tell me what to do, Christofer Petersen. I am a grown woman and if I want to hire someone to come live with me and help me then that is exactly what I'll do!" He noted her accent becoming more pronounced the way it did whenever she was angry.

"This is my house, Marta. I decide who comes and who goes," he reminded her.

She folded her hands in her lap and for a moment said nothing, making him think that he'd won. He really should have known better.

"Then I'll use my money and move out. I'll rent a two bedroom apartment closer to town and Cloe can come live with me."

He threw his hands up in frustration. "You're not leaving, Marta. We don't need anyone. I take good care of you."

She snorted.

She actually snorted.

"What's that supposed to mean?" he demanded, noting that his own accent was starting to come through. Damn it. Hadn't that *woman* done enough today? First she nearly makes him lose control in the store and now she was messing with his home life. Clearly the woman needed to leave and soon.

"You do not take care of me, Christofer," she said firmly.

He gaped at her. What the hell? "I put a roof over your head," he started, holding up one finger to give her a visual of just how much he did for her. "I put food on the table, which I cook I might add," he pointed out, adding another finger. "I do the laundry," he said as another finger joined the party. "And I run all the errands for the house," he said firmly as the fourth finger went up, proving without a doubt that he took great care of her.

She shifted in her seat. "I would not call what you do cooking."

"What's that supposed to mean? You never had a problem with it before!"

"You make watery tea. Your idea of breakfast is lumpy oatmeal or a piece of fruit and burnt toast," she announced, holding up a finger. "Your idea of lunch is a sandwich, and they're not very good. I'm tired of bologna," she said, earning a glare as she held up another finger. "Your idea of dinner is whatever's in a can or one of those disgusting frozen meals," she said, adding another finger. "You run errands only when you have time and you never bring me along," she snapped as the fourth finger went up, but she didn't stop. "You never spend any time with me. You're always in the barn and when I ask you to do something you make me feel like I'm nothing but a burden," she announced, wiggling all five fingers to get her point across.

"What do you mean, I don't spend time with you? I sit down with you for every meal and I check on you several times a day!"

She scoffed. "You sit at the table, reading or fixing one of your sketches and your idea of checking on me is to listen to my heartbeat from the barn."

"That's not true!" It was.

Marta smoothed her skirt down. "I'm tired of being a burden to you, Christofer. I know you gave your word to Papa and you've kept it to the best of your ability, but now I am releasing you from your promise. I know you would rather be anywhere else but here and with Cloe here you can do that now."

That gave him pause. "You hired her to get rid of me?" That actually hurt. It was true that he didn't want to be in this town, but he wanted to be with her. She was his sister, his family, his friend and without her he would be all alone in the world.

"That's one of the reasons."

He began pacing the room. "I'm not leaving, Marta. This is my home and you are my family. So, if that's the reason for this woman's presence then you might as well send her away, because I'm staying."

"So is she if she still wants the job after all of your yelling."

"I did not yell!"

"You're doing it now!"

He groaned as he picked up his pacing. An idea hit him. He stopped and faced her. "What do you really know about this woman? More to the point, how did you hire her? For all you know she could be a thief or an ax murderer."

"I hired her through an agency. They did a background check on her, drug testing *and* I contacted all her former employers and they couldn't say enough nice things about her."

Damn.

He started pacing again.

"She's very nice. She let me go for a ride, took me out to eat and-"

"*I* paid for you both to go out," he pointed out.

She smiled. "No, you didn't, Christofer. Cloe paid, not you."

He eyed her, not liking that smug expression on her face one bit. "She can't stay and that's final."

"Why?"

Because if Cloe stayed he would end up breaking the vow that he'd made to his sister and the one that he'd made to himself. He wanted Cloe's blood so badly that he actually ached with the need to go after her. He also wanted to fuck her while feeding from her then fuck her again and then probably fuck her again, he thought, but he couldn't tell his sister *that.* So he gave her a lame answer instead. "Just because."

She snorted as she stood up and headed for the door.

"Good, go tell her to leave," he said, confident that his word was law.

She laughed at him.

Good God, what the hell?

"I'm going to bed, Christofer. I will see you *and* Cloe in the morning."

"She won't be here!" he called after her.

"She better be."

He growled softly as he watched his sister disappear into her room. That woman was not staying. He didn't care what Marta threatened him with. If Marta tried to move out he would either drag her back here or follow after her. Either way Cloe was not staying a moment longer. He couldn't tell Marta this, but she was risking the young woman's life by keeping her here. He'd never wanted anyone's blood or body more in his life. His self-control was good, but it wasn't perfect.

Cloe had to go.

He walked into the kitchen only to find it empty and....clean? What the hell? His eyes dropped to the floor. It was shiny and white with rose petals. He frowned down at the floor. He could have sworn that it had been a dull gray this morning. The room no longer smelled of old food, dust and a thousand other odors. It smelled of chemical and oranges. Every surface was clean and shining. He could have done that, he thought with a grumble.

He closed his eyes and listened. He heard two heartbeats. One on the first floor, which was Marta's and the other was on the second floor, which meant that Cloe had made herself at home.

Oh, hell no....

He took the back stairs two at time and raced towards the sound of her heartbeat. It came from a closed door at the end of the hallway. Without slowing down, he threw the door open and quickly stumbled forward, tripping over his own two feet from the sight that greeted him.

"Don't you knock?" Cloe snapped as she grabbed a towel to hold up in front of her.

He opened his mouth to speak, but nothing would come out. His eyes were fixed on that damn towel that she was now using to cover up heaven. He glared at the damn thing, willing it to drop or shift to the side a foot or two so he could see that beautiful body again. Large breasts tipped with dark pink nipples, a flat stomach with just the slightest swell, wide hips and soft (he was willing to bet his life they were soft) butterscotch curls between her legs that were just begging for his devotion and he would give it too.

Gladly.

"The towel's not going to disappear and I'm not dropping it."

She couldn't know that for sure, he decided as his gaze on the towel intensified. For another moment he stared, more like silently pleaded for it to move.

"You really need to get laid," she said dryly.

His eyes snapped up to hers. Holy shit! Was that an offer?

Cloe rolled her eyes as she managed to wrap the towel around herself and tucked it in between her breasts without giving him a show.

Damn.

"Is there something that you wanted?" she asked.

You. "I-I wanted to…" he stammered before his voice trailed off. His gaze had dropped back down to the cleavage that he wanted to run his tongue over and he was back to willing the towel to drop.

She sighed as she walked over to him. Thank God because his feet wouldn't move and he was practically screaming at them to go to her. She was taking the initiative. That was fine with him. He'd let her set the pace and then he'd take over and probably take her on every surface in this room.

Cloe gripped his arms, tightly. *Oh, yeah.* He leaned down to kiss her when he was unceremoniously shoved from the room. A split second later, the door closed in his face.

"But…but…."

He heard her soft laughter from behind the door. He stared at the door for another moment before he came to his damn senses. It was probably a good thing the door was between them so that his blood, well most of his blood, could return to his head. He was fucking weak, he thought with disgust.

For fifty years he'd been able to keep the promise that he'd made to himself for his sister's sake, but one look at a woman's beautiful body had him ready to say the hell with it and take what he wanted, what he couldn't have. It only proved that she needed to get the hell out of this house and out of this town before he lost his good sense and gave in, destroying his sister's life in the process.

He pounded on the door. "Cloe!"

With an exasperated sigh, she answered the door. Thankfully, she was dressed. His gaze skimmed over the tight tank top and oddly arousing green and blue flannel pajama bottoms. To his utter delight, the two pieces of clothing didn't meet, giving him a glimpse of that taut little stomach and navel. Damn, he'd love to trace that with his tongue.

He was fucking pathetic, he thought helplessly.

Two warm fingers gently gripped his chin and pulled his attention away from his new obsession. He may have whimpered.

"Hi, nice to have you back," Cloe said with a wry smile. "Now, what is it that you wanted to talk to me about?" She released her hold on his chin and he had to fight not to drop his eyes back down. From the look on her face he knew that if he did that he would be looking at the door again.

He gave himself a mental shake. Right, he needed to get her out of his house and soon.

"You're fired," he said firmly in a tone that brokered no argument.

She yawned. "Okay, see you in the morning." She moved to close the door.

Christofer pressed his hand against the door to stop her. "Didn't you hear me? I said you're fired."

"That's two times," she said with a small smile.

"Yes...yes, I did say it twice."

Was she insane?

"I'll make sure to tell Marta that in the morning."

"Wait, what?"

Cloe gave him a coy smile. "Marta told me to tell her if you tried to fire me and how many times. Something about a cane....not really sure." She shrugged.

Aw, shit.

This was not happening. He was the man of this family. This was his house goddamnit.

"You're fired!"

She rolled her eyes. "That's three."

Damn it!

"Are you going to let me go to bed or not? I have a big day tomorrow."

"No! You're fired."

"And you're repetitive," she snapped back. With another sigh, she released the door, walked into the room and shut the light off. He was on automatic when he followed her inside.

"What are you doing?" he asked although he could see everything without a problem, even in a supposedly pitch black room. Everything took on various shades of blue in the darkness, making it easy for him to see. He watched as she climbed into bed.

"Going to bed," she answered as she curled up on her side.

His hands fisted with the need to climb in behind her and hold her. That startled him. As much as it pained him to admit it, he'd never had a problem keeping his vow to himself to put off living his life for his sister's sake before. It was one of the reasons he didn't want her here. His baby sister was asleep downstairs, defenseless. Allowing this woman to stay here would be exposing his sister to a possible threat.

He sighed. "You're fired."

"Five," she muttered into her pillow.

He growled his frustration as he stormed out of the room. Somehow he was going to get her out of his house sooner rather than later. Perhaps if he showed Marta that Cloe wasn't needed around here she'd agree to let Cloe go. A slow grin spread across his face as he headed down to the basement. Oh, the little smart ass was as good as gone.

FIVE

Williams Mansion

"We're going to be late," she moaned, arching her back and lifting her ass off the bed so that she could ride his tongue in a sensuous move that had his fangs sliding down and the head of his cock pushing past the waistband of his jeans.

"Don't fucking care," Ephraim said, tilting his head slightly to the side so that he could leisurely lick his wife out.

"Ephraim!" Madison gasped in pleasure and pain, tilting her hips and trying to force the tip of his tongue inside her core, but other than sliding the tip over it to tease her, he didn't give in to her demands.

"They can wait," he said, refusing to be rushed.

Thanks to a slow night on patrol, he'd had plenty of time to fantasize about all the very naughty things that he wanted to do with his wife. Licking her out was phase one. Fucking her with his fingers was naturally phase two and that would bring him to phase three where he planned on fucking her in nine different, fully thought-out, positions before he pulled out and allowed her to finish him off with her mo-

"Hurry the hell up!" Kale suddenly demanded and Ephraim didn't need to use his Pyte abilities to know that the annoying shifter was standing right outside their bedroom door.

Madison whimpered as she moved back and tried to close her legs, frustration pouring off her in waves. He didn't bother telling her to ignore the bastard, because he knew that she wouldn't be able to do that. Even though she could normally ignore the fact that there were at least three people living here that could hear what they were doing no matter which room they used, she wouldn't be able to ignore someone with razor sharp hearing standing right outside their bedroom door.

"We'll be down in a minute, asshole!" Ephraim snapped, grabbing Madison by the ankles and pulling her back where she belonged.

"Are you crazy?" Madison hissed, slapping at his hands as she tried to crawl away from him, but he wasn't having that.

He yanked her right back and leaned down, sliding his tongue through her wet slit. She let out a choked moan as her fingers threaded through his hair, alternating between pushing him away and pulling his mouth tightly against her.

"I'm still waiting!" Kale growled.

"Keep waiting!" Ephraim shot back, beyond annoyed with the pain in the ass shifter. Next time the bastard left for one of his trips, Ephraim was having all the locks and security codes changed.

The bastard had to go, Ephraim decided as Madison once again tried to shove him away as she attempted to crawl out of his reach. He'd waited all night to touch her and he wasn't about to let that bastard wreck this.

"*Just ignore him,*" he hissed as he pulled Madison back towards him.

"*Are you kidding me?*" Madison hissed back, slapping at his hands.

"*He'll get bored and eventually leave,*" Ephraim hissed back, managing to pull her closer.

"No, I really won't," Kale announced cheerfully, effectively ruining what had promised to be a very satisfying morning.

He wasn't exactly surprised when everything suddenly took on shades of red as he watched Madison scramble off the bed and race for the bathroom. He practically shook with rage as he slowly got to his feet, his arousal a thing of the past as he focused all of his anger on the soon-to-be dead bastard on the other side of the bedroom door.

Killing the shifter would piss Izzy off, but he was pretty sure that she'd eventually forgive him if he kept her well supplied with sweets. It would probably take her a few years to forgive him, but tearing Kale apart with his bare hands would be worth her cute little glares. Then again, he could just simply lie to his daughter-in-law and tell her that he'd gone into bloodlust and "accidentally" torn the bastard apart.

At the moment it sounded like a reasonable plan, so he decided to go with it. He unlocked the bedroom door and yanked it open, smiling grimly as he spotted his prey leaning against the far wall.

"About fucking time," Kale muttered in disgust as he pushed away from the wall and started heading down the hall, taking him by surprise.

The fact that the shifter hadn't taunted him over the interrupted sex and goaded him into a fistfight caught him off-guard. Putting off his need to kill the bastard for the moment, he reluctantly followed.

"What's the rush?" he asked, realizing that this was the first time since the shifter had invited himself to move in that he was not only willingly attending a meeting, but that he was in a rush to get to it.

"A member of the council is here," Kale said, not bothering to slow his pace as he turned down the left hallway.

"Are you in a rush to beat the shit out of this one too?" Ephraim asked, catching up with the shifter as he descended the stairs to the main foyer.

"He shouldn't have come between me and the last cupcake," was all Kale said, lying his ass off and trying to downplay the real reason why he'd made a bloody and bruised Sentinel Council representative flee from the mansion as fast as his dislocated knee would carry him.

The representative had been sent to the mansion to check on their security, look in on the children, and to make sure that their newest inhabitants, a Pyte couple, were following the rules. Caine was still on probation for the destruction he'd caused years ago as well as for turning his mate, Danni, without the Council's permission.

Not that they would have given him permission had he asked. From what he'd heard and knew about the Council, they didn't trust Caine. The only reason that he wasn't at this moment encased in cement and rotting for eternity in the bottom of the ocean or in a volcano somewhere was because his mate was the daughter of Sentinels and had been a well-respected member of their human squad. They also wanted to keep her now that she was a Pyte.

They all knew that the Sentinel Council had released Caine in the hopes to use his mate to control him and keep him working for the Council. As long as Danni depended on the Council to supply her with demon blood to keep the cancer that had followed her into immortality at bay, the couple didn't have much of a choice. He hadn't said anything, but he seriously doubted that the Council was in much of a rush to cure Danni and lose the only hold they had over the Pyte couple.

The representative the Council had sent last time had made it more than obvious that the Council didn't trust Caine. The little bastard followed him around, taking notes on everything that Caine said or did until the Pyte finally had enough, grabbed his mate and took off for a few days. With his main reason for visiting gone, the representative had turned his attention on the rest of them.

When the little bastard had started to pay a little too much attention to his sons and made suggestions that he should talk to Madison and consider sending their young children to one of the Sentinel compounds in Europe for training, Ephraim had calmly listened to the man before he grabbed him by the scruff of the neck and hung him upside down from the second floor balcony.

After that, the representative had focused his attention elsewhere for the remainder of his stay, not that it had been very long once the dumb bastard had made the mistake of describing Izzy as a useless cripple in what he probably thought was a private phone conversation with one of his superiors. Then again, if the representative had known that the shifter had been standing behind him at the time, he probably would have waited until he was well away from the mansion before he called his superior to give his report.

"I don't understand why you don't believe me," Izzy said with an adorable pout as Chris carried her into the hallway and joined them as they headed towards the large conference room in the basement. "It was him!" she said in exasperation as she pointed an accusing finger in Kale's direction.

"Uh huh," Chris sighed absently, obviously not believing the little sugar addict.

Ephraim didn't need to ask to know what the two of them were fighting about. He'd caught part of the conversation going on in Kale's room about an hour ago when he'd walked into the foyer. When he'd realized that Izzy had been caught binging again, he'd blocked out the rest of the conversation and focused on a hot shower and getting his mate to do all the naughty things that he'd been fantasizing about all night.

"I'm really hurt that you don't believe me," Izzy said softly, sounding upset as she looked up at his son with doe-like eyes as she allowed her little chin to tremble.

Ephraim had to turn his head and force a cough to hide his chuckle. He knew that she was lying. He could smell the chocolate and sugar smothering her scent. She was so damn adorable sometimes.

"You're not getting cake for breakfast so just drop it," Chris said firmly, probably hoping that his tone would be enough to put an end to the sugar addict's pleas.

"But-"

"Drop it."

"It wasn't me, I sw-"

"Let it go."

"If you would just ask him, he'd tell you!" she protested, gesturing wildly to the shifter who simply sighed and continued walking ahead of them towards the conference room.

"This is just getting sad," Chris mumbled, shaking his head in disgust before he leaned down slightly so that he could kiss the tip of her nose.

"Then put me down if you don't believe me," Izzy said in a huff, no doubt planning on storming off to get her next sugar fix.

"Nope, sorry can't do that. I like carrying my munchkin around," Chris said with a shrug, instead of pointing out that the conference room was a good five minutes away and that Izzy wouldn't be able to make it there without hurting herself.

As long as no one pointed out the reason behind their obsession with carrying her, Izzy was fine with being carried around. They all came up with some bullshit story to do it and as long as the story was somewhat believable, Izzy accepted their piss poor excuses. It was the only way to save her pride and allow her to pretend that they weren't all worried about her or that the sounds of her weeping quietly in a corner somewhere didn't break their hearts.

"I don't want you carrying me if you don't believe me, Chris," Izzy said, crossing her arms tightly over her large chest as she pointedly glared off. "You may hand me over to my Daddy."

"Izzy-"

"You heard me," Izzy said stubbornly.

"But-"

"I said good day, sir!"

With an annoyed sigh, Chris turned and handed her over to him. He gladly took her. He loved her a great deal, adored her really. It didn't matter to him that she was his daughter-in-law, he thought of her as his baby girl, which was probably why she'd requested to be handed over to him, he realized with an inward groan.

"He's not going to give you any junk food," Chris pointed out as he walked past them to catch up with the shifter.

Izzy didn't say anything as she looked up at him with adoring eyes and a sweet smile that had him resigning himself to a junk food run after the meeting.

SIX

"Tell me again why we're here?" Danni asked as she sat down next to Caine at the large conference table.

"Because the Council called a meeting," he said, taking her hand into his so that he could press a kiss against her knuckles, noting that she was still wearing the gauze bandage around her wrist.

He considered asking her about it, but decided against it since she would only lie to him. She'd been wearing the bandage for over a week, a week more than she should need it. Although the cancer in her body caused problems and slowed the rate of healing, it didn't slow it down that much. Whatever injury she had should have healed within a day, especially since he made damn sure that she fed every day, twice a day.

She rolled her eyes as she pulled her hand back, taking his with it so that she could place it on her lap where he knew that she'd spend the next half hour, or however the hell long this meeting was going to last, absently tracing his hand with her fingertips. It was a nervous habit that she'd recently developed when she wasn't feeling well and didn't want to tell him, but he knew.

He always knew when she wasn't feeling well, but he didn't say anything, not unless the stubborn woman tried to push herself too hard. Then he'd step in and do whatever it took to keep her in bed until he could get his hands on some more demon blood. Not that the demon blood was helping much these days and the knowledge fucking terrified him.

When he'd changed Danni into a Pyte he'd truly fucked up. He hadn't known that she was dying of cancer. She should have been given more blood during her transformation, but he hadn't had enough to give her. They'd been held captive by a Master at the time and as a result his blood had not only given Danni immortality, but the cancer as well. Now his mate was going to live for eternity dying from cancer.

"Since when are we invited to Council meetings?" Danni asked, voicing the question that had been bugging the shit out of him since the damn shifter had started banging on their bedroom door, demanding that they move their asses.

At first he'd ignored the bastard and focused on Danni who had been moaning his name as he took her from behind, but when the banging wouldn't stop and the bastard told them that their presence was requested, he'd been admittedly too curious to refuse.

Not once in all the years that he'd worked with the Sentinels had he ever been invited to a Level One meeting. That was usually reserved for Leaders, Council members, Sentinels and human squad leaders and not for Pytes like him who'd fucked up over the years and were on probation. Since he normally used his enhanced hearing to eavesdrop on the meeting, he'd never really cared enough to bitch before, but since moving into the Williams mansion he started to care, a lot.

The Williams treated them like family, like equals and he'd never realized before just how good that felt. The Council on the other hand was still having problems trusting them since he'd turned Danni without their permission. His mate beating the shit out of a Council member hadn't helped either. So while he was officially on probation the Council members had decided that his probation extended to Danni as well now that they were mated.

"Since I was able to get the Council to take you both off probation," Eric, the Sentinel Leader for New England, said with a wink as he walked into the large room, flanked by five other men. Technically they should be under the watch of another Sentinel leader since they lived in New York, but Ephraim and Chris had refused to work with anyone else.

"We're off probation?" Danni asked with a mixture of surprise and caution.

Not that he could blame her since it had only been two months since he'd been released from his punishment for turning Danni and he seriously doubted that he'd done anything spectacular enough to earn this. That of course meant....

"We need your help," Eric said, confirming his suspicions.

"Am I off probation for good or just until whatever bullshit assignment that the Council needs help with is completed?" Caine asked, moving to clench his hand tightly into a fist when he remembered that his mate needed the comfort of tracing his hand with her fingertips.

"Well," Eric said, not one to bullshit him, as he sat down across from him, "you're off probation, but if you fuck up again you'll be punished as though you'd never been released from it."

"They can't do that!" Danni argued, her movements on his hand increasing with her agitation.

"So basically if I fuck up there's no warning whatsoever?" Caine guessed, closing his hand around Danni's trembling one and giving it a small squeeze to tell her that everything was going to be okay.

"Basically, yes," Eric said with a nod as he gestured for the other men to sit down.

"How exactly is that different from being on probation?" he demanded, entwining his fingers with Danni's as he noted that the other men sat on the opposite side of the table with Eric.

"You'll both be given Leadership status, pay, and-"

"We don't give a flying fuck about any of that," Caine said, cutting off the man that he respected. "I want to know what happens to my mate if I fuck up."

"Her status will be revoked," Eric said, reminding him why he liked this man so much.

He didn't play games, didn't make promises to Caine that he didn't plan on keeping in order to get what he wanted and wasn't afraid of him. That didn't mean that Caine was going to sit back and let the Council fuck them over, because he wasn't.

"You're not punishing my mate over something that I did."

Eric shook his head. "The Council can't keep her at Leadership status and risk giving her access to information that would aide you."

"I've *never* betrayed the Council," Danni snapped, sounding pissed and if her tone didn't give her away, her shimmering red eyes sure as hell did. "I've worked my ass off since I was a child to aid the Council. I have never done anything to give the Council reason to question my loyalty. I-"

"You broke a Councilman's nose when he came to arrest your mate," Eric pointed out dryly, cutting her off.

"Are we still on this?" Danni demanded with a snort of disgust that had him biting back a smile that she probably wouldn't appreciate at the moment. "I'm getting punished for something that healed in less than an hour?"

Eric's lips twitched, but he managed to bite back a smile as well. "Yes, well," he said, pausing to clear his throat and hide a chuckle before he continued, "they're afraid that you'd use your position to free your mate."

Danni opened her mouth to argue, but quickly closed it with a shrug before she admitted, "Well, that's probably true."

"The only thing that I care about is my mate getting the blood she needs. Is the council planning on withholding the demon blood from her?" Caine demanded, already deciding that if it was a condition that he would tell the Council to go fuck themselves. He'd focus his time on finding a cure for his mate instead of helping the Council for one more day. He would never risk her being left dependent on a group that could let her suffer just to punish him.

But before Eric could answer, Chris was there picking Danni up and dropping her on Caine's lap. With a sigh, Chris sat down in Danni's freshly vacated seat, leaned back and relaxed as he studied the men sitting across from them.

"Jackass," Danni said, glaring at Chris as she adjusted herself on Caine's lap.

Chuckling, he shot Danni a wink as he continued to study the men sitting across from them. "Oh, I doubt they'd do something that foolish," Chris drawled, letting Caine know that he'd heard a good portion of their conversation and wasn't happy.

He saw the pain in the ass shifter sit down on the other side of Chris. The man didn't say a word on their behalf and Caine didn't expect him to. Everyone in the mansion knew how the shifter felt about Pytes and would probably volunteer to take him down if the time ever came. Kale sure as hell wasn't about to bitch about one of them suffering when he wanted nothing more than to see every last Pyte wiped off the face of the earth.

"No," Ephraim said, taking the seat to Caine's right with Izzy in his arms, "I doubt they would."

Caine nearly sighed with relief. Ephraim saw Danni as a sister and if anything ever happened to him, he knew that the other man would gladly step up and take care of her. He'd move heaven and hell to make sure that Danni didn't suffer. She was part of the Williams family and they viciously protected their own.

"Do what?" Izzy asked, shifting to get more comfortable on her father-in-law's lap.

"Relax, gentlemen," Eric said, taking over the conversation before it could turn ugly. "Even if you broke every single condition of your old probation and Danni broke the nose of every Council Member, we're not going to make her suffer. She'll get her blood."

Caine nodded as relief coursed through his veins. Even though he had no plans of fucking up anytime soon, it was good to know that his mate would be well taken care of in his absence.

"What's this about hunting Pytes?" Kale asked, sounding hopeful as he managed to shock the hell out of him and apparently Ephraim if the man's startled expression was any indication.

"What?" Danni asked, frowning in confusion.

Eric sighed heavily as he leaned back in his chair. "The Masters are at war again."

"They're always at war," Caine pointed out, wondering why all of a sudden a war between Masters was enough to grant him his freedom.

"True," Eric nodded as he gestured to them, "but this time they're fighting over Pytes."

"Fuck me," Chris breathed, obviously realizing exactly what that meant for everyone in the room and for the innocent children living in the house that meant the world to them. "I thought the Council wanted the Pytes to expand their numbers."

"Have they found any yet?" Izzy asked, voicing their fears.

"We're not sure yet," Eric admitted. "We're hoping that we can use your program to find out."

"Of course," Izzy murmured, carefully climbing off her father-in-law's lap so that she could go to her mate, who would need the comfort that only Sentinel mates could provide.

As Chris picked Izzy up and carefully placed her on his lap, Caine watched as Danni reached over and took Ephraim's hand into hers, knowing the man was probably seconds away from losing control and going into blood-lust. Ephraim had three young children, young Pytes that were defenseless until they reached their sixteenth year and welcomed their Pyte transformation. They would also be the perfect targets for Masters looking to get their hands on Pytes.

No one bothered asking why the Masters wanted to get their hands on Pytes. They all knew, had feared this happening for years. They wanted to create an army of faster, stronger vampires and they needed Pytes to do that. Some would kill for a chance at true immortality and would do anything and everything to get their hands on a Pyte with the hopes that they would be turned into a Pyte as well, but most of them would be content with just having a Pyte under their control.

It was something that they could never allow to happen.

"What are the Council's plans for them?" Kale demanded.

"Right now?" Eric asked, before shaking his head. "We have none. Our only plan right now is to remove every Pyte from the Masters grasp that we can before it's too late."

"Are you going to force them to work for the Council?" Caine asked, taking his mate's other hand into his as he prayed that the Council wasn't going to try to do something so monumentally stupid as to try and force a Pyte to work for them.

"No, but if they want to fight, we won't stop them," Eric said and God help him, but Caine wanted to believe him.

"What's the reward for bringing in Pytes?" Kale, always the mercenary, asked.

"Ten million dollars a piece," Eric said, not missing a beat.

"Twenty," Kale said, his intense gaze never leaving Eric as the man turned to glare at him. "And this mission is under my control."

"Agreed," Eric said softly, letting everyone in the room know just how far the Council was willing to go to stop the Masters from winning.

Kale Quinn was a vicious bastard and they'd just given him free reign over the Sentinels.

SEVEN

Townson, MA
One week later…..

Cloe ducked her head to hide her smile as Christofer glared at her. Out of the corner of her eye she could see him rubbing his arm. One would think that after a week he'd learn to control his mouth, but sadly he hadn't. At least it was providing her with endless hours of entertainment.

For the past week they'd seemed to be in a competition. Well, he seemed to think that they were at least. Christofer had taken it upon himself to try and take over her job. She had to admit that it was really interesting to watch him try. Every morning she got up to find the kitchen a mess and a cursing Christofer trying to make breakfast for his sister.

She would hide her smile as she quickly put together breakfast and allowed Marta to choose between the two. For some reason Marta always picked her breakfast over Christofer's burnt and somewhat distorted versions. Same thing happened at lunch and dinner. Sometimes he would simply give up when he saw her at the stove and storm off to the barn for a few hours. Every time he lost his patience, which was pretty much every time that he saw her, he would say the two words that would guarantee him a sore spot. It was like a compulsion with him now.

Cloe would do something like the laundry before he could and he would get pissed when Marta thanked her. Those two little words were always followed by the *thump* of Marta's cane and a few choice words from Christofer as he glared accusingly at her. About five days ago she'd stopped counting how many times she'd been fired. She was pretty sure it was up to two hundred and fifty, give or take a few cane swats.

"I can see you smiling," he bit out.

She simply shrugged as she focused on her blueberry muffin.

"Fucking tattle tale," he muttered followed by, "Ow!"

Cloe smiled sweetly as she looked over at him, holding up the plate of muffins she'd made and with an innocent expression asked, "Muffin?"

He glared first at her and then at the plate of muffins before his eyes shot to the burnt French toast that he'd tried to make. He opened his mouth and she knew what was coming.

"Don't even think about it, Christofer," Marta said. "My arm is starting to get sore from tapping you."

"Good! Then maybe you'll stop!"

For a moment, Marta looked thoughtful while she broke off a chunk of muffin and made a show of eating it. Christofer's eyes narrowed on the action before he glared accusingly at Cloe.

"No, I don't think that I will," Marta said before she focused back on her paper.

Christofer mumbled something under his breath while he stared at her. Cloe sighed as she picked up the muffin plate and brought it to the counter, knowing he wouldn't eat any of it. He never did. According to Marta, he was on a special protein diet. She didn't question it since she knew what a bitch a metabolic disorder could be on a person.

"Cloe, could you please give me a ride into town this morning? I would like to spend most of the day at the Senior Center."

Cloe smiled. For the last four days Marta had spent her mornings at the Senior Center. She suspected that a certain Mr. Goodfellow had something to do with it, but she wasn't going to say anything, mostly because of the man sulking at the table.

"Sure, I can do that on my way to the hardware store," Cloe said, immediately regretting the slip when Christofer's head snapped back in her direction.

"Why are you going to the hardware store?" Christofer demanded.

Marta of course answered. Cloe was willing to bet the woman was enjoying thumbing her nose up at her brother.

"She's picking up the supplies to paint the house."

"The hell she is! That's *my* job."

"Uh huh," Cloe sighed. Just like everything else, he only wanted to do it so that she couldn't. "I'm ready to go if you are, Marta."

Marta pushed her empty plate towards Christofer and grabbed her purse and cane. "I'm ready."

———

Christofer dug his hands into his pockets to keep from strangling little Miss Perfect whose muffins always came out looking like muffins, making his look like dog shit on crack cocaine.

He almost ran into Cloe when she suddenly stopped in front of him. "Marta, do you want me to pack you a sandwich?"

No, she doesn't, Christofer thought smugly. Granted, it was his fault that his sister couldn't stomach eating sandwiches any longer, but that was beside the point. There was finally something that little Miss Perfect could offer his sister that Marta wouldn't accept.

"No, thank you, dear," Marta answered from the front hall.

"Guess she doesn't like your cooking after all," he whispered close to her ear, deciding to rub it in.

Cloe looked over her shoulder at him, giving him a knowing smile. "I bet she never asked for seconds when you used to cook, now did she?"

He glared at her, feeling his teeth try to push through. She was getting on his last damn nerve. He should just do the world a favor and put her over his knee and spank that beautiful ass of hers.

She reached back and petted his cheek with a coy little smile that instantly set his blood on fire. "Just because she eats my cooking doesn't mean that she likes yours any less," she said, somewhat appeasing him. She started to walk away only to pause and look over her shoulder with a teasing smile as she added, "Of course, it doesn't mean that she likes it any more either." She gave him a wink before walking away, leaving him fuming.

He was still fuming a minute later when he followed Cloe and Marta outside. Cloe raised an eyebrow in his direction. "And what do you think you're doing?"

"I'm coming with you," he said as he walked past her, snatching her keys out of her hand. "And I'm driving."

"That's fine with me. I never turn down a cute chauffer," she said teasingly as she climbed in the backseat, leaving him stunned.

Did she just call him cute? The horn honking startled him and brought his glare to Marta who gestured at her watch impatiently.

"They start Bingo in twenty minutes. Hurry, Christofer!"

He rolled his eyes as he climbed in the driver's seat and adjusted it and then readjusted it. Damn, she was a short little thing. Of course he liked that. He liked that she looked small and made him want to wrap his arms around her and-

"Comfy?" she asked wryly from the backseat.

-strangle her.

His eyes met hers in the mirror and she smiled sweetly and, definitely, innocently back at him.

"Christofer!" Marta said impatiently.

"Give me a minute, woman, while I adjust the seat from midget to man-sized," he grunted as he shifted the seat again.

"Too bad everything in the driver's seat isn't man-sized," Cloe muttered under her breath, too low for the human ear to catch, but not for him.

"I heard that!"

Her brows arched as she frowned at him. "No, you didn't."

"I assure you, sweetheart, *everything* is sized correctly," he said, looking in the rearview mirror, shooting her a wink as his words hit home.

Christofer decided then and there that he really liked it when she blushed. Marta sputtered something about him moving his butt and Cloe looked out the window. Her cheeks were still bright red when he pulled in front of the Senior Center ten minutes later. Before he could get out and help her, Marta was climbing out and a man in his seventies was standing there smiling at her and giving her a hand.

Before Christofer could demand an introduction to the man who was manhandling his sister, Marta waved him off and headed inside the building.

"Stop it. I think it's cute," Cloe said as she climbed between the two front seats to get to the front passenger seat. No doubt she feared that he would drive away if she stepped out to switch seats. He probably would, he thought with a smirk.

"I don't know why, but that little smile is making me nervous," Cloe mumbled.

"As it should, sweetheart. As it should," he said with a grin as he pulled out of the parking lot and headed for the hardware store.

———

"What about-" Cloe started to say only to be immediately shot down.

"No, I want white," Christofer, the most stubborn man on earth, said.

"Don't you even want to look at any other colors?" she asked, gesturing to a plethora of color samples set up on the back wall.

He pursed his lips up thoughtfully as he stepped closer. Instead of stepping around her to look at the samples though, he stepped up right behind her.

Cloe tried to step away only to find herself boxed in by his large body. He put a hand on her hip and leaned over her like it was the most natural thing in the world to do. She sucked in a breath and closed her eyes, trying to force herself to remain calm.

"Hmmm, these are okay I guess," she heard Christofer say, sounding as though he was far away instead of right behind her.

She could feel her heart pounding against her chest as she tried to convince herself that she was not locked in place. She could move. She could. She had the entire store to move around. There was no way that she was trapped in this small space. None. If she wanted to move she could.

"Are you okay?" Christofer suddenly asked, breaking through the tension that threatened to bring her to her knees.

"Yes, I'm fine," she lied, stepping away from him and headed towards the paint accessories. "Why don't you think about it before you decide?" she suggested, trying to sound casual as she tried desperately to calm her frayed nerves. "It's going to take a while before the house is ready to paint anyway."

"But I want white," he said in a sulky, somewhat cute, tone that made her smile and somewhat calmed her nerves.

She looked over her shoulder at him to find him looking at her curiously. "What?" she asked self-consciously, fighting back the urge to squirm under his probing gaze.

After a moment he shook his head. "Nothing. Why don't you get what you need and I'll meet you up front?" he offered, walking off before she could respond.

With a sigh, she returned her attention to scrapers, wondering what the hell that was about. For a second there she thought he'd looked hurt, but just as quickly the hurt expression was gone, leaving her to wonder if she'd just imagined it.

She quickly selected several scrapers and a large tarp and headed towards the front of the store, wondering where Christofer had wandered off to. When she spotted him outside leaning against her car and looking bored, she couldn't help but frown and wonder what his problem was. During the entire ride here he told her that he was doing this and that she didn't need to bother and now he'd lost interest?

What a jerk.

"Miss? I can help you over here if you're ready," a man said, drawing her attention to the counter by the far wall where a man dressed in a shirt and a tie stood, patiently waiting for her.

"Thank you," she said, pasting a smile on her face as she walked over and placed her items on the counter.

"Did you find everything you needed?" he asked as he scanned her items.

"Yes, thank you," she said, pulling some money out of her pocket.

"You're new in town, right?" he asked hesitantly, taking his time to add up her purchases.

"I just moved here last week," she answered politely, wishing he'd hurry up so she could leave. She was still feeling a bit jittery and desperately needed to step outside and get some fresh air.

He smiled. "You know, I think I heard that somewhere. You're staying with the Petersens, right?" he asked her as his gaze darted past her. Unable to help herself, Cloe followed his gaze to find Christofer watching them through the window.

"Just a little friendly advice, but I would stay away from him," the cashier said and Cloe could have sworn from the angry expression that crossed Christofer's features that he could hear them, which was ridiculous since they were a good thirty feet away with a wall of thick glass between them.

"How much?" she asked, returning her attention back to the cashier.

"Fifteen-fifty," he said. "Look, I know it sounds like small town drama, but there is something seriously wrong with that man. He's-"

"Keep the change," she said with a forced smile, cutting him off. The last thing she needed in her life was small town bullshit. She grabbed her small bag and walked outside, relaxing when she took her first breath of fresh air.

She walked towards her car and nearly dropped the bag when Christofer tossed the keys to her.

"Wow, you're going to let little ole' me drive? I'm honored," she said dryly.

"Tell Marta that I'll be home sometime later tonight," Christofer said evenly as he pushed away from her car.

"What are you talking about? I thought you wanted to help."

"Changed my mind," he said with a shrug, walking away without giving her another glance.

She couldn't help but shake her head in disbelief. "What an asshole," she muttered, climbing into her car. He really needed to figure out what he wanted, because these little mood swings were seriously starting to annoy the shit out of her.

Not that she couldn't use the extra money, she definitely could, but it was the middle of September and it was already starting to get chilly. At least with his help she could have cut half the time off the project, but now she'd be lucky to have it finished before the first snowflake fell.

"Fine, whatever," she said, sighing as she drove the short distance back to the house. If he didn't want to help then that was more than fine with her. She wasn't about to lose any sleep over it.

A few minutes later she pulled into the driveway and was kicking herself for not asking Christofer to grab the ladder out of the small shed in back when she had the chance. Then again, knowing his mood swings he probably would have agreed to do it and then stormed off to glower somewhere, she thought, laughing at the image of him doing just that. Not that she would admit it, but she found his little glares and pouts kind of adorable even if he did occasionally irritate the shit out of her.

Wanting to get this over with so she could relax for at least a few hours, she headed to the backyard, hoping the ladder wasn't too heavy. The last thing she needed was to throw her back out and depend on Christofer to take care of her. She pulled the key that Marta had given her yesterday out of her pocket and unlocked the door. She shoved it open until she made sure that it caught on a few clumps of grass and stayed open.

She stepped inside the small shed and looked around the dimly lit space, wondering if she should go back inside and get a flashlight so that-

The door slammed shut behind her, startling her as everything went pitch black. Forcing herself not to panic, she turned around and blindly searched for the doorknob. When she found it, she tried to turn it, but it wouldn't budge. She yanked on the door several times before she slammed her shoulder into it as she tried desperately to turn the knob.

"Oh God, please no," she cried softly as she pulled at the door as old terror surfaced, threatening to overtake her. She could almost hear the screams and the growls as she pounded against the door. This could not be happening, not again. "Help! Somebody, please help me!" she screamed as she slammed her fists against the door.

"Please!"

EIGHT

"**Y**ou want another beer?"

Christofer didn't bother looking up at the waitress as he nodded. She sighed heavily with annoyance as she walked away, probably hoping that he'd just leave. Hell, at the moment he wished he could do just that. He wished that he could get into his truck and forget that this small town even existed and live the life he craved.

There were so many things that he wanted to do and see, but never had the chance because of his duty to his sister. He didn't blame her for the way his life turned out. He blamed himself. If it hadn't been for him, their parents would have lived and his sister would have lived a full happy life instead of a life filled with sorrow and disappointment.

He'd lost count over the years of just how many ways he'd truly fucked his sister over. He was the reason she'd spent four years in that hell being poked, prodded and experimented on by those monsters. He was also the reason why they had to hide after their escape and the reason she never had the childhood that she'd deserved. If it hadn't been for him, she could have been adopted out after the war to a nice couple, but he'd been unable to let her go.

When they came to the States he'd planned on finding a couple that would take Marta in and love her as their own. Through a priest, he'd found a young couple that would have done just that. They would have given her everything that he couldn't, a home, stability and, most of all, a childhood, but in the end he hadn't been able to part with her. He couldn't trust anyone with her care. It was one of the most selfish things he'd ever done.

She meant the world to him and he'd thanked her by destroying hers. There were so many things in life that she'd given up to stay with him. Instead of a life with dolls, schoolwork and games, she'd lived a life on the run. They never stayed in any area long enough for her to make friends, because they were always afraid of being discovered.

He knew that he should have destroyed the lab and all evidence of their existence when they'd escaped, but there hadn't been enough time. He'd been too afraid to find out what they'd do to his sister if they'd been caught. Instead, he'd grabbed his sister's weak body and ran and never stopped running it seemed until about forty years ago when Marta finally had enough.

It was the first time they'd ever truly argued. She was tired of running and wanted a home, a real life and he wanted to keep her safe. It hadn't mattered what he said or did, she'd refused to listen to him. He tried, God, how he'd tried to convince her to stay with him, but she wouldn't. She'd said she loved him, but couldn't live like a fugitive any longer. She needed some peace in her life and in the end he'd been helpless to do anything but see to her wishes.

So he'd bought her a house and stepped back, allowing her a chance at the life he knew that she deserved, but he was never far from her. He took any job he could find, jobs that no one else wanted and sent her every last cent. The only thing he seemed to need was blood in his stomach and that was easily handled with a visit to the seedier side of whatever town or city he happened to be living in at the time.

For years he'd slept in abandoned buildings, garages and woods, too afraid to make any place permanent. Even though he'd missed Marta a great deal, he was glad that she no longer lived that life alongside him. As much as it hurt to watch her go on with her life, he was glad that he could finally do the right thing by her. In time it gave him comfort to know that his little sister was happy, had friends and had even fallen in love.

He'd never seen her happier than on her wedding day when Richard promised to love, honor and cherish her for the rest of their lives. Although it had frightened him to entrust another man with her care he did it, because he truly believed Richard loved her. For the first five years of their marriage, Marta was always smiling. Then one day her smile dimmed and she didn't seem to have as much energy anymore until one day she could hardly get out of bed.

The next five years were a struggle for her and hell for him. No one knew what was wrong with her. Her doctor tried to convince her that it was all in her head and for a while she believed him. Richard certainly had. Her husband started to pull away from her, leaving her alone, in pain, and not caring that she wasn't eating or able to even get out of bed.

Christofer left a construction job in Canada when he'd stopped receiving letters, couldn't get her on the phone, or a straight answer from the man he'd entrusted with her care. The day that he came home and found her practically living on the bathroom floor caused something inside of him to snap.

For the first time since he'd woken up and found himself chained inside a cage, he hadn't fought to keep the monster inside him buried. After settling his sister in her bed he went after the bastard that was supposed to care for her. It hadn't taken him long to find Richard's scent and hunt him down. When he found Richard in that motel room two towns over God himself wouldn't have been able to save him.

While his sister had been struggling to survive on the bathroom floor, the bastard that he'd trusted to care for her was off fucking another woman. In two minutes he'd made his sister a widow and hadn't cared, because he would never allow another person to harm her.

After that, he'd made Marta his world once again. He'd brought her to specialists who'd discovered that the damage done to her from the experiments he'd been helpless to stop had done far more damage to her than anyone had realized. It took years of surgeries and almost constant care before Marta was able to function once again. The damage had left her weak and vulnerable. Christofer hadn't had the heart to ask her to move from the only home she'd ever known and loved when he knew that he shouldn't stay. There had been so many reasons for him not to stay, but none of them had been more important than Marta's happiness and wellbeing.

During the first year, Marta made him promise to stop feeding off people, afraid that he'd draw attention to himself and he'd be taken away. He'd reluctantly agreed even though he knew the pain from hunger would be unbearable thanks to his time spent in the lab, but for her, he happily did it.

For that first year, he managed to keep most of the hunger pains at bay by drinking animal blood he'd purchased from butchers in town. It was the vilest thing he'd ever put into his body, but he hadn't had much of a choice. If he let himself go hungry for too long the monster inside him would take over and leave him with no choice but to attack someone and he was afraid that someone would end up being his sister.

He'd hoped his purchases would go unnoticed, but they hadn't. People in town began talking about them. Not long after that, their attention shifted to the fact that he wasn't aging. It wasn't long before men he used to work for started refusing to hire him and women and children would go out of their way to avoid him by crossing the street or running into the nearest building when they spotted him.

He quickly went from being a welcome member of the community to the town freak and there hadn't been anything that he could do to stop it. He'd already cost his sister so much. He refused to take her away from her home. Since leaving her wasn't an option, he'd learned to ignore the glares, whispers, and looks of revulsion.

He'd also managed to make a living doing what he loved, something he doubted would have happened if the people in town were still willing to hire him and he hadn't been forced to turn back to drawing out of desperation to support his sister.

The only other good thing that came from his position as town freak was meeting Seth. Seth had heard the rumors of a man that didn't age and lived off animal blood. Seth decided to come to the house late one night and introduce himself. At first, Christofer had denied the rumors and threatened to tear the man apart if he didn't get off his property, but Seth had been persistent. Just when Christofer was about to make good on his threats, Seth had thrown him a toothy grin.

It was the first time he'd ever seen anyone like himself. For the longest time he'd truly thought he was a freak of nature, especially when the doctors in the lab failed time and time again to replicate his abilities in soldiers who'd volunteered for the chance at becoming stronger and indestructible. No matter how much of his blood they took or how they gave it to the soldiers, none of the experiments had worked. Within minutes of receiving his blood, every single man had died, violently.

That hadn't stopped the doctors from trying. They'd refused to give up until they had an army of soldiers with all of his abilities, and they made damn sure they knew all of his abilities. For four years he was tortured in every single way imaginable and he'd had no choice but to allow it so that he could keep Marta safe. The only thing that gave him peace was the fact that they'd failed to duplicate him.

For the first sixty seconds after Seth had displayed his fangs, Christofer had been terrified that one of the experiments had worked, but that thought left almost as quickly as it came when he realized that Seth could not enter his house without an invitation. During that meeting he'd learned that vampires truly did exist and that some of the old wives' tales were true.

He led Seth to believe that he'd been recently turned so that he could garner information about their world. At first Seth had been reluctant to share any information with him, claiming that Christofer didn't give off the earthy scent of a vampire. It wasn't until after Christofer had shown off his own fangs, careful not to allow his eyes to shift, that Seth had been more than happy to share information with him.

He'd learned that some of the Hollywood hype had been right and that vampires couldn't tolerate sunlight or holy relics. He'd also learned that garlic didn't bother them. He'd been shocked to discover that most vampires were loyal to a leader called a Master, but that there were others like Seth, who didn't belong to anyone. They led a different life than most vampires. Instead of feeding from the source, humans, Seth and other vampires like him survived on bagged blood.

When Seth offered his blood delivering services to Christofer, for a price, he'd jumped at the chance, desperate for human blood and half afraid that he was close to finally losing control.

"John said you're cut off," the waitress suddenly announced, pulling him away from his rather depressing thoughts.

Christofer shoved the hood off his head and looked past the waitress to find the bartender taking a nervous step back. They might not know exactly what he was, but they knew enough to be wary around him. Now Cloe did as well, he thought, the realization leaving a bitter taste in his mouth.

"Why am I cut off?" he asked the waitress, returning his attention back to her.

"Because you drank twenty beers already," she bit out in a bitchy tone, folding her arms over her small chest as she glared down at him.

Christofer did a quick mental tally of all the beers he'd drank since he stepped into the bar ten hours ago and shrugged. It wasn't like he could get drunk off the shit. The fact of the matter was that it wouldn't affect him one way or the other. His body wouldn't even be able to digest it.

"I'm not drunk," he argued, not because he really wanted another beer, but because he really didn't feel like heading home and dealing with Cloe looking at him the way everyone else did. Whether Marta wanted her to leave or not no longer mattered. She was leaving. It was bad enough that he had to deal with living in this bullshit town, he'd be damned if he put up with the looks of disgust in his own home.

"Doesn't matter. John said you're cut off," she said firmly. One look at John and Christofer knew this hadn't been the man's idea. He looked close to pissing himself.

With a heavy sigh, Christofer took pity on the man and stood up. The waitress, for all her bravado, jumped back and quickly scurried off to hide behind the bar and John.

Yeah, living with this constant bullshit at home would just be so much fun, he thought dryly.

After throwing a few twenties on the table, he headed towards the men's room, chuckling when several wait-resses and a few big beefy guys tried to look casual as they jumped out of his way. His reputation did have its benefits, he decided a minute later when several men, in mid-pee, jumped out of his way when they spotted him walking into the bathroom.

Ignoring their theatrics, he stepped up to the uri-nal, unzipped and pulled himself out. Without a second thought for the guys that were practically running over each other to leave, he relieved himself. Seconds later the scent of warm beer filled the tiny bathroom as it left his body, still in its original form. It was one of the rea-sons why he stayed away from drinking hard liquor since it stung like a bitch when it came out.

He finished up and turned around, surprised to dis-cover that he wasn't alone after all. One of the men that had jumped out of the way when he'd walked into the bathroom squirmed from side to side as he held both hands over his junk.

"I really have to go," the man stressed.

Christofer's lips twitched. "Don't let me stand in your way."

"Thanks," the man said, practically running to the urinal, but damn careful to stay away from Christofer, effectively killing the tiny ounce of humor he'd felt from watching a grown man doing the "pee pee" dance.

He washed his hands and stormed out of the bathroom, uncaring that he sent half the bar's occupants jumping to the side. He was in no mood for any more bullshit tonight. The sound of his phone ringing did nothing to help his mood. He pulled the phone out of his pocket and answered a little more abruptly than he normally would have since only one person had this number.

"What?" he demanded.

"*Christofer?*" Marta said, sounding unsure.

"*Yes,*" he snapped before he took a deep calming breath and reminded himself that Marta hadn't done anything to deserve his anger. "Yes?" he said more softly as he walked out of the bar, rolling his eyes in exasperation as several bikers he'd seen around town, jumped out of his way.

"Is Cloe with you?" she asked, sounding anxious.

"No. Why would she be with me?" he asked, heading towards their house and wishing that he didn't have to wait until he was out of sight before he could use his speed to run home. Not that he was in any rush to deal with Cloe. He wasn't. He just wasn't in the mood to stay in town for longer than was necessary tonight.

"Oh dear," Marta mumbled.

"What's going on, Marta?" he asked as he watched a small group of women rush across the street to get away from him.

"She's not here," she answered, hesitantly.

"*What do you mean she's not there?*" he barked, frightening another group of women into running across the street and almost getting hit by a car. At the moment he was simply too pissed to be aggravated by their stupidity. "Where did she go after she picked you up?" he demanded, quickening his stride.

There was a heavy pause before she answered. "She didn't pick me up, Christofer. I wasn't sure if she was running late or not."

"Where are you?" he demanded, feeling his temper rise as his fangs throbbed in anticipation. He ran his tongue over his teeth to keep them at bay.

"Home, but I can't find her anywhere, Christofer. I'm very worried." she rushed out, her accent becoming more pronounced with each passing second.

"How did you get home, Marta?" he asked with barely restrained fury.

"I-I took a taxi," she whispered nervously and for good reason.

"She's fired," Christofer bit out as he broke out into a run, no longer caring that he was still in view of the town.

"But, Christofer-"

"This is no longer up for discussion, Marta. She'll be leaving tonight," he said firmly, not bothering to tell his sister that he'd be draining the bitch's body dry for failing to keep her safe.

"But, Christofer-"

"*Tonight,*" he bit out coldly, cutting his sister off before he hung up. He was in no mood to argue with his sister tonight. Allowing his sister to keep Cloe around had been a mistake, one that he wouldn't allow her to repeat. It had been foolish to bring someone else into their home when she had him.

He slowed his pace to a walk once he came in view of his house. His eyes shot over to Cloe's parked SUV as he allowed his fangs to finally slide down. Tonight he was going to drink the blood that had been tormenting him for over a week and he was going to fucking savor every last drop of it, he decided with a predatory grin when he heard the second, more frantic, heartbeat coming from the backyard.

He headed towards the backyard, more than eager to fire the bitch.

NINE

He followed the sounds of her erratic heartbeat to the old shed and growled in anticipation as the scent of her fear hit him, hard. His cock hardened painfully just thinking about sinking his teeth into her beautiful skin, but he knew that he wouldn't do anything more than drain her. She wasn't worth more than that.

She'd fucked up big time and he was not the forgiving type. Against his better judgment, she'd been entrusted with the care of his sister and had failed miserably. Marta had been abandoned and left to fend for herself, something he hadn't allowed in over forty years and he wouldn't tolerate now.

Another wave of her fear hit him and his knees nearly buckled in ecstasy. He inhaled deeply, savoring the aroma. It had been so damn long since he'd fed from the source. He could hardly wait to rip open the shed door and tear into her throat, but he forced himself to savor the moment.

He considered thanking his sister for warning Cloe that she was in danger, but knew it would probably be a long time before Marta spoke to him again. At the moment he simply didn't care. Marta had known the danger she was courting when she'd invited the young woman to live with them. Nobody knew better than Marta what he was capable of.

If she really thought warning Cloe to make a run for it would save her then she'd been sadly mistaken. Marta would have been better off keeping the woman protectively by her side. He would never release the monster inside of him in front of his sister, not again, and she had to have known that. Warning Cloe so that she could run only fueled his need and with Marta out of the way there was nothing in this world that was going to stop this.

He reached out and turned the doorknob, chuckling darkly when he found it locked. Did she really think that she could keep him out with a flimsy lock? Marta must not have explained the situation very well. Otherwise, Cloe would have tried to escape him by using her car instead of trying to hide from him. Not that it would have made much of a difference in the end. After what she did tonight he would have gladly hunted her down.

With a small flick of his wrist he broke the lock and jerked the door open. Even in the pitch black shed it didn't take him long to find her. The darker an area, the brighter everything appeared to him. She sat against the opposite wall with her arms wrapped around her indrawn knees. She looked absolutely terrified, Christofer noted with morbid satisfaction.

"Cloe," he said softly, wanting to watch her fear explode before he took her. She was going to suffer for every second of fear that she'd caused his sister. He would make sure-

"Christofer?" she mumbled around a small sob as she awkwardly got to her feet and rushed him. He didn't even bother preparing himself for her attack, knowing there was absolutely nothing she could do that he wouldn't heal from.

"Christofer!" she cried softly as she......

Threw herself into his arms?

What. The. Hell?

Her legs wrapped tightly around his waist as her arms circled around his neck, damn near cutting off his air supply, not that he needed it. She panted quietly against the crook of his neck as her body trembled almost violently in his arms.

Christofer stood there for a moment, stunned. After a slight hesitation, his arms came around her and held her tightly against him, unable to help himself. It had been so damn long since someone willingly went to him, never mind touched him like this. He closed his eyes and inhaled deeply, savoring the aroma of adrenaline and fear as it poured off her. The combination mixed with her already enticing blood was too much for him to take.

He licked his lips in anticipation as his eyes latched onto a patch of beautiful tan skin just below her neck as he moved in for a taste. As much as he wanted to savor the moment, he knew that he'd probably tear into her throat and lose control when the first drop of her blood hit his tongue. It had been far too long since he'd fed from the source and Cloe's blood was too damn-

"Ow!" he snapped, startled as he realized that something hit him upside his head. Pulling his head back, he quickly turned around, expecting to see his sister standing there only to discover that they were still alone. Which meant....

"Why the hell did you hit me?" he demanded as he stepped out of the shed and into the pitch-black backyard.

As if to answer his question, she slapped him upside his head, again.

"What the hell is your problem?" he demanded, gripping her hips to pull her off only to find her legs locked in a death grip around his waist. She had him so damn confused that he had no idea what he should be doing with the infuriating woman.

"I w-was st-st-stuck in the shed all d-d-day b-because of you!" she managed to get out through her chattering teeth as her arms somehow managed to tighten further around his neck. If he'd been human he'd probably be on the ground gasping for air by now.

"How is that my fault?" he demanded, wondering if he should just go ahead and rip into her throat and save himself from the bullshit that she brought into his life.

"You were supposed to help today," she said tightly, sounding more in control, but her body's violent shivering and the desperate way she clung to him told a different story. The badass woman he'd met in the pharmacy was scared out of her mind and oddly enough, it wasn't because of him.

Surprisingly, she seemed to be seeking comfort from *him* when most women stayed away from him. Suspicious of her actions, he narrowed his eyes as he glared down at her.

"You didn't purposely abandon my sister, did you?" he asked, knowing that if he sensed any hesitation or deception in her answer that he would take her behind the shed and drain her. He'd happily deal with the consequences

R.L. MATHEWSON

of having a pissed off sister. Better to be pissed off at him than to be harmed or dead, he decided.

"No, you jerk!" she said, accompanying her denial with another slap.

"What the hell is it with you women and hitting me?" he demanded in a half growl. "A simple answer would have been enough."

"Maybe if you hadn't acted like an asshole today and ditched me, you wouldn't be getting slapped upside the head," she pointed out, sounding furious, but he noted that she was still clinging to him.

He felt his temper snap with that accusation and the reminder of why he'd left her alone. "I wouldn't have ditched you if you hadn't made it so fucking obvious that you didn't want me around!"

"What the hell are you talking about? I never acted like I didn't want you around," she said, shivering violently against him as she tried to shift in his arms to get closer, confusing him even more.

"You couldn't get away from me fast enough in the hardware store," he snapped even as he released his hold on her hips and wrapped his arms around her, simply because he couldn't help himself.

The only person in his entire life that had sought him out for comfort and accepted him unconditionally had been Marta. As a small child she'd always preferred to go to him for company, attention, and comfort. Even his father, who he knew loved him, held him at an arm's length, probably because he blamed him for his mother's death.

According to the midwife and the physician that had overseen his birth, his delivery had been the most violent birth they'd ever witnessed. His mother had died in agony as she gave him life. As much as his father had tried, he hadn't been able to stop the tale of his birth from reaching the small village they'd lived near.

Things probably wouldn't have been so bad if he'd grown at a normal rate, but he'd been small for his age and grew at an alarmingly slow rate. The villagers took that as a sign that there was something wrong with him and avoided him, although not outright. No one would have done anything to anger his father since they counted on his generosity for their livelihoods.

His family had been one of the richest and oldest families in Germany. At the time, owning more land, homes, and businesses than even Hitler, but none of that had meant anything when the shit hit the fan.

"What the hell are you talking about? And can't we have this discussion in the house?" she demanded through chattering teeth.

"Fine!" he snapped, walking towards the house. He didn't miss her tiny sigh of relief. What had scared her this badly? he wondered as he took the back steps two at a time.

Once they were in the dark kitchen she didn't release him as he'd expected. Instead, she reluctantly raised her head to look around, her heartbeat increasing even faster as a new wave of fear hit him hard.

"The light?" she whispered harshly.

Frowning down at the woman trembling in his arms, he reached out and flicked the switch on, encompassing the kitchen in bright light. As soon as the light was on, Cloe was out of his arms and across the room in what seemed like a matter of seconds, further pissing him off.

"Maybe you should just leave if my presence disgusts you so much," he said tightly, running his tongue over his fangs as they threatened to shoot out. He was pissed.

Beyond fucking pissed.

She hadn't run off and abandoned his sister, he understood that, but it seemed as though she still had a problem being around him. He wasn't about to put up with the same small town bullshit in his own home. After a lifetime of being treated like a pariah he was done.

If Marta needed extra companionship so badly then maybe they should move so that she could have it without his pride taking another hit. He really couldn't fathom anything more insulting than the woman he was stupidly falling for thinking that he was lower than dog shit. Call him crazy, but it wasn't exactly a flattering comparison.

"What are you talking about?" Cloe asked absently as she wrapped her arms around herself and looked around the kitchen as if she expected something to jump out at any second and attack her.

"Every time I come within touching distance of you, you can't get away from me fast enough. If I had known that you were going to buy into the little town drama I would have saved us all the trouble by throwing your ass out the first day you came here," he said, running his tongue over his fangs as they poked out of his gums once again. The scent of her fear wasn't going anywhere and he was having a hard time ignoring it.

She paused in her wild search to roll her eyes at him. "I don't have a problem with you, you jerk. Well, besides screwing me over so you can have a hissy fit."

"I don't throw hissy fits," he cut her off, but she continued as if she hadn't heard him, which was damn frustrating.

"My problem is space," she finished, bending slightly so that she could shoot a nervous look beneath the kitchen table.

Frowning, he couldn't help but do the same. "What exactly are we looking for?"

"Nothing," she said quickly, too quickly, but he decided to let it go.

For now.

"Uh huh, and what are you talking about? Space? What the hell does that have to do with anything?" he asked, wondering when she was going to relax. They'd been in the house for over five minutes and she was still giving off the scent of fear as she shivered her ass off.

She shot him a glare as she said, "I don't like being cornered or trapped in small spaces. I need space."

Her words ran through his head as he remembered that she hadn't taken exception to his presence, other than annoyance, until he'd crowded her against the paint samples, which he'd done because she'd been driving him crazy at the time and he kind of enjoyed pissing her off.

"Oh," he said, feeling like an ass.

"Yeah, *'Oh'*," she snapped back. "If you hadn't gone off pouting and had stuck around to help me, I wouldn't have been locked up in that shed all night," she bit out, making him wince.

Shit.

"So……," he trailed off not exactly sure how to broach the subject, "I don't disgust you?" he asked, immediately wishing that he hadn't.

"The only thing that disgusts me about you is the food you try to serve Marta," she said, shooting a nervous look at the door and damn near jumped to the ceiling when it was suddenly thrown open.

Marta stormed into the room, shooting him a narrowed eye glare that instantly disappeared when she spotted Cloe.

"Are you alright, dear?" she asked Cloe, walking as quickly as her cane would allow her over to the young woman who was still shivering as she held herself tightly.

Cloe forced a reassuring smile for Marta. "I'm fine. Just a little cold. I was stuck in the shed all day," she explained and he couldn't help but notice that she hadn't blamed him, but apparently that wasn't going to stop Marta from placing the blame squarely at his feet.

"This would not have happened if you had helped her," she said accusingly as she took a step towards him, her hand noticeably tightening around the top of her cane.

"Marta," he warned tightly. He was done with *all* the bullshit.

"You should have been helping her today instead of sulking!" Marta snapped, further testing his patience. He was not about to stand there and allow his younger sister to yell at him like he was an errant child.

"I'm so upset with you, Christofer!"

"Marta, it's not his fault," Cloe said, coming to his defense and further shocking him, but Marta wasn't done.

"You should have-"

"Marta, go to bed!" he snapped, having had more than enough for one night.

She drew up rigid, glaring at him. When she opened her mouth, probably to promise to whack him with her cane if he didn't behave, he added, "Now."

After a moment of glowering at him, she nodded slightly. "Fine. As long as Cloe is okay."

"I'm fine, Marta. I'm sorry that I worried you."

"There's nothing to apologize for," Marta said, giving him a look that he knew all too well. There would be hell to pay in the morning and God help him, but he would probably just suck it up and take it as long as it meant that Marta got it out of her system. He didn't like to see her upset. Every time she was stressed, her heart worked over-time, scaring the hell out of him. So for her, he would take it, but not in front of Cloe.

Not again.

"Good night, Marta," he said, not at all surprised when she acted as though she hadn't heard him.

"You didn't need to yell at her. She was only worried," Cloe said, rubbing her hands up and down her arms, try-ing to create friction to help warm herself.

"Don't worry about Marta," he said, gesturing for her to leave the kitchen. "She's fine, just angry. I assure you that she will not hesitate in telling me just how furi-ous she is in the morning," he said dryly.

Cloe's lips twitched, the first sign of humor since he'd found her. He hated to admit that it calmed something inside of him. Seeing her upset and vulnerable made him feel helpless, a feeling he detested. "She does seem to enjoy doing that," she said just as a violent shiver tore through her body, making her cringe into herself.

"Let's get you warm," he said softly as he pushed the guilt away that was threatening to take over. He watched her nod stiffly as she walked past him on shaky legs.

None of this would have happened if it weren't for him. Instead of feeling sorry for himself he should have owned up to his responsibilities, not left them to this young woman. As he followed Cloe up the stairs a sense of shame surrounded him when he realized that he'd once again failed to keep the promise that he'd made to his father.

TEN

"Get in the tub, Cloe," Christofer said, sighing heavily as he pinched the bridge of his nose as if she were the one acting insane.

She tightened her grip on her towel as she stubbornly shook her head. "Thank you, but no thank you, Christofer. I can handle taking a shower by myself," she said through chattering teeth, wishing he would get out of her bathroom so that she could stand under the hot water without an audience.

"I'm not leaving, Cloe," he told her, leaning back against the doorframe. When he'd first followed her inside the bedroom and opened the bathroom door for her, she'd been relieved. Right now she couldn't deal with any enclosed spaces and he seemed to understand that.

That didn't mean that she appreciated the little alpha male routine he was pulling on her at the moment. She was more than capable of taking care of herself. She'd been doing it for more than thirteen years and one night of hell was not going to change that.

"I'm not getting in that shower with you standing there," she bit out through clenched teeth when he didn't make any move to leave after a few minutes. She was freezing her ass off and so damn tired, but she knew that she wouldn't be able to sleep tonight. Hell, she'd be lucky if she could sleep in a few days when exhaustion finally took over.

"Fine," he said, shrugging as he pushed away from the doorway.

She nearly sighed with relief. That is until he said, "You're leaving me with no choice but to drag you in there." As he spoke, he pulled off his sweatshirt and tossed it aside, revealing a simple gray tee shirt that molded to his perfectly sculptured chest and abs, leaving Cloe momentarily stunned.

That is until he pulled the tee shirt off and tossed it to the side as well.

Living near the beach for the past few years, she'd seen some very drool worthy bodies, but none of them, and she meant none of them, had anything on Christofer. Every muscle was perfectly defined and tanned. Even the light dusting of dark hair on his chest and trailing down his stomach didn't mar the perfection. If anything it added to it. Thankfully he dragged her out of her thoughts before she did something stupid like drool.

"Let's go," he said, picking her up before she realized what he was doing.

"Hey! Put me down!" she snapped just as a violent tremor tore through her body. God, she was so damned cold.

"No problem," he said, carefully placing her in the shower, just out of reach of the water.

"Thank y—*hey!*" she may have screeched when he surprised her by snatching her towel away and tossing it over his shoulder.

He ignored her outraged glare and simply pointed towards the water that was even at this distance giving off a delicious warmth. "Get under the water or I'll put you there," he said evenly and she knew that he'd do just that.

With a small sigh, she gave up and moved beneath the water, making sure to keep her back to the wall. She was too tired to care that she was naked in front of a man that on a good day made her a little nervous. At the moment the only thing she cared about was getting warm, making sure that he didn't see her back, and keeping the lights on. Anything else was too much work for her frayed nerves.

"I'm going downstairs to check on my sister. Do you think you'll be okay for a moment?" Christofer asked, reaching over and pushing her now soaked hair out of her face.

"I-I'm f-f-fine," she stammered through her chattering teeth. "Y-you don't n-need to c-come back."

Of course he ignored her. "I'll be back in a few minutes, Cloe," he said firmly as he walked out of the bathroom, leaving her alone.

As the hot water streamed down her body, delivering much needed warmth, she fought against the urge to close her eyes and simply savor it. Although she doubted he would get a chance to come back before she was out of the shower, she didn't want to take the chance of him coming back and getting a glimpse of her back.

He would either react with pity or disgust and right now she didn't have the energy to deal with either. She didn't know which reaction she hated more, but she knew that she didn't want to see either expression on his face. She wasn't sure why it mattered what Christofer thought since it was more than obvious that he didn't want her here, but it did.

The boyfriends she'd had over the years, granted there hadn't been many, either tried to play it off like it was no big deal or flat out lied, but she never missed the looks of pity or revulsion on their faces whenever they saw her back. While most women would probably hide their scarred backs, she didn't. She didn't exactly flaunt it or make a big deal out of it, but she did use it to see just what kind of man she was dealing with.

There were a few guys that took one look at her back and walked away and although their reaction disappointed her, it never really bothered her. If they couldn't deal with the scars covering her back, making her less than perfect, then that was more than fine with her. She wasn't looking for "Mr. Right" anyway. She just wanted someone that she could spend a little time with every now and then to forget her troubles. The guys that managed to pretend that her back didn't bother them had provided her with the only thing she allowed herself, casual companionship.

That is until she'd met Aidan. In the beginning he'd been great, fun, kind and unbelievably great in bed. He hadn't seemed to mind her scars. In fact, they'd actually seemed to turn him on. At first she'd thought it was sweet, but soon after they began sleeping together it started to creep her out just a little bit. When she tried to pull away and end things he became possessive and she hated to admit this, but he actually started to scare her a little bit.

Not too long after she'd ended things with him the late night phone calls began. When she spotted him when she left the house she was a little weirded out, but didn't think much of it. It wasn't until she'd noticed that she couldn't even go out to grab the mail without seeing him that she realized that she had a little problem on her hands and decided to cut her losses and get out of Florida.

It had been past time to go anyway. She never stayed anywhere for very long and she'd already stayed in Florida a year longer than planned. So she'd contacted the agency that she worked for and looked into what they had available before she'd decided to give New England a try.

Now she was living in a house with a man, who admittedly pissed her off a lot and amused her, but one that for some strange reason actually mattered. He could be a real jerk sometimes, well most of the time, but the thought of *him* looking at her with revulsion had her stomach churning. She didn't know why it mattered. It really shouldn't, but it did.

If she were going to be honest with herself then she'd admit that she liked the way he looked at her when he didn't think anyone was watching, but she always knew. It didn't matter what she was doing, the moment his eyes landed on her she sensed it.

The way he watched her made her feel desirable and beautiful. She knew that she was being ridiculous and that nothing would ever happen between them. His sister was her employer and that made him a complication. Not to mention Aidan. After dealing with him, she needed a break from men, but that didn't mean that she wanted him to suddenly look at her with anything close to pity or disgust.

Still shivering, she shut the water off and stepped out of the bathtub. Why couldn't she get warm? She reached for one of the folded towels she kept stacked on the corner of the sink counter and ended up knocking the small pile onto the floor with a trembling hand.

With an annoyed sigh, she knelt on the floor to pick the towels up. Her hands only trembled more violently when she tried to grab them. She needed to get it together and stop freaking out. Nothing happened. She was fine. It had been a horrible experience, but she'd had worse, much worse.

A towel was suddenly draped over her shoulders, startling her and she reacted. She swung back, barely registering the grunt of pain as she pulled her fist back to do it again. She kept on swinging until she found herself pinned against the tiled wall, panting hard as her body shivered violently.

"Calm down!" Christofer snapped and it was then that she realized that she was still fighting him. "It's okay, Cloe. *Shhhh*, it's okay," he said soothingly as he released his hold on her arms to gently cup her face in his hands. "Are you okay?" he asked softly.

She almost snorted at that. Right now she was so far from okay that it wasn't even funny. He'd surprised her, scared her and any other day she probably would have been able to laugh it off, but not today. Not when old memories were threatening to take over and suffocate her.

"Don't sneak up on me!" she snapped, shoving him back, surprised when he complied.

He held his hands up as he took a step back. "I didn't mean to scare you," he said softly. She noted the red marks on his face and the blood dripping from a small cut on his lip, but if he noticed it didn't show. As badly as she felt about hurting him, she wouldn't apologize. He'd scared the hell out of her by sneaking up behind her and she'd reacted like any other woman would when a man who had no business being in her bathroom startled her.

"You didn't scare me. You surprised me," she snapped, snatching one of the towels off the floor and wrapping it around herself. She was relieved when he didn't follow the movement with his eyes. The last thing she needed right now was one of his smoldering looks that usually set her body on fire. Right now it would make her feel too damn vulnerable and she didn't need that. She needed to get it together and push through this.

He frowned down at her. "You're still shivering," he said on a sigh as he headed for the door. "Get some clothes on and I'll see if I can find another blanket for you."

"I'm fine!" she yelled after him. She was fine, more than fine. Everything was fine. The important thing was that she was alive and no longer stuck in that old musty shed. As soon as she was able to stop shivering she'd be better than fine.

Ignoring her trembling legs, she walked into her room and quickly pulled on a long-sleeved t-shirt, a pair of sweatpants and a pair of socks all while keeping an eye on the door. When she was done and didn't feel even an ounce of additional warmth, she crawled in bed, pausing only long enough to turn on the lamp by her bed to brighten the already bright room up a little more, and then snuggled beneath the covers.

Why couldn't she get warm? She was wearing clothes and there was a mountain of blankets on top of her, but it felt as though she was only covered by a thin layer of tissue. She was so damn cold, she thought miserably as another shiver rocked her body.

"I found another quilt and a blanket," Christofer announced as he walked back into the room. Without another word, he placed the blankets over her.

"T-thank you, Christofer," she stammered, closing her eyes as she willed her body to stop shivering. "I'm fine now. Thank you," she said, hoping that he would leave. She just needed a little time to pull it together. By morning she'd be as good as new. She just needed to get warm first.

"We'll see if that helps," he said just as her mind registered the sound of wood creaking. She opened her eyes to find him sitting in the old wood rocking chair in the corner of her small room, watching her.

"You can go now, Christofer. I'm fine," she promised him even as another tremor tore through her body, leaving her with no choice but to grind her teeth against the pain racing up and down her muscles.

She heard him sigh heavily and looked up in time to see him pull off his shoes and the t-shirt he'd pulled back on at some point, leaving him bare from the waist up. If she hadn't been shivering so damn violently or trying to calm her nerves she'd probably take a moment to simply enjoy the sight before her.

Had she ever seen anything more beautiful? She really didn't think so. Her eyes quickly took in his tanned muscular chest, ropes of muscle and perfectly sculpted abs. Okay, so maybe she took a moment between tremors to appreciate the sight before her. She was human after all. Thankfully another tremor tore through her body, helping her to focus.

"What are you doing?" she asked, hating the way her voice shook.

"Body heat," was all he said as he pulled back the covers of the small double bed and climbed in beside her.

It took her a moment to register what he'd said and when it did she was moving to climb off the bed. Unfortunately for her, he was a lot faster than her and had her yanked back into his arms before she could put up a proper fight. Of course, once she felt the delicious heat that he was giving off she didn't want to fight it anymore.

With a little grumble and a grunt, she turned in his arms and plastered herself against him. She ignored his hiss of surprise as she pressed her cool cheek against his shoulder. If he hadn't invited himself into her bed she might have felt bad, but then again, she wouldn't even be in this mess if he hadn't ditched her ass today. This was his fault, she reminded herself as she placed her cold hand on his chest and nearly smiled when he released another hiss.

"Better?" he asked, sounding almost concerned, but she knew that he really wasn't. He was probably doing this out of guilt more than anything. Marta was mad at him and he was probably being nice to her to earn his sister's forgiveness.

If she hadn't already known that Christofer was the one that owned the house and had the money she would have suspected that he was using his much older sister. She'd seen it enough times to recognize the signs. She hated when relatives who didn't give a damn showed up occasionally just to get on the good side of the elderly person she was working for to gain a spot in their wills. It was sickening and she was glad that it wasn't going on here. She really liked Marta, probably more than she'd liked any of her previous employers, and she didn't want to see her hurt.

The real reason, and something that actually stunned her once she'd realized what was going on here, was that Christofer genuinely cared about his sister even if he was lazy about showing it. In a way it was actually kind of odd. The two of them acted as though they'd been raised together when they had be at least fifty years apart. Sometimes Marta treated Christofer like the older sibling. That is, when she wasn't going out of her way to torment her brother. It was a little odd, but she'd seen odder things over the years.

"Go to sleep, Cloe. You're safe," Christofer said, earning a snort from her.

Yeah, right. Like she'd be able to sleep. She knew it would be several days before she managed to fall asleep. She'd be too damn afraid to close her eyes, but she appreciated the offer all the same and of course the body heat.

She snuggled tightly against him as her eyes began to droop, noting that she felt oddly safe in his arms.

ELEVEN

"What's wrong, Christofer?" Marta asked, appearing concerned as he made his way quickly down the stairs.

"Everything is fine. I'll be back in a minute. Grab your purse," he said, desperately struggling against the urge to go back upstairs and rip into Cloe's neck.

If he didn't get downstairs within the next minute he knew there would be nothing to stop the monster inside of him from taking over. Holding her in his arms all night had been heaven and hell for him. Being that close to someone was something he usually never allowed for himself. He'd pleasured women before, but he'd never been able to relax his guard enough to hang around long enough to hold them afterwards or cared enough to do it. The only woman he'd ever cared about was Marta.

When they'd first escaped the camp, she'd been scared, traumatized, and in no shape to face the world alone. Every night he'd held her in his arms, singing all those songs that used to annoy him, but that she loved. He sang them until his voice was raw and she was sleeping deeply. Whenever she woke up in the middle of the night, he started all over again. He did that until she was a grown woman and no longer needed him.

Before he'd made his promise to Marta, he'd resigned himself to seeking a temporary escape in the arms of women. No matter how many women he'd pleasured, he couldn't escape the bitter loneliness or the creeping sensation that always reminded him that he couldn't trust them. He couldn't trust anyone but Marta and that knowledge made it damn difficult to focus on the woman begging for more. More often than not, old panic would surge through him as he tried to take a woman and he'd have no choice but to leave. It was the main reason why he hadn't sought out a woman to warm his bed in over fifty years.

Last night while he'd held Cloe in his arms he'd willed her to fall asleep before the panic could take over and force him to flee her bed, but it never came. Instead, he found himself enjoying the feel of her in his arms. While she'd slept, he took his time studying her face, running his fingers carefully through her hair and breathing in her unique scent. Until a few hours ago he'd been able to ignore how enticing her blood was, but once hunger hit, it had become a struggle that he'd almost lost several times.

The sun hadn't been able to rise fast enough for him. When the cravings began a few short hours ago, he should have just left to save himself the torture of being near her and not being able to have her, but he hadn't been able to forget the fear that he saw in her eyes last night. That alone kept him in her bed and his arms wrapped around her. When the sun had risen high enough that he'd felt it was safe to leave her, he hadn't been able to get away fast enough.

Another minute and he would have ripped into her throat without a second thought. As he made his way downstairs, he had to fight against the urge to do just that. His stomach growled viciously as he caught a hint of her mouthwatering scent coming off his clothes. His hand shot out and grabbed the railing as he struggled for control. In seconds, the hardwood banister snapped beneath his hand as he fought his body's demand to go take what was rightfully *his*.

He shoved that disturbing thought away as he forced his feet to carry him the rest of the way to his refrigerator. In seconds, he had a bag of blood stuck on his teeth and another two in his hands, ready to take its place before the last drop was gone. By the time he'd moved onto his sixth bag, he was already calculating the amount of blood that he was going to need to order to make sure that there were no more close calls.

Even as he decided that the only safe way to do this was to triple his order, he realized that the smartest thing to do would be to send her away. It wouldn't be too difficult. After the scare she'd had last night it probably wouldn't be tough to make her want to leave. If he hadn't realized just how badly he'd fucked up last night that's exactly what he would be doing.

Instead, he was making plans to binge on blood to keep her safe so that she could stay. If she'd had family, someone that he thought would take her in and care for her, he wouldn't hesitate in sending her packing, but she didn't. After Marta had refused to fire her the first night, he'd done a little investigating of his own. All of her family had been killed years ago in a lodge fire. She'd been the only one to survive, but she hadn't come out of it unscathed. Her back was proof of that.

She'd spent three months in a trauma center after the fire and then two and a half years bouncing around in the foster care system. Once she'd turned eighteen, she'd started to work a string of shitty jobs while she'd put herself through school. Once she had her nursing degree, she used it to travel the country. It wasn't difficult to figure out that she didn't seem to like to stay anywhere for long. He doubted that she'd stay here for very long, but until he felt that she would be okay and he found her a new position that was safe for a young woman with no family, she was staying.

TWELVE

Before last night, Cloe could have honestly said that she didn't embarrass very easily, but now…..

Now, she was actually looking forward to Christofer firing her this morning so that she had the excuse she needed to leave without looking like the coward that she truly was. Last night had been a mortifying experience, one that she fully planned on forgetting. The faster that she put distance between her and this house, the better.

She had no idea where she was going yet and she didn't really care. She just wanted out of here. She wanted to get away from that damn shed, away from the nightmares that were even now threatening to destroy her and away from the memories of how pathetic she'd been last night. The only thing that she wished that she didn't have to leave behind was Marta, but she knew that it was for the best.

Marta was such a sweet, caring woman and it was going to kill Cloe to have to leave her. In just a few minutes she was going to be fired and really, what choice did she have in the matter? She'd been hired to take care of Marta and she wasn't doing it. Yesterday the poor woman had been left on her own and that had bothered Cloe almost as much as being trapped in that shed.

Actually, knowing that Marta was all alone with no way of getting home had cranked up her desperation to get out. She'd only known the older woman for a week, but she knew how stubborn Marta could be about protecting her from Christofer. There was no doubt in her mind that Marta would have done anything and everything to keep Christofer from finding out that Cloe wasn't doing her job, including walking home instead of calling Christofer to come pick her up.

Cloe had been terrified that the older woman would do just that. In between dealing with her own fear, she'd been terrified that Marta had walked home instead of asking for help. She'd hoped that Marta would ask someone at the center for a ride or call a taxi, but Cloe hadn't been sure that Marta had any money on her. When she saw the feisty older woman storm into the kitchen last night, healthy and whole, she'd felt herself relax, somewhat.

She'd still been on edge and it should have only gotten worse during the night, but somehow Christofer had managed to do what therapy, pills, time and prayers hadn't been able to do. He'd chased away her fear, made her feel safe for the first time in years and she didn't know how to deal with that. The only thing that she was sure of was that Christofer was a dangerous man.

He made her feel things that she had no business feeling and made her want things that she could never have. She was glad that he was a complete jerk. It helped keep things in perspective and kept her from doing something foolish like falling for a man that she could never have.

Long-term relationships weren't possible in her life, not with the need to move hitting her every couple of years. She couldn't handle anything permanent in her life, mostly because there was no such thing as forever. She'd learned that lesson the hard way.

She liked to live for the here and now and with anything permanent in her life she wouldn't be able to do that. That's why she didn't keep jobs for longer than was necessary or stayed in any one area for too long. She liked the freedom of being able to go where she wanted, when she wanted and right now she really wanted to leave.

She'd never been fired before, never wanted to be fired before, and she wasn't exactly looking forward to this. She'd always prided herself on working hard, being on time and giving a hundred and ten percent into everything she did the way her father had-

No, she wasn't going to think about him. Not right now when she needed to keep it together and get through this. This time when he fired her, she would nod in understanding, thank him and Marta. She'd make her goodbyes quickly before she grabbed her bags and made a run for it.

Decision made, she picked up her duffle bag and threw it over her shoulder, grabbed the handle of her oversized suitcase and headed for the stairs. Pausing at the top of the stairs, she looked down at her watch and nearly sighed with relief. It was well after one o'clock in the afternoon, which meant that she'd slept through breakfast and lunch. Christofer now had more than enough reason to fire her, not that he really needed it today.

Telling herself that it was better to get this over with, she started down the stairs. When she walked into the kitchen she was relieved to find Christofer washing his hands at the kitchen sink since it saved her from having to hunt him down to get him to say his two favorite words.

"Is there something that you needed, Cloe?" he asked, not bothering to look up at her as he slowly scrubbed his hands clean.

A little taken off guard that he hadn't spoken those two words that he seemed to be in love with, she softly cleared her throat as she set her bags down. She opened her mouth and then abruptly closed it when she realized that she had absolutely no idea what to say. This was the first time that she'd ever tried to get fired and she had no idea how to go about achieving that without pissing him off enough to call up the agency that she worked for and complain.

Since she decided which jobs she would accept, she wouldn't get in trouble for quitting if that's what she had to do now. For safety reasons they were allowed to abruptly quit. Normally they were expected to stay on until a replacement could be found, but if she told Marie, her contact at the agency, that she was uncomfortable with staying here a minute longer she would be allowed to leave immediately and still get work through the agency.

Getting fired wouldn't cause any problems for her since she'd never been fired before and there weren't any criminal concerns along with her termination. The only caretakers that had to worry about termination from the agency were the ones that were habitually fired, quit every job abruptly, were accused of stealing, elderly abuse or one of a dozen offenses that the agency specifically prohibited.

If he called up and filed a complaint about her, she wouldn't get fired, but she would have a black mark against her that could be used against her later and that wasn't something that she was comfortable with. She needed him to fire her without getting pissed so that she could apologize, thank him for the opportunity to work with Marta and leave.

"How are you feeling?" he asked, still not looking at her as he turned off the faucet.

"Fine," she said, which was mostly true thanks to the sleep she'd been able to get last night. Her nerves were frayed and she was still slightly on edge, but it was manageable.

At least for the moment.

Right now she had two choices to keep it together, leaving or going back on her medication. Since she refused to go back on her medication that made her choice pretty simple. She was leaving. He could fire her ass or she'd quit and hope that he didn't try to get back at her by calling up the agency. Either way she planned to put at least ten hours between her and this house by tonight.

He nodded absently as he dried his hands on a dish-cloth. "Are you hungry?" he asked, looking at her for the first time since she'd stepped into the kitchen.

"No," she said, watching as he glanced down at the bags by her side.

"Why don't you go back upstairs and lay down? I'll bring you something cold to drink," he suggested, already grabbing a clean glass from the dishwasher to do just that and confusing her more than she ever thought possible.

For the past week he'd been firing her over every little thing and now that she'd made it more than obvious that she wanted to leave, he was letting a golden opportunity to fire her ass slip by him. Worrying her bottom lip, she watched as he filled a glass with the lemonade that she'd made yesterday.

"I'm not tired," she said, deciding to give him another minute so that he could properly fire her.

"I see," he said with a slight nod as he set the glass of lemonade down on the counter.

Good, she thought, nearly sighing with relief as she leaned over to grab her bags. Before she could manage to do more than brush her fingertips over the handles, the bags were yanked away from her and carried past her. More than a little surprised, she turned to follow him outside.

At least he wasn't gloating, she thought, ignoring the slight disappointment that she felt that he hadn't at least tried to talk her out of this. He was no doubt relieved to finally be rid of her. Then again, he was probably waiting until they were outside, by her car and out of earshot of Marta so that he could gloat.

She should say goodbye to Marta, she realized, opening her mouth to ask him to hold up a minute when he took her by surprise and walked past the backdoor and headed upstairs with her bags.

"What the hell are you doing?" she asked, following him upstairs to take her bags back.

"Helping you bring your bags back to your room," he said, taking the stairs two at a time and forcing her to practically run up the stairs to catch up with him.

"I'm leaving," she pointed out, rushing after him as he headed down the hall towards the bedroom she'd been using.

"No, you're not," he simply said, not bothering to look at her or even slow his pace as he stepped inside the bedroom.

"Yes, I am," she bit out in exasperation as she finally caught up with him.

"You're staying," he said, tossing her bags on the bed before she could grab them.

With an annoyed sigh, she walked past him and grabbed her bags. "I'm really not, Christofer. You can either fire me or I quit, but I'm out of here."

"Wow, I didn't know that you hated my sister that much that you'd willingly subject her to my cooking," he said conversationally as she turned around and discovered that he was blocking the only exit from the room.

As much as she appreciated the fact that he'd left the door open, it didn't make her feel any less trapped. Normally she could deal with having someone standing in the doorway, but not today.

"Move," she said, shifting the heavy bag over her shoulder as she moved towards the door and the large man blocking it.

Christofer shook his head. "Not until you promise not to leave."

"If you're not going to fire me, Christofer, then I quit. So please move away from the door so that I can say goodbye to Marta and be on my way," she said, forcing herself to ignore the panic that began crawling up her spine and the breaths that were coming too quickly to do her any good.

"Cloe?" Christofer said, sounding worried and so far away.

"I'm leaving, Christofer," she said, noting that her words sounded slurred right around the time that she stumbled slightly to the right.

Her arms and legs went numb, the bags dropped to the ground seconds before her legs gave out to join them. The room spun violently as the floor rushed up to greet her, but before she could become better acquainted with the hardwood floor, she found herself rising and moving towards the door.

"You're not going anywhere, mein Schatz," Christofer said as he headed for the stairs. As much as she would have loved to have been able to come up with a smartass remark to tell him exactly what she thought of his high-handed ways, sadly all she could come up with was a muttered grumble that had the bastard chuckling.

THIRTEEN

"I'm fine. You can put me down," Cloe said calmly and he probably would have believed her if she hadn't been squeezing her eyes shut or gone deathly pale on him.

He didn't bother arguing with her as he carefully placed her in a chair at the kitchen table. When she leaned forward and laid her head on her folded arms instead of getting up and storming off to make another attempt to leave, he wasn't exactly surprised. She hadn't eaten since yesterday morning and now that she was over the initial stress and drama from last night, her body was finally making its demands for food known.

Now that she'd stopped giving off the scent of fear and anxiety, he could smell how low her blood sugar actually was. She needed to eat something before she made herself sick or passed out again. Instead of coming up with a bullshit story to explain how he knew that her blood sugar was low, he simply focused on getting some food in her.

After he made sure that she wasn't going to fall out of the chair, he grabbed a glass, a bottle of orange juice from the fridge and the sugar bowl. Keeping an eye on her, he quickly filled the glass with orange juice and dumped in a large scoop of sugar and mixed it before placing it on the table in front of Cloe.

"Drink it," he said softly as he returned to the counter to clean up the small mess that he'd made.

"What is it?" Cloe asked, not bothering to raise her head as she opened her eyes and shot the glass of juice a wary glance.

"Orange juice and a little bit of sugar," he said, replacing the cap on the orange juice bottle and returning it to the fridge. "Drink it. It will make you feel better," he said absently as he looked over the contents of the fridge.

It was practically overflowing with food that he didn't recognize, never mind knew how to cook. Milk, juice, water, a jar of mayonnaise, cheese, eggs, and what appeared to be some kind of brown deli meat were the only things that he recognized. Deciding to keep it as simple as possible, he grabbed the cheese, mayonnaise, and deli meat and placed them on the counter.

After hunting down a half loaf of bread, he started making a sandwich. He grabbed a large serving spoon and scooped up a big spoonful of mayonnaise and dropped it on a slice of bread, careful to make sure that the mayonnaise didn't pour out onto the plate. That was followed with a half-inch of cheese, an inch of deli meat, and a few good shakes of salt and pepper between every layer.

He wasn't an expert on sandwiches, but he thought it looked pretty good. It would at least fill her up, he mused as he topped the sandwich with the second slice of bread. For a moment he considered cutting the sandwich in half, but he didn't want to risk any of the mayonnaise escaping.

Cloe was slowly sipping the orange juice when he placed the sandwich down in front of her. Her brows pulled together as she looked down at the sandwich.

"This will make you feel better," he said, gesturing to the sandwich as he leaned back against the counter.

"I'm not so sure about that," Cloe murmured, her lips twitching with amusement as she inspected the sandwich, layer by layer.

"Did, um," she said, clearing her throat as she bit back a smile that had his eyes narrowing, "did you make Marta's sandwiches like this?"

"Yes," he answered defensively, wondering what her problem was. The sandwich had everything that she liked to eat and would fill her up quickly. It was the perfect meal in his book. It was easy to make, cheap and provided everything that she would need; bread, meat and cheese. What more could she ask for?

"I see," she said as a smile broke free before she managed to pull it back. She lightly touched the top of the sandwich which caused an obscene amount of mayonnaise to seep out and pool on the plate.

Sighing in irritation, he grabbed a spoon from the drawer and grabbed the plate away from her so that he could fix the sandwich for her. He pulled the top layer of bread off and quickly scooped up the mayonnaise that had escaped and put it back in the sandwich. When he was done, he pushed the plate back to her.

"Um, thank you," she murmured as she looked around the kitchen. "Where's Marta?"

"I dropped her off at the Senior Center this morning," he said, moving to clean up the mess as he waited for her to finish her sandwich.

"Oh," she said, looking oddly disappointed as she slumped in her chair and focused her attention back on the sandwich where it belonged.

"They're having a spaghetti dinner there tonight and she wanted to help," he explained, frowning when he caught her poking the sandwich and watching with fascination as more mayonnaise poured out.

He was just about to demand that she eat the wonderful sandwich that he'd made when he heard her stomach growl, demanding that she eat the sandwich and doing his job for him. Since she was now his responsibility that meant that he had to make sure that she was well taken care of and he had to admit that he was doing a damn fine job of it so far.

"I guess I could hang around to say goodbye to her," she said with a sigh as she got to her feet.

"What about your sandwich?" he asked, gesturing to the home cooked meal that he'd slaved over for her.

"I'm afraid that I can't handle eating something that delicious, Christofer," she said with a sigh of regret, which somewhat appeased him. "It would wreck me for all future sandwiches."

That was true, he had to admit. He was just about to offer to make her a bowl of cereal when she took him by surprise and did the one thing that he'd truly never expected. She walked over to him and….

She hugged him.

"Thank you for everything that you did for me last night," she said softly, pulling away only to pause long enough to press a kiss against his cheek. Then she was moving away from him before he could stop her or at the very least, wrap his arms around her and savor the warmth that she was offering him.

"You're welcome," he said softly, not sure what to make of this woman. One thing was for damn sure, she wasn't like any other woman that he'd ever met.

And he wasn't ready to let her go.

———

"May I help you?" Cloe asked, pausing at the top of the stairs even as she made a backup plan just in case the large, grumpy man in front of her decided to play caveman with her luggage again.

"That depends," Christofer drawled, crossing his arms over his chest as he leaned back against the wall and momentarily drew her attention to the bulging muscles flexing beneath the tight gray tee shirt that he wore.

"On?" she found herself asking as she forced herself to look up and focus on the stubborn man that refused to let her quit.

"On where you're going," he said, gesturing to her luggage with a slight nod.

"Well first, I thought I'd go to the diner and get a bite to eat before I pass out. Then I'm going to head over to the Senior Center and say goodbye to Marta. After that I thought I'd head south for a while and see where life takes me," she said, picking up her luggage and moving to take a step down the stairs when, surprise, surprise, he blocked her.

"I made you lunch," he said accusingly as he pushed away from the wall and blocked her path.

"I know and it was sweet, really, but I really don't think that I could handle something that delicious," she said with a heartfelt sigh even as she did her best to bite back a smile.

It really had been a sweet gesture even if it had grossed her out to an unbelievable degree. She'd never in her life seen so much mayonnaise and pepper in one sandwich before. It had oozed out of the sandwich, reminding her of pus and that had pretty much killed any cravings for sandwiches for a while.

"I tell you what," Christofer said, reaching over and gently removing the bags from her hands and the one on her shoulder, "let me buy you lunch and we can talk."

"I'm not staying, Christofer," she sighed, moving to pick her bags up, but instead found him taking both of her hands in his and giving them a gentle tug that had her reluctantly following him down the stairs.

"And we can discuss that while we eat," he said, giving her a hopeful smile that had her narrowing her eyes on him.

"And if I decide to leave afterwards?" she asked, eying him suspiciously.

"Then you can leave," he said with that damn smile that did funny things to her. "No worries."

"Uh huh," she said, letting him lead her towards the front door. "And why don't I believe you?"

"Because you're paranoid?" he offered with a wink as he released her right hand and grabbed his sweatshirt off the coatrack.

"Fine," she said, pursing her lips up in thought as he released her other hand so that he could pull on the sweatshirt, "I'll have lunch with you, but on one condition."

"And what's that?" he asked, starting to pull his sweatshirt on.

"That you leave the sweatshirt home," she said, knowing damn well that he didn't leave the house without his sweatshirt, pretty much guaranteeing that she would never have to see him again.

———

"H-h-how m-many?" the waitress finally managed to ask after a full minute and a half of blatantly staring at Christofer, who was looking decidedly uncomfortable and making her feel kind of bad.

She still couldn't believe that he'd agreed to her terms. He hated this kind of attention and honestly, if she'd known that he was going to say yes, she never would have made the request in the first place. Instead of doing what she'd expected, he'd gone completely still, staring down at the sweatshirt in his hands, his life support, before reluctantly nodding and returning the sweatshirt to the hook.

"We don't have to do-" she started to say, giving him the escape that he clearly needed.

"Two," he said tightly, cutting her off.

"O-okay," the waitress said, wide-eyed stare still fixed on Christofer as she blindly reached out and grabbed a handful of menus. "Right this way," the waitress said numbly, reluctantly turning around so that she could show them to a booth.

Looking decidedly uncomfortable, Christofer gestured for her to walk ahead of him. She opened her mouth to once again offer him an escape, but with a resigned sigh, shook her head and followed the waitress. He was a grown man and if he wanted to put himself through this hell then that was his choice. Who knows, maybe the whole thing would piss him off enough that he'd willingly let her leave without an argument, she hoped as every conversation in the small diner stopped and every head turned to gawk in Christopher's direction.

She'd be on the road within the hour since she doubted that he'd be able to last more than ten minutes before he ended up making a run for it.

FOURTEEN

"I'll give you a few minutes to decide," the waitress said hollowly, her eyes never leaving him as she slowly backed away from the table.

Christofer did his best to ignore her and the rest of the patrons who were now openly staring at them and focused on the woman sitting across from him. Other than throwing the gawking customers a curious look, Cloe didn't seem to care one way or the other about their audience.

"What's good here?" she asked, picking up her menu and turning her attention to ordering food, the rest of the customers clearly forgotten.

Hell, he wished that he could forget them, but the eerie silence that had taken over the small diner made it impossible. He could hear every startled breath taken, every heartbeat racing with excitement, and every subtle shift on the vinyl covered seats as they did their best to get a better view. When the hushed whispers broke through the silence he wasn't sure if he should feel relieved or pissed.

Definitely pissed, he thought a minute later as he was forced to sit there and pretend that he couldn't hear what they were saying about him.

"I can't believe he's here!"

"He never goes anywhere without his hood!"

"He's such a freak!"

"Oh my God! He looks exactly as he did thirty years ago! Wait until I tell Mavis!"

"I hear she's living with them!"

"I wonder if she's a freak like him."

"I thought he didn't eat. What's he doing here?"

"They should have run him out of town years ago!"

"Hank needs to kick him out. He doesn't belong here!"

"You don't have to stay here," Cloe said, bringing his attention back to her and away from the whispers that seemed to be getting louder with each passing second.

It took him a minute to realize that most of the customers had stopped whispering and were now talking loud enough for Cloe to hear what they were saying. They were probably hoping that he'd take the hint and get the hell out. If it weren't for the woman sitting across from him, he'd probably do just that.

What the hell was wrong with him? He hadn't left the house in over forty years without a hat or a sweatshirt, because he hadn't wanted to deal with this bullshit. He still earned stares and whispers wherever he went, but never to this degree. Then again, they'd probably still be reacting like this even if he had brought his sweatshirt, he realized. He hadn't stepped foot in a restaurant since he'd moved here over forty years ago. He was also out with a woman who wasn't his elderly sister, something that he'd never done before since most women in this town took one look at him and ran screaming the other way.

"I'm fine," he said, opening his menu and forcing himself to ignore everything going on around them.

"Do you know what you'd like?" their waitress asked as she approached the table, sounding normal and giving him some hope that at least one person was going to stop treating him like a freak.

When he looked up and met the waitress's petrified gaze he was forced to bite back a few words that would have probably had the terrified woman screaming for help. Instead, he looked back down at the menu filled with food that he'd never even heard of before, never mind tasted. What the hell did humans eat these days?

"I'd like a chocolate frappe with extra ice cream, a cheeseburger with fries and coleslaw, please," Cloe said, saving him from playing a guessing game.

"I'll have the same, please," he said, taking Cloe's menu from her and handing it over to the waitress who seemed too stunned to do anything but stare at him.

"You're going to eat?" she finally asked, sending a pleading look over her shoulder at the equally stunned waitresses cowering behind the counter.

"Yes," he said evenly as he prayed for patience.

"O-okay," the waitress said woodenly as she turned around and walked off, but not before she threw a cautious look over her shoulder, probably making sure that he wasn't following her.

"You really know how to turn heads," Cloe said, earning a glare from him. "Wanna tell me about it?"

"No," he bit out.

"Alrighty then," she said with a careless shrug as she opened her purse and pulled out her phone, leaving him to frown as she started typing something on the small keypad.

"What are you doing?" he found himself asking.

"Sending my contact at the agency an email and asking her if she has any job openings on the west coast," she said, never taking her eyes off her phone.

Scowling, he plucked the phone from her hand and shoved it in his pocket. "I thought we were going to talk," he said, ignoring the hand that she held out for the return of her phone.

"No," she said with a sigh as she dropped her hand away when it became painfully obvious that he had no intentions of returning her phone, "I came to eat. *You* came to talk."

Still wondering why she hadn't eaten the sandwich that he'd made for her if she was so hungry, he forced himself to focus on getting her to stay without having to resort to kidnapping her. It would probably draw more unnecessary attention his way, he mused as he watched her every move. He needed to figure out a way to make her stay without her finding out that she really didn't have a choice.

"What will it take to get you to stay?" he asked, deciding to go with bribery first. Giving her a raise or buying her something would be a hell of a lot easier than convincing her to stay, he decided as he waited for her demands.

"Nothing," she said with a shrug, making him wonder if she was trying to play hardball and see just how much she could get out of him.

"You're going to be difficult about this, aren't you?" he asked, rubbing his hands down his face and wondering just how many hoops she was going to make him jump through to get her to willingly stay.

"Not at all," she said, shaking her head as she looked around the restaurant, "I'm just not staying."

"Why not?" he demanded, hoping to buy himself a little more time so that he could think up a better approach, one that didn't involve chaining her to the house.

"Because this job just didn't work out for me," she said with a shrug, not quite meeting his eyes, he noticed.

"This job or because of what happened last night?" he demanded, having a pretty good idea that if he hadn't fucked up yesterday and ditched her that she would still be willing to stay and drive him out of his fucking mind.

"What happened last night?" the woman sitting behind him asked, startling him and bringing his attention to the fact that the forty-something year old woman sitting directly behind him was turned around in her seat and shamelessly eavesdropping on their entire conversation.

Before he could tell her to mind her own fucking business, Cloe beat him to it. "I forgot the safe word last night and was brutally punished for it," she said dryly, staring at the nosy woman until she got the hint and turned back around in her seat.

"It has nothing to do with last night," she said, pulling her hair back into a ponytail as she looked away.

"You're lying," he said, because he knew without a doubt that she loved her job. She loved working with his sister and she sure as hell loved driving him crazy.

"So what if I am?" she asked, sitting back when a large plate of food was placed in front of her.

"Is there anything else that I can get for you?" the waitress asked as a large plate of food was placed in front of him.

He was just about to tell her that they were fine when he looked up and realized that they had a different waitress. Frowning, he looked past their new waitress to find their old waitress standing just outside the kitchen doors with a small brown paper bag stuck to her face and two women trying to get her to calm down before she passed out.

"We're all set," Cloe said, following his gaze with a frown.

"Just yell if you need anything," the new waitress said, sending him a curious look before she walked away.

"This is a very weird town," Cloe mumbled as she grabbed a bottle of ketchup and squeezed an insane amount all over her fries.

"You have no idea," he muttered as he took the bottle of ketchup from her and squirted the red stuff all over his fries before setting the bottle down and wondering what he was supposed to do now.

With a sigh, Cloe picked the bottle back up and squirted some on her burger before placing the bun on top. Deciding that it was probably a good idea, he took the bottle from her again and did the same to his burger. When she cut her burger in half, he did the same.

"Are you going to tell me why this town treats you like a leper?" she asked, taking a bite out of her burger.

"Are you going to tell me what freaked you out last night?" he asked, cocking a brow as he took a bite out of his burger, but not before he discreetly smelled it, making sure that they hadn't put anything extra in his burger.

"Touché," she said with a nod as he struggled not to gag.

Although it had smelled pleasant enough, it tasted like garbage and his mouth desperately wanted to get rid of it. Instead of spitting it out, he forced himself to chew a few times before he swallowed the entire bite. When it landed like a ball of lead in the pit of his stomach he was reminded of what he'd be forced to do later. It was not something that he was looking forward to, he mused as he forced himself to take another bite.

"I thought you were on a special diet," Cloe said, gesturing to his plate with a ketchup-smothered French fry.

"I am," he said evenly, picking up a French fry and forcing it down his throat.

"Is this going to make you sick?" she asked, pausing with a fry halfway to her mouth, sounding concerned.

"No," he lied, well, not technically since the food wouldn't make him sick. He'd be the one forced to make himself sick to rid his body of this crap before it started to rot in his stomach and caused a few other problems that he'd really rather not have to deal with.

"How's your frappe?" she asked, picking up her own and taking a long, slow sip of it all while watching his every move.

"Delicious," he forced himself to say as he picked up the glass of what looked like liquid shit and copied her, doing his best not to cringe when the overly sweet, cold, thick liquid hit his tongue.

"You don't look like you're enjoying it," she pointed out, returning her attention to her burger.

"I'm in heaven," he said dryly, earning a smile from her as he forced another bite of his burger down his throat.

She rolled her eyes as she picked up another fry and dipped it in a puddle of ketchup. "You could have ordered something else."

Not unless she was on the menu, he thought wistfully as he picked up another fry and forced it in his mouth. She smelled mouthwatering, he thought, nearly groaning when his stomach growled in agreement. His fangs actually ached for a taste of her as his eyes latched onto her pulse, mesmerized by the beautiful thrum of her artery as it danced in tune to her heartbeat. What he wouldn't give for a taste of her, he thought miserably as he stuffed yet another fry in his mouth.

"What time will Marta be done with her dinner tonight?" Cloe asked, managing to draw his attention away from her vein.

"Late," he said, returning his attention to his burger when the thought of stuffing one more grease soaked fry into his mouth had his stomach turning in disgust.

"Maybe I should come back to the house and prepare a few casseroles to carry her over for a few days until she can find someone to replace me," Cloe said, frowning with worry and providing him with a better, and more private, opportunity to convince her to stay.

"Yes, yes you should," he said, biting back a grin as he took another bite of his burger.

FIFTEEN

"I swear to God that if you don't open this door and give me back my purse that I will kick your ass!" Cloe snapped, slapping her hands flat against the basement door before she followed it up with a small kick when her threat was once again met with silence.

She still couldn't believe that the bastard had done it.

If she had known that he was going to steal her purse when she went upstairs to grab her bags, she wouldn't have left it on the kitchen table. Hell, if she had known that he was going to use the last three hours to try and convince her to stay, she never would have come back here.

"Asshole!" she growled, shoving away from the door as she tried to figure out what she was going to do now.

Staying here wasn't an option, not unless she could manage to ask Christofer to crawl in bed with her tonight and keep her safe without dying of mortification. Since she was pretty sure that she couldn't manage that, leaving was her only choice. She wasn't weak and she'd be damned if she let anyone think that, especially the bastard that she was going kill as soon as she got her hands on him.

Last night had been a fluke for her. She'd been taken off guard by old memories and she'd reacted. It wasn't something that she was proud of, but at least she hadn't broken down and sobbed hysterically no matter how tempting it had been. She hadn't cried, hadn't taken her pills, run screaming into the night or begged Christofer to take care of her.

He'd done that all on his own and right now she hated him for it.

She didn't want to need someone the way that she needed him, not when it would hurt too much to lose him and she would lose him. One day she would have to move on. The need to leave, to put some more space between her and her past would take over and leave her with no choice but to accept a new job in another state. She'd be forced to say goodbye to him and the longer she stayed, the harder that would become. That was only if he didn't leave her first, which he probably would.

He'd either get sick of dealing with her baggage, get sick of her, find someone else, or die, leaving her behind to deal with no longer having him in her life. She couldn't do it. Didn't want to do it. There was a reason why she didn't allow herself to get close to her clients. It was also the reason why she'd cut ties with everyone as soon as she moved on to a new job. She never wanted to deal with the kind of pain that went along with losing someone that she cared about again. She'd already dealt with enough loss in her life and didn't need anymore. She should have remembered that this morning instead of looking for an excuse to prolong her goodbyes.

Now the bastard was downstairs with her purse. He had her ID, money, credit cards, and keys and she was left here fuming as she tried to figure out a way to get her stuff and get the hell out of here. She needed to do it before he figured out another way to keep her here and she was left with no choice but to beg him to stay with her for another night. Since that wasn't going to happen, she needed to figure out a way to get the basement door open and quickly. It was times like this that she wished she'd made friends with the criminal sort so that she'd know how to pick this damn lock. Then she could go downstairs and kick his ass!

"Asshole," she muttered again, simply because it gave her something to do as she tried to think of a way to-

"Now, that wasn't very nice," the bastard that she was going to kill with her bare hands said as he opened the basement door and leaned against the doorframe.

Eyes narrowing, she quickly looked him over, hoping to find her purse, but there was nothing in his hands. That was fine with her, she thought as she pushed past him, half-expecting him to stop her. When he simply stepped aside and let her walk past him, she decided that she could just as easily ransack his room as she could kick his ass.

"You'll never find it," he said, chuckling as he followed her downstairs.

"Uh huh," she said, pausing at the foot of the stairs as she surveyed the large finished basement.

Unlike the rest of the house that looked like it was stuck back in the 1950s, this room looked modern. It looked more comfortable and it definitely was more guy friendly. The loveseat by the back wall was large and looked comfortable, as did the bed, which was neatly made. That shocked her, but not as much as the fact that the rest of the room was clean and tidy. Given how much Christofer seemed to hate doing household chores, she'd assumed that his room would have resembled something out of a frat house.

Instead his room was clean and everything seemed to have a place. There were no posters of scantily clad women on the walls, empty beer cans littering the floor or the smell of food rotting away somewhere in the corner. Then again, there wasn't much to leave on the floor, she realized as she looked around the room and noted that besides the laptop computer, some art supplies and an insane amount of books lined up against the walls, there wasn't anything personal in the room.

The only furniture in the room was the bed, a small dresser, a large refrigerator in the corner and a few bookshelves that were crammed full of books. She'd seen hotel rooms that looked homier than this room. As far as she knew, he'd been living here all of his life, but it didn't show. It looked more like he was just passing through. It made her heart break a little more for him.

He was living in a town where he was obviously not wanted, had no friends, hid out in the barn most of the time working, and spent whatever free time that he had making sure that his sister was taken care of. Well, his version of taking care of her, she amended, pursing up her lips in thought as she looked the room over again.

"How exactly do you plan on finding it?" he asked, walking past her as he pulled off his shirt, revealing the incredible torso that she may have enjoyed snuggling up against last night.

"By tearing your room apart piece by piece until I find my purse. Then I'm going to beat you with it, say goodbye to Marta, kick your ass again and then leave," she said, somehow managing to look away when all she wanted to do was to walk up to him, wrap her arms around him, and soak in the comfort that only he could give her one last time before she left for good.

"That sounds like fun," he said around a yawn as he flopped down across the bed on his stomach. "Just try not to wake me up, okay, mein Schatz?" he said, sounding amused when he should be frightened.

And what the hell did mein Schatz mean anyway? She considered asking him, but she didn't want to take a chance giving him something else to torment her with. Sending one last scowl in his direction, she made her way to what she assumed was his bathroom. After a quick check, she decided that her purse wasn't in there so she moved on to his closet with no luck.

Fifteen minutes later she was ready to kill the bastard. She'd searched everywhere with absolutely no luck. Well, that wasn't entirely true, she thought as her gaze narrowed on the refrigerator in the corner, the refrigerator that was currently locked and no doubt held her purse.

"Open the fridge," she demanded as she walked over to the bed.

"No," he said, shifting onto his back with a sigh as he settled in once again for a nap.

TALL, SILENT AND LETHAL

"Just give me my purse so that I can leave," she bit through clenched teeth, praying that he cut the shit and just let her go, because she seriously didn't know how much longer it would be until she snapped and did something that would require her to apologize to Marta and probably face a little jail time.

"Let me think about it for a minute," he said, folding his arms behind his head, not even bothering to open his eyes as he added, "No," with a little smirk that had her eyes narrowing to slits and her hands twitching with the need to grab a pillow and smother the bastard.

"Christofer," she said, pausing to close her eyes and take a deep breath before she continued, "I'm seconds away from killing you with my bare hands. Just give me my purse so that I can be on my way and you can continue breathing."

"No," he simply said, leaving her with no choice but to kill him.

Furious, she stormed over to the bed, grabbed a pillow and climbed onto the bed. She straddled his thighs just as she shoved the pillow down on his face. She held it over his face for a good thirty seconds or so before she asked, "Are you going to give me my purse?"

"No," came the muffled reply and God help the bastard, but it sounded like he was laughing.

"Last chance," she warned, giving the pillow a slight shake to show him that she meant business.

With a sigh, Christofer pulled his arms out from behind his head and grabbed the pillow. Before she could stop him, he flipped the pillow back and raised his head as he settled back more comfortably against it.

When she went to grab the pillow away from him and finish the job, he grabbed her hands and carefully entwined their fingers.

"Let go," she demanded as she tried to pull her hands free, admittedly not trying very hard and hating herself for it.

She liked where she was a little too much, which was just a reminder that she really needed to leave before she did something stupid like let herself fall for the jerk. As it was, she was already too close to liking him. It probably wouldn't take much to push her over the edge and make her come up with a lame excuse to stay.

"No," he said, gently caressing his thumb over the back of her hands.

"I need to go, Christofer," she said, feeling herself soften as she looked down into his beautiful baby blue eyes.

"No, you really don't," he said with a simple shake of his head as he continued to caress his thumbs across the back of her hands.

"Yes, I really do," she snapped in aggravation as she sat back on his thighs and glanced around the room again.

"Then leave," he said with a careless shrug that she really didn't care for, not one bit.

"I can't," she ground out even as she wondered if he'd snuck out of the house and hid the purse somewhere else.

"You could if you really wanted to," he explained before adding, "Clearly you don't want to leave," just to piss her off.

"Really?" she asked, looking back down at him and cocking a brow. "Why don't we put your little theory to the test then?"

"And how do you propose that we do that?"

"Give me back my purse," she suggested in a challenging tone.

"And what would that prove exactly?" he asked as his gaze slowly left her face to do a slow perusal of her body and she swore that she could actually feel it moving down her body.

"Well, after I kick your ass and take off, I think it will prove that I wanted to leave," she explained, noting the way her voice started to tremble at the end even as she prayed that he'd missed it.

Why did he have this affect on her? It wasn't right. It sure as hell wasn't normal. No man had ever made her feel like this, like she'd die if she had to go another minute without touching him. She liked men, loved sex, and enjoyed spending time with men and the excitement that led to jumping into bed with them, but this was different.

She loved the way Christofer looked at her, the way he touched her without any hesitation like it was the most natural thing in the world. She loved the way she felt when she was near him, like she was safe and nothing bad could touch her as long as she was with him. She even loved how he could set her body on fire with one simple look even while she hated the fact that he had that much power over her.

"It would only prove just how badly you wanted to stay," Christofer said, voicing her fears.

"I need to go, Christofer," she said, pointedly ignoring him as she moved to climb off him and search the room one more time before she tried to come up with a plan B.

"No, you need to stay, Cloe," he said, giving her hands a gentle tug that had her ass landing back on his thighs.

She sighed, long and heavy, as she shot another glance around the room, hoping that her purse would suddenly appear. When her gaze landed on the small alarm clock by the bed she felt her stomach drop. It was after five o'clock, which meant that even if she managed to find her keys tonight, she'd be forced to drive well into the morning to put any real distance between herself and another bad memory.

Maybe she should-

"Shit!" Christofer snapped as her cellphone rang loud and clear right above her head.

Smiling in triumph, Cloe stood up, making sure to put one foot on his stomach and one on his thigh in the process, loving the little pained grunt he made as she put all of her weight on the leg currently getting its support from his stomach. "Looks like someone forgot to shut the ringer off," she pointed out with a relieved sigh as she reached up and pushed the aged ceiling tile aside. She spotted her purse hanging just over the edge and grabbed it before the bastard seething beneath her could knock her on her ass and take it away from her.

Making sure to earn another one of those pained grunts that she was beginning to love, she ground her foot in his stomach one last time as she stepped off him and jumped off the bed. As she pulled her phone out of her purse, she ignored the glare that he was sending her way. She didn't know him well, but she knew by the expression on his face that he was already thinking up another bullshit plan to keep her here. Knowing that it was probably best to leave before he had a chance to stop her, she headed for the door as she looked down at her phone and nearly sagged with relief.

It was Marta calling, most likely looking for a ride home. Perfect timing. This phone call provided her with the opportunity that she needed to say goodbye and put this nightmare, and the overbearing bastard coming after her, behind her once and for all. Then she could-

Let out an embarrassingly high squeal as the bastard that she was going to kill with her bare hands took her by surprise and swept her off her feet.

SIXTEEN

Williams Mansion

"**P**lease tell me that you're fucking kidding me," Kale said, sounding frustrated as he rubbed his hands down his face.

If she'd been anyone else delivering the bad news to the shifter, she knew that he would have probably sent her screaming from the room. Instead, he was forcing himself to stand where he was and take a deep breath. It was something that she definitely appreciated about their close friendship, she mused as she opened the bag of peanut butter cups she kept hidden in her desk where her overbearing mate couldn't find them.

She wasn't too surprised when the bag was suddenly snatched away from her or when she looked up to find Kale tearing into the bag, sending her a look that dared her to bitch. Normally she would have snatched the bag back from him, but she just didn't have the energy today.

For the last week she'd been working day and night on *Tattletale*, teaching it how to decipher the Sentinel blood supply system. It had broken into the system and grabbed all the information that she'd requested, quickly fitting it into categories within the first hour, which was what she'd expected it to do. What she hadn't expected, and she really should have, was that all the information was fake.

Well, the drop off locations, the amount of blood ordered and delivered, and the deposits made to cover the blood delivery orders were real, but that wasn't really helpful when the rest of the information was fake. Not only that, but it seemed that once a customer moved out of an area they apparently would set up a new account with a new fake name and contact information.

Was the Council surprised when she'd informed them of the problem? Not at all. They'd set it up like this. They wanted to make sure that vampires, demons and all the lovely creatures that relied on human blood had easy access to bagged blood to keep them from attacking humans. It was something that she understood and normally would have fully supported, but not now, not when she was depending on their information to weed out the Pytes.

"Are there any descriptions? Notes? Anything to clue us in on the identity of the customers?" Kale demanded as he unwrapped a peanut butter cup and shoved it in his mouth.

Izzy shook her head, biting back a wince when the movement sent sharp pain shooting through her throbbing hip. Ignoring it, because it was either that or break down and cry, she focused on the large monitor in front of her. "No, there aren't any notes. No clue into their species, nothing."

Kale growled out something unintelligible as he shoved another peanut butter cup in his mouth. He'd been on edge all week, eager to start this job only to discover that it wasn't going to be that easy. Every attempt they'd made to hunt down Pytes had been met with roadblocks. First, he'd been denied access to the files that the Vatican held on suspected Pytes, because the Council refused to agree on just how much information Kale should have access to.

Then they'd discovered that all those files that the Council were protecting were hand written, kept in an underground tomb where they were protected by a security system. *Tattletale* could have shut it down, but that wouldn't have helped since there was no record of the location of the tombs in the files. Until the Council could come to an agreement over the files, they had to use what they had, which wasn't a hell of a lot.

"Vampires can't smell Pytes," Kale suddenly announced, sounding thoughtful.

"True, but they also can't smell most demons," she felt the need to point out, wondering where he was going with this.

"We need the delivery personnel to start identifying the species of every customer," Kale said, dropping the now-empty bag of peanut butter cups on the desk. He grabbed a chair and pulled it up to her workstation and settled in.

"What are you thinking?" she asked, even as she hacked into the Sentinel blood supply system and added a new column in the database and labeled it, "Species."

"If we can start eliminating vampires off our list, we can narrow it down," Kale said, opening the mini-fridge that she kept beneath her workstation.

"Vampires can't distinguish between most demons and Pytes," she pointed out, again.

"It doesn't matter," Kale said, pulling out two bottles of orange juice and handed her one. "If we can manage to shorten the list, we'll have something that we can work with."

Izzy pursed her lips up in thought as she looked back at the database. After a moment, she added another category, "Special Notes."

"What's that for?" Kale asked, taking her orange juice back so that he could open it for her.

"We might be able to cut the list down further if we get clues that will help us sort through the rest of the list."

"Good idea," Kale agreed with an approving nod.

"I'm going to break into the message center and send out a general message requesting the deliverers to identify the species of their customers and take note of anything unusual about the customer," she explained even as she did it.

"We don't want them cluing anyone in on our plans," Kale warned.

She shook her head. "I'm going to make sure that they know that this is observation only, no questions asked."

"What if they don't comply?" Kale asked, but she could tell by his tone that he already had an idea or two to make sure that they complied.

"I'm going to give them some bullshit administrative excuse to get the job done. If I offer them information, an incentive or make a big deal out of this in any way, it will tip them off and make them curious."

"Curious is bad," Kale agreed with a nod.

"Exactly."

"Are you going to be able to filter out Pyte abilities?" he asked, getting to his feet.

"I should be able to as long as I get decent information," she said, wondering if perhaps she should set up a form for the deliverers to check off for each customer, something mixed with Pyte and demon abilities so that the deliverers were kept in the dark about their real intentions.

"Let me know when you have something concrete," he said, heading to the door.

"Where are you going?" she asked, keeping her attention on her monitor as she readjusted the database.

"To get my team together."

——

Orlando, Florida

"She's definitely left the state," Brock, his beta, said in way of greeting as he stepped into the office and shut the door behind him, blocking out the noise from the busy kitchen.

"Where is she?" Aidan asked, not bothering to look away from his computer as he double-checked last night's figures.

"We're not sure yet," Brock admitted on a heavy sigh as he walked around the large mahogany desk that they shared. "Did your balance match mine?" Brock asked, nodding towards the computer screen.

"Yes, but we'll handle that in a minute," Aidan said, pushing back from the desk and turning the chair around so that he could face his beta. "Were you able to cut off her support?"

Brock nodded, not looking particularly happy about it. Then again, none of his pack was happy about this, but he didn't care. He wanted his property back and until he got it, they would continue to do whatever was necessary to ensure that happened.

Of course this time he wasn't demanding that his pack uproot their lives again and move across country. This time he was done chasing after his property, watching her from afar, especially after he'd so freely been allowed to taste her. This would be the very last time that she would run away from him.

"We've hacked into her bank accounts and froze them. We also have someone trying to get information from the nursing company that she works for. We should have something within the week if not sooner," Brock explained, making Aidan smile for the first time in a week since he'd discovered that the bitch that he'd claimed as his own had taken off sometime during the night.

"Good," Aidan said, nodding approvingly as he looked back at the computer screen and the small problem that needed his attention. "Are you keeping track of her bank and credit card activity?" he asked as he opened up the file for last week's sales figures.

"So far she hasn't tried to use her ATM card or credit cards. According to her bank records, she took out a thousand dollars the morning that she left. So-"

"It's only a matter of time before she tries to use her bankcard," Aidan finished for him as he headed towards the thick black door that he'd had specially installed two years ago when he bought the restaurant.

"What if she calls someone to ask for money or a place to stay?" Brock asked as he waited for Aidan to unlock the door and open it.

Aidan, smiling more than he had in years, simply shook his head. "She cuts everyone out of her life as soon as she moves on. When she realizes that she has no income or money in the bank, she'll have no choice but to accept what I'm willing to offer her."

Her place in his Pack and in his bed.

His cock hardened painfully at the memory of the last time that he'd had her. Her wet, willing pussy clenching tightly around him as he took her from behind while he'd licked the marks that he'd left on her all those years ago. He'd waited a long time for her to ripen and it had been worth it.

The only thing that he regretted was not being the one who'd taken her virginity, but he'd known then that if he had, he wouldn't have been able to hold back. He would have marked her again as he forced his blood down her throat, forcing her into his Pack and making her able to take him without the risk of breaking her fragile human body before she was ready. She'd been too young then and would have fought him, and as much as he loved a good fight, he didn't want to take the risk of ruining that beautiful body of hers any more than was necessary.

Soon she'd be able to take him, all of him, and he would finally be able to let go and enjoy her without holding back, he promised himself as he opened the door and headed down the dimly lit staircase, absently adjusting the tent in his pants as he went. The sounds of muttered whimpering met his ears as he stepped into the large room that he'd had specially made for those nights when his Pack couldn't get out of the city and away from the watchful eyes of the Sentinels.

"Please!" the young woman he'd had his men chain to the wall only a few hours ago pleaded around her gag.

Sighing in annoyance, Aidan reached over and yanked the gag out the woman's mouth since the muttered noises would only irritate him. True, his men could have removed the gag and allowed the woman to scream her head off without worry that she would alert the customers dining above them, but then they would have chanced her screaming until her throat was raw and she was unable to answer his questions.

Not that he had many, not after he'd gone through his records for the past three weeks since she'd been hired to wait tables. The only thing that he didn't know, and cared about, was where his money was. He wasn't poor, far from it, but that didn't mean that he was willing to look the other way when someone stole from him.

He couldn't afford to show weakness, not with his Pack watching his every move, looking for a sign of weakness. Like most Alphas, he was very strict with his Pack. He didn't tolerate defiance on any level, because that would only lead to chaos among his Pack. It would give them ideas that they didn't need him, could ignore his commands, or worse, that they should get rid of him and welcome another Alpha to lead *his* Pack.

Since he had a low tolerance for bullshit and had no intentions of allowing another shifter to take over his Pack, he ruled with an iron fist. He had a three-strike system, one that his Pack understood and followed. Unless they severely pissed him off, he gave them three chances to stay on his good side.

The first time they fucked up, he forced them to spend the three nights of the full moon in a small metal box, just big enough for them to shift. It was pure hell for any shifter not to be able to run and hunt on the nights of the full moon, but not being able to do anything more than breathe was a form of hell that he made damn sure that all of his Pack experienced at least once.

The second time they fucked up, he had them placed in a box, much smaller than the first so that when they shifted, their bones would dislocate and as they continued to expand, they would break, one by one, leaving the shifter in agonizing pain. They'd suffer the same torment for three nights until the third morning when they shifted back to human for the last time.

Then he, still in shifted form, would drag the offender out by using his fangs. While the rest of the pack was still experiencing the high of a shift, he would teach them a new lesson that they would never forget. If they earned a third strike.....

Well, not many earned a third strike and those that did never lived to regret it.

"Please let me go!" the young woman pleaded between choked sobs as she yanked at her chains.

"Where's my money?" he simply asked as he reached down and pulled off one shoe.

"I-I d-don't know what you're talking about!" she cried, but the way that she yanked at her chains and her tone became panicked said otherwise.

"Where's my money?" he asked again as he reached down and pulled off the other shoe. He scented the air, noting the scent of adrenaline pouring into her bloodstream. It awakened the beast inside of him, making him hunger for a taste.

"I-I don't have it!" she cried, the scent of her fear tripling as he pulled off his socks and pants.

"Where is it?" he asked, taking his shirt off and leaving him in a pair of boxer shorts that encased the evidence of his thoughts about Cloe.

The young woman's eyes landed on his drawers and stayed there only to shift to his erection when he yanked the boxers down low enough so that he could kick them off.

"I-I spent it all, but I can pay you back! I swear that I'll pay you back! Please just let me go!" she begged, sobbing hysterically.

Aidan gave her a small smile as he walked over to where she sat on the metal floor. He crouched down in front of her, tilting his head to the side as he reached out and ran a finger down her jaw. She flinched back as though he'd struck her, which was pretty fucking insulting since he'd never hit a woman in his life. Tearing one apart with his fangs and claws…..

Well, that was an entirely different story altogether.

"Now, what kind of message would that send to my Pack if I let you go?" he asked with a *tsk* as he allowed his eyes to shift silver and his fangs to descend.

She opened her mouth, probably to beg him for another chance only to release a blood chilling scream as the finger that he was tracing down her jaw suddenly sprouted a claw, leaving a trail of blood behind as he moved his hand down to her throat.

"Now," he said, pausing as his hand shifted into something out of a horror movie, "you were telling me where my money was?"

SEVENTEEN

"Oh my God, you're insane," Cloe said, sounding frustrated as she rubbed her hands down her face.

"Most likely," he agreed, not because he really thought that he was insane, but because arguing with her right now wasn't possible, not with her straddling his lap.

He'd be the first one to admit that this hadn't been one of his best ideas, but he hadn't been left with much of a choice, not with the damn woman trying to leave every other second. When he'd picked her up to stop her from leaving, he'd considered tossing her in his closet or in his bathroom. He'd planned on keeping her there until he was able to talk some damn sense into her, but the reminder that she didn't like enclosed spaces or feeling trapped had him making a last second adjustment to his plan.

"Let me go," she demanded.

"I'm not holding you," he pointed out, technically not lying since he wasn't holding her.

Granted, he did have his arms resting along her thighs and his hands on her hips, ready to stop her if she tried to climb off his lap, again, but he really didn't think that counted as holding her. She'd be flipping out a hell of a lot more if she really thought that he was holding her in place. So, since she was only straddling his lap and glaring at him, she clearly didn't feel trapped.

"Really?" she asked, cocking a brow in disbelief as she tried to move off his lap only to have his hold tighten on her hips, keeping her in place before she could do more than lift her ass.

"Really," he said, settling back on the love seat, relaxing even as he tightened his grip on her hips.

"You do realize that this is considered kidnapping in most states," she pointed out, crossing her arms over her chest as she narrowed her eyes to slits on him, no doubt trying to come up with a way to escape his hold and get out of the house before he found another way to stop her.

"You're the one that has me trapped on this couch," he explained innocently with a shrug, knowing that it would piss her off.

So, when she closed her eyes and took several deep breaths in an obvious attempt to calm down, he couldn't help but smile. She definitely made his normally tedious life interesting, he thought as he leaned in and fucked up his plans to convince her to stay without having to resort to chaining her to the house.

He kissed her stubborn little chin and nearly groaned from the contact. It was such a simple, innocent kiss, but it had him wanting more, wanting her. She felt so good in his arms, too damn good. Christ, he wanted her, he realized with a pained groan. He'd do anything to have her, to touch her, to hold her, to have her in his life.....

Hell, he just wanted her.

Knowing that he was close to fucking this up and making her want to leave for good, he pulled back and-

Somehow found himself leaning forward and kissing the tip of her nose. As he pulled back, admittedly not to do the right thing, he realized that she was watching him through half hooded eyes and that her breaths were coming a little faster than normal. Releasing his hold on her hips, he raised his hands and gently cupped her face, barely aware that his hands were trembling as he lightly caressed her cheeks.

"Do you have any idea how beautiful you are?" he whispered as he ran his thumb over her bottom lip.

"Is this another attempt to get me to stay?" she asked, sounding breathless as she leaned into his touch as though she couldn't help herself.

"God yes," he whispered, gently pulling her closer as he moved in and pressed a soft kiss against the corner of her mouth.

"What if I don't want to stay?" she asked, reaching up and placing one of her hands over his, curling her fingers around his palm and holding it where it was.

"Do you?" he asked, leaning in and pressing a kiss against her bottom lip, loving the way she shifted on his lap, but loving the little startled gasp she released when she realized that he was hard, even more.

"Want to stay?" she clarified on a sexy little whisper that had his cock straining against his jeans to get inside her. Reaching up with her free hand, she ran her fingers through his hair until she had the back of his head cupped in her hand and was able to keep him right

where she wanted him. Licking her lips, she leaned in closer until their lips were barely touching and said, "Not on your life, Hoodie."

"Little liar," he said with a chuckle as he dropped his hands away from her face, letting them trail down her sides and hips until he was cupping her bottom.

Leaning back just enough so that he could watch her reaction, he used his hold on her and pulled her closer. The movement caused her to gently grind against his erection. Her lips parted on a soft moan, her hold on him tightened as she arched her back slightly, putting more pressure in that one move that had him running his tongue over his teeth to stop his fangs from dropping.

The scent of her arousal had him biting back a groan even as he gripped her ass and ground her more force-fully against his erection. She was so damn wet, he could smell it, could hear it and it was driving him out of his fucking mind. Every time she moved against him, more of her juices rushed to coat her core, preparing her for his invasion and he'd never smelled anything sweeter.

He groaned long and loud when Cloe took over, hesitantly grinding herself against him at first as though she wasn't quite sure how they'd got to this point, but seemingly helpless to stop. Every time she rubbed against him, her movements became less stiff and more sensual, making his cock swell to the point of pain and his breaths come faster.

Cloe wrapped her free arm around his shoulders as she cupped the back of his neck with the other hand, using her hold on him to grind herself against him harder. With each flex of her hips, the scent of her arousal became stronger, her breaths became soft pants as little moans and needy whimpers escaped her. When she licked her lips invitingly, he leaned in and finally covered her lips with his.

The kiss turned hungry and out of control within seconds. He sucked and licked her tongue, not caring that he was probably fucking this up and should be taking this slower to seduce her properly, to make this good for her. It had been over fifty years since the last time that he'd tried to seduce a woman and it showed.

He couldn't get enough of her, of the way that she tasted, the way she moved against him, the sweet smell of her sex, the feel of her hand running over his bare chest or the way that she held his hair in a death grip as she returned his kiss just as desperately, like she'd die if he didn't fuck her soon. When she moaned his name, his hips shot up against her, earning a strangled gasp as her head dropped back and she licked her lips in pure pleasure even as she continued to grind against him.

Struggling not to come, he wrapped his arms around her and gritted his teeth as he pressed his forehead against her chest. This was too much. It felt too fucking good, too fucking good to have any hopes of staying in control, he realized with a touch of fear. She wrapped her arms around his head, holding him where he was as she continued to ride him, continued to drive him out of his fucking mind and unfortunately for her, awakening another hunger that he had no hope of controlling........

Not with her.

Her scent was so much stronger now, thicker, causing his breaths to come a little faster as he desperately searched for a breath of untainted air so that he could clear his head and gain some semblance of control, but with each breath, her scent saturated his lungs. He was losing control, so fucking fast and heaven help him, but he didn't want to stop it.

———

"*Christofer*," she gasped on a strangled moan as she felt her body clamp down, searching for something, anything to hold onto as-

Christofer suddenly stood up, which wouldn't have been a problem, except for the fact that as he did it, he shoved her away, causing her to fall back and land on her ass. Dazed, she sat there trying to figure out what just happened as Christofer finally said the one thing that she'd been waiting all day to hear as he stumbled past her.

"Get the hell out of here."

"What are you-"

"*Get the fuck out of here!*" he roared, taking her by surprise and causing her to jump back as she struggled to get to her feet to do just that when he suddenly grabbed his stomach.

"*Fuck!*" he snarled as he stumbled forward a few feet and dropped down on his knees.

Forcing herself to ignore the way that her body still trembled from his touch and the painful ache between her legs, she rushed over to his side as her training kicked in. He was sick, most likely from the diner food that he shouldn't have eaten and he was embarrassed, not that she could blame him. Losing your lunch during a heavy make out session was probably a life-altering event, one that she was secretly relieved that she hadn't been forced to experience.

"Christofer, let me get you a-"

"*Run!*" he snarled, but that wasn't what had her stumbling to a stop or struggling to take her next breath.

It was the bright red eyes glaring up at her that froze her on the spot and had her heart racing. This couldn't be happening, not now, not again. Swallowing back a scream, she staggered back, her eyes never leaving Christofer's face.

"This can't be happening," she mumbled, barely aware that she'd said the words as she continued to stumble back when her mind was screaming at her to run and get the hell out of there.

"*Fucking run!*" he snapped, giving her a good view of a set of fangs that had her heart pounding in her chest. It also gave her the wakeup call that she needed to make her finally turn around and run away.

Unfortunately, by then it was too late.

EIGHTEEN

Williams Mansion

"**I** want a Coke," Izzy sighed pathetically even as she smiled down at the three little boys curled up next to her on the nursery floor, fast asleep.

Her baby boy, Chris Junior, affectionately known as CJ, was curled up next to her on the soft Winnie the Pooh blanket that Madison had laid out earlier. Madison and Ephraim's twin boys Deven and Hunter were fast asleep on her other side, curled up next to each other with a plush Eeyore doll between them. A soft snore drew her attention to the corner of the nursery where Marc was fast asleep with little Jessica in his arms.

She really didn't know what she would do without him. He was such a sweet kid, always helping her, watching after Jessica and the boys without having to be asked. He never complained about Jessica following him everywhere or constantly demanding his attention. No matter what he was doing he would immediately stop when Jessica demanded his attention. It was really sweet....

And something that she needed to put a stop to, soon.

Guilt was tearing Marc apart and no matter what they said or did, he wouldn't let it go. It wasn't his fault, none of it was, but he couldn't see that. He took the blame for her injury, Jessica's scar, what had happened to Joshua, everything. He spent every minute of the day trying to make up for what happened, exhausting himself to the point that he was making himself sick.

They'd all tried to talk to him, to explain to him that none of it was his fault, but he wouldn't listen. He thought he'd failed and he was doing everything that he could to make up for it. He was losing weight, had dark circles beneath his eyes and she couldn't remember the last time that one of the babies had woken up crying, because Marc refused to leave them. They'd barely get the chance to open their mouths to let out a healthy cry and Marc would be there with a bottle and a clean diaper to take care of them and make sure that the adults were able to work and sleep throughout the night, undisturbed.

Ephraim and Chris had banned Marc from the nursery at night, telling him to get some damn sleep, but the kid never listened. As soon as his father and brother went off to patrol the town or had a meeting, he would sneak right back in the nursery. He'd give into Jessica's demands and snuggle up with her in the rocking chair or on the floor where he would watch over the younger children for the rest of the night.

It was too much for a young child to bear and she was going to put an end to it just as soon as she figured out how to get through to the kid. The problem was, every time that she tried to talk some sense into Marc, he wasn't able to look past her injury to hear what she was saying to him. Most of the time, it would actually make matters worse. He would get a tormented look on his face when her injury made itself known and storm out of the room, only to double his efforts to make it up to her.

What she wouldn't give to hear Marc give one of them a smart-ass remark or find him slacking off and playing video games. She would love to see him-

"What the hell?" she murmured when an unexpected chime brought her attention back to the laptop perched on her lap.

"You've gotta be kidding me," she mumbled in disbelief as *Tattletale* opened a file to the left of the screen and then systematically grabbed every file, image and video that it could match to the image that it had found and grabbed from Facebook less than thirty seconds ago.

She watched in disbelief as old grainy images were posted in documents only to be cleaned up seconds later. Handwritten script and typed documents appeared beneath the pictures in what appeared to be German and a few other languages that she didn't know. Before she could even consider running the documents through an interpreter program, *Tattletale* was translating everything in the blink of an eye even as it continued to search the internet, grabbing government documents, personal documents, bank account information, immigration documentation, only to finally end with another chime as it made its last match against the Sentinel blood supply system, letting her know that there was nothing left to find.

Not that she needed anything more, not with this much information. She hadn't expected to find anything when she'd started her search a few hours ago, mostly because of her father-in-law, who'd never stayed in one area long enough and had constantly changed his name to avoid discovery. She'd assumed that other Pytes would develop the same habits, to keep people from noticing things like the fact that they didn't age, but apparently there was at least one Pyte who didn't give a damn about keeping his identity a secret.

Christofer Petersen, better known as, Christofer Herrmann according to the SS file opened on the right side of her screen, didn't appear to be trying to hide what he was at all, she realized. Swallowing back a curse, she picked up her Sentinel phone and swiped her finger across the screen. A split second later she unlocked the phone with a code, praying that it wasn't too late.

———

Townson, Massachusetts

"Stop!" Cloe screamed as she struggled to break free, but the bastard wasn't letting her go.

His arms tightened around her, constricting her breathing to small gasps as she struggled to shove him away, but it was impossible. No matter how hard she tried to push him away, there was no give. The grip that he had around her was suffocating her to the point that each hurried breath her body desperately tried to take in pulled in less oxygen. Black spots were already dancing along the edge of her vision, but she wasn't sure if that was because of the constrictive hold that he had on her or the blood that she was losing, the blood that he was taking from her.

She hadn't been given the luxury of confusion or disbelief when he'd attacked her and sank his fangs into her neck. The pain of those sharp teeth tearing through the flesh of her neck hadn't allowed any delusions. The memories of having her back sliced open all those years ago had also taken over, forcing her to acknowledge what was happening to her.

Christofer was the thing nightmares were made of and right now he was gorging on her blood as she struggled to shove him away, but it was no use. The hold he had on her wasn't allowing her to shove him away. He had her arms trapped between their bodies and no amount of screaming, scratching, shoving or trying to yank her arms free worked. She used her legs and tried to move, to kick him, knee him, push off the floor to try and shove him away, but she couldn't move, not with him lying on top of her the way that he was.

"Christofer, stop!" she gasped, struggling in vain to break free from his hold only to have his arms tighten around her to the point that she thought her ribs were going to break and breathing became a thing of the past.

Then it hit her.....

She was about to die.

The realization should have triggered tears, panic, prayers for help, pleading for another chance, making promises to do whatever it took to save herself, but instead all it did was piss her right the hell off. This had to be a fucking joke. After everything that she'd gone through this was really how it was going to end?

She couldn't believe that she'd survived hell, lost her family, struggled to survive, lived her life always watching over her shoulder, careful about who she let get close to her only to be attacked and killed by the only man that she had stupidly allowed herself to believe made her feel safe and protected. It was just so goddamn wrong, her mind registered as she bit down hard on his bare shoulder and dug her nails as far as she could in his chest, needing the action to get through the next few seconds when the bastard violently shook his head, tearing into her throat.

She ignored the agonizing pain, the blood pouring down her throat forcing her to swallow or choke, the bastard on top of her, and the fact that she was going to die. She put every last ounce of energy that she had into biting down harder and digging her nails in as far as they would go, deciding that if she was going to die like this that she would inflict as much damage as she could to the asshole on top of her. Right now she hated him more than anything, even the monsters that had killed her family, because he'd made her feel safe and it had all been a lie, an illusion that she'd foolishly believed when she'd known better.

Now she was paying the price.

Why hadn't she left the first night when he'd made it more than obvious that he hadn't wanted her there? She should have just called up the agency, arranged to have someone replace her and found another job. It would have been quick and painless for everyone involved. For any other job she would have done just that, but there was something about Christofer that had grabbed her attention and held it.

At the beginning she'd told herself that she was staying to help Marta, but that had been a lie. She hadn't stayed because of Marta no matter how much she liked the older woman or how much she wanted to help her. She'd stayed because of the man that she'd met in the pharmacy, the one that had made her smile, eased the fear that ruled her life.

She'd stayed for herself.

She'd been drawn to him from the start-even when he'd been a jerk, she'd still craved being around him. She'd wanted more of it, needed it and she'd been willing to tell herself a thousand and one lies in order to get it. Needing someone, anyone, was dangerous and something that she'd never allowed herself until the day that she'd walked into that pharmacy and sat by a man wearing a gray hooded sweatshirt.

A choked cry escaped her as she felt his teeth tear through her throat. She closed her eyes, squeezing them tightly shut as she used every last ounce of energy that she had to dig her nails further into his skin and bite down harder on his shoulder, hoping, hell praying, that he choked on her blood. If he thought that she was going to go quietly then he was wrong.

She might be quickly fading away, but she wasn't going to go easily. She was going to keep this up until she passed out or he realized that he was hurting her and released her.

Then she was going to kill him.

She might not have been able to stop the monsters that had killed her family from hurting someone ever again, but if she got the chance, she would do that with this monster. She'd end this here and now if she was given a chance, but as her energy began to drain, her hands trembled and the effort to bite down became too much, she realized that she wasn't about to get that chance.

Her eyes flickered open as her body went boneless. She stared aimlessly ahead, barely seeing the ceiling hovering several feet above her. The sounds of Christofer growling as well as the sounds of her choppy breaths coming too quickly slowly muted out until all she could hear was a soft humming noise. The pain of having her throat torn open evaporated, leaving her feeling oddly numb and tired.

"Cloe?" the choked whisper drew her attention to the beautiful blue eyes staring down at her in horror. "Oh………God………"

It was funny, she thought as everything slowly faded away, all the times she'd thought about dying and how it would happen, she'd been right.

She'd always been destined to die in the arms of a monster.

NINETEEN

"**D**on't fucking die on me, mein Schatz," he whispered harshly, shifting his attention from the blood soaked towel he had pressed against the side of Cloe's neck to the alarm clock by his bed.

"Come on......*come on!*" he growled, waiting impatiently for another minute to go by and when it did, he couldn't help but sag with relief.

"Thank fucking God," he mumbled, pressing a quick kiss against Cloe's cold forehead as he placed her on his bed, gently laying her down as he stood.

She was deathly pale, her heartbeat was sluggish, he'd taken too much blood and her throat had been viciously ripped open, but he couldn't help but feel relieved. Somehow she'd made it to the ten-minute mark after consuming his blood, something that had never happened before. Whenever he'd been forced to watch as some unsuspecting volunteer received his blood he'd always kept his attention on the large clock hanging on the wall across from his cage, counting down the minutes as he waited for the inevitable to happen.

Before the clock managed to tick off ten minutes, the foolish volunteer who had been lured to his doom with promises of immortality and unimaginable power had been screaming in pain, begging for help and eventually praying for death. While the doctors had stood around, taking notes and clearly frustrated that their plans had failed again, he'd sat in his cage, torn between relief and horror that people reacted so violently to his blood. Those experiments had made it impossible to deny what the doctors had claimed the moment that he'd opened his eyes to find himself locked up in a small metal cage and chained to the bars.

He was a monster.

He was also a freak accident, one that couldn't seem to be repeated no matter what they tried. The only thing that they'd managed to reproduce was a horrifying death. This time shouldn't have been any different, but somehow Cloe had managed to escape the violent death that his blood should have delivered.

Not that he was going to complain. She had a chance and he was going to make sure that she took it. He didn't care what he had to do to make it happen. After rushing to the bathroom to grab a small stack of facecloths, he shoved his keys in his pocket, replaced the blood soaked towel with the small pile of facecloths and gently picked Cloe up. He was careful not to shift the cloths away from her wound that was barely bleeding any longer, not a good sign, but for the moment he ignored the implications and moved his ass.

He headed for the back door, shifted her in his arms and opened the door, praying that he was able to-

"I have your........," Seth started to say as soon as Christofer yanked the door open only to let his words trail off as his gaze fell to the bleeding woman in his arms before shifting back up to his face. Seth closed his eyes in resignation and shook his head with a sigh as he murmured, "Please tell me that you really didn't mark that bitch."

———

"Whoa!" Seth snapped, holding his hands up in surrender as he backed away quickly only to manage to stumble over the coolers that he'd stacked near the backdoor.

"What did you just call her?" Christofer demanded between clenched teeth as he descended on the bastard, barely aware that the monster inside of him was struggling to take over and rip the vampire's throat out.

"I didn't mean it like that!" Seth rushed to explain, getting back to his feet and moving to put some distance between them.

"Then what did you mean?" Christofer snapped, moving to go after him when the sound of a small groan drew his attention back to the woman in his arms, reminding him that he had more important matters to deal with than a prick with a death wish.

"Where the hell are you going?" Seth demanded, moving quickly to his side, deciding that a peek at Cloe was worth the risk of having his throat torn out.

"To the hospital," he gritted out, praying that the precious seconds that he'd just wasted wouldn't-

"You can't do that," Seth snapped, quickly moving in front of him to block his path.

"Watch me," Christofer said, stepping past the vampire and heading for his truck.

"No," Seth said, once again blocking his path, his hands held up, but this time to stop Christofer, "I mean you really can't do that."

"*She's dying*," Christofer bit out, losing the tenuous hold he had on his patience as he tried to move past the determined vampire only to once again find his path blocked off.

"Then let her," Seth said, shooting nervous glances around the poorly lit yard.

Let her die?

Not fucking happening.

He'd been forced to watch a lot of people die over the years and he wasn't about to add Cloe to their ranks. She deserved better than this and he would do whatever it took to make sure that she got it. He'd royally fucked up, lost control and he'd be damned if Cloe was going to pay for that. He'd promised himself that he was going to take care of her and that was exactly what he was going to-

"She's been fucking marked!" Seth shouted, placing his hands on Christofer's arms where they cradled Cloe and shoved him back.

"I don't have fucking time for this!" Christofer shouted back, the sounds of Cloe's heartbeat slowing down even further, making it harder with each passing second not to give into the monster inside of him, but he fought it with everything that he had.

It would be so easy to give in and let it take over, but he knew that if he did that Cloe wouldn't survive. He didn't know why the monster had given her up when it had, but he wasn't about to give up control a second time and give it a second shot at finishing off Cloe.

"What the hell are you?" Seth suddenly asked, gesturing to his face and making him realize that he'd fucked up for the second time that day as he noted that everything had taken on shades of red.

"No fucking clue," Christofer bit out, shifting back so that he could move around the vampire when his next words stopped him.

"If you bring her to a hospital they'll kill her."

"What are you talking about?" he snapped, moving to take another step towards his truck, but fear for Cloe made him hesitate.

"She's a shifter's marked property, a bitch," he explained with a sheepish shrug when Christofer narrowed his eyes on him.

Ignoring the bitch comment, for now, he asked, "What's a shifter?"

Seth opened his mouth to answer, shut it, shook his head and then ran his palms down his face, sounding tired as he said, "This is going to be a long fucking night."

———

"She needs to go to the hospital," he stubbornly said even as he gently laid her back on his bed.

Seth simply shook his head as he leaned over Cloe and carefully peeled back the blood-soaked facecloths. "You can't bring a marked human to the hospital bearing your….." his words trailed off with a frown as he peered down at Cloe's wound. "Why are you so goddamn hell-bent on bringing her to the hospital for a scratch?"

"What are you talking about?" he demanded, shoving the vampire aside so that he could look at Cloe's wound. What he saw had his stomach twisting in dread.

"Please tell me that you didn't turn a shifter's property," Seth grumbled, but Christofer was barely listening as he ran his fingers over what should have been torn flesh.

"This has to be a mistake," he mumbled, running his fingers over the scratch on Cloe's throat as he struggled to understand what he was seeing.

She was healing before his eyes. He watched in disbelief as the rest of her wound quickly knitted itself back together until the only evidence of his attack was the dried blood staining her skin. After all this time and all those failed experiments and this happens.......

"What are you?" Seth asked him, gently cupping Cloe's face in his hand and moving it to the side to get a better look at Cloe's face and neck only to have his hand slapped away.

"Don't touch her," Christofer said, not liking the idea of anyone, especially another man, touching her and not really understanding why. She wasn't his wife, girlfriend or even really a friend, but he couldn't stop himself from thinking of her as *his*.

Seth sighed heavily as he stepped back from the bed. "Okay, so that answers one question at least. Whatever you are, you're possessive over your turned. Add that to the red eyes and you're definitely not a vampire," he said as he headed towards the door.

"Where are you going?" Christofer absently asked as he continued to trace Cloe's smooth skin with his fingertips, mesmerized by what he was seeing.

"I'm going to go get the blood that you ordered since we're obviously going to need it," Seth explained, drawing his attention away from Cloe.

"What are you talking about?" he asked with a frown as he glanced over his shoulder just as Seth stepped back inside carrying one of the large coolers that he'd tripped over earlier.

"We may not know what you are, but we do know that you drink blood, which means that she's going to need it and probably a lot of it during her change," Seth said as he headed for the locked refrigerator.

With a frown, he looked back at Cloe. "Will she be able to eat food?" he asked, hating the idea of a woman who loved food so much suddenly being forced to live on a diet of cold blood.

"That depends," Seth said absently as he reached over and picked up an old hardcover copy of *Huck Finn* and opened it, revealing a hollowed out space where Christofer kept the small key for the lock on the refrigerator.

"On what?" he asked, gently brushing a few strands of hair away from Cloe's face.

"On whether or not you can eat food," Seth said, removing the lock and opening the refrigerator.

Shaking his head, he headed for the bathroom. "I can't digest food."

"Not at all?" Seth asked from the bedroom as Christofer searched for a clean basin and more facecloths.

"No," he said absently, frowning as he filled the small plastic basin with warm water and soap as he tried to remember if he'd ever been able to handle food since his change.

He remembered that his appetite, something that hadn't been very big to begin with, had started to dwindle around the time that he'd turned fourteen. It had disappeared almost completely by the time he'd turned fifteen and had been completely gone by the time he'd turned sixteen. He'd managed to hide it from his family, but that was probably only because he hadn't appeared to be starving.

He hadn't lost any weight, had any problems functioning or any of the symptoms that should have accompanied his lost interest in food. Instead he found himself hungry for something that he couldn't name, but not to the point that he couldn't function. By the time that he'd opened his eyes and discovered that he'd somehow become the property of the SS, that hunger had consumed him.

It only took him a few minutes to realize what his body craved and when he did, he'd panicked. He'd curled up into a ball on the cold, metal floor of his cage and struggled to ignore the mouthwatering aroma coming off the doctors, guards and vials that lined the tables set up in the center of the large lab. Instead, he'd tried to tell himself that it was all a bad dream and that he'd simply fallen asleep in front of the fire again and as soon as he woke up everything would be okay. Instead, one of the guards had noticed that he was finally awake and they'd done their best to redefine his definition of hell.

"What about liquids other than blood?" Seth asked as Christofer returned to Cloe's side and began carefully washing away the blood.

"No," he answered, his attention never leaving Cloe's beautiful face as he wondered if she was going to turn out like him or if they'd simply found a way to heal her with his blood without destroying her life.

TWENTY

"She wants to talk to you," Seth announced as he jogged down the stairs, another large cooler in his arms.

"She'll have to wait," he said even as he opened up his senses and listened to Marta's heartbeat, making sure that her heart wasn't stressed. After a minute he blocked out everything, focusing back on Cloe. Her breaths were still shallow, but they'd evened out, giving him some hope.

"Can I ask you something?" Seth asked, sounding genuinely curious as he set up an IV pole, something that Christofer was unfortunately quite familiar with thanks to all the surgeries that Marta had been forced to endure over the years.

His first impulse was to tell Seth to mind his own fucking business, but then he remembered that he was in no position to refuse the vampire, not when he had so many questions of his own that needed answers. "What do you want to know?" he murmured as he sat by Cloe's side, taking her cold hand into his.

"Why didn't you change Marta?" Seth asked, his attention focused on the small rubber tube that he was carefully attaching to the bag of blood that he'd hung from the IV pole.

"Because my blood kills," he explained without much thought.

Seth pointedly glanced down at Cloe. "Looks like she's doing okay."

"She should be dead," he said softly, reaching over to run his knuckles gently along her jaw, needing to touch her to prove to himself that she was okay.

"What did you do differently this time?" Seth asked, leaning over to gently pry Cloe's mouth open.

Shaking his head, Christofer forced himself to move his hand away from Cloe's face, afraid that he'd tear the bastard's hands off for touching her. "I don't know."

"Were you trying to change her?" Seth asked, applying some clear gel to the tube before he slowly and carefully began feeding the tube down Cloe's throat.

"No," he said, forcing his attention away from what Seth was doing to her.

"Then how did she get your blood?"

"I don't know," he answered, frustrated that he still didn't know how he'd fucked up so badly.

More than that, he was furious with himself for not figuring it out sooner. If he'd known that it was possible to turn someone, to save them from dying, from suffering unnecessary agonizing pain that wouldn't go away no matter how many surgeries or pills doctors suggested, then he would have changed Marta as soon as she'd turned eighteen. He could have saved her, made up for all the time that she'd been trapped in that lab with him, forced to undergo experiments even though the doctors had figured out early on that she was nothing like him.

He could have saved her.

His gaze shot back to Cloe as a thought occurred to him. Maybe he still could. If Cloe pulled through this, he could ask her what happened and then he could-

"It's too late," Seth said quietly.

"You don't know that," Christofer bit out, refusing to look at the vampire and see the pity that matched his tone.

"There's a reason why we don't turn children or the elderly," Seth began to explain while Christofer watched the clear tube turn red as blood flowed down the tube until it reached Cloe's lips and he had to once again force himself to look away, his stomach turning at the reminder of what he'd done to her.

"When they're changed," Seth continued, "they're trapped the way the world saw them as they were when they were mortal. That means that a child will forever remain a child even while his mind continues to develop into adulthood. The world will always see him as a child, weak and dependent and no amount of time will ever change that. He'll never grow up."

"Marta's not a child," he needlessly reminded the vampire through clenched teeth, trying to pretend that he didn't know where Seth was going with this.

"I know that she's not a child," Seth explained softly as he double-checked Cloe's line. "She's an old woman whose body is struggling to make it through each day. Her body is broken down, her bones weak, her skin thin, her organs slowly failing and her mind is tired, unconsciously accepting the fate that awaits her. It's the natural process and her body's preparing itself for what's coming."

"I can stop it," Christofer bit out, looking down at the proof that anything was possible.

"If your blood doesn't kill her, there's always a chance that she won't survive the change. With her age and health problems it's doubtful that she'd survive it and if she did you'd be condemning her to an existence of dying from old age."

"You said it yourself, I'm not a vampire. My blood might affect her differently. She might-"

Seth chuckled without humor. "Might? Are you really willing to take that chance? You could end up killing her immediately or dooming her to a life of hell, living each day like she was dying, too weak to protect herself in our world and leaving her helpless to protect herself against humans if they discovered what she was."

"I'd protect her," he bit out through clenched teeth. He'd always protected her, that would never change, but if he could do this, if he could change her into what he was then he would never have to lose her.

"Do you really think that she wants to continue living like this? She'll always be weak, always tired, making her more dependent on blood just to get through the day. Is that really what you want for your sister?"

No, it wasn't.

He wanted Marta to have the chance at the life that she'd been robbed of. He wanted to go back in time and fix everything. He'd leave long before that night when the SS stormed their home and dragged them off, because they'd heard a rumor about a teenage boy who wouldn't grow. He'd lead them away from his family and if they still caught him, then so be it as long as his family was spared the hell that Hitler's men had unleashed on them.

His father never would have been shot in the back of the head while trying to protect him. His pregnant stepmother never would have been shipped off to a concentration camp, suffering unimaginable horrors before she'd finally perished. Marta would never have been forced to live with a lifetime of reminders from her time in that lab. All he wanted to do was fix this…

But it seemed that he couldn't.

His sister had suffered her entire life and now that there might be a way to save her, he couldn't use it because it was too late. There would be no saving Marta no matter how badly he wanted to and God, did he want to.

"Don't waste what precious time you have left with your sister living with regrets," Seth said after a slight pause, drawing his attention to the man that was looking down at Cloe with a haunted expression.

Christofer didn't respond and Seth didn't seem to expect him to. For a long time they watched over Cloe, quietly switching out the empty bags with fresh blood when the time came while Seth explained a few more things about their world to him. Within a few hours, Cloe's color improved and her skin warmed while his mind reeled from everything he'd learned.

"Were you born this way or were you changed?" Seth asked while Christofer watched the vampire change out another bag, memorizing everything he did so that he wasn't forced to feed Cloe by pouring blood down her throat later.

"Born," he guessed, still not sure after all these years what went wrong.

Seth nodded, appearing to file that information away. "That definitely rules out vampire."

"I thought we'd already established that," Christofer said dryly, biting back a yawn when his gaze flickered to the clock and he noted the time.

"I'm going to have to leave soon," Seth said, noting the time as well.

Christofer absently nodded as he picked up Cloe's hand and brought it to his lips so that he could press a kiss against her palm.

"She might not be happy if she wakes up," Seth said, pointing out the obvious.

"She's going to be furious," he murmured, already knowing that she was going to hate him and was damn well going to wake up from this.

"The shifter that you stole her from will-"

"*She doesn't belong to anyone,*" he snapped, cutting the vampire off.

"Whether you like it or not, she was a shifter's property. Someone marked this woman, claiming her as his property and that same someone is going to be pissed when he finds out that you stole her," Seth snapped right back.

"I don't fucking care," he said, not giving a damn whether some fucking werewolf, and he'd been shocked when Seth had explained that they really existed, was mad that he'd changed Cloe.

The bastard could go fuck himself, because he'd be damned if he allowed anyone to treat Cloe like shit, especially since Seth had explained exactly what shifters did to their property. When he'd discovered what those marks on her back meant he'd barely been able to contain the rage inside him. The only thing that had helped was the promise he'd made to himself that one day he would find the shifter that had ripped her back to shreds so that he could tear the piece of shit apart with his bare hands.

"You'll care when he brings his Pack after both of you, especially if Marta gets caught in the middle," Seth said, making everything in him go still even as his vision dimmed out, taking on shades of red. "You're going to have to accept the fact that you can't protect them both, Christofer. One day that shifter is going to come for her and when he does, he's going to make you pay and if Marta is around........," he let his words trail off, but Christofer didn't need him to finish his sentence to know that if the shifter ever came sniffing around, he was going to be forced to make a choice, protect his sister, the person he loved most in the world, or the woman that he couldn't stop thinking of as his.

—

It was time, Marta realized with a sad smile as she carefully ran her fingertips over the yellowed piece of creased parchment that she'd been carrying with her since she was a child.

The fact that it had survived a toddler carrying it everywhere, the time she'd spent locked up in that tiny room off the lab, their escape through Europe, their time living on the run and all the years she'd carried it in her purse, still amazed her. Christofer had been mad when he'd realized that she'd taken this picture, she remembered with a small smile.

Papa had forbidden her to go into Christofer's room, but he'd been her favorite person in the world and sometimes when she got too lonely while he was having his lessons or when the nannies were vexed with her, she'd sneak into his room, sit in front of the fire and look through all of his drawings. She loved looking at his artwork. Even as a child she'd known that it was special. She used to think that Christofer used magic to create his drawings and statues the way that he could capture the exact detail of someone's face, every perfection and flaw with such ease. It didn't hurt that he'd agree with a chuckle and a wink as he worked, creating works of art that rivaled masters. To this day, she'd never seen any piece of art come close to her brother's skill.

It wasn't just because he could capture someone's likeness perfectly and without a single flaw, but that he seemed to be able to capture the heart and soul of a person. It was in their expression, the tilt of their lips and the way they held themselves that made you believe that Christofer had found a way to turn people into images on paper and into stone and marble. She loved to watch him work, loved everything that he created, but this piece of aged parchment......

This was her favorite.

The paper was simple, the kind that he used to use when he was doodling. Some of the graphite had smudged over the years, but it was still just as perfect as it had been the day that she'd found it stuck inside of one of Christofer's school books. It was a drawing of Christofer holding her when she was just a baby, probably only a few hours old, but the look of adoration on his face as he peered down at her had made her feel special, safe. He'd always made her feel that way even those times when she'd probably deserved a swat on the bottom, she thought, smiling as she ran her fingers one more time over the picture that she'd cherished for most of her life.

"*I'll protect them,*" Christofer's words carried up through the grate in her floor just as more pain sliced through her tired body, "*I'll protect them both.*"

No, he couldn't, she thought with a wistful smile as she picked up another bottle of the pills that Christofer didn't know about. One by one, she began to swallow them, taking small sips of water every few minutes to help the pills go down. Once the bottle was empty, she carefully lowered herself to the floor and pushed aside the small throw rug that Christofer had given her one Christmas so that her feet wouldn't have to touch the cold floor in the winter.

As quietly as possible, and praying that Christofer was still focused on what was going on downstairs, she pried open the loose board that she'd discovered after Christofer had bought the house for her, with trembling fingers and removed it. She was taking a chance by doing this while Christofer was home, something that she'd never done before, but right now she didn't have a choice if she wanted a chance to tell him how much she loved him.

She reached for the shoe box that she kept in the space just as another shot of pain surged through her stomach and down to her legs, almost making her do the one thing that she'd been struggling not to do for the past year, cry out in pain. Gripping the edge of the opening tightly, she closed her eyes and calmed her breathing, knowing that if she didn't Christofer would hear her heart racing and he'd rush up here to check up on her.

After a few minutes when her body started to go numb and the trembling worsened, she finally managed to calm her breathing enough so that she could reach down with an unsteady hand and push the lid off the box. On top was the letter, the one that she'd written a year ago when the doctor had told her the news.

She picked it up and held it against her chest as she used her other arm to help pull herself up and back onto the bed. Sitting on the edge of the bed, she closed her eyes and tightened her grip around the letter, wishing that she'd been able to say more, to make things right for Christofer, but there was no time.

If what she'd heard coming from the vent was true, then everything had just changed for Christofer. He had a chance now, a chance to live, to have someone of his own who could make him happy and she refused to take that away from him. He'd sacrificed enough for her.

Opening her eyes, she released a shaky breath, laid back on the bed and placed the letter on the bed by the drawing. Sending up one last prayer for Christofer and Cloe, she closed her eyes for the last time.

TWENTY-ONE

"Look, I've gotta get going before the sun......."
Seth's words trailed off. He shot Christofer a
questioning look just as a rather sweet and enticing aroma
teased Christofer's senses, making his stomach growl.

"What is that?" Christofer asked even as he opened
his senses. What he heard had him taking a step towards
the stairs. The instinct to protect his sister was so well
ingrained that he found himself heading towards the
stairs, but for the first time in his life, he hesitated. He
looked over his shoulder at the pale, defenseless woman
that needed him and growled out a vicious curse.

He couldn't leave her.

"Pull the tube out," he ordered Seth as he quickly
moved back to the bed to scoop Cloe up in his arms, but
before he could pick her up there was a knock at his door.

"Oh, this can't be good," Seth grumbled, sounding
drained as he plopped down on the edge of the bed and
dropped his head in his hands.

"What the hell is going on?" Christofer demanded,
not really sure how he should be reacting.

Seth just sat there, looking tired and a little annoyed
as the knocking continued. There wasn't a hint of fear or

anger coming off him to alert Christofer to any impending danger. He just looked…….

Resigned.

"Sentinels," Seth said, seconds before he tilted his head to the side, scented the air, frowned, shook his head and cursed softly before adding, "and a shifter and humans."

Before Christofer could react to the knowledge that a shifter was at his door, Seth added, "I wouldn't worry about the shifter though since he's with Sentinels."

He started to nod in the process of absorbing that information before a thought occurred to him. "What the hell is a Sentinel?"

Pursing his lips up in thought, Seth asked, "I didn't tell you about Sentinels?"

"No," he bit out, his patience wearing thin.

"Oh," Seth said, sighing as he lazily gestured towards the back door when the pounding started. "Those are Sentinels."

"That's really fucking helpful!" he snapped, putting himself between the door and Cloe.

He welcomed the shift in his eyesight and the tingle of his fangs sliding down. His gaze constantly shifted between the door and the stairway. *This was wrong*, his brain screamed, demanding that he go to Marta and protect her, but the rest of him….

The rest of him demanded that he keep his ass right where it was and protect what was *his*. Cloe was defenseless and needed him. The idea of leaving her like this, even with Seth to watch over her, felt wrong. His gaze shifted back towards the stairs and he felt his body jerk in that direction, the instinct to go to his sister, to protect her so well ingrained that he couldn't simply ignore it. Marta was his sister, his responsibility and he knew that she would always come first. He'd made a promise to his father and he planned on keeping it.

"Protect her!" he snapped, ignoring the panic and terror that shot through him at the idea of turning his back on Cloe, but for his sister he did it.

Ignoring Seth's long-suffering sigh, he took the stairs two at time as he opened up his senses. Before he made it hallway up the stairs he knew three things, there were three people in his house, they weren't human and he couldn't hear Marta's heartbeat.

———

"Wake up, sweetheart," Ephraim said, giving the frail hand in his a small squeeze, already knowing that it was too late. He carefully pushed back a strand of gray hair away from the face that held the unmistakable expression of peace that he knew too well.

She was gone.

"Cancer," Caine suddenly announced, confirming his suspicions.

"Can you tell what kind?" Ephraim asked, unable to pinpoint exactly where the scent was coming from. He could smell hints of the deadly growth all over her body, which surprised him since it wasn't normally something that he could detect until it hit the skin. Then again, he'd been living with a woman who was doomed to die for eternity from the horrible disease so perhaps his senses were sharpened because of Danni.

"Brain, heart, bone, stomach, uterus and kidneys," Danni listed hollowly by his side.

"How bad was the growth?" Ephraim asked as his gaze moved away from the frail old woman to settle on the note and drawing on the bed beside her.

He didn't need to open it to know what it was. It also confirmed his belief that the male downstairs had no idea that this woman was dead. If he had, that note wouldn't be crisply folded by her side and placed neatly on the pillow still. His gaze moved over to the nightstand that was covered in prescription bottles, the five bottles by the edge were empty with their covers placed by their sides.

"We need to warn him," Ephraim said, giving the quickly cooling hand another small squeeze as he said a quick prayer for her soul, hoping that she'd found some peace.

"He already knows," Caine mumbled softly as he slowly backed up and moved away from the door, pausing only long enough to grab Danni's hand and pull her back with him.

With a small nod, Ephraim stood and stepped back away from the bed, wishing that they'd broken into the house sooner so that this woman hadn't been all alone when she'd taken her last breath. Being with his brother Marc as he'd drawn his last breath had been the only thing that had made his death somewhat tolerable. He hadn't been able to save Marc from the fever, but at least he'd been there to give his brother some comfort in his last moments. It was something that the Pyte they were here for was going to regret not being able to do for his sister for the rest of his unnatural life.

"Marta?" the man they were here for said, his tone laced with desperation and dread. He stumbled into the room, no doubt already knowing what to expect, but still fighting it with every fiber of his being, not that Ephraim could blame him.

"Marta?" Christofer murmured, confirming his suspicions that this was the woman listed as his sister. Christofer moved towards the bed, his voice cracking with emotion when he spotted her lying on the bed with her hands resting on her stomach. His gaze moved from the empty prescription bottles and then the note on the bed. "Oh.........God........."

Danni took a step towards the grieving man, but Caine smartly kept her with him. Ephraim shifted to the side, putting himself between the Pyte dropping to his knees by the bed and Danni. Without taking his eyes off Christofer, he held up a hand and gave the signal for Caine to take Danni out of the room. Thankfully this time Danni didn't argue. Instead, she allowed her mate to push her gently in front of him and left the room.

Never taking his eyes off the Pyte trying to rouse Marta, Ephraim opened his senses and listened as Danni and Caine headed towards the woman, a marked woman judging by the scent that he'd picked up a half mile down the road, and a vampire in the basement. A few seconds later he heard Chris mutter a curse as he registered the *click* of a lock, letting him know that his son and the pain in the ass shifter that they were stuck with were now inside.

Knowing that the situation downstairs was handled and that his son was safely away from the Pyte that was most likely seconds from losing it, he was able to focus on the man in front of him. His hair was shorter and his clothes were just as simple as they had been in the old black and white images that Izzy had sent to his iPad. This was definitely Christofer Petersen, the Pyte they'd been sent to retrieve before Masters saw that Facebook post and came after him.

"Marta? Marta!" the Pyte cried, a sob breaking free as he gently shook the woman. "No! Goddamnit, no!"

His grief was so raw that it damn near knocked Ephraim on his ass. If it had been anyone else he would have stepped out of the room and given the man some time alone with his sister, but this wasn't anyone else. This was a Pyte who could lose it at any second and make the world pay for his pain and with his son in the house that wasn't an option.

Chris was a Sentinel. He was a hell of a lot stronger than humans. He could probably go a few rounds with a Pyte under normal circumstances, but once the Pyte lost control and went into bloodlust Chris was just as vulnerable as any human. Even though Chris had the ability to heal faster than humans, there were still some things that he would never be able to heal from and a Pyte on a rampage was one of those things.

"*Don't leave me, Marta!*" Christofer begged, gently pulling the woman's frail body in his arms. "Don't leave me," he sobbed, gently rocking the woman in his arms as though she were a baby seconds before he began singing what sounded like a lullaby in German.

Ephraim swallowed, wishing that he could be any-where but here. God, he didn't think that he could take another minute of this, because he knew without a doubt that one day that he would be in the same position when Madison's grandmother passed away. He cared about that woman a great deal and it killed him that he couldn't save her. Her loss was something that he wouldn't be able to avoid, but his children…..

He'd be damned if he was going to be forced to sit around and wait for any of his children or grandchildren to take their last breaths. When it was time, he was going to change Jill, his grandchildren and hopefully Chris and Izzy whether or not the Council approved. This wasn't their call to make no matter what they believed.

Christofer didn't even look his way, no doubt blinded by his grief as he moved to sit on the bed and hold his sister in his arms. He squeezed his eyes shut, tears stream-ing down his face as he continued to rock the woman in his arms as he sang to her. As Ephraim watched, he couldn't help but wonder why Christofer hadn't changed her years ago when she'd been young enough to handle the change. Then again, maybe he already had a mate or he simply didn't know how to change someone without killing them. The way that Christofer held his sister in his arms told him that it was the latter. He probably would have done anything to save her.

They should be leaving, putting as much distance between themselves and this house as quickly as possible, but he just couldn't force himself to interrupt this man's grief. He needed a chance to say goodbye and he was going to give it to-

A vicious growl suddenly tore through the small bedroom as Christofer's head snapped up. His red eyes focused on the open doorway as he bared his fangs in another vicious snarl. Wondering if they were too late, Ephraim opened his senses expecting to hear a small army descending on the house, but there was nothing. He was just about to go outside and do a quick sweep of the area just in case they were being descended upon by demons when he heard it.

"She needs to be moved to the van," Chris said, just as Ephraim heard a bed dip beneath someone's weight. With a curse, he detected the unmistakable scent of his son's scent mingling with the marked woman's. His son had seriously fucked up.

"Relax," Ephraim said, stepping in front of the door as he held up his hands, hoping to talk some sense into the Pyte before it was too late, "we're here to help you, Christofer."

The vicious snarl that followed wasn't exactly encouraging. Neither was the fact that the Pyte seemed to be looking right through him, oblivious to the fact that he was standing there, trying to stop him from tearing his son apart. So much for this being an easy extraction, Ephraim thought. He watched the Pyte press one last kiss against his sister's forehead as his attention remained fixed on the door. With one last mumbled goodbye to his sister, Christofer headed for the door.

"*Christofer,*" Ephraim said, stressing the Pyte's name as he held up his hand in a stopping motion. "I'm going to need you to calm-*oh, fuck,*" he said, the last part leaving him in a pained grunt as a very large, and very pissed off,

Pyte in bloodlust slammed into him, knocking him off his feet and sending him flying across the hallway into the living room where an old television and a wall broke his fall. He heard several sickening cracks as bones broke and his head was whacked against what felt like a fireplace before he was dropped on his ass with a weak grunt.

"That's the last fucking time that I ever try to negotiate with a Pyte in bloodlust," he muttered, wincing in pain as he forced himself to get to his unsteady feet. Ignoring the black dots cascading his vision, he pulled his weapon free from its holster at his back and went after the Pyte.

"Calm the fuck down!" he heard Chris shout as he made it into the kitchen.

"I told you not to pick her up, you dumb bastard!" Kale snapped just as Ephraim headed down the stairs.

When he made it down the last step, he found Kale standing in front of Chris. Holding the marked woman in his arms, Chris tried to back up towards the door where the vampire stood, looking terrified and for good reason.

"*Mine!*" Christofer snarled as he backhanded Kale, sending the shifter flying across the room and getting rid of the one thing that was standing between him and Ephraim's son.

"Shit!" Chris groaned, looking torn between placing the innocent woman down so that he could fight the furious Pyte and keeping her in his arms so that he could protect her.

Deciding that enough was enough, Ephraim released the safety off his weapon, raised the gun, aimed it at the back of Christofer's head and pulled the trigger.

TWENTY-TWO

"We're not bringing her back to the house!" a man shouted, jolting Cloe awake.

Gasping for air, she opened her eyes and quickly scanned the room. Terror sank in as her mind registered her last waking moment, the moment she'd accepted death and the fact that she would never get the chance to kill the son of a bitch that attacked her. Her hands shot up to her neck, frantically searching for the torn skin and blood that she knew should have been there, but instead her fingers met only smooth, sticky skin. Anxiously licking her dry lips, she sat up and scooted back as she quickly glanced around the room only to discover that she was in a hotel room. The second thing she noticed was the large bastard that had attacked her lying on the bed next to her with his hands cuffed to the headboard, appearing dead to the world and looking hotter than ever with several days of beard growth.

The bastard!

She took a shaky breath as memories assaulted her. He'd attacked her. He'd actually attacked her! The man that she'd stupidly allowed herself to feel safe with had attacked her, she fumed, her anger building to a dangerous degree. Every muscle tensed, her jaw clenched tightly until she was literally seeing red, which only told her just how pissed she was if she'd actually managed to burst the capillaries in her eyes.

Moving off the bed, she got to her feet, not really surprised that her legs were trembling since she was literally shaking with rage. That son of a bitch! She forced herself to move closer as she glared down at the bastard who looked nothing like the monster that had attacked her. Right now he somehow looked handsome and peaceful even though he was handcuffed to a bed and covered in dried blood.

Dried blood.....

Her blood!

Furious at the realization, she looked around the hotel room, hoping to find a weapon that she could use to pay the bastard back for what he'd done to her. When she didn't find anything weapon-worthy she grabbed the closest thing to her. Not really caring that it was a pillow and that it wouldn't do any serious damage, she started to beat the shit out of him with it. Barely two hits in and the damn thing practically disintegrated in her hands, clumps of cheap cotton filling and torn pieces of the pillow casing covered the bastard, the bed and floor, but he didn't stir, pissing her off even more!

With a frustrated growl, she looked around again for something else to beat the shit out of him with when something occurred to her. It was something that probably should have occurred to her as soon as she woke up to find herself in a strange hotel room and Christofer was handcuffed to the bed. Someone had grabbed them and dragged them off to wherever the hell they were.

They'd obviously realized that Christofer was dangerous, something that she'd apparently missed, and had
handcuffed him to the bed. They either hadn't expected
her to wake up at all or they'd assumed that she wasn't
going to be a problem. Yeah, they were wrong about that,
because if they didn't let her go, promise her that Marta
was okay, give her back her phone, keys, etc. and bring
her ass back to the house so that she could check on
Marta then she was going to be a very big problem for
them.

Her hand went back to her neck, ran over the smooth
skin again, and for a split second she had to wonder if
she'd dreamed the entire thing, but she knew deep down
that it hadn't been a dream. It had been too detailed,
too real and the fear and pain had been too much for a
dream. The memory of the attack was solid with none of
the weird pauses or missing details that a dream, a nightmare really, would have created.

No, the attack definitely happened and based on how
well the wound had healed it had been a while since it
happened. Keeping her hand where it was, she sent one
last glare at the bastard out cold on the bed and walked
into the bathroom, flicking the light on as she went.
Maybe there was a scab or bruises left, something that
would give her a hint of how long……of how…..

"*No, no, no, no, no, no, no, NO!*"

The denial rushed out of her mouth as she shook her
head frantically. She stumbled back the short distance
until her back slammed back against the wall, leaving her
with no where else to go, nowhere to hide from the ugly
truth that stared back at her in horror.

This couldn't be happening. It couldn't. There was no way. This part was definitely a dream, a horrible dream that she would wake up from at any minute. She'd most likely be in a lot of pain, her neck still torn apart and the bastard would still be tearing into her throat, but it would save her from this nightmare and right now that was okay with her.

She stared in horror at the image in the mirror as it stared right back at her, looking terrified. This wasn't her. She didn't have red eyes and she sure as hell didn't have fangs in her mouth. This was not happening.

"Please don't let this be happening," she mumbled, feeling desperate as she raised a trembling hand to her mouth, praying that this was someone's idea of a sick joke. She touched the tip of one fang with her fingertip, hoping the pressure would be enough to knock the obviously fake tooth out of her mouth.

Instead, she pulled her finger back with a wince as the sharp tip pricked her finger, drawing a drop of blood. This was real. It wasn't a dream. It was either that or her mind was registering pain that her unconscious body was experiencing at the moment and carrying it into this dream. Please let it be-

"You're not dreaming," a deep voice suddenly announced, cutting into her panicked thoughts and drawing her attention to three very large, and very gorgeous men, standing in the hotel room behind her.

"Yes, I am," she said weakly, hating how her voice cracked, but hating the way her chin trembled even more.

"Why don't we have a seat and I'll see if I can explain everything without scaring you," the tallest of the three

men, the one with jet black hair and baby blue eyes, suggested with what appeared to be a friendly smile, but
that's not what had her reluctantly nodding and doing
what he asked.

He had the tone of a cop, a seasoned one at that. He
appeared professional, calm and understanding, which
made her relax just enough to agree to sit down and
hear him out. It was either that or losing it and right now
she didn't think that she could handle losing it. She was
afraid that if she lost it that there would be no coming
back this time. In the back of her mind she realized that
she was most likely in shock, which was probably the real
reason why she was going along with this so calmly.

Never taking her eyes off the three men that made no
secret of watching her every move, she took the seat by
the door, needing to know that she could leave if she had
to. With another one of those reassuring smiles, the tall,
devastatingly handsome man sat opposite her while the
largest of the three men, the one with dark brown hair,
killer green eyes and a nasty pink scar on his neck, sat
down on the corner of the bed she'd found herself lying
on barely a half hour ago.

His attention was on her, but she could tell by the
way he'd angled himself that he was keeping an eye on
Christofer as well. When he raised his right hand to rub
the back of his neck, she noted the white gauze wrapped
around his wrist. She quickly noted that the man sitting
across from her also had white gauze wrapped around his
right wrist. Frowning, her attention shot to the man leaning back against the wall, his murderous glare focused on
her. Feeling a little unnerved by his attention, she quickly

noted that he didn't have any white gauze on his right wrist and focused her attention back on the man sitting across from her.

"How are you feeling, Cloe?" he asked, leaning back in his chair, his attention never leaving her, his expression curious as though her answer was important to him.

"Fine," she mumbled absently as she caught the sound of a cart being pushed past their room, the noise of a squeaky wheel had her wincing and wondering just how thin the room's walls were.

If she screamed for help, would anyone hear her, she wondered, trying not to cringe as that same cart came to a stop in front of their door. The sounds of overly starched cotton rubbing together and sneakers shifting on gravel had her wincing at the sudden assault to her ears. Before she could recover or even wonder what that was about, the assault on her nose immediately followed.

The coppery tang scent of old blood, expensive aftershave, sweat, dust, old cigarette smoke, body odor and a thousand odors that she could have happily lived her life without ever smelling together again, seemed to be hitting her all at once. Just when she didn't think that she could handle anymore, an extremely sweet fragrance hit her, making her stomach growl in hunger and her gums throb painfully. She tried to breathe through her mouth, but that just ended up making her gag when she realized that she could actually taste the scents in the air. The assault on her ears intensified. The shades of red that refused to go away seemed to sharpen, become brighter and darker until she couldn't take it anymore. She was forced to squeeze her eyes shut, cup her hands over her ears and hold her breath, gagging again as the sounds around the room seemed to explode, shooting sharp pain through her head.

"When was the last time she ate?" the man sitting across from her suddenly seemed to shout.

"Please don't yell," Cloe whispered, too afraid to raise her voice, but even the sound of her whisper was too much to take. Thankfully, he didn't say anything else.

The sounds of the cart being pushed away, of the men breathing and moving, ricocheted through her head, made staying upright impossible. She needed to lie down or find a bathroom, she decided as the pain shooting through her head had a nasty effect on her stomach. Opening one eye just so that she could get a general sense of where the bed was, she quickly shut it. She stumbled to her feet and hauled ass across the room, not stopping until she was curled up on the bed, her face buried against Christofer's chest. She grabbed a fistful of his shirt and held on, terrified that one of the men was going to drag her away.

Right now it didn't matter that he was a monster or that he'd tried to kill her. The only thing that mattered to her was the way he made her feel, safe. She knew that the feeling was false, but right now she really didn't give a damn, not when being next to him helped. It also didn't hurt that his scent seemed to make everything better. She could still smell the old coppery smell of blood coming off him, but just barely. Needing an escape from this sensory overload, she kept her face buried against him, her hand fisted in his shirt and worked on ignoring everything else until she finally felt herself relax and drift off.

This time she decided not to fight it, not even when she felt the bastard beneath her begin to stir.

———

"Try not to move," a man whispered before Christofer had a chance to open his eyes. "She just fell asleep and unless you want her in pain, you'll let her stay that way."

He didn't need to ask to know that Cloe was lying on top of him, holding onto him for dear life. Slowly, he opened his eyes, opening his senses and taking in his surroundings. His gaze shot down to Cloe, needing to make sure that she was really okay. Her hair was a mess, her clothes were worse, but her skin color was good, she felt warm against him and her heartbeat was strong and steady, which meant....

That she'd survived.

Cloe had taken his blood and not only survived, but if what Seth said was correct, then she was going to be just like him. She'd never age. She'd heal from anything as long as she drank blood. The best part, she would be strong, strong enough to protect herself against the bastard that had marked her. He was relieved that it had worked, but another part of him, the part that was struggling to accept the memories forcing their way to the front of his mind felt like a part of him was dying.

Marta was gone.

Jaw clenched tightly, he forced himself to breathe through his nose as he squeezed his eyes shut, trying to retain the weak grip that he had on his control. His sister, his best friend and the person that he'd loved more than anything was gone. Not only that, but she'd been the one to take herself away from him, leaving him alone. If he'd thought for one second that the men in this room had been the ones that took her away from him, nothing on this earth would have been able to keep him calm, not even Cloe.

He hadn't been ready to lose her. He'd never got the chance to tell her how much he loved her and now he never would. He wanted to scream at the injustice of the situation, unleash his anger on the world, but he couldn't. The woman lying on top of him needed him to keep it together long enough to figure out who these people were and why he was handcuffed, from the feel of it, to a bed in what smelled like a cheap hotel room.

"Just relax, Christofer," one of the men said in a calm, soothing tone that he didn't trust for one goddamn minute.

It was the same tone that the doctors had used on him when he'd first opened his eyes in that lab and realized that he'd changed. They'd wanted his cooperation and answers to their questions. As long as Christofer had told them what they wanted to know, they'd been nice to him, which of course had lasted for all of five seconds. He didn't know who these men were and he honestly didn't care. All that mattered was keeping Cloe safe until he could take her someplace-

"I'm going to remove your handcuffs," the man said, taking him by surprise.

He opened his eyes and met the icy blue eyes of the man looking down at him with so much pity that

Christofer had to force himself to look away, afraid he'd really lose it.

"We ran out of blood a few hours ago," the man explained apologetically as he unlocked the cuff holding Christofer's right hand immobile. "We had just enough to see Cloe past her transition and you through the worst part of your healing. Caine and Danni are getting more blood to help Cloe with the changes and some to take care of that headache that you probably have," he explained as he removed the last cuff, making Christofer realize that his head was pounding.

"You shot me," Christofer said a few seconds later, remembering the last time that he'd woke up with his head hurting this badly.

"You were going after my son," the man said unapologetically, tossing the cuffs on the bed by his side where they could easily be grabbed and used to cuff him back to the bed if he stepped out of line.

"He had Cloe," Christofer muttered, wincing as the pain in his headache intensified.

"Which is why I had to put you down," the man said with a shrug as he sat down on the other side of the bed.

"Oh," Christofer asked, carefully shifting so that he could sit up without disturbing Cloe, "and why's that?"

The man sighed heavily as he said, "Because if I hadn't, you would have killed my son for touching your mate."

TWENTY-THREE

"Just relax!"

Was he fucking kidding?

There was a tube down her goddamn throat, pumping blood into her stomach! There was no way in hell that she was going to be able to calm down, especially not in *his* arms.

"Just calm down, mein Schatz," Christofer said, his arms tightening around her, pinning her arms to her side and stopping her from thrashing.

"Uck..ooooo!" she snapped at him, wanting to kick the bastard in the balls when he sighed heavily.

"Just swallow, Cloe," he said, tentatively pulling one arm away after making sure that she wasn't going to fight him and grabbed hold of the tube.

Realizing that he wasn't going to let her up until she did what he'd asked, she narrowed her eyes on the water stained ceiling above her and swallowed. Within seconds he had the tube out and she was coughing her damn head off. With a muttered curse, he sat up and pulled her into a sitting position beside him. Before she could ask for something to drink, a bottle of ice-cold water was pressed into her hand. Coughing uncontrollably, she twisted the cover off, pressed the bottle to her lips and swallowed as she thought over everything that he'd put her through.

That….son…..of………..

"*You bastard*!" she snarled between coughing fits, launching herself off the bed to put some space between them, but the son of a bitch wouldn't give her an inch. As soon as she turned around to tell him exactly what she thought of him, he was off the bed and standing only a few feet away from her, looking miserable.

"I'm sorry," Christofer croaked, standing there with his arms by his sides, looking completely lost as he waited for her to strike.

She took a step towards him and then another until she found herself standing less than a foot away from him, trembling with the urge to slap him. She stared up at him, grinding her jaw shut to the point of pain, but she barely felt it. She couldn't believe this was the man that she'd trusted and allowed herself to care about when he was nothing more than a monster.

"Do it," Christofer whispered hoarsely, his expression pained as he waited for her to strike like that would somehow make them even.

Nothing ever would, she realized with disgust, forcing herself to walk away from him.

"Cloe, I-"

She cut off his apology with a slam of the bathroom door in absolutely no mood to hear any of his bullshit apologies. There was nothing that he could say or do that would make up for what he'd done to her, what he'd made her.

———

"Cloe-"

No answer.

Not that he'd expected one. He'd royally fucked up. There was no excuse for what he'd done to her. He'd viciously attacked her, could have killed her, probably technically had and now she was-

"*Oh my God! Oh my God! Oh my God!*" Cloe muttered frantically as the bathroom door was suddenly thrown open and Cloe was rushing out, a towel loosely wrapped around her.

"What's *wrong?*" he ended his question in a pained groan as Cloe turned around and dropped the towel, taking his breath away.

"*My ass!*" she snapped accusingly, her eyes flashing a crimson red as she shot him a murderous glare that had his hands reflexively twitching to cover his defenseless balls. "Look at my ass!"

Against his better judgment, he allowed his gaze to move down her scarred back, over her curvy hips and finally land on the body part in question. Somehow he found the willpower not to lick his lips, knowing that she wouldn't appreciate the gesture. He forced himself to look over her ass, taking in every curve, the beautiful tanned skin, the fullness of each cheek, looking for a flaw, something wrong, but all he saw was perfection.

"What am I looking at exactly?" he asked after a minute of staring at her ass and finding absolutely nothing wrong.

"It's bigger!" she snapped, looking more pissed by the second.

He opened his mouth to answer her, but he really had no idea how he was supposed to respond to that so he just stared at her beautiful ass. It was full and round and definitely not something that he should be looking at or fantasizing about right now. He'd just lost his sister, had fucked up Cloe's life and they were in the middle of some fucked up situation with absolutely no clue on how to fix it.

"Doesn't it look bigger to you?" she demanded, looking all kids of pissed. She peered over her shoulder to glare down at the offending body part while he tried to come up with some way to tell her that this was the first time that he'd actually seen her ass in all its glory since she'd purposely kept her back to the wall the last time he'd seen her naked.

He cleared his throat, deciding that it was probably best not to remind her of that incident and asked, "Is anything else different?"

"*Everything!*" she snarled as she turned around and faced him, damn near making his knees buckle

Damn……..

Her breasts looked fuller, her nipples larger, darker, her athletic stomach that he'd admired in the pharmacy looked more defined, but no less feminine, the thatch of butterscotch curls between her legs looked silkier, more inviting, her hips a bit fuller, her legs looked smoother, toner and damn him if her toes didn't look cuter.

"It's Saturday," she said accusingly, dragging his attention away from the adorable toes and back up to her face and the reminder of what he'd done to her as she glared up at him with shimmering red eyes.

"Okay," he said, because he had no idea what day it was and absolutely no idea what else he should say.

"I've been out cold for three days," she said, gesturing to her beautiful legs, "and they're smooth!"

"And that's a problem because.....?"

"I haven't shaved since Monday!"

"Still not seeing a problem," he mumbled, his gaze running over every inch of her.

She opened her mouth, no doubt to point out something else just to confuse him when they heard a throat clearing outside their door.

"It's the changes," Ephraim explained from the other side of the door, reminding them both that they weren't alone. "Your body is at its peak now. It's part of your natural allure."

"By making my ass fatter?" she demanded, shaking her head in disgust as she snatched up her towel and stormed back into the bathroom, slamming the door shut behind her and saving him from having to stumble his way through another apology.

"Poor bastard," he thought he heard Chris mumble as he pinched the bridge of his nose, wondering how in the hell he expected to handle a mate when he'd never been able to handle his sister.

TWENTY-FOUR

Manhattan, New York
Later that day...........

66 **G**et that away from me," Cloe bit out as she glared at the bastard holding a bag of blood out to her.

"You need to drink this," Chris, aka Kidnapper Number Two, as she liked to think of him, said in clear exasperation as he gave the bag a little shake to entice her.

"And you need to shove that bag up your ass, because I'm not drinking it!" she snapped, having had more than enough of this bullshit for one day.

No, actually that wasn't true.

When she'd woken up in Christofer's arms a few hours ago to find a tube shoved down her throat and blood being pumped into her stomach was when she'd finally had enough. All the crap they added afterwards was just icing on the cake that made her already fucked up life even worse.

Apparently the bastard, Christofer, had not only lost control and gone into bloodlust, meaning the prick hadn't been able to keep his fangs in his pants, but he'd also managed to turn her into a Pyte. She still wasn't clear on what that was except for the fact that it wasn't exactly a vampire and now, she was a monster that needed blood

Anyone else and it would probably feel like they'd won the lottery, but for Cloe it meant that she was the same as the monsters that had destroyed her family now. It made her sick to realize that her very survival depended on drinking human blood like some parasite.

"Alright," Chris said, tossing the bag of blood across the small space of the cargo van, where they'd tossed her ass in when she'd refused to willingly go with them, to Caine, aka Kidnapper Number Four. "Listen up, cupcake, because I'm only going to explain this to you once. I need to get you into that building," he said, pointing towards the tinted side windows and the large building they'd been parked in front of for the last half hour.

"I'm not going in there," she ground out even as she absently wondered when her vision would go back to normal, because this whole seeing everything in shades of red thing was really starting to freak her out a bit.

Ignoring her, as he had been doing for the last six hours, Chris continued. "The plan is to get you inside and up to the penthouse without notice and preferably before the sun sets in twenty minutes. Once inside-"

"I'm. Not. Going. In. There," she bit out, sick and tired of being ignored and bossed around.

They swore up and down that they weren't kidnapping her, but every time she tried to leave or asked them to just let her go, they'd refused. She just wanted to go off somewhere by herself and process everything, to mourn

Marta, make peace with what happened to her, but they refused to let her do that. She understood their fears, well, most of them, but she wasn't going to hurt anyone and she sure as hell wasn't going to go around announcing that she was now a freak of nature. She just....

She just wanted to be left alone.

"Okay," Chris said, nodding as he pursed his lips up in thought. "Then let me put it this way, I want to get home to my very pregnant mate and children. I can't do that until I have you and your mate," he said, gesturing towards Christofer, who was sitting in the back of the van, still staring down at that creased paper in his hands while she tried to secure their freedom and seriously pissing her off, "secured in that building. The longer that you drag your ass and pout, the longer that my mate and children go without my protection," he snapped, sounding seriously pissed off and startling her, because up to this point he'd been relaxed and even tried to coax a smile from her a time or two.

"Chris," Ephraim sighed heavily from the front of the van, sounding like an exasperated father dealing with his child, which if everything they'd told her was to be believed was the case.

Chris rubbed his hands over his face as he muttered a, "Sorry."

"Izzy is only a few weeks away from having twins," Danni, the only female of the group, explained absently as she pulled out a gun and double checked the barrel. "Prolonged time away from her and their babies turns this big baby into a prick," she finished, shooting Cloe a wink as the rest of the men, all but Christofer and the man sitting across from her who wouldn't stop glaring at her, chuckled.

"We'll explain everything once we get inside," came the muffled announcement from her left, which had her turning her head to her left and her jaw dropping.

"Sorry," Caine said with a shrug as he paused in draining the bag of blood that she'd refused, "but I skipped lunch."

"T-that's okay," Cloe mumbled, not really sure what to say as she swiftly turned her attention straight ahead at the bastard glaring at her, but that was definitely better than watching a man slurp down some O positive, she decided, trying not to cringe or gag.

"We need to get inside," Danni announced once Caine had managed to drain the bag.

With a nod, Caine tossed the empty bag back to Chris who caught it with a flick of his hand and shoved it into the front of the black backpack sitting between him and the seriously pissed off man who wouldn't stop glaring at her. At this point she seriously had to wonder what that was about. She opened her mouth to ask him what his problem was, but a slight growl and a flash of silver eyes had her rethinking that decision and deciding that perhaps getting out of the van and away from the perpetually angry bastard was for the best. Of course, that didn't mean that she was planning on going along with their plans to lock her up.

With a feigned sigh of resignation, she nodded and said, "Fine. Let's go inside," making sure to sound putout.

"Let's do it," Chris said, gesturing for Caine to unlock the door and climb out.

She forced herself to sit there, waiting for her turn to jump out when all she wanted to do was to shove her way to freedom and make a run for it, but she knew better. They'd just grab her and carry her ass inside and she wasn't having that. Trying to hide her excitement, she waited and watched as Christofer stepped out of the van, looking somber as he stood there, hands in his pockets as he stared down at the pavement while he waited for everyone else to climb down. If he hadn't come close to killing her, she'd probably feel bad for him, but-

Okay, fine. She did feel bad for him. He'd just lost his sister, someone that Cloe knew that he loved very much. She still didn't know all the details, mostly because he'd refused to talk to anyone right now and no one else would say anything except that it had been unexpected. Cloe certainly hadn't expected the feisty old woman who'd made her laugh to pass on so soon. She'd been so full of life, so kind and sweet. She hadn't even known Marta that long and she was going to miss her terribly. She couldn't even begin to fathom what Christofer was going through right now.

"Let's go, princess," Chris said, gesturing rather impatiently for her to step out.

"That's not my name," she said evenly as she carefully climbed out of the van, keeping her eyes downcast to hide the red glow as well as to hide her intentions.

"Aw, but you're such a dainty little princess," Chris said mockingly, petting her head condescendingly as she stepped out of the van. He reminded her of an older boy in foster care she used to know named Brian, who used to love nothing more than to torment her when none of the adults were around.

So, of course she felt obligated to handle the over-bearing bastard the same way that she used to handle Brian when the jerk used to pin her down and let his spit hang a mere inch away from her face before he sucked it back up and did it again.

She went for his balls.

"Mother fucker!" Chris growled, cupping his balls as he dropped unsteadily to his knees even as he glared at her, not that she was waiting around to watch his reaction.

She wasn't.

She tried to make a run for it as soon as she'd managed to take him by surprise. By take him by surprise she of course meant that she'd taken advantage when his phone started chiming and he'd rushed to answer it. As soon as he had the phone in his hands, she'd turned around and brought her knee up, sending his balls up through his throat. Startled that it had actually worked, she'd decided to press her luck. Unfortunately for her, she'd barely managed to turn around when she found herself picked up.

"Let me-*Hey*!"she started to demand her freedom only to squeal at the end when Ephraim, the bastard that interfered with her escape attempt, tossed her a good ten feet over pavement that she seriously did not want to land ass first on, to the brooding bastard standing off to the side.

She opened her mouth to demand that Christofer put her down, but could only gasp as she struggled to catch her breath. She grabbed onto his shoulders and buried her face against his chest, in no way admitting defeat. She just needed a minute or two while she struggled to catch her breath and calm her racing heart before she made another run for it.

"*My balls,*" Chris croaked.

"Quit your bitching," Kale, who seemed to love to glare, said with a touch of an Irish brogue that she refused to find sexy. "You should have seen that coming," he snapped, stepping up to the side, blocking off one of her escape routes as he shot her a look that practically dared her to try something.

"I expected it," Chris managed to get out as he sucked in a breath.

"It really shows," Caine said dryly as he moved to block her other side while Danni moved past him, obviously intent on blocking her from the back.

"*I got distracted,*" Chris snarled, holding onto his father's arm while the two of them took the position in front of her to complete the trap. As soon as they were in position, Chris bent back over, gasping for air and keeping a tight hold on his father's arm.

Meanwhile, people came and went, walking past them as though they weren't there. It was a little unnerving that that no one seemed concerned about a woman being tossed about or kidnapped. They did however seem putout with the fact that their group wouldn't move and they were forced to alter their path and walk around them.

"*You got distracted,*" Kale mimicked with obvious disgust.

"Izzy texted me and-"

The name Izzy was barely out of Chris' mouth when the scowling jackass to her right and Ephraim were both on Chris, trying to tear the cellphone out of his hand.

"Let go, you bastard!" Kale snapped, trying to wrestle the phone out of Chris' hand while his father simply reached down, pinched the back of Chris' hand, which earned a yelp from Chris before he was forced to release the phone. Ephraim pressed his finger to the screen seconds before he typed something.

"She's fine, you insensitive bastards!" Chris snapped, shaking off his hand as he got to his feet with a glare aimed at the men focused on his phone and stumbled past her to take up Kale's abandoned spot.

Both men sighed heavily with obvious relief as Ephraim tossed the phone back to Chris. "Just a reminder to pick up some fudge from that shop that she likes," Ephraim muttered, rubbing his hands down his face.

"Which I would have told you if you hadn't attacked me, you betraying bastard!" Chris practically snarled as he continued to shake off his hand with a wince as he shifted his legs.

"I thought you told her not to text you unless it's an emergency," Ephraim grumbled as he gestured for Christofer, who was still oddly quiet throughout this whole exchange, to precede them inside the large, and obviously, upscale building.

"I did," Chris gritted out, keeping stride with Christofer as they headed inside.

"She's pregnant," Danni said dryly. "To her, fudge is an emergency."

Ephraim chuckled as he pulled up the rear alongside Kale, who was once again glaring at her. How did she know this? Because while everyone else was chatting away and Christofer was voluntarily walking them to their doom, she was struggling to get free. She kicked, shoved, pinched and squirmed, but nothing worked. He'd barely even grunted when she'd kneed him in the chest when she'd tried to climb over his shoulder to take a chance with a pavement dive.

"Let me go, Christofer!" she said, squirming wildly in his arms, but other than tighten his hold around her, he didn't seem to react at all.

Fed up, Cloe decided to take a chance that someone, anyone, might actually give a damn in this city. "Somebody, please help me! They're kidnapping me!" she shouted as Christofer stepped inside the opulent building and the gold encased glass door closed behind her with a *whoosh*.

"Scream all you want," Kale said, smiling smugly as he gestured to the men and women moving all around them and making her frown when she realized that they all wore various forms of black combat clothing much like that of her captors. "It won't do you any good, not in a Sentinel compound."

TWENTY-FIVE

"**Y**ou son of a bitch!" Cloe snapped as he stepped inside the large penthouse.

Without a word, and because he needed some space to clear his head, he put her down, dropping her beautiful ass on the leather love seat as he passed by it. He kept walking until he found himself standing inches away from the floor to ceiling windows overlooking Central Park. Other than releasing a little surprised squeal that teased a small twitch from his lips, she didn't say anything about the rude way he'd handled her.

He knew that he should have pulled her away from the group and tried to explain things to her, at least of what he knew, but he just.....he just couldn't. Too much shit had happened in the last couple of days and he wasn't handling it very well. To be honest, he'd rather be anywhere but here. He should be accompanying his sister's body back to Germany and seeing that she had a proper burial in the family cemetery, but instead he was here in New York making sure that the woman whose life he'd ruined was tucked away somewhere safe.

Goddamn Marta for leaving him like this, he inwardly raged, grinding his teeth together as he forced his hands to stay by his sides when all he wanted to do was to pull out that damn letter again. She'd fucking lied to him. She'd known that she was dying for a goddamn year and she'd never said a word to him. She'd fucking played him, telling him that she had a serious female problem that needed frequent treatment. It was the only way she'd been able to convince him to drop her off at the doctor's office and leave her there until she called to be picked up after her appointment.

He never should have left her there, but he'd wanted to respect her request for privacy. She'd been humiliated enough in that fucking lab and he hadn't wanted to take away what little self-respect she had left so he'd left her at the medical office and drove off far enough away so that he wouldn't be able to overhear what was discussed during her appointment. If he had known that she'd been diagnosed with cancer he never would have left her.

Never.

She had no business leaving him the way that she had, taking her own life and saying goodbye to him in a fucking letter! He'd deserved to know what was going on, deserved to be there to hold her hand and tell her how much he loved her, but most of all he deserved a fucking chance to try to save her! He would have taken her to every expert that he could find and made them fix her.

She'd left him too soon. He hadn't been ready to say goodbye to her, not when he knew that they should have had several more years together. He would never forgive her for doing this to him, goddamn her for leaving him like this and goddamn her for doing this to Cloe. It made him sick knowing that Marta had purposely brought an innocent woman into this mess. She'd put Cloe's life in danger, and for what? So that he wouldn't have to worry about being alone for a few more decades?

Marta thought she was giving him someone to care about and love when all she ended up giving him was another responsibility. He might not have been ready to say goodbye to Marta, but he'd been prepared for it. He'd been prepared to learn how to live on his own, to have no one to worry about, to finally explore the world around him, and to figure out how he was going to manage to live forever without losing his goddamn mind. Now it seemed that he couldn't even do that, because he was already losing his goddamn mind.

He had a mate........

A fucking mate that he didn't want and who sure as hell didn't want him, but none of that mattered, because she was his now and he'd be damned if he failed one more woman in his life.

"Why haven't you tried to run yet?" Ephraim asked as he moved to join him in front of the large window.

"Why do you care?" Christofer asked, staring out the window at what other people would probably call a breathtaking view, but he barely noticed it, lost in his thoughts the way that he was.

"I'm just curious," Ephraim admitted.

"Were you expecting a fight?" Christofer asked, already having noted that this little misfit group had been heavily armed when they'd come to retrieve him.

They'd probably expected him to fight them tooth and nail and if it hadn't been for Cloe, he would have done just that. Throw in the fact that they hadn't resorted to bullshitting them, threats of violence, and he didn't count Ephraim being forced to shoot him in the back of the head to protect his son, and the fact that they seemed genuinely concerned about Cloe's safety and he didn't see a reason to fight them.

Not yet anyway.

Once he knew that Cloe was going to be okay and he'd figured out how to keep her safe that was a different story altogether. He didn't need or want their protection. From what they'd told him, he knew that Masters, demons and shifters were searching for others like him, hoping to use them to make an army or whatever the fuck they were after. He didn't care what they did, as long as they left him alone.

He didn't want any part of their war, wasn't interested in getting involved, but he did appreciate the heads up about what was going on. He'd be more careful from now on, use a different name, wouldn't stay in one area for too long, not again. Not that there was a reason for him to stay anywhere now. Not with Marta gone, he thought as he felt his eyes begin to shift. With a simple thought he made his eyes return to their normal blue, refusing to clue this group in on just how badly he was hurting right now.

He'd learned long ago that his eyes gave away too much, let the doctors know just how badly they hurt him, pissed him off and frightened him. It had taken some time, but he'd eventually learned how to control the shift in his eyes and teeth. They might have been able to make him wish for death, but he'd refused to let them know just how helpless and terrified he'd really been.

"I still am," Ephraim admitted, not really sounding all that worried about it and probably for good reason.

The man was just like him, a Pyte. He couldn't even begin to describe his reaction to finding out that there were others like him. All these years he'd thought that he was a freak of nature, a mistake, but he wasn't. There were more of them out there, a product of a vampire and a human woman in most cases. Unfortunately, it had also confirmed what the doctors had claimed all those years ago.

Marta wasn't his sister.

At least not by blood. Not that he really cared, because the little girl he'd gone through hell with, raised, protected and loved would always be his sister. He didn't give a damn what anyone said, Marta had been his baby sister and he would always love her and miss her. Learning that his father hadn't really been his father, however, had damn near killed him.

He'd loved his father more than anything. More than that, he'd respected the man for his kind heart and his dedication to his family. When he'd been a child, he'd always hoped that he'd grow up to be a man just like his father, but now he knew that was impossible. The man that he'd thought was his father had simply been the man who'd taken over the responsibility and care of raising the child that his wife had left behind.

Christofer wondered if the man that he'd been raised to think of as his father had known the truth. If he had, he'd never showed it. He'd treated Christofer like his son, accepting him for who he was and never expecting or demanding anything more. His father had given his life to protect him and he would not dishonor him by thinking of him as anything less than his father.

"Is that why you brought us here?" Christofer asked, forcing his mind away from things that he'd rather not dwell on right now.

"To this compound?" Ephraim asked, shaking his head. "No, we didn't bring the two of you here because we were expecting a fight."

"Then why are we here?" Christofer demanded, turning to face the man that seemed to hold all the answers.

"That's what I'd like to know," Cloe announced, apparently giving up on trying to "glare" her way to freedom as she joined them, making damn sure to put some space between them.

A few days ago, that little action would have seriously pissed him off, but today......

Today, it sounded like a good plan.

———

"Why don't we have a seat?" Ephraim suggested, gesturing back towards the sitting area where the rest of her captors now reclined, obviously waiting to get this over with. Well, all but one. Kale, the bastard that she'd already decided that she didn't like, was leaning back against the kitchen island, looking bored as he played with his iPhone.

She pretended not to notice when Christofer turned his back on her, pretended that it didn't hurt or feel like he was abandoning her when she needed him to help her get through this. She hated needing him this badly. He'd attacked her, changed her into this monster and here she was, hurt because he wanted nothing to do with her. She was pathetic, but she wasn't going to beg him for anything. Instead, she forced herself to focus on Ephraim. He was the clear leader of the group, which meant that he was her best bet to get out of here.

"Are you going to let me go afterwards?" she demanded, not really sure that she could handle anything more right now.

Ephraim shot her a sympathetic smile as he said, "No, I'm afraid that's not an option. At least not yet."

"That's the only option that I'm giving you," Cloe snapped back, the shades of red sharpening as her fangs shot down through her gums, cluing her into the fact that her eye color and fangs were tied in with her emotions. It was something that she was definitely going to have to work on if she didn't want anyone to figure out that she was a-

"Don't worry about your eyes and your fangs right now," Ephraim cut in with a sympathetic tone. "You'll learn how to control those with time."

"I wasn't worried," she snapped, lying her terrified ass off.

"If I promise to answer all of your questions first, will you hear me out?" Ephraim asked, gesturing for her once again to go have a seat.

"What if after I hear you out, I still want to leave? What then?" she asked, wondering just how hard it would be to get past those security panels attached to the elevator doors and the fire escape she'd spotted at the other end of the small hallway when Christofer, the bastard, had carried her inside.

"I tell you what," Ephraim said, glancing over his shoulder at the quickly darkening sky before looking back at her, "if you still want to leave after everything's been explained to you, then I'll let you go."

She stilled as she considered him, obviously suspicious of this sudden turnaround. "I hear you out and you'll let me go? Just like that?" she asked, narrowing her eyes on him, looking for a sign that he was lying.

He met her gaze head-on as he nodded. "You have my word."

Nodding, she turned around and headed for the leather chair closest to the door, making her intentions clear from the start. She'd listen to him and then she was leaving, and she didn't care what she had to do to make that happen.

———

"Ow! Ow! Ow! *Stop that!*"

Fucking Pytes, Kale thought with disgust.

He watched Caine and Chris force Cloe's hand beneath the stream of cold water while Danni did her best to hold Cloe near the sink when she clearly wanted to bolt away from Ephraim and that damn bag of blood that he was trying to get her to drink. Letting Ephraim take the lead on this one had been a mistake, one he wouldn't be making again, he decided, sighing heavily as he shut off his iPhone and shoved it in his back pocket.

Not that he could fault Ephraim with the way he'd handled retrieving the Pyte, he couldn't. He'd gotten everyone in and handled a situation that you couldn't pay him to touch. He didn't do emotional bullshit, didn't have time for it, so when they'd realized that one of the heartbeats in the house was slowing down and who it belonged to, he'd been more than happy to leave it up to Ephraim to deal with.

It had given him the distraction that he'd needed to see what was going on in the basement. He'd have to admit that he hadn't expected to find a vampire, one of the Sentinel's blood deliverers, switching out a bag of blood for the unconscious woman lying on the bed. He sure as hell hadn't expected to find a freshly turned Pyte on his first retrieval mission for the Council.

He'd come for one Pyte and had instead discovered two. While Chris had been playing twenty questions with the vampire and checking to make sure that the woman was okay, Kale had stood by the bed, gun in hand while he'd struggled against the urge to kill her before the turn was final. He'd had a chance to rid the world of one of them, he'd been tempted, oh so fucking tempted to take it.

If Chris hadn't stepped in his way and picked the woman up, he would have killed her. If it had been any-one else who had taken up the responsibility of protect-ing her, he would have killed them just to get to her and kill her before it was too late, but Chris was untouchable for a reason.

Izzy.

She loved her mate, adored the annoying bastard so when Kale was on patrol with Chris or on a mission, he made damn sure to return the bastard to Izzy without so much as a scratch on him. So, for Izzy, he hadn't gone through Chris to get to the woman. The fact that he'd doubled his pay without lifting a finger should have comforted him, but it didn't.

He had no problem wrangling in the Pytes that were already in existence, especially if it meant making sure that they were kept out of Masters' hands, but he had a real fucking problem with creating new Pytes. If it was up to him, he'd rid the world of every last one of them, but since it wasn't up to him or evenly remotely possible, he'd settle for making a few bucks by delivering them to the Council....

As long as the Council didn't try to build its own army that is.

If they ever tried that bullshit, Kale would make every last Sentinel pay for unleashing that horror on the world. But, for now he was going to content himself with being paid to hunt Pytes, retrieve them and deliver them to the Council. This way he would know how many of them there were, where they were and of course, bring him that much closer to his goal.

At least he didn't have to worry about these two Pytes creating any little bastards that he'd eventually have to put down before they hit their immortality, he mused, shaking his head in disgust at Ephraim's attempts to explain their world to this woman. He really should have saved the whole "we heal from everything" part of the speech until the end. Even Kale knew what the woman was going to do as soon as Ephraim had made that little announcement.

Sure enough, as soon as Ephraim had finished explaining how Pytes could heal from absolutely everything, and he would know, the seriously pissed off, but curious, woman had stormed into the kitchen to find out for herself. He'd known exactly what she was planning when she'd eyed that large butcher knife and he could have easily stopped her, but....well, he really hadn't cared enough to try.

"Lying bastard!" Cloe yelled, struggling to get away from Ephraim, who was still trying to get her to drink some blood.

He probably should have explained that Pytes only heal quickly if they'd fed recently or drank blood after they were injured. Otherwise it could take a while for their injuries to heal. Since this woman had only been turned a few days ago and refused to drink blood, she didn't have enough blood stored away to handle even a tiny scratch never mind that huge gash on her palm.

"Get the hell away from me, you bastard!" Cloe snapped at Ephraim as she continued to struggle to get away. The trio, who were only fucking this up more, were trying to slow the bleeding down before Cloe could slip into bloodlust from blood loss and they had to deal with more bullshit.

A small chime brought his attention back to his phone and the job that was waiting for him. He didn't have time for this bullshit. He had a job waiting for him and he needed to get going. He looked over at the Pyte who should be handling this and sighed.

The bastard sat on the loveseat, looking bored. Christofer's focus was on the floor to ceiling glass window and his eyes were a calm crystal blue instead of the fiery red that he'd expected. Kale was curious how the Pyte managed to control that reaction, looking as though he didn't give a rat's ass that his mate was being manhandled by three other men, but he knew the truth. The Pyte was just barely holding himself back. The scent of fury poured off him in waves. His heart was pounding against his chest even as he appeared relaxed, bored.

Interesting…..

Curious to see if he could break through that façade, and admittedly a little bored himself, Kale walked over to the small group, keeping his attention on the Pyte in front of him, reached out and with the very tip of his finger. He'd barely touched Cloe's arm when he suddenly found himself soaring through the air courtesy of a seriously pissed off Pyte.

TWENTY-SIX

"**G**et him off me!"

"Man the fuck up!" Chris snapped as he tried to pull Christofer off Kale and failed, judging by the way he was suddenly sent flying through the large room.

"Grab his legs!" Ephraim ordered Caine as he moved to grab Christofer by the arms and-

Went flying across the room to join Chris, who was just getting to his feet before stumbling and falling back on his ass next to his father. With a muttered, "Should just let him tear the shifter apart," Caine grabbed Christofer by the legs and yanked him back and-

Landed on top of Chris and Ephraim with a pained grunt just as the two of them struggled to get back to their feet. Sighing heavily, Danni moved to make an attempt to pull Christofer off Kale, but all three men on the floor yelled, "No!" in unison.

Sighing in disgust, Danni walked past Christofer and Kale, and picked up the bag of blood that Ephraim had dropped in order to rush to Kale's aid. With another roll of her eyes and a muttered, "pathetic," she walked past the trio still struggling to get to their feet, plopped down on the couch and tossed the bag of blood on the coffee table.

"Fucking hell!" Kale groaned as he shoved Christofer back in order to gain some ground, but within seconds Christofer was back on top of him, beating the shit out of him.

"Is he in bloodlust?" Chris asked, panting heavily as he shoved Caine off his legs and finally managed to get to his feet.

"Don't you ever fucking touch her again!" Christofer snapped, laying punch after punch on Kale's face and chest as Kale returned the favor, punching Christofer, landing several nasty blows that had Cloe wincing and wondering what she should be doing. Then she remembered that she was supposed to be standing there, bleeding all over the kitchen because the bastard just getting to his feet had lied.

"Does that answer your question?" Ephraim asked, groaning as he stretched his back, a loud *crack* accompanying the action.

"He's coherent," Chris said, sounding impressed as he gestured for his father and Caine to get back in there.

With a snort, Caine stumbled past them and headed to the fridge to grab two bags of blood before returning to the living room section of the large open space. He tossed Ephraim a bag as he joined Danni on the couch. Ephraim watched the fight for a good minute while he drank the blood, at which time Cloe had to force herself to look away before she got sick. Not because the sight of him drinking blood disgusted her, but because her stomach actually growled viciously at the sight.

She closed her eyes and took a deep breath. She tried to focus on the pain in her hand, but the cold water had numbed it by this point. It made it difficult to focus on anything but the tantalizing scents around her. They teased her, making her realize just how hungry she was. She didn't want to notice how good the air smelled. Even the overly sweet scent coming from Chris was mouthwatering. She'd never considered herself one of those girls with an uncontrollable sweet tooth before.

As she slowly inhaled, savoring his scent, she had to wonder just how much sugar he had to ingest to end up smelling like pure sugar. She didn't know much about Sentinels other than they weren't human, but she couldn't imagine that ingesting sugar like it was going out of style could be good for him. Turned off by the idea of eating something overly sweet, she moved onto the other scents competing for her attention.

She scented a heavily metallic odor and immediately wrinkled her nose in distaste. It didn't take much to figure out that she'd smelled the bagged blood the trio on the couch was drinking. If they thought that she was going to willingly subject herself to that crap then they were out of their-

An enticing aroma grabbed her attention. Her stomach growled viciously as she breathed in the slightly spicy scent with just a hint of that metallic odor, but this time her stomach didn't turn in disgust. Instead her stomach rumbled, demanding the delicious treat that she was scenting. Confused, and really hoping that she was smelling a medium rare steak cooking somewhere in the building, she opened her eyes to find her focus already zeroed in on its source.

And that's when she finally lost it.

———

"Cloe, open the door," he said, sighing heavily in exasperation as he reached up and wiped away the blood dripping in his eye.

"Just leave me alone," she said softly, too soft for the human ear to pick up, but he didn't have that problem.

He could hear everything going on in that room, which was how he knew that Cloe, the woman terrified of enclosed spaces, was hiding in a closet. It was enough for him to know just how poorly she was handling this new situation. It also made him feel like more of an asshole for not helping her. She hated him and if she didn't, she should.

He'd destroyed her life, attacked her like some sort of animal and would have killed her if she hadn't decided to fight back and unintentionally taken his blood at just the right time. Turning her had been an accident and one he deeply regretted, more so right now that the poor thing was stuck hiding in a closet as she.....

His brows arched in confusion as he zeroed in on the odd grinding noise coming from the closet. It took him a good minute to figure out what she was doing. Sighing heavily, he shook his head in disgust. He ignored the bleeding bastard leaning against the wall next to him and grabbed the doorknob, twisting it until the lock broke.

"I want a rematch," the sore loser growled, looking furious as glowing silver eyes narrowed on him.

"Anytime, asshole," Christofer said, looking forward to beating the shit out of the shifter again as he walked into the room and slammed the door shut behind him. He headed straight for the closet where those odd grinding noises were growing increasingly louder.

He wasn't exactly surprised to find Cloe hunched down in the closet trying to make a stake from what appeared to be a broken chair leg. Although, he was surprised to discover that she'd already managed to wrap a ripped piece of lavender sheet around her hand, made a large cross by tying two broken chair legs together with what looked like a shoelace from her sneakers in the short time since she'd fled the living room. What he couldn't figure out was the bathroom trashcan filled to the brim with water. Besides getting him soaked, he rectified a minute later when Cloe spotted him, squealed and grabbed the trash can and sent the cold water flying across the short distance to soak his crotch and legs.

"Shit! Holy water doesn't work!" she muttered with alarm, anxiously grabbing her makeshift cross and holding it up like a shield as she got to her feet. "Stay back!" she ordered, giving the cross in her hand a little shake for emphasis that had him biting back a smile that she probably wouldn't appreciate at the moment.

"What are you doing?" he asked, pinching the bridge of his nose, struggling not to laugh. It surprised him that he actually had the urge to laugh after everything that happened.

"I'm making my escape," she said firmly, shifting her attention to the closed bedroom door.

She moved ever so slightly towards the door, homemade cross still firmly raised in his direction. She held the stake with the splintered end in the other hand, probably thinking that it would be enough.

"I see," he murmured, reaching out and placing his hand against the cross.

Her eyes widened in surprise before narrowing with disgust as she tossed the useless item aside and held the stake higher. "I don't want to have to hurt you, Christofer, but if you don't let me go I'll-"

"Give me a splinter?" he finished for her as he absently reached up and scratched the back of his neck. He nearly cringed when he realized that except for washing up quickly in the hotel sink this morning, he hadn't showered or shaved in days.

"I don't want to have to hurt you, Christofer!" she repeated, licking her lips nervously as she gave the stake a little jab in his direction. She didn't even come close to his chest, which surprised him considering everything that happened.

He scented the air around them and frowned. He didn't smell anger coming off her. The only thing that he could detect was her anxiety and fear and even that had gone down since he'd opened the closet door. If anything it should have gone up with him in the room. He'd attacked her, destroyed her entire world and instead of attacking him like she had every right in the world to do, he could smell her fear diminishing and her heart rate slowing down to a normal tempo.

It had to be the fucking blood exchange, he thought with a sigh as he reached back and grabbed the back of his shirt. He yanked it off and tossed it aside.

"W-what are you doing?" Cloe demanded, shifting anxiously as she moved her gaze from his bare chest to the closed door.

"Getting out of these dirty clothes so that I can take a shower," he said, toeing off his shoes as he undid his pants.

"Well stop!" Cloe said, waving her sad little stick even as her eyes ate up every inch of him.

"Yeah, I'll get right on that," he said around a yawn, wondering if he should try to get her to drink some bagged blood before her bath or just go straight to plan B, and she was definitely taking a bath.

He needed her relaxed, very relaxed if he was going to convince her to eat. She needed to eat soon or she'd lose control and that would only make things worse for her. There was nothing quite like losing control of your mind, your actions and giving into rage and need. It left you feeling helpless, weak and frightened of doing something, anything that would make it happen again.

At some point it would happen to Cloe. It was inevitable, but he didn't want it to happen when she was still struggling to deal with everything else that happened to her. She needed to get strong, learn to control her reactions, learn to feed and learn to hide what she was, especially since their kind apparently held the number one spot on some fucked up wish list.

He'd planned on leaving her education on her new life in the hands of Ephraim and the ragtag group that had brought them here since they obviously knew more about their world than him, but seriously? Who in their right mind starts off by telling someone that they'd heal from absolutely everything, especially to a woman as pig-headed as Cloe?

As soon as Ephraim made that little announcement, Cloe, obviously curious and eager to see if it was true, had stopped listening to Ephraim as he'd tried to explain her new abilities and walked over to the kitchen island to see for herself. It had taken everything he had in him to continue sitting there when all he wanted to do was to tackle the woman and kick the shit out of Ephraim.

He'd also wanted to kick the shit out of Chris for rushing after her and making a grab for the knife, startling Cloe and making the cut a hell of a lot worse than she'd probably intended. At least one good thing came from this experience. Cloe now knew that she wasn't invincible and that she could still experience pain. It would hopefully stop her from doing something stupid like climbing to the roof and doing a header in an attempt to escape. She'd survive, yes, but by the time she'd hit the ground below she'd be wishing that she hadn't.

"Seriously, what are you doing?" Cloe asked, absently waving that stake at him as she ran her eyes, hungry eyes, he noted, down his body.

He ignored her question as he shoved his pants, along with his boxers, down and stepped out of them. "Come on," he said, reaching out and taking her empty hand into his. With his other hand, he reached over and gently plucked the stake that was more splinters than anything, out of her hand and tossed it aside.

"I don't want a shower," she protested even as she allowed him to lead her into the bathroom. "I just want to leave."

"You don't think you'll be noticed dressed like that?" he asked, pointedly looking at her blood stained shirt and pants.

She frowned down at herself. "But I don't have anything else to change into," she murmured, sounding a little lost.

"Ephraim had our stuff sent here while we were recovering," he told her, pushing the bathroom door open and flicking on the light, making sure that she followed him inside before he closed the door behind them.

"He did?" she mumbled with a frown, looking deep in thought and a little confused as she asked, "What do you mean by when 'we' were recovering?"

Deciding that now was not the time to inform her that Ephraim had been forced to shoot him in the back of the head to stop him from killing his son because he'd lost control, he instead gestured towards the shower. When she threw a hesitant glance at the door, he knew that she was worried about the others coming in.

"They've already left," he gently explained, lying his ass off, but he knew that one of the Pytes in the other room would hear him and take the hint.

He knew that they were eager to continue explaining things to Cloe, but not tonight. Tonight she needed a break, some time to relax and accept what happened to her. Tomorrow......

Tomorrow they could finish destroying what was left of her world.

TWENTY-SEVEN

"Tell me that you really didn't start with the whole, 'you'll heal from anything,' bullshit," Caine grumbled, rubbing his palms down his face while Danni wrapped her arms around his waist and leaned into him.

He dropped his arm around his mate's shoulders and kissed the top of her head as he closed his eyes and savored her touch, welcoming the peace that just being near her gave him. The last couple of days had been grueling and he was starting to feel it. Right after they'd come back from patrol on Monday morning, the asshole, a.k.a. Kale, had barked orders for them to hurry their asses up and get in the van.

After telling the bastard to go fuck himself and he'd finished explaining exactly where the shifter could shove his orders, he'd taken Danni, who'd been dragging ass by that point, inside. He'd badgered her until she'd finally given in and drank the demon blood the Council supplied her with. Once he'd made sure that she'd consumed enough demon blood and he'd managed to consume five bags of bagged blood, he'd pulled her into his arms and held her while she took what she needed from him.

It hadn't been enough, not nearly enough, but Danni, stubborn as always, had been in a rush to get on the road. She'd needed to rest, but she'd refused to listen, promising him instead that she'd sleep on the drive. He hadn't exactly been surprised when she'd broken her word to him.

Instead of doing as she'd promised, she'd spent the entire ride going over the files that Izzy had sent to their iPads. He had to admit that he had as well. The files the Nazis had left behind of what those sick fucks had done to Christofer and his sister had turned his stomach and had him seeing red the entire ride. His own captivity and torture was hard enough to deal with, but Christ, he didn't have shit on what they'd put Christofer through.

Ephraim hadn't said anything, but the way his jaw had clenched tightly every few seconds and his eyes had glowed red as he'd read through the file lead him to believe that Christofer's time spent in the lab had been just as bad as Ephraim's time spent in the dungeon. The sick fucks had cataloged absolutely everything that they'd done to Christofer and Marta, *everything*.

There'd been pictures of doctors smiling while they'd congratulated each other on a job well done as they'd stood over Christofer's eviscerated body, of them looking at a loss when their experiments had failed, but mostly, there had been pictures cataloguing every humiliating moment that Christofer had endured to keep his sister alive. The worst pictures, the ones that had him wishing that he could hunt every last one of those sick fucks down, were the ones where Christofer had been forced to watch as they'd experimented on his sister.

The pictures had been bad, but the journals and notes they'd kept......

There were no words to describe the revulsion he'd experienced when reading over everything that they'd done to Christofer. The way they'd detailed everything from Christofer's reaction to being dipped in acid to having his balls cut off with a straightedge razor was almost as bad as the pictures. One thing he'd realized early on in the notes, the doctors performing the experiments had gotten a kick out of making Christofer react.

It appeared that a few of them had turned it into a game. They'd wanted to see who could make Christofer lose control the fastest and had even encouraged the guards to torture him. They'd been immensely pleased each and every time Christofer's eyes had turned red and his fangs had made an appearance. They'd taken the changes as a sign that their experiments were working, that they could sneak past the façade of the perfect blonde haired, blue-eyed male and drag the red-eyed monster to the surface.

He had to smile when he'd realized that Christofer had figured out their sick game and started to deny them the reaction that they'd craved. They'd perform tests on Christofer, but they'd mutilate what they'd deemed the "monster" inside him. Whenever Christofer eyes shifted and his fangs dropped, the scientist believed that they'd released the monster inside of him and hadn't held anything back.

By the end of the first year of Christofer's captivity in that lab he'd started fighting back by not giving them what they'd wanted. It started off by Christofer managing to briefly put off allowing his eyes to shift and his teeth to descend. At first he'd only been able to hold back the shift for a minute at a time, but slowly he gained control for several minutes, hours, and days until finally, Christofer had stopped reacting at all.

At least that's what Caine had assumed at first.

But after seeing him beat the shit out of Kale, Caine knew better now and of course, couldn't help grinning every time he thought about it. An untrained Pyte, one without any military training as far as he knew, had beat the shit out of Kale Quinn, packless Alpha shifter, deadly mercenary and pain in the ass without having to go into bloodlust. It should have been damn near impossible for Christofer to land a blow against Kale, never mind beat the shit out of him.

Kale was a very old and very powerful shifter. His control was legendary. He could harness the strengths and abilities of his werewolf form without actually having to shift. It was something that no one else had been able to accomplish….

Until now that is.

It seemed as though Christofer not only had the ability to keep a tight leash on his control, but that he could harness the uncontrollable strength that bloodlust provided without actually having to fall victim to it. That is of course, unless his mate was involved. She seemed to have the uncanny ability to rattle him, but then again, Caine's mate had the same effect on him.

"I didn't realize that she knew absolutely nothing about our world. I thought she'd already figured out that part from her recovery," Ephraim bit out, glaring straight ahead as they waited for the elevator doors to close.

"You know what they say when you assume......." Caine murmured, chuckling when Ephraim shot him the finger as he leaned back against the elevator wall. He pressed the button for the fifth floor, the guest floor, when the door still hadn't shut a few seconds later.

"Madison didn't become cut happy after she'd been turned," Chris pointed out in a helpful tone, but Caine caught the familiar glint of mischief in the Sentinel's eyes. He knew Chris was just trying to push his father's buttons, something the Sentinel seemed to really enjoy doing.

Ephraim's eyes narrowed on his oldest child as he snapped, "That's because she knew what to expect, asshole."

"*Asshole?*" Chris repeated back, doing his best to sound hurt as he pressed a hand over his heart. "Is that any way to speak to your favorite child?"

"Izzy's his favorite child," the shifter, who'd gotten his ass handed to him, grumbled as he stepped into the elevator to join them. He looked as though he'd like nothing more than to go back inside that penthouse and beat the shit out of the Pyte who'd kicked his ass.

"Puhlease," Chris said, closing his eyes as he leaned back against the elevator wall. "He fucking loves and adores me. Worships the very ground I walk on and would be lost without me," he finished off the familiar litany with a loud yawn.

After another minute of just standing there, too tired to torment Ephraim for his fuckup, Kale snapped, "Why aren't we moving?"

"No fucking clue," Ephraim said around a loud yawn as he reached over and pressed the button for the fifth floor again.

Muttering obscenities in Gaelic, Kale reached over and flicked open the cover for the first floor button, revealing a fingerprint scanner. He gestured for Ephraim to press his finger against the smooth piece of glass. "You can't get off a restricted floor in a Sentinel compound without requesting access," Kale explained as though they were all idiots and at that moment, he sure as hell felt like one.

He'd been working with the Sentinels for over twenty years and this was the first time that he'd heard about this. Granted, he'd never even been allowed on a restricted floor before so he had no reason to know about this security measure, but still.....

"How do you know about this?" Caine demanded, knowing that the shifter standing in front of him was the last person on earth that the Council would willingly share their security secrets with.

"I make it a point to know everything about my enemies," Kale said, meeting his gaze head on and delivering the unmistakable message that the shifter definitely counted him as an enemy.

"Me too," Caine said with a wink, letting the cocky prick know that he more than shared the sentiment.

In fact, that was one of first things he did upon deciding to stay at the Williams' mansion with his mate. He'd investigated everyone living there, even the prick who came and went as he pleased. He knew all about Kale Quinn, probably more than most people. He definitely knew things that the shifter wanted kept secret and as long as the shifter stayed away from his mate and didn't try to fuck her over, he'd keep those secrets.

Ephraim pressed his finger to the scanner and held it there for a minute before he dropped his hand away and sighed. "What time are we leaving in the morning?" he asked, sounding almost as tired as Caine felt, which was pretty fucking exhausted.

"Don't fucking care," Kale said, pulling out his iPhone. "I'm leaving tonight."

"Tonight?" Chris asked, opening his eyes as he shot a frown at the shifter that they all tolerated for Izzy's sake.

"*Tonight,*" Kale confirmed, looking bored as he scrolled through his messages.

"What about the Pytes we just left upstairs?" Caine snapped. "They need to know what's going on. They need-"

"That's not my job," Kale said, barely sparing him a glance as he shoved his phone back in his pocket as he reached over and pressed the button for the lobby.

"*Not your job?*" Danni repeated in disgust. "How is that not your job? You're supposed to-"

"Find them, capture them and deliver them," Kale fired off rapidly, cutting her off. "Babysitting them and making them feel good about their fucked up existence isn't part of my job description."

"So, that's the game plan?" Ephraim asked in a deceptively bored tone. "You're going to hunt them down and deliver them to the Council with no questions asked?"

"Not a one," Kale answered absently, pulling his phone back out when it chimed again.

"And what about Pytes like Christofer and Cloe who have no fucking clue what they are or what they're getting themselves into?" Ephraim pressed on, asking the questions that they were all wondering.

"Pytes like Christofer can get their answers from whatever Sentinel is assigned to hold his hand," Kale drawled, once again putting his phone away.

"And newly turned Pytes like Cloe?" Danni demanded, moving to get in the shifter's face, but Caine knew his mate well enough to keep her right by his side.

"Will be exterminated before they draw their last mortal breath," he said in that same bored tone that let them all know that he wasn't fucking playing around.

"*You fucking prick,*" Chris growled, all signs of the playful exhaustion he'd been displaying only seconds before gone and in its place was the deadly Sentinel that most people learned not to fuck with.

Chris moved to get in Kale's face, but before he could move so much as an inch, Ephraim was standing between them and in the shifter's face. His eyes flashed red as he stared the shifter down. A muscle ticking in his jaw as he bit out, "Not. Fucking. Happening."

"The Council won't agree to that," Danni hissed, struggling to get away from Caine and as much as he would love to tear the bastard apart, he couldn't allow it.

He was still technically on probation and Kale, the fucking piece of shit, was the Council's golden boy at the moment. He couldn't chance getting his ass back on probation, not when he needed the Sentinel's resources to make sure that Kale never got a chance to put his fucked up beliefs into action. He knew the shifter well enough to know that he wouldn't hesitate in killing a child or a woman just to make sure that they never got the chance to reach their immortality.

"Really?" Kale asked, chuckling darkly. "Do you really believe the Council's going to care if I kill a few unauthorized turns?"

No, he didn't.

TWENTY-EIGHT

"**O**w! Stop!"

"Hold still," Christofer demanded with an expression of determination that actually frightened her as he-

"*Ouch!*" she hissed as more shampoo seeped into her eyes.

"Stop opening your eyes," he said, sounding drained as he continued to tangle his fingers in her hair, somehow forcing more shampoo to drip down her face and seep into her eyes and mouth.

"I can do this myself!" she snapped. She moved to take over when he stopped what he was doing to gently, yet insistently, push her hands away so that he could continue with the torture.

"Not with your hand still bleeding," he patiently pointed out with a touch of exasperation, throwing the body part in question a pointed look that had her sighing and reluctantly moving her hand to hang over the side of the tub where he'd told her to keep it when he'd started this line of torture more than twenty minutes ago.

"About that," she said, cringing when he accidentally yanked out a strand of her hair. He muttered a, "sorry,"

but continued, unfortunately, with his self-appointed task. "Don't you think it's about time that we accepted the fact that I haven't fully turned into what you are and go to a hospital for some good old fashioned stitches?" she suggested, raising her injured hand in front of his face and wiggled her fingers. Well, tried to wiggle her fingers, but the gauze that the bossy bastard had insisted on cocooning her hand in prevented her from moving any of her fingers.

He took her hand in his and gently placed it back where he'd had it, hanging over the tub before he continued washing her hair. At least, that's what she'd assumed he was doing. He shifted by the side of the tub where he knelt and if her hand hadn't been killing her, and she wasn't starving and struggling to ignore the mouthwatering aroma that Christofer was giving off, she'd probably be able to appreciate just how good he looked in those black boxer shorts.

God, did he look good, so good, that all she wanted to do was to run her hands over him, caressing his skin as she mapped out every delicious muscle. She wanted to lick every square inch of his body, starting with that happy trail of dark blond hair that disappeared beneath his shorts and end with the spot on his neck that she constantly found herself staring at as she tried not to lick her lips, the spot where she could see his pulse beating just beneath the skin. Her stomach growled loud enough to draw her attention away from his neck and back to her biggest problem.

She needed to escape and ummmm, and..... ummmm..........

God, he smelled soooo *good*! Licking her lips, she allowed her gaze to drift back towards his neck, but the realization of what she was doing and thinking had her quickly shifting her attention back to the soapy water and squeezing her eyes tightly shut. She counted to ten and when that didn't help, she counted to a hundred all while she tried to convince herself that the mouthwatering aroma that was assaulting her senses was coming from a double cheeseburger with the works and a side of crinkly fries and not from the man that was pouring more soapy water into her eyes and that she had every reason in the world to hate.

"Your hand will heal as soon as you drink some blood," Christofer softly explained even as he poured more of that soapy water that was stinging her eyes over her head.

Annoyed, she moved to open her eyes to glare at him as she told him exactly where he could shove his advice, but was instantly forced to squeeze her eyes shut and squeal as a full cup of soapy water was poured over her face. It seeped into her eyes, causing her to do a combination of gasping and cringing as she frantically tried to wipe soap out of her eyes. She opened her mouth to ask for a towel so that she could wipe her face, but unfortunately, Christofer had chosen that moment to turn the shower on.

At full blast, making her squeal as she was hit with ice cold water.

"Shit!" Christofer groaned as he, thankfully, shut the shower off.

"Could I-abadowel?" she started to ask, only to have the rest of her question muffled as Christofer pressed a large, fluffy towel against her face and proceeded to smother her.

"What the hell are you doing?" she demanded, pretty sure that he was trying to kill her as she somehow managed to push his hands away.

His frown was *not* adorable! she told herself with a glare as she snatched the towel out of his hands. When he went to help her with the towel, self-preservation kicked in and she slapped his hand away.

"Ow!" he grunted, but didn't take the hint and get the hell away from her before she was forced to do bodily harm to him. "Let me help you," he said, moving to grab the towel away from her again, this time ignoring her mad slaps.

"Ow!" she cried as he somehow managed to pinch the side of her left breast when he wrapped the towel around her and secured it. She opened her mouth to tell him to get the hell away from her, but as soon as she opened her mouth she ended up gasping for air and frantically yanking at the towel that he'd somehow managed to wrap around her so tightly that breathing became impossible.

It took a few frantic attempts, but once she finally managed to yank the towel off and sucked in several deep breaths, she shot him a murderous glare that quickly gave way to panic as she saw him sorting through a pile of combs and brushes. Knowing and fearing where this was going, she scrambled to get out of the tub and bathroom before he could get his hands on her, but sadly, he was a hell of a lot faster than her.

"Put me down!" she demanded, struggling in his arms as she did her best to fight her way to freedom, terrified for her precious hair and scalp that had no chance of survival if he got anywhere near them with the large plastic comb in his hand.

"Shhh, just relax, mein Schatz," he murmured as she sat down on the edge of the bed and placed her down rather roughly on his knee. Before she could take advantage of the move, he had his arm wrapped tightly around her waist and was bringing that comb down towards her hair.

"Stop!" she demanded, grabbing hold of the hand that wielded that dangerous weapon and held it away from her.

With an exasperated sigh, he pulled his hand away from her and brought the comb closer and closer to her hair until she was left with no other choice but to scream like a girl.

"What the hell is wrong with you?" he demanded, cringing even as he moved to continue with his sick plans.

"What the hell is wrong with me?" she repeated in disbelief, slapping at the hand coming at her until she finally managed to knock the comb out of his hand. "What the hell is wrong with *you*?" she demanded.

"Nothing!" he snapped, shooting her a glare as he tossed her onto the bed and moved to go get the-

Oh, hell no!

Before the thought even had a chance to form in her head, she found herself on his back as she attempted to place him in a chokehold so that she could-

"What are you doing?" Christofer asked as he easily peeled her off his back and placed her on the bed.

"Stopping you from your next attack, you sick bastard!" she snarled, more than ready to attack him again if he so much as looked in the direction of that comb.

"Next attack?" he murmured, looking adorably confused. "What the hell are you talking about?"

"You are not scalping me!" she snarled, the shades of red sharpening as she felt the tip of one fang scratch her tongue, and for the first time since she'd woken up to discover that he'd turned her into a monster, she welcomed the creepy changes, hoping that she could use them to her advantage.

"Scalping you?" he repeated back as he shot a questioning glace at the comb before looking back up at her. "I'm not trying to scalp you."

She snorted at that, shaking her head in disgust. "Just like you weren't trying to strangle me when you helped me take off my clothes? Or you weren't trying to drown me when you dunked my head under water? Or blind me when you kept pouring soapy water in my eyes? Or suffocate me when you-"

"I was trying to help you relax!" he snapped, looking so damn disgruntled that she was surprised to find herself fighting back a smile.

But, then his words sank in and she couldn't help but frown as she asked, "Relax? How in the hell was being mauled relaxing?"

"I wasn't mauling you!"

"Yes, you were!" she snapped back, tightening the towel around herself as she climbed off the bed, careful not to give him a peepshow, not that he hadn't already seen everything.

"I was giving you a relaxing bath!"

She snorted at that as she stomped over to his bags and without bothering to ask for permission, tore through them until she found a grey tee shirt and a pair of plaid boxers that she could pull on. Once she was dressed, she stomped past him, picked up the comb off the floor and sat back down on the bed. She set to work on carefully combing the snarls out of her hair all while glaring at the bastard that was glaring right back at her.

For several minutes they continued like that, her combing her hair while they glared, until with a muttered, "Marta never complained," Christofer turned his back on her, picked up her discarded towel and threw it in the bathroom. When he turned back around and found her gaping at him, her mouth wide open as she looked at him with unmitigated horror, he asked, "What?"

"You...," she started to say, only to pause so that she could swallow back the revulsion that was sending her already queasy stomach into turmoil, "you did that to Marta?" she finally managed to get out, horrified at the thought of Marta being forced to suffer through that kind of torture. She'd barely survived it and couldn't imagine a woman in her eighties surviving such an ordeal.

"Of course," he said with a frown as though there was nothing wrong with what he was admitting to doing.

"Y-you sick bastard!" she snarled, horrified on Marta's behalf.

"What?" he asked with a puzzled expression on his otherwise handsome face, which did nothing but make her shake her head in disgust.

"How could you do that to an eighty year old woman?" she demanded, wondering how she'd missed Marta's screams for help those times that Christofer had helped his sister with her shower routine, the one thing that Marta had refused to allow Cloe to help her with.

Now she wished that she had ignored Marta's wishes and taken over that chore. It would have added another hour or two to her day, but at least Marta would have been able to enjoy a pain free bath for at least a little while.

"*Eighty?*" Christofer repeated back, looking as though he had no idea what she was talking about. Then with a sigh and a shake of his head, he explained, "I haven't bathed Marta since she turned twelve."

"You helped bathe her every morning," Cloe pointed out even as her brain struggled to register what he'd just said and what that meant.

"No, I just helped her get in and out of the shower," Christofer explained just as she realized what he'd said only a few seconds ago. "She needed help, but she was embarrassed about.....some marks on her body," he said, shifting his gaze away.

"You bathed Marta until she was twelve?" she asked, wishing that she'd misheard him, but she had a sneaking suspicion that she hadn't.

Which meant......

"How old are you exactly?" she asked, swallowing back dread as she looked him over, really looked him over as though she was seeing him for the first time.

The man was utterly perfect. There wasn't a single flaw marring his face or body. There didn't seem to be a single ounce of fat on his body. His hair was a healthy golden blonde, his eyes crystal clear blue, and his skin perfectly tanned. He didn't look a day over twenty-five, but could probably pass for a thirty year old with the right clothes. But if he'd been able to bathe Marta when she was twelve, that meant that he was-

"I'm ninety-nine years old," he announced with a shrug as though it was no big deal and to him it probably wasn't.

Unfortunately for her, she couldn't just shrug it off, not when the realization that she'd made out with a senior citizen had her running for the nearest toilet.

TWENTY-NINE

"Cloe," he said with a heavy sigh as he hunched down in front of her and moved to push a strand of damp hair out of her face.

"Go away," she muttered angrily, pulling her knees up and hugging them tightly to her chest. She looked so damn lost and scared that all he wanted to do was pull her in his arms and tell her that everything was going to be okay, but he couldn't do that.

Right now Cloe was terrified and confused, not to mention getting closer and closer to losing control of the monster inside her, and he was afraid of doing anything that would make it worse for her. He'd hoped that she would be relaxed after her bath. It would have made the transition to drinking blood easier, but somehow that plan hadn't worked. He still couldn't figure out where he'd gone wrong.

Women loved baths and they especially loved being pampered. At least, he'd always thought so. His step-mother had always seemed to enjoy it when his father would pamper and spoil her as did his aunts and the servants that had worked for his family. He'd seen more than one maid giggle and blush under the attentions of an admirer when they were surprised with bouquets of flowers, chocolates and gifts. But Cloe, as he was begin-ning to understand, was not a typical woman. She hadn't appreciated his attempts to help her relax. Every time he realized that she wasn't enjoying herself he tried harder to help her relax, but nothing seemed to work.

Now they were out of time and he was running out of options. If he didn't do something soon she was going to fall prey to what Ephraim had referred to as bloodlust and if that happened, he was afraid of what that kind of loss of control would do to a woman like Cloe. He couldn't take back what he'd done to her, but he could make this transition easier for her, but only if she let him.

"Just leave me alone," Cloe mumbled, absently shov-ing his hand away, clearly intent on continuing to sit on the bathroom floor feeling sorry for herself.

With another sigh, he sat down in front of her. He ignored the murderous glare that she shot him since acknowledging that she had every right to go for his balls was counterproductive at the moment. He decided to try another approach to get her to listen before he was forced to finally give up, drag her to the kitchen and force feed her a half dozen bags of blood before this fucked up situation got any worse.

"Cloe," he said, pausing as he tried to figure out what he could possibly say to convince her to listen to him and trust him when Cloe gave him the opening that he needed.

"I just want to go home," she mumbled pathetically, averting her eyes as she roughly rubbed the back of her arm across her eyes, letting him know just how upset and terrified she really was and breaking his heart. More than anything he wished that he could take her in his arms, hold her tightly and make all of this go away, but he couldn't.

"Cloe-"

"I'm not going to tell anyone about any of this. I just can't deal with being here, Christofer," she said slowly, clearly struggling not to lose what little control she had left.

He thought about lying to her, telling her that everything would be okay and that this wasn't really a big deal, but he couldn't lie to her. It killed him to see a strong woman like Cloe breaking down like this, but if it helped him explain to her why it was so important for her to stay here then he was going to be blunt with her and pretend that it didn't kill him to be the one to destroy her last shred of hope.

"If you leave right now, Cloe, you will kill someone before the night is over," he explained softly, praying that his tone was enough to soften the blow. Judging by the way that she'd flinched as though he'd struck her along with the absolute look of horror on her face, he realized there was nothing that he could say or do that would make this easier.

So he stopped trying.

"I would never-" she started to protest with a determined shake of her head, but he didn't allow her to finish, knowing that the words would come back to haunt her one day.

"Yes, you would," he said firmly, reaching out and taking one of her trembling hands into both of his. "You think that you can control this, that you can control what you are, but the truth of the matter is, Cloe, that right now you pose a danger to every man, woman and child that makes the mistake of crossing your path."

"You don't know that," she bit out tightly even as her stomach rumbled viciously as if to give credence to his words.

"Yes," he said, looking up and meeting her terrified gaze, "I do."

———

"I would never hurt anyone," Cloe said weakly as the truth of his words sank in.

But that's not why she was starting to believe him.

The reason that she was starting to believe everything that he was telling her was quite simple. The tenuous grip that she had on her self-control was quickly slipping away with every passing second. If she didn't get away from him or figure out another way to get through this, any other way, she wasn't going to be able to ignore Christofer's scent for much longer and that would destroy her last hope that she wasn't really a monster.

She refused to accept this.

She didn't want to be like this, didn't want to crave something so wrong and she sure as hell didn't want to worry about losing control and-

"I can help you, Cloe," Christofer said, cutting into her panicked thoughts before they could take her to a place where she had no hope of escape. "I can help you get through this, learn to live with the changes. I

can show you how to stay in control, but I can't help you unless you let me."

She released a mortifying sniffle as she forced herself to focus on the way that his hands gently held hers. She refused to meet his gaze, terrified that he'd see just how afraid she really was.

"You're the one that did this to me," she lamely pointed out, struggling to hold onto the last strands of her humanity even though she already knew that it was a losing battle.

He gave her hand a small squeeze, but it was enough to make her look up and meet his determined gaze. "And if you give me a chance, I'll be the one to fix this."

Terrified of what she would become without his help, she reluctantly nodded. "Just don't let me turn into a monster," she said, forcing herself to meet his gaze head on.

"I'll do my best," he said, giving her hand another gentle squeeze that was probably meant to be reassuring and surprisingly, it was.

———

Christofer sighed heavily.

He couldn't help it.

"That's not going to work," he pointed out, but she refused to listen to him.

With a mutinous glare aimed in his direction, Cloe picked up the piece of toast slathered in peanut butter and strawberry jelly and took a huge bite out of it. After a few seconds of chewing, her glare shifted to shock, disbelief and finally disgust as she turned around, grabbed the trashcan with both hands and spit out every last crumb. When she was done, she turned on the sink, cupped her hands in the water and proceeded to rinse her mouth out while he stood there, sighing heavily as he wondered just how much longer it would be before she finally listened to him.

"You need blood, Cloe," he said for what was probably the hundredth time since he'd decided to try and fix the fuck up that the others had created.

"I want to see if this works first," she stubbornly argued as she pushed the offending plate of toast away and with the same look of determination that had accompanied every single "test" as Cloe liked to call them, she grabbed the box of wheat crackers that she'd found in the cabinets, opened a sleeve of crackers, grabbed a small stack and shoved them into her mouth until it became obvious that this test had failed as well and she was reaching for the trashcan.

"Stop doing this to yourself," he said, his exasperation clear as he watched her go through the process of rinsing out her mouth before that look of determination returned and she forced herself to reach for a can of beef stew.

"No one told you that you had to watch," she said, keeping her focus on the small can as she grabbed a can opener and removed the lid. Cloe cringed when the aroma of cold, chemically preserved beef hit her, causing her to gag a little, but it apparently wasn't enough to make her give up this asinine plan of hers. He watched as she went through the process once again, this time pausing to rinse her mouth out twice as long to get rid of the taste of chemically preserved beef from her mouth.

"Are you about done yet?" he asked, noting that she was quickly running out of food to test.

Looking determined, she picked up a can of tuna fish and nibbled on her bottom lip as he watched her try to force herself to go through with the next test. Reluctantly, and a with a cringe, she picked up the can opener, secured it to the can and with a muttered curse, dropped the can and the can opener on the kitchen island and finally said, "Fine, we'll try it your way."

Making damn sure to hide his triumphant smile, he went to the refrigerator and grabbed two bags of blood. As he closed the refrigerator door, he contemplated heating up the blood, but then he decided against it since the heat had a tendency of making the rusty smell worse. He did however grab two coffee cups, hoping that by placing it in something normal like a cup that it would help Cloe pretend that she wasn't drinking blood.

"How much b-blood am I supposed to drink a day?" she forced herself to ask.

"Four bags a day should help you stay in control," he answered, knowing damn well that's what she was worried about, losing control.

She seemed to consider his words before she asked, "And you're sure that there are no other options?"

His gaze lingered on the kitchen island covered with open food containers and shook his head, wishing that there was another way to do this for her. "This is the only way."

"Okay," she said, shifting nervously as she watched him cut a small hole in one of the bags and pour the red liquid in two cups before he carefully placed the opened bag of blood in a plastic bowl by the sink.

"And this will stop the cravings?" she asked, sounding hopeful and he should have lied to give her this small amount of comfort, but he didn't.

"No, but it will make things more tolerable," he said, deciding not to use the fact that the scent of her blood probably still had the power to shred every last ounce of his control if he allowed it.

Since that most likely wouldn't comfort her, he handed her a cup of cold blood and held his up in a mock salute. "Cheers," he said, chuckling as she shot him another glare.

"I hate you," she ground out as he hid his grin behind his cup and took a long, leisurely sip of his blood. He watched her every move, afraid that she would balk at the idea of drinking blood and he'd be forced to-

"Oh my God!" she choked out as she pulled the mug away from her lips after taking him by surprise and swallowing a large gulp of the cold, metallic liquid that admittedly took some time getting used to. "That's disgusting!"

"Yes, it is," he agreed with a pleased chuckle as he took another sip of his blood just as she did, further shocking him.

He'd expected her to throw the cup in the sink and go back to her "experiments" or play twenty questions with him again, no doubt hoping that she'd stumble across something that he'd missed, but Cloe it seemed, was determined to get through this. She wanted control of this thing and was willing to do anything to get it. Although he knew that she hadn't fully accepted what happened to her or was even happy about it, he was relieved that she was no longer fighting him on this.

It was going to make taking her with him a hell of a lot easier if he knew that she could take care of herself or at the very least, he mused as he took another sip of blood, keep herself from attacking everyone in sight.

THIRTY

"Are you sure that you're okay?" Christofer suddenly asked and she'd just barely stopped herself from flinching.

"Yeah, I'm fine," she said absently as she pulled her legs up and shot another nervous glance around the large penthouse, her gaze pausing on all the doors and the large windows before reluctantly returning to the large flat screen television above the fireplace where some horrible romantic comedy was playing.

"Are you planning on staying up?"

"Uh huh," she murmured, struggling not to glance around the large open space to make sure that everything was still as it should be.

"Do you want some company?" he asked, pushing away from the kitchen island.

She shrugged, trying not to let him know just how much she wanted him to stay with her. She didn't want him to know how badly their little "talk" had affected her. When he'd volunteered to answer her questions, she'd been relieved and admittedly a little excited to find out what else she could do now. A lot of the stuff that she'd learned like being able to see in the dark, being able to float and having inhuman strength had definitely helped take the sting out of her new predicament, but the other things that he'd explained to her had scared the hell out of her.

Not that he knew that.

As he explained things to her along with the new dangers that went hand in hand with her new existence, she'd forced herself to sit there and listen, making sure to nod at the appropriate times while she'd struggled to make sense of what he was telling her. She knew that there was still a lot of information that she didn't know, that he most likely didn't know either, but what she knew now had her terrified to take so much as a step outside of this building.

The monsters that had haunted her dreams and memories all these years, the ones that everyone including her therapists had claimed were just a figment of her traumatized imagination were in fact, real. Christofer hadn't been able to give her much information about them other than they were apparently very real. A part of her had always wished that the therapists and doctors had been right, that her injuries were just an unfortunate circumstance from the fire, but deep down she knew that she hadn't imagined the terrifying memories from that night.

Until Christofer had explained what he'd learned, she'd been able to pretend that there was a possibility that those monsters really didn't exist, but now there was no point in pretending any longer. She'd been attacked by shifters, aka werewolves.

When he'd shared that bit of information with her, she'd had to force herself to pretend that the news didn't bother her when all she wanted to do was run to the rooms where her bags had been placed and tear through her stuff until she found her medication and make everything go numb. She hadn't taken them in years, because she hated the way that they made her feel. She should have just thrown them away years ago when she'd decided to stop taking the damn things, but part of her had been afraid that she'd need them again.

So, she kept them in her bags, refilled them when they expired and pretended that she was fine. Only now, things weren't fine and she couldn't stop thinking about them. The only thing that stopped her from getting them was the knowledge that she would need a level head if she was going to get through this and the fact that Christofer had explained that medicine, drugs and alcohol would no longer affect her.

After digesting that depressing information, she'd asked him more questions, hoping to distract herself from the knowledge of what waited out there for her. A few hours later she had more than enough information to keep her busy freaking out for a while. Now she was freaked out, stuffed from drinking too much blood, exhausted and too damn nervous to close her eyes.

She tried to tell herself that the worst was over now, but she had a feeling that Ephraim and his group were going to prove her wrong. They'd brought them here for a reason and tomorrow morning she'd no doubt find out that reason and probably tumble headlong into a nervous breakdown.

It was something to look forward to, she thought with a sigh that was quickly cut off by a yawn as she picked up the remote and-

"Where are you going?" she demanded anxiously when she spotted Christofer heading towards the hallway.

"I'll be right back," he said softly, giving her a reassuring smile that he probably thought would comfort her.

It didn't.

Since the only thing that seemed to comfort her right now was his scent and presence, she couldn't help but freak out a little bit as she watched him walk out of the room. There was definitely something wrong with needing the man that had not only attacked her, but had also turned her into this *thing*, and later she'd probably berate herself for her reaction to him, but for now she was too frightened to lie to herself.

She needed him.

Not that she planned on letting him know that. That would give him too much power and right now, he already had more than enough power over her. She was new to their world, unsure of herself and completely dependent on him. It wasn't something that she was comfortable with, but for now she would endure it.

Biting her lip, she watched him disappear around the corner. It took everything that she had to keep her butt on the couch, which apparently hadn't been all that much, because not even two seconds later she was moving to get off the couch and follow him and-

Scream her head off!

"What's wrong?" Christofer asked, looking puzzled as he sat down next to her, shifting the large sketchpad on his lap as he got comfortable.

Still gasping for air, she looked from him towards the hallway where she saw him disappear only a few seconds before and then back to him to find him shooting her a curious look as he opened the sketchpad to a blank page. Having absolutely no idea what just happened or how he got back so fast without her seeing him, she decided to just sit there, struggling to catch her breath as she shot another curious look between him and the hallway.

"Oh," Christofer said with a frown. "Did I forget to mention that we could move pretty quickly when we need to?"

Gaping at him, she nodded her head, because she was pretty sure that she would have remembered being told that she now had the Road Runner's skills.

With a shrug, he said, "Well, we can move pretty quickly for short periods."

"Apparently," she mumbled, shooting one last look between him and the hallway. For about thirty seconds she flirted with the idea of seeing just how fast she could move, but with a shrug she returned her attention to the television, deciding that with her luck she'd most likely end up running through a wall.

A few minutes later her breathing had calmed down and she'd managed to find an Indiana Jones movie to watch. She relaxed back and focused on the movie while Christofer continued to scribble in his sketchpad. This was actually nice, she thought as she shifted on the couch and-

Let out another embarrassing squeal as all the lights went out and she suddenly found herself enveloped in hues of blue.

"Did I forget to mention that everything turned blue in the dark?" Christofer asked conversationally, but she didn't miss the amusement in his tone or the way his lips twitched.

"Bastard," she muttered with a scowl as she decided that her sanity couldn't take another surprise tonight and got off the couch and headed for the hallway, forcing herself to keep moving no matter how badly she wanted to turn around and run back to the couch and into the bastard's arms.

———

"This isn't so bad," she mumbled, squeezing her eyes shut even tighter as she pulled the blankets all the way up to her chin and shifted onto her side as she tried to convince her brain to fall asleep quickly with promises that everything would be back to normal by tomorrow morning.

Apparently her brain wasn't buying a single syllable of bullshit that she was giving it. Tomorrow wouldn't be fine and most likely the day after wouldn't be either. She wasn't sure that anything would ever be fine, not when she was now confined to a life of secrecy and drinking blood out of coffee mugs.

How exactly was she supposed to hide what she was? she wondered with a disgruntled groan as she shifted onto her side and-

Let out another scream!

"Shhh, it's just me," Christofer whispered soothingly as he gently pushed her hair out of her face and gently cradled her face in his large, warm hand.

"That's why I was screaming!" she snapped, reaching up and shoving his hand away even as she noticed that her heart wasn't beating frantically against her ribs and her breathing was normal when she should be freaking out and struggling to take her next breath after finding a man suddenly lounging in bed next to her.

She shouldn't be feeling her body start to relax, but that's exactly what it was doing. As soon as her body registered that Christofer was in bed next to her, she'd felt herself begin to relax, her breaths evening out and her eyelids becoming increasingly heavy in a matter of seconds as she struggled to remain awake so that she could finally give him a piece of her mind for all the bullshit that he'd put her through and for continuing to scare the shit out of her. It soon became apparent that finally telling him off wasn't going to happen, at least not tonight.

Not when it felt so good to lie next to him.

But her pride refused to accept this situation, needing to put up the façade of a fight for self-preservation, because even as she muttered, "Get out," she knew that if he tried to leave her right now that she would tackle his ass to the ground and make him stay. At least, for tonight, she told herself, once again more than willing to lie to herself so that she could take the comfort that Christofer was offering without hating herself.

"Is that what you really want, mein Schatz?" he asked softly as he lightly ran the back of his knuckles along her jaw, sending a wave of pleasure through her body that had her unconsciously shifting closer to him, greedy for his touch.

"Yes," she whispered harshly. She reached out to push him away, but as soon as her hand touched the warm bare skin of his shoulder, she found herself wrapping an unsteady hand around the back of his neck in a desperate attempt to keep him close.

"I'm not going anywhere," he promised her as she registered the feel of his large warm hand mimicking her hold on him. He gently pulled her closer until his forehead was touching hers.

"Yes," she said, opening her eyes to find herself staring into glimmering blue eyes, "you will."

For a moment he didn't say anything as he stared into her eyes, his hold on the back of her neck turning caressing as she waited for him to lie to her and to make promises that he would never be able to keep. Just when she prepared herself to call him out on any bullshit promises that left his mouth, he took her by surprise.

"Everyone leaves you, don't they?" he whispered softly in a tone that should have softened the blow of his question, but nothing could have stopped her from flinching from his words.

"No, they don't," she bit out, releasing her hold on him so that she could put some much needed space between them.

His hold on her tightened as he kept her from fleeing as his gaze bore into hers, searching for an answer that he had no right to demand.

"No, they don't," he murmured softly after a painfully long moment as he pulled her closer and pressed a kiss against her forehead. "You leave them before they get a chance," he said against her forehead as she struggled to breathe.

"That's not true," she lamely argued, unaware that she was once again holding onto him, refusing to let him go.

"You'll never have to worry, mein Schatz. I'm not going anywhere," he promised her.

"Don't make promises that you can't keep," she whispered helplessly as she closed her eyes and savored his touch, the warmth from his body and the feeling of being enveloped in a protective pocket where nothing and no one could harm her.

"Why do I feel so safe with you?" she found herself asking him, hating how much she needed him even as she prayed that she never had to endure another day without him.

"I don't know," he whispered as his hold on her gentled and he was once again caressing her nape.

She gave a humorless chuckle at that. "Well, that makes two of us then, because I honestly don't know why I'm not doing everything in my power to get away from you."

He pressed another kiss against her forehead as he confessed, "I'm still waiting for you to kick my ass for everything that I've put you through."

She heaved out a sigh as she admitted, "I should have kicked your ass a hundred times over by now."

"Yes," he said, pressing another kiss against her brow, "you should have."

"Especially for that sandwich," she said, cringing at the memory of all that mayonnaise pouring out of the sandwich like a-

"There was nothing wrong with that sandwich!" Christofer argued, softening his words with another kiss.

"I'll probably have nightmares for years to come thanks to that sandwich," she teased with a laugh when he released a sexy little growl that had her toes curling in pleasure.

"That sandwich was perfect!"

"That sandwich was terrifying," she said solemnly, loving the sexy glare that he was giving her, surprised that somehow through all of this they'd managed to slip back into taunting and teasing each other, something that she'd truly enjoyed before her world had been destroyed.

It gave her hope that one day everything would be okay.

THIRTY-ONE

"**A**re you awake?"

"Mmmhmm," Cloe murmured as she lay there, staring out the large window at the beautiful city sky as she continued to absently trace her fingers over Christofer's arm where it rested around her waist.

"Are you hungry?" he murmured, pressing a soft kiss to the back of her head, something that he'd been doing a lot tonight. Not that she was going to complain, because she wasn't.

It felt too good in his arms to complain or find fault with the way that he held and touched her. They'd talked for a little while about absolutely nothing at all, neither of them wanting to broach on a subject that would jeopardize this overwhelming sense of peace that they'd somehow managed to stumble across. For about two hours now, they'd been lying there, staring out at the night sky, the tranquility broken only by murmured questions and a gentle touch.

A few times she'd found herself wanting to ask how he was holding up, but at the last second she'd decided against it. She didn't want to bring up Marta until he was ready and she knew that he wasn't ready. So instead, she'd laid there in his arms offering him what little comfort she could.

"No, I'm fine," she finally answered, closing her eyes and savoring the touch of his lips as he once again pressed a kiss against her hair.

"Do you need anything?" he asked, his voice slightly muffled against her hair.

Answers.

Reassurance that everything was going to be okay.

Promises that she didn't think that he'd be able to keep.

A time machine so that she could go back and fix everything before her world was destroyed and her family was taken from her.

The ability to enjoy a double cheeseburger with the works.

But, she didn't say any of that, because it would force her to face a future that she wasn't sure that she could handle. Instead she continued to trace her fingers over his arm, enjoying the feel of his body pressed up against hers. She'd been with several men in her life, probably more than she should have, but she'd never allowed any of them to hold her the way that Christofer was holding her.

Not that any of them had ever tried.

The ones that hadn't been put off by her scars had treated her like a fuck buddy. There had never been warm smiles, flowers, romantic dinners or flattering words. She'd enjoyed herself for the most part, enjoyed the momentary escape that they'd offered her, but it had never been more than just sex to her. Sometimes she'd wished that it had been more, that she'd been with the type of man that could make her feel wanted and loved, but it had never happened.

Until now.

It was crazy, beyond crazy. She'd only known Christofer for a few weeks and in that time he'd fired her, irritated her, taunted her, ditched her, attacked her and aided with her kidnapping, but somehow during all that he'd become everything to her. He made her smile, made her feel safe even as she fought to ignore what was happening between them, made her feel wanted and could make her smile. She could happily spend the rest of her life in his arms, she thought as she snuggled back against him, determined to soak up every last ounce of comfort that he had to offer before she was forced to face an uncertain future.

"No," she said, shifting back against him as she laid her hand over his where it moved lazily against her stomach, "I'm fine."

For several minutes they just laid there, staring out the large windows as Christofer lightly caressed her stomach with lazy movements of his thumb. She closed her eyes and inhaled slowly, allowing the peaceful moment to wash over her. She savored his comforting scent, his touch and the warmth that his large body enveloped her in and couldn't help but wonder just how long this reprieve would last.

Not very long as it turned out.

———

Five days later.........

"It's not going to happen!"

"Cloe-"

"No!" the stubborn woman snapped, glaring at him from the other side of the couch that she'd dodged behind ten minutes ago in a sad attempt to keep him from forcing her to do what needed to be done.

"You don't have a choice in the matter," he said, struggling against the urge to jump over that couch and end this bullshit.

"Yeah, I really do," she said, shifting to the left when he shifted to the right, preparing to make another run for it.

"We don't have time for this, mein Schatz," he said with forced patience as he closed his eyes and slowly inhaled, praying for a modicum of patience that didn't seem forthcoming.

"Really?" Cloe said mockingly. "Because it seems to me that we have all the time in the world for this."

His eyes snapped open to glare at the woman standing across from him. "As soon as you do what I asked, we can leave!" he snapped, coming to the terrifying conclusion that he'd finally found a woman more stubborn than his sister.

It was a truly frightening thought, but one that he was going to have to push aside and dwell on later, because right now he had more important matters to deal with, like finding a way to escape without putting Cloe in danger. It wasn't going to be easy. They were too far from the ground for him to risk trying to descend down the side of the building with her. They were also unarmed and trapped on a heavily secured floor in a building filled to the brim with armed military personnel.

To make matters worse he had a newly turned woman with a chip on her shoulder, a temper almost as bad as his, absolutely no clue what could happen to her and she was driving him out of his fucking mind! He'd never wanted a woman the way that he wanted her, needed her and the reminder that he could never have her only pissed him off.

She was his responsibility and he wouldn't fuck that up by letting his dick call the shots. The last time had been enough for him. Not only had he hurt her, changed her life, but he'd been so fucking focused on her that he'd failed his sister. Because of him, his sister was gone. It wasn't likely a lesson that he'd forget anytime soon.

"One more day isn't going to kill us," the brat pointed out.

"We can't afford to give them another day," Christofer explained as patiently as he could, praying that she wouldn't start another argument about leaving.

Of course he should have known better.

"I'm not going anywhere until we get our answers," Cloe said as she started up the same argument that she'd been using since yesterday when the blood finally ran out and he'd announced that it was time for them to leave.

"We haven't had blood in twenty-four hours, mein Schatz," he bit out slowly, shifting to the left only to have the stubborn woman shift to the right. "The longer that we go without blood, the weaker we'll become. If we don't go today, now, then we might not get another chance until they decide to give us more blood."

Which he doubted they planned on doing anytime soon.

He'd fucked up by trusting Ephraim, believing that he would do everything within his power to keep Cloe safe. Thankfully, it was something that he'd planned for. What he hadn't planned on was the woman in front of him suddenly acting like a pain in the ass and making their escape more difficult than it needed to be.

"For all you know they could be sending up blood at this very minute," Cloe pointed out as she folded her arms over her chest, bringing his attention to her large breasts before he forced himself to look away with a curse.

For the last five days she'd been driving him out of his fucking mind. Every night he held her in his arms, forcing himself to ignore just how good she felt or how badly he wanted to run his hands over her and use his mouth on her while filling her with his fingers, tongue and cock. During the day she sat next to him while he drew whether it was on a bed, a couch, chair or the floor. She never bothered him or asked him what he was doing, apparently happy just to be near him.

He was glad that she was feeling more comfortable with him, because it meant that she felt safe with him. What he didn't like was just how fucking comfortable she felt with him. She didn't see any problem with walking around in just her panties and a small shirt most of the time or heaven help him, walking around naked in front of him. He wasn't sure when exactly she'd started viewing him as a eunuch, but for the sake of his sanity and his dick, he really wished that she'd go back to viewing him as a monster. Spending this time with her was driving him out of his fucking mind and without blood to help combat his hormones he was struggling every second not to grab her, bend her over and fuck her until they both passed out.

Driving. Him. Out. Of. His. Fucking. Mind.

"I'm not willing to take that chance," he told her, in no mood to argue about this for another minute.

"They probably didn't realize that we'd end up going through the blood so quickly."

"We're wasting time arguing about this," he said, shifting to the right and this time when she shifted to the left he made his move. He was over the couch and had her in his arms before she could react and once she realized what he'd done, she fought him tooth and nail to get away from him.

"Let me go!" she demanded, struggling in his arms and damn near making him lose his hold on her, reminding him that she was a hell of a lot stronger now.

"Not until you feed!" he snapped with a wince when she managed to elbow him in the gut, but he refused to release her.

"I'm not hungry!" she snapped right back, struggling to push away from him, but he wasn't going anywhere, not until she fed.

"It's for your own good!"

"No, it's not!"

"We don't have time for this!" he pointed out, biting back a pained grunt when she managed to slam another elbow in his side.

"I'm not drinking your blood, you sick bastard!" she yelled, ramming her backside into him in an attempt to dislodge him, but he held on even as the move made him stumble back.

"Yes, you are!"

"No, I'm not!"

"You need it!"

"No, I don't!" she said, twisting in his arms so that she could shove him away, but he wasn't giving up that easily, not when he needed to do this so that he could keep her safe.

"I can't take you out of here until you've fed!" he snapped, sick of arguing over this bullshit. She needed to feed if they were going to have any chance of getting her out of this safely, but the stubborn woman refused to listen to reason.

If they tried leaving right now a single injury would have the power to knock her on her ass and keep her there. Feeding wouldn't save her if she was shot in the head or the heart, but it would give her some protection. At least if she fed now, she would have a chance to heal from her injuries and keep moving her ass. As long as she could make it to the exit, he would do the rest, but in order to do that he needed the stubborn pain in the ass to feed!

It didn't matter what he said or did, Cloe refused to feed from him. When he'd suggested this plan last night, he'd assumed that she would just suck it up and do whatever she had to so that they could escape, but he'd been wrong. She'd argued with him all night, refusing to feed from him no matter what he said. He'd flat out refused to take her out of here until she fed, thinking that would help, but she wouldn't listen.

"I'm not drinking your blood so let it go already!"

"Yes, you are!" he growled down at the woman in his arms as she glared right back up at him through narrowed red eyes.

"I'm not drinking your goddamn blood and I'm not leaving here without my answers!" she snapped as she tried to shove him away, but he refused to budge, refused to let this damn stubborn woman go until she'd fed and was moving her ass through the front door.

"Fine!" he snapped back, realizing that there was only one way to get her to move her ass.

He had to take the choice out of her hands.

THIRTY-TWO

"**N**ow that we have that solved, why don't we……..
what are you doing?" Cloe demanded as she
found herself suddenly scooped up in Christofer's arms.

"Helping you get your answers faster," was all
Christofer said as he carried her to the bedroom that
they'd been using for the past week.

He kicked the door shut behind them as she wracked
her brain, trying to figure out how exactly they'd gone
from arguing to *this*. For about ten seconds she'd thought
that she'd finally managed to make the stubborn bastard
listen to reason, but now, as she went flying through the
air and landed with a soft "*ooof*" on the plush bed, she
wasn't so sure.

"What the hell is wrong with you?" she demanded
even though she was pretty sure that she could come up
with a decent list on her own.

"You want your answers, don't you?" he asked with a
careless shrug that she didn't care for, not one bit.

"And how exactly is tossing me on the bed going to
accomplish that?" she demanded, pushing herself up
into a sitting position so that she could glare at the bastard as he-

"Why are you taking off your shirt?" she suddenly found herself asking as he tossed the shirt over his shoulder.

"Don't want to get any blood on it," he reasoned as he climbed on the bed and headed for her, moving with the grace of a predator as she struggled to register what he'd just said and when she did, she turned over and tried to scramble off the bed as quickly as humanly possible, praying for some of that elusive Pyte speed to help aide her escape.

Somehow she managed to make it to the edge of the bed and even succeeded in getting one foot on the floor before he dragged her right back on the bed. But she didn't go easily.

"Let me go!" she yelled, shoving at the hands that gripped her hips as he dragged her back on the bed.

"As soon as you've fed," the irritatingly stubborn son of a bitch calmly explained as he shifted his hold on her and maneuvered her onto her back.

He smoothly shifted over her until his weight had her pinned to the bed, but unlike the last time that he'd had her in this position, her arms and legs weren't pinned beneath him. She did her best to kick him as she gripped his shoulders and shoved, but the only response she got was a bored sigh as he shifted his weight onto his elbows so that he could look down at her, effectively trapping her.

She gasped, shifting beneath him as she licked her suddenly dry lips while she waited for the panic to hit, but......

It never came.

Instead of freaking out or feeling like the world was closing in on her, she felt safe, protected and if the bastard on top of her wasn't trying to force her to drink his blood, she'd probably allow herself to enjoy this moment.

"I'm not moving until you've fed."

"I don't need to feed to get my answers!" she snapped, frustrated that she'd once again been manhandled.

"Yes, you do," Christofer murmured, propping his chin on his upturned palm as he continued to gaze down at her, looking bored.

"No," she gritted out, trying to shove him away, "I don't."

"I can't take you out of here until you've fed," he murmured, clearly biting back a yawn, which only pissed her off more.

"You lying son of a bitch!" she said, shifting until her feet were pressed against the bed before she did her best to dislodge him, but other than jostling him a little and earning another yawn, he didn't appear to notice.

"The sooner you feed, the faster we can get out of here," he explained, somehow managing to sound rational.

"What about my answers?" she demanded, slightly winded, which had her narrowing her eyes on the bastard and wondering if he'd lied to her before. "Why can't I kick your ass? You said that I would be stronger."

"And you would be if you fed more," he said with a slight nod against his palm as he reached up with his free hand to push a loose strand of hair out of her face. She slapped the offending hand away and fixed it herself, all while sending the bastard a murderous glare.

"I've drank more blood than you over the last couple of days so according to your little theory, I should be stronger," she said accusingly as she pointedly shoved at his shoulders again to no avail.

He simply shrugged as he explained, "I'm older and need less blood."

Narrowing her eyes on him, she let out a frustrated growl as she tried once again to shove the bastard away.

"If it makes you feel any better, you're still stronger than a human," he said with an amused glint in his eyes that she chose to ignore.

"It doesn't!" she snapped back, wishing that she was strong enough to kick *his* ass.

"All you have to do is take a little nibble," he said, lazily gesturing to his neck, "and we can go get your answers."

"I'm not feeding from you!"

"You will if you ever want to get off this bed," he said with another careless shrug that had her seeing red.

"Get. Off. Me," she bit out, hating him for doing this to her, but hating herself more because right now, she wanted nothing more than to sink her teeth into the tantalizing tanned skin above her and finally find out if his blood tasted as good as it smelled.

"Just as soon as you have a small bite, we can go," he promised her with a teasing smile that made it difficult to hate him.

Seeing him smiling or carefree in any way shouldn't affect her, but it did. She liked this side of him a hell of a lot more than the brooding version of him that treated her with kid gloves and acted like she was a chore that he got stuck with. She enjoyed spending time with him when he was relaxed like at night when he held her in his arms or when he was focused on his sketchpad, but other times....

She wanted to kick him in the balls.

"I know you're hungry, mein Schatz," he murmured as he played with a strand of her hair.

"I'm fine," she lied, squirming wildly beneath him as she struggled to ignore just how good he smelled.

"I'll even make this easy for you," he said, lowering himself on her and turning his head to the side so that his neck was bared to her. "Just sink your fangs in me, mein Schatz, and take what you need."

She closed her eyes tightly and shook her head. "No!"

"Yes," Christofer said, turning his head so that he could look at her. She opened her eyes to glare at him. "You need to eat, mein Schatz."

"Not like this!" she snapped, in no mood for another lecture about what could happen if she went too long without drinking blood. She'd accepted the fact that she had to drink bagged blood for the rest of her life, something that she wasn't happy about, but she would do it if it meant keeping other people safe. But this.......

No, she couldn't force herself to do this, not when there were other options, options that would keep people safe and allow her to keep whatever was left of her humanity.

His gaze turned tender as he looked down at her. "This won't turn you into a monster, Cloe," he murmured softly as he gently caressed her jaw with his fingertips.

"You don't know that," she mumbled, hating the way that her voice shook, giving away just how scared she was that she was about to lose this battle.

"Yes," he said, turning his hand so that he could trace her bottom lip with his thumb, "I do."

She stubbornly shook her head. "I don't want to lose control," she said, remembering the look on his face when he'd lost control, the fear that shot through her when she'd realized what was happening. It was something that she never wanted to experience again, not if she could help it.

So, no matter how hungry she was or how badly she wanted to give in, she wouldn't do it. She wouldn't let herself lose control like that and-

"How about a compromise?" Christofer suggested softly, moving his fingers back to trace the line of her jaw.

"What kind of compromise?" she hesitantly asked, her eyes narrowing suspiciously on the bastard above her.

"The kind that lets me take care of you without you having to worry about doing something that you'll regret," he promised her softly.

"You can't promise-"

"Yes," he said, leaning down to brush his lips against hers, "I can."

"How?" she asked with a sigh, giving up on trying to push him away since it was obvious that he wasn't going anywhere until he was damn well ready. She wrapped her arms loosely around his shoulders. Unable to help herself, she began running her fingers through his hair, needing something to do as she laid there struggling not to get her hopes up.

"You're going to drink from me and only me," he said like that solved all her problems.

It didn't.

Not even a little bit.

"And that helps me how?" she demanded, spreading her legs further apart when she felt him shift to get more comfortable. The move settled him more deeply against her.

"Because you'll never have to worry about hurting me, mein Schatz," he whispered as he shifted so that he could gently cup her face in his hand.

She opened her mouth to argue with him, but he cut her off with another tender kiss. "My blood can make you stronger, keep you safe and will cut down on how much blood you need to consume," he whispered against her lips.

"How do you know that?" she asked, continuing to run her fingers through the hair on the back of his head, using the motion to hide the way her hands shook.

"Caine and Ephraim explained a few things while you were sleeping," he said, tracing his thumbs over her cheeks.

"I don't want to drink from you," she stubbornly mumbled, her breaths coming faster.

"You don't have a choice any longer, mein Schatz," he said, brushing his lips against her forehead. "I need you to do this, Cloe. I need to keep you safe," he said hoarsely.

"Why?" she asked, unable to understand why he cared so much.

"Why what?"

"Why do you care?"

He looked down at her, a small smile tipping his lips. "Because," he said, leaning down until their lips were barely an inch apart, "you make me happy, mein Schatz."

With that he sealed her fate and took the decision out of her hands.

THIRTY-THREE

"Just do it!"

"Don't rush me!" Cloe snapped back, chewing her bottom lip as she gazed at Christofer's neck with uncertainty.

She'd agreed to do this, because he'd made her realize that this connection between them wasn't one sided. He made her feel safe, protected and cherished and she apparently calmed something in him as well. It wasn't something that she could ignore, not when she cherished that connection too much to risk it.

The other reason that she was doing this was simple. She liked the idea of needing less blood and not having to worry about hurting anyone. She'd been prepared to binge on that cold nasty bagged blood for the rest of her unnatural life even though it was without a doubt the nastiest stuff she'd ever consumed. So now, she was lying on a bed with the hottest man that she'd ever met laying on top of her, waiting for her to sink her fangs into his neck and drink his blood.

Yeah...........

"Do you need help?" he asked with a sigh as he shifted slightly on top of her.

"No!"

"Are you sure?"

"Yes!" she snapped back, wishing he would just be quiet so that she could focus on what she was doing.

"If you need help........." he said, letting his words trail off meaningfully.

"I don't!" she said, deciding to just get this over with if it meant shutting him up.

With a slight cringe and a prayer that this wasn't going to scar her for life, she leaned in, opened her mouth and moved in to just get it over with when something occurred to her. Her fangs weren't down and she had no idea how to make them come out on command. Refusing to ask for help, at least not until after she'd tried, she pictured bagged blood, hoping it would be enough to make her fangs slide down.

It wasn't.

Finally after a few more minutes of trying to force her fangs down, she gave in with a heavy sigh and admitted, "I need help."

"What's wrong?" he asked, pushing up and turning his head so that he could look down at her.

She answered with a grumpy mumble.

"What was that?" he asked, sounding amused.

"I said I can't get my fangs down!" she snapped, quickly shifting back to her previous desire to kick his ass.

Chuckling, he leaned down and pressed a kiss against her forehead. "Is that all?"

"Is that all?" she repeated tightly with frustration. "It seems kind of important at the moment, doesn't it?"

His lips twitched with more amusement, making her scowl deepen. "Well, since anger obviously isn't helping to get the job done, why don't we try a different approach?" he suggested.

She opened her mouth to tell him exactly what approach she'd like to take when he took her by surprise. One second his eyes were the beautiful crystal blue that she loved and the next second they were a fiery red and his fangs were down. Stunned by how quickly he'd managed to accomplish something that she'd been struggling to do, she was barely aware of what he was doing until it was too late.

While she'd been trying to figure out how he'd managed to do that so quickly, he'd pressed the tip of one of his fingers to a fang and drew a large drop of blood. The delicious aroma hit her nose just as she realized that he'd traced his bleeding fingertip across her bottom lip, leaving a trail of that mouthwatering liquid behind. She'd barely registered the action before the tip of her tongue darted out to taste the warm liquid. The first taste of his blood tore a moan from her lips, the second a groan and by the time that she'd realized that there wasn't a single drop left, her control snapped.

"Oh, *fuck!*" he snarled, his hands fisting in the comforter as he struggled not to flinch away from her sudden attack.

He clenched his jaw tightly as he forced himself to remain still so that Cloe could take what she needed from him. He considered asking her to gentle her bite, but thought better of it when he realized that would make him an asshole. He'd attacked her without any finesse, ripping into her throat and drained her without a thought for her comfort. He deserved this, deserved more and he would gladly take it.

For her.

After a few minutes her bite gentled and he found himself taking a shaky breath. He felt himself relax above her as her greedy pulls at his neck turned to gentle suckling motions that allowed the torn skin around her fangs to heal, taking away the sharp sting of her bite and leaving only pleasure.

Shit!

His fingers flexed around the comforter as he closed his eyes and tried to shift his thoughts away from the gentle suckling at his neck and the soft moans muffled against his skin. He counted to one hundred in German in his head and when that didn't work, he counted back from a hundred in French. He forced his mind on all the projects that he still needed to finish, the emails he needed to respond to, the.........the......the.......

The way Cloe ran her hands over his back, her fingers threading through his hair, the warm press of her body beneath his, the way her breasts pressed up against his chest, the way her legs cradled him, the way her hips arched and caused the most intimate part of her body to rub against the erection that he couldn't make behave, but mostly, he focused on the scent of her arousal. She smelled so good, fucking fantastic, he amended a second later while he licked his lips in pure ecstasy as she rubbed up against him, caressing the underside of his cock. The combination of the material from their jeans only added to the delicious friction.

She felt so good, so fucking good as she suckled at his neck, ran her hands all over his body and rubbed herself against his cock. As he held himself still above her, he couldn't decide what was better, the sounds of her moans or the sweet scent of her sex. He inhaled deeply, savoring the smell of her aroused sex and came to the decision that the smell of her arousal was the clear winner of the two.

Although he did love the way she moaned against his neck, the sound a mixture of pleasure and need. He wondered what kind of sounds she would make if he ground himself against her, or pulled down her pants and panties and fucked her with his tongue and fingers. Would she scream his name? Scream for more when he pushed her over the edge or simply lay there, panting and moaning as he licked every last drop from her slit.

But, it was pointless to wonder, because he would never allow himself to find out. She was his responsibility, his to protect and care for, not to fuck when-

She reached between their bodies and ripped his pants open, gripped his boxers, tore them from his body and grabbed hold of his eager cock. He opened his mouth to stop her, but the only sound that came out was a strangled groan as she gripped his cock by the base and stroked him. It nearly had him coming, but his desperate cock refused to give in so easily. The greedy little bastard withstood the first stroke and jerked in rapture with the second.

"*Cloe*," he started to say only to realize that her name came out as a strangled moan and a plea for her to keep going. He needed to stop her before it was too late and they did something that she'd regret later, because with the third stroke of her talented hand on his cock, he realized that there was no fucking way that he would ever regret this. Cloe on the other hand, would probably kick his teeth down his throat when she realized that she'd lost control because of him.

She was reacting to the scent of his arousal and the taste of it in his blood. He should have thought about this before he decided to feed her from his vein, but when he'd made the decision to feed her, sex hadn't been on his mind. He wanted to get her out of here safely not fuck her.

He should have known this would happen, but it had been so long since he'd tasted arousal from a woman's blood that he'd forgotten the power it held. If he'd thought about it, he would have taken a cold shower or taken himself in hand first, but he hadn't. Now Cloe was losing control and giving into the hormones that his aroused body was flooding into her system, leaving with her no other choice but to react.

"Cloe, stop!" he gritted out as he reached between them, sending a silent apology to his poor cock, to gently remove her hand. "We have to stop."

"Mmm, I don't want to," Cloe murmured against his neck as her talented hand evaded his capture and stroked him from tip to balls and back again.

Realizing that she'd released her bite on him and that she wasn't going to stop, he pushed himself up on the bed and started to move away. He should have moved faster, a hell of a lot faster since it appeared that his blood had helped unlock Cloe's new abilities.

In one swift move, she had him pressed back down on the bed and her mouth wrapped around his cock in the next. His hands actually shook as he reached down to stop her when all he wanted to do was to thread his fingers through her hair and force her mouth further down his cock, but he couldn't do it, not when he knew how much she'd hate him if he didn't stop her now.

———

"Mein Schatz, you have to stop," Christofer said as he gently cupped her face and guided her mouth away from the largest erection that she'd ever seen.

She allowed him to guide her away, but only far enough until she could lean forward and take his mouth with her own. She moved her lips against his stunned ones as she wrapped her arms around him and settled herself back on his lap. She released a moan of pleasure when she felt his erection press up against her.

God, he felt so good……

No, correction, she felt good, really good.

It felt like every cell in her body had come to life with Christofer's blood. She felt stronger, energized and more alive than she ever had before. She'd noticed changes in the way that she felt when she'd woken up after the attack and even more changes after she started to drink the bagged blood, but this was different, more intense. It also made her realize something.

Christofer really hadn't meant to hurt her.

Ephraim and the others had explained that over a dozen times to her and she'd believed them. For the most part, but it had still been hard to accept when she'd wanted, needed, someone to blame for what happened. She'd blamed Christofer even as she'd craved contact with him, which did nothing more than to confuse her and made what she felt for him feel wrong.

But now…..

Now she couldn't get enough of him and refused to fight what she wanted any longer. The moment she'd tasted his blood she'd lost control and had given in to attacking him and taking what she wanted without a second thought. She hadn't lost control and gone into bloodlust, that much she was sure of, but she had lost control. She remembered the look on his face, the sound of his voice as he'd yelled at her to run and knew that Christofer never would have hurt her. He had fought against it. Knowing that didn't take away the pain and terror from the memory of that attack, but it allowed her to trust the man beneath her. She knew without a doubt that he would do anything to keep her safe even if it meant that he had to deny himself something that he wanted.

"Cloe," Christofer said, gently grabbing her by her shoulders to pull her away and for the moment, she allowed it. "We have to stop."

She simply shook her head as she said, "No."

He closed his eyes, his expression pained as he took a slow, deep breath, no doubt trying to regain his control. "You're reacting to me, Cloe. I'm sorry, but if we don't stop now you're going to regret this later."

"How exactly am I reacting to you?" she asked in a sultry tone as she reached up and cupped the back of his head, allowing her fingers to thread through his short silky hair as she ran her fingertips down his chest and stomach, marveling at the feel of smooth skin over hard, lean muscle. He caught her hand before it could stray any closer to the large erection jerking against his stomach in an attempt to reach her wandering hand.

"My blood," he bit out between clenched teeth. "You're reacting to my blood."

"So," she said, pulling her hand away from his so that she could return to exploring his chest, "are you saying that I would react to anyone that I drank from?" she asked, even though she already knew the answer.

She was reacting to Christofer and the knowledge that he hadn't betrayed her. He turned her on and inside out. He pissed her off even as he made her smile and he made her want things that she never thought were possible.

"Only if they were turned on when you drank from them," he explained in the same hard tone.

"I see," she said, biting back a smile as she dropped her hands away from him and leaned back away from him.

"I'm sorry," Christofer said, tightly averting his eyes so that he could glare at the wall as she slowly got off his lap and climbed off the bed.

"No need to apologize," she said casually as she kicked off her shoes and released the button on her pants so that she could push them down.

"You're not mad?" he ground out, still glaring at the wall as she pulled off her tee shirt, tossed it aside and reached back to unsnap her bra.

"No, I'm not mad," she replied, hooking her thumbs in her panties and pushed them down. "But, I do have a question for you," she said, knowing him well enough now to know that he took his responsibilities very seriously. Marta had been proof enough of that and since it was obvious that he saw her as another responsibility, she knew that he wouldn't allow himself to do anything that would hurt her.

Unless she gave him no other choice.

"What do you want to know?" he asked, a muscle ticking in his jaw as she purposely strode in front of him, giving him no other choice but to look at her as she strode naked towards the bathroom.

Pausing by the bathroom door, she looked over her shoulder to find a pair of red eyes devouring every inch of her. "What makes you think that you weren't reacting to me?"

THIRTY-FOUR

"That's Nolan," Chris said with a tilt of his head towards the large Sentinel male walking through the lobby. Ephraim and Caine nodded as they headed towards the elusive compound leader.

For the past five days he'd been putting them off with bullshit promises and excuses until finally, they'd had enough. They'd wasted enough time sitting on their asses waiting for answers that the compound's leaders didn't seem to be in any rush to give them. Even a call to Eric hadn't garnered them the answers they wanted or reinstated their access to the secured floors.

If it had been up to Chris, he would have asked his little mate to unleash *Tattletale* on the compound and taken the choice out of the compound leaders' hands sooner, but his father and Caine wanted to give the compound leaders a chance before they did anything that would start any bullshit and make their jobs more difficult. But even his father had a limit, and this morning he'd reached it.

"Nolan," his father said in way of greeting as they reached the large Sentinel.

"I'm busy, Williams," Nolan said as he gestured to several Sentinels to join him.

"I think you can spare ten minutes to explain why you've decided to deny us access to the Pytes that we brought in," his father said, keeping stride with the man while Chris moved up to Nolan's other side, leaving Caine to flank them, effectively cutting the compound leader off from his men.

"Not today," Nolan said, not bothering to spare them a glance as he walked towards the double doors to the right of the front desk.

His father didn't bother to say another word as they walked with the Sentinel leader, because there was no point. The man had made his decision, but unfortunately for him, so had they.

"What the hell?" Nolan muttered a moment later, frowning with confusion as he pressed his thumb against the security pad that controlled access to the double doors of the conference rooms and was answered by the telltale sounds of a sharp beep, denying him access. He tried several more times and was met with the same results. "Get IT on the phone and have them fix this goddamn door!" he snapped over his shoulder as he made one last attempt.

"Phones are down!" one of the women manning the front desk announced with a perplexed expression as she switched her attention from the dead phone to one of the computers lining the front desk.

"Internet is down, too!"

"What the fuck? My phone won't work!" one of the Sentinels standing next to them snapped.

"Elevators aren't working!"

"The front door won't open!"

"None of the doors will open!"

"What the hell is going on?" Nolan demanded, giving up on the door as he turned his attention on the men and women standing around the large lobby, looking confused and kind of pissed.

He moved to storm past them when Chris spoke, not bothering to hide his shit-eating grin. "It appears that a very pregnant genius got pissed that you were fucking with her mate and took matters into her own hands."

"*What?*" Nolan demanded harshly, his confused expression shifting as a play of emotions crossed his features from weary, to outraged and finally ending on resignation as he closed his eyes and growled, "Fucking hell."

"Oh, look at that," Chris mused as his father pressed his thumb to the security pad, the alarm chirping as the door unlocked, "it looks like you have ten minutes after all."

Nolan leveled a glare on him as he stormed past him, "Asshole."

"Caine," his father said as he opened the doors, "why don't you invite our guests to this meeting since this involves them"

Nolan cleared his throat, drawing everyone's attention as he said, "That might not be such a good idea."

"Why not?" Caine asked, pausing by the front desk.

Nolan sighed heavily as he rubbed the back of his neck and admitted, "Because we haven't fed them in five days."

———

"You're driving me out of my fucking mind," Christofer whispered in her ear as he wrapped his arms around her and pulled her back against his body.

"Are you complaining?" she asked, moaning as his hands covered her breasts.

"God no," he said, leaning down and pressing a kiss against her neck as he gave her breasts a gentle squeeze. "Not as long as you're willing to put me out of my misery."

"Gladly," she said on a choked moan as she slapped her hands against the bathroom wall and pushed back against him, biting her lower lip in pleasure when the move forced the large erection pressed up against her back to caress her skin. Christofer moaned in her ear as he pressed a hungry kiss against her skin, his hands gripping her breasts tighter as he gently thrust against her back.

"How are you feeling?" he asked, pressing a kiss between her shoulder blades.

"Good," she moaned, tilting her hips back against him, "Really good."

She could feel him smiling against her back. "Good. Then maybe it's time that I teach you how to use some of your other abilities," he murmured seductively as he pressed another kiss against her back. She was so caught up in that kiss that she almost missed what he'd said.

Almost.

"What are you-" her question ended on a panicked gasp as she suddenly found herself turned around, picked up and pressed back against the wall.

"Stay there," he said, releasing his hold on her only to catch her a few seconds later when she started to slide down the wall.

With a chuckle, he raised her right back to where he'd had her. "I see that you're going to need some help with this," he said in a conversational tone as she numbly nodded, nervously wondering what he was doing. Excitement shot through her as she enjoyed his touch and from the anticipation of learning one of the skills that she supposedly now had.

"What should I do?" she asked, reaching out to hold onto his shoulders only to find herself pushed up higher against the wall until her head was less than an foot away from the ceiling.

"Just hold onto me, mein Schatz," he said, pressing a kiss right above her navel as he slid one hand down her thigh and placed it over his shoulder. He kissed her just below the navel as he did the same with her other leg until she found herself propped up on his shoulders with her back flat against the wall. When she started to tilt forward, she grabbed onto his head and held on.

"Now spread your legs wide for me," he whispered, pressing another kiss against her stomach as he spread his arms and placed his hands flat against the wall. Biting her lip, she did just that, spreading her legs open until they were dangling over his large biceps.

"Now close your eyes, mein Schatz," he whispered softly, his warm breath caressing her stomach and after a slight hesitation, she did just that, giving him the one thing that she'd never given to another man.

Her trust.

She felt the muscles in his arms bulge beneath her legs as they shifted, pushing her up higher against the wall.

"Now," he said, pausing only long enough to press a kiss against her thigh, "I want you to relax and just focus on what I'm doing to you."

"And what exactly will you be doing to me?" she asked, gentling her hold on his head so that she could thread her fingers through the short, silky locks that she loved so much.

He pressed a kiss against the opposite thigh before he turned his head and leaned forward, pressing another kiss beneath her navel. "Everything I've been fantasizing about and more," he said as he slowly kissed his way down.

"Oh my God!" she gasped as she felt the very tip of his tongue tease the bottom of her slit.

Slowly, he moved the tip of his tongue over her slit, just enough to tease, but not enough to part her and reach all the places that craved his tongue. When he reached the top, he pressed a kiss against her wet slit and started all over again, teasing her with the same light touch that had her breaths quickening and her body trembling.

"You taste so fucking good," he whispered when the tip of his tongue once again reached the top of her slit and he pressed another soft kiss against her slit before he started the torturous process all over again.

"Christofer," she moaned, too far gone to care how desperate she sounded.

"Hmmmm?" he said, not even bothering to pause in his slow swipe of her slit.

"Stop teasing me," she groaned, her grip in his hair tightening as she struggled not to squirm and try to take what she wanted.

"I'm not teasing you, mein Schatz," he said just before he pressed that teasing kiss against her slit just above her swollen clit, but too lightly to give her any relief.

"What do you call this?" she demanded, choking back a sob as he started the process all over again.

"Savoring you," was the only answer he gave her as he ran the tip of his tongue through her wet slit, but this time dipping his tongue in just far enough to run it over the tip of her clit.

She groaned, long and loud as he did it again. Squeezing her eyes shut, she dropped her head back and licked her lips, enjoying the feel of his tongue teasing her. It was torture and bliss all wrapped in one leaving her wanting more.

"Christofer!" she pleaded, licking her lips as she struggled against the urge to open her eyes just so she could glare down at him as she demanded that he stop teasing her and get on with it.

"Do you want more?" he asked casually as he started the torturous process all over again.

"Yes!" she moaned just as the tip of his tongue flicked over her clit.

"Then put your feet on my arms and open up more for me, mein Schatz," he explained, pressing a kiss against her slit as she moved to do just that. She quickly raised her knees up and placed her feet on his locked elbows.

A loud moan broke free as Christofer rewarded her with a long leisurely lick through her now exposed lips, hitting every spot that craved his touch. He ran his tongue over her core, under the small hood of her clit before his tongue flicked over it, once, twice and then brushed down her clit and back over her core where he traced the rim with the tip of his tongue.

"Keep your eyes closed, mein Schatz," he whispered.

She opened her mouth to argue, but simply found herself nodding in agreement as he dipped his tongue inside her. At the same time she felt his mouth close over her core. He gently suckled just as she felt the slide of his tongue retreat with the movement, leaving her gasping and moaning for more.

Over the years she'd realized something very important when it came to men and sex. There were two types of men when it came to oral sex. There were men who used oral sex just to get what they wanted, but didn't take much pleasure in the act. Then there were men who loved the act almost as much as the woman if not more and Christofer was clearly one of those men who loved nothing more than to go down on a woman.

The thought of him doing this to another woman was not pleasant. Anger surged through her, making her fangs throb as she imagined ripping apart any woman that-

"I could lick you out all day," Christofer growled, bringing her murderous thoughts to a quick halt before they could really begin. "Do you have any idea how many times I've imagined doing this to you? How many times I wondered how you tasted? How many times I've wondered how it would feel to slide my fingers inside you? How many times you made me hard over the past couple of weeks? How many times I imagined fucking you?"

Squeezing her eyes shut, afraid that he'd stop if she opened them, she licked her lips, shaking her head as she imagined him stroking himself as he thought about her. It was almost too much to bear.

"I never imagined you'd taste this sweet," he groaned against her swollen wet flesh as she felt his hands gently clasp her ankles and pull them off his arms. He guided her feet to the wall as he slid his tongue inside her.

As soon as he released his hold on her, she pressed her feet flat against the wall and spread her legs wider, desperate for more. As his tongue slid inside her, his hands caressed her legs, moving down her thighs and then up over the gentle curve of her belly and over her breasts, teasing her swollen nipples with his barely-there touches.

He let his palms skim back down and over her nipples before he settled his hands around the heavy curve of her breasts and gently squeezed. His large hands cradled her large breasts as his thumbs moved to caress her aching nipples. As his tongue slid out of her only to slide back inside, further than before, his thumbs caressed the swollen skin around her sensitive nipples, careful not to touch the nipples themselves.

Moaning softly as she licked her lips, enjoying the sensation of having his tongue inside her and his very capable hands on her breasts, Cloe ran her fingers through his hair, silently encouraging him to continue and rewarding him for his very talented tongue. She'd been with several men that enjoyed going down on a woman, but none like Christofer. She never thought a man's tongue could feel so good.

As he continued to leisurely lick her out, his right hand gave her breast one last squeeze before it slid back down to join his tongue. She gasped when she felt the first caress of his thumb. His thumb teased the very tip of her clit, spreading the warm liquid over it before he gently pressed down and drew it back and forth, thrumming her perfectly as he stiffened his tongue inside her.

Before she knew what was happening, Christofer had changed the pace and the pressure of his touch, his gentle tongue no longer licking her out but fucking her with quick hard strokes. His thumb showing no mercy as it sped up to match the strokes of his tongue until she found herself gripping his hair tightly between her fingers, desperate to hold his mouth against her as her breaths sped up, her body began to tremble and then convulse as a scream was ripped from her lips.

She felt herself tighten around his tongue, her body desperate to keep him inside her. His tongue remained firmly inside of her as he somehow found a way to flick the tip inside her, hitting her in just the right way and ripping another scream from her lips as his thumb suddenly pressed down on her clit, sending her over the edge once more as his fingers gently pinched her nipple.

When the last tremor left her body, she found herself panting and her hips gently rocking against his mouth, greedily taking every last ounce of pleasure that he could give her. Gasping for air, she allowed herself a few more seconds of his touch before she released her death grip on his hair and allowed her hands to drop limply by her sides and her legs to fall open in surrender.

She felt Christofer press one last kiss against her slit as he pulled away from her. She wanted to reach out and pull him back, wanted him to hold her in his arms as she worked her way through the pleasure induced haze that he'd left her in, but she couldn't find the strength or the willpower to do it.

"Open your eyes, mein Schatz," Christofer whispered softly.

Wanting to see his face as she worked through the last tremors, she slowly opened her eyes, looked down at Christofer and then abruptly squealed as she found herself falling face first towards the tiled floor below.

THIRTY-FIVE

Before she could hit the floor, he had her in his arms and was heading for the bedroom, desperate to be inside her.

"You did great, mein Schatz," he told the trembling woman in his arms as he pressed a kiss against her forehead.

"You….," she said, pausing to gasp for air, "*bastard*!"

"Is something wrong?" he asked innocently, hoping that it would be enough to make her forget that he'd manipulated her into floating for the first time and that she'd opened her eyes to find herself with an unobstructed view of the tiled floor below. Then again, if he'd been paying attention and had stopped her from sliding up to the ceiling when she'd lost control she probably wouldn't have been so pissed to find herself pinned against the wall instead of lying flat against the ceiling.

Ah, live and learn, he thought with a sigh as he placed the visibly angry woman on the bed. When she opened her mouth, no doubt to tell him to go fuck himself, he decided that it would probably be for the best for everyone concerned, meaning his aching cock, to distract her for a minute.

"You son of-*oh, God*! Not again!" she ended with a strangled cry as he buried his face between her legs.

He hadn't been lying when he'd said that he could happily lick her all day. Just the thought of doing this for the rest of his life had his balls drawing up tight and his cock aching for release, and he would be doing this for the rest of his life, he'd decided about twenty minutes ago when he got his first taste of her. She was his. It was as simple as that. Since Ephraim's announcement that she was his mate worked in his favor, he'd decided to just go with it. He didn't care about the "whys" or "hows," he just cared that she was his, forever.

He was forced to run his tongue over his fangs when they tried to slide down, eager for a taste of the blood swelling the feminine flesh beneath his mouth. When time hadn't been a factor and he hadn't had to worry about Marta's safety, he used to pleasure a woman just like this, methodically hitting each pleasure point and pushing a woman past her endurance to make the blood rush between her legs. Once she was properly distracted, he would slip a finger inside her and keep her distracted, fucking her with his fingers while he slid his fangs in her thigh and took his fill. He'd never enjoyed the act before. The women he'd pleasured had been nothing but a meal to him and a way to escape his life for a short time, but this…..

God, he could do this all fucking day, he thought as he outlined her core with the tip of his tongue and flicked it over her swollen clit. He shifted over her, working his tongue on her clit while he reached between her legs with his hand as he settled on his stomach. He closed his lips around her swollen nub as he traced her opening with his finger, loving the way that she squirmed and moaned.

Her fingers threaded through his hair in that way that drove him out of his fucking mind. He'd noticed that she did it when she was turned on and she liked what he was doing. He wasn't even sure that she was aware that she was doing it, but he loved it. He loved the way it felt to have fingers running through his hair, the gentle way she did it as though she was rewarding him with a soothing touch for pleasing her.

"Christofer," she moaned his name as her legs fell open, her fingers running through his hair as she slowly arched her hips, riding his finger in a slow sensual pace that was making it more difficult with each passing second to hold back, but he wanted to hear her scream his name one more time before he was too distracted to savor it.

He gave the sweet little nub between his lips one last suckle and a kiss before he moved up her body, dying to take one of the large pink nipples between his lips as he took her with his finger. Cloe continued to run her fingers through his hair as he kissed and licked his way to one large breast. He savored the warm firm globe, nuzzling it with his face as he kissed every inch of skin that he could reach until finally his mouth found the prize.

She gasped with pleasure as he ran his tongue over her nipple. Her fingers ran through his hair even as she rode his finger almost desperately. He pulled his finger free of her honeyed core and added a second finger and slid them back inside the smooth channel as he pressed his thumb just above her clit.

"*Christofer*," she said his name like a plea as he suckled her nipple into a hard point and moved to the other one all while his thumb slowly moved around her clit, teasing the little nub as his fingers slid inside her.

"Now," Cloe demanded on a gasp, her hips riding his fingers in a way that made his cock jealous.

"Now," he agreed, pressing one last kiss against her nipple, he pulled his hand away from her and placed it on the bed near her head as he settled between her legs.

Her fingers paused in their soothing motions to cup his face and pull his mouth down to hers. She brushed her lips against his as he settled more firmly between her legs. When his erection came to rest against her wet slit they both moaned.

"You feel so fucking good," he said hoarsely, forced to close his eyes and hold his breath, terrified that this was going to be over before it began.

But, Cloe was having none of that.

She nibbled at his lips, licking the slight sting away before she teased his lips open and invaded. He groaned long and loud as her tongue slid over his, teasing an involuntary thrust of his hips, but that was enough to keep his hips rocking between hers. With every thrust of his hips, his cock slid further and further between her swollen, wet lips until the underside of his cock was gliding over her core and swollen little clit, earning the sexiest little moans from Cloe. The scent of her arousal intensified, making it more difficult with each thrust of his hips to resist finally giving in and allow his cock to slide inside her, but he wanted to savor this for as long as possible.

He'd waited so long for this moment, for this woman and he didn't want to ruin it by rushing in too quickly, especially since he didn't think he'd last that long, not if being inside Cloe felt as good as he'd imagined. It had been so long since he'd touched a woman, since he allowed himself to believe that he could be with a woman like a normal man. She felt too damn good to care about anything, especially with the way that she was suckling on his tongue as he moved it against hers.

His hand snaked between them and found one of her large breasts. He caressed the soft skin, groaning as the move caused her hard nipple to tease his skin. Christ, he wanted her. He wanted to slide inside her, kiss her, lick her breasts, suck her nipples and fuck her until his cock exploded and then he wanted to do it again and-

"Christofer?" Cloe said, sounding uncertain even as her hands ran all over his body as she mindlessly arched beneath him, desperate to be filled.

"Yes, mein Schatz?" he said, moving against her, the need to be inside her overshadowing old fears until all he could think of was shifting between her legs and sliding inside her.

"Y-you're not going to," she said on a hoarse whisper, pausing only long enough to release a moan when the underside of his cock hit her core in just the right way, "lose c-control are you?"

"Hmmm?" he murmured, absently as he shifted his hips, dragging his cock down through her wet slit until

he found the tip of his cock settled at her core, ready to finally slide home.

"You won't lose control, will you?" Cloe demanded, fisting her hands in his hair and yanking his mouth down for another kiss that had his head spinning and robbed him of his ability to think past how good it felt to be in her arms.

He pushed the tip inside her, groaning in pleasured agony as smooth velvet skin surrounded him, coating him in warm liquid as he slowly pushed inside her. Finally, he thought, damn near laughing in relief to feel her close around him.

Finally.........

"Oh, God," Cloe groaned, her fingers tightening in his hair, her breaths coming faster as he pushed inside her another half inch. "Just......oh, God......*just don't bite me, Christofer,*" she half moaned, half pleaded, lost to the sensation of having him slide inside her. He-

Had to stop before he hurt her.

———

"Christofer?" Cloe mumbled in confusion when he pulled away from her.

"I can't hurt you," he said tightly, sounding pained as he climbed off the bed and when she saw that large, angry erection bobbing with every movement she couldn't help but wince in sympathy.

"And you'll do that if we go any further?" she asked, hesitating on the last part and wondering why she hadn't just said have sex or fuck to describe something that she'd used to do to burn off a little energy and some of the bitter loneliness that used to plague her.

She could pretend all she wanted that she didn't know the reason behind the hesitation, but it was difficult to do even that with the reason gently caressing her face as he pressed a tender kiss against her forehead.

"I would rather die than hurt you again, mein Schatz," he whispered against her forehead.

"Do you lose control when you're intimate with a woman?" she forced herself to ask, the words leaving a bitter taste on her tongue as her sight flickered red several times, making her realize that for the first time in her life she was jealous.

It wasn't a pleasant emotion.

"I never have," he admitted, looking away from her as he moved to stand, but she cupped his face, stopping him as she brought his mouth back down to hers.

"So then why do you think you'll lose control with me?" she asked, teasing his lips, nibbling on them and gently sucking on them as she moved to get on her knees and wrap her arms around his broad shoulders, more than ready to pick up where they'd left off.

"Because I've never wanted another woman the way that I want you, mein Schatz," he confessed, setting her body on fire and making it difficult to care about the dangers of making him lose control.

Well, almost.

She couldn't forget the way that he'd lost control the last time they'd played this game no matter how badly she wanted him, and God did she want him. Feeling him start to slide inside her had been the most incredible experience of her life. It had quickly put her on the verge of another powerful orgasm and if he hadn't stopped, she probably would have been screaming for mercy by now. But he had stopped, and now she was torn between thanking him and wanting to kick his ass as her body demanded more of him.

"And you think that means that you'll lose control?" she asked, following his lips with her own as he started to move away from her, curious about something that he probably wouldn't appreciate her asking.

His answering growl was beyond sexy. "You make me lose my fucking mind."

He pulled away and this time she let him. She looked up, searching bright red eyes for the monster that had destroyed her life, but he wasn't there.

"So, this is it?" she whispered, surprised by just how badly she was willing to say the hell with it and take a chance on him, but she couldn't.

The memory of those eyes glimmering seconds before he'd attacked her wouldn't let her. She just couldn't-

"Hell no," Christofer said, leaning back down and taking her lips in a swift kiss that left her a little dazed.

"Then what are you suggesting?" she asked, reaching for him even as she had to wonder if he was about to show her another trick to help her stay in control, something that she should be focusing on right now, not pulling him back in her arms and taking off where they'd ended. She should-

"Lock me up," he said with the sexiest grin that she'd ever seen as he dropped a pair of handcuffs on the bed next to her, making her bite back a smile as she realized that she might just be getting her curiosity assuaged after all.

THIRTY-SIX

"Are you sure?" Cloe asked as he felt her hesitate.
Fuck no, but he didn't have much choice in the matter, not if he wanted to make love to her. It wasn't a perfect plan, but it was one that he felt confident would work, or at the very least, give her a chance to put him down before he could get a chance to hurt her if he lost control.

"Yes," he heard himself answer as he forced himself to stand there as Cloe reluctantly handcuffed his hands behind his back.

When he felt the last cuff click in place, he had to close his eyes and just breathe as he reminded himself that he wasn't in the lab anymore. The panic that tried to take over was from long ago memories better left off forgotten and that he was doing this for Cloe, his mate.

"We don't have to do this," Cloe said, pressing a kiss against his bare shoulder as she reached up and ran her fingers through the hair on the back of his head, soothing him.

He chuckled without humor as he looked down at the angry appendage that was about ready to explode. His chuckle quickly turned into a drawn out groan when

Cloe wrapped her arms around him, bringing her body flush against his.

"Where did you get these cuffs?" she asked, pressing another kiss against his back as she ran her hands over his chest and stomach, making it difficult to think.

"I swiped them at the hotel," he said, not bothering to point out that he'd taken them just in case she lost control since the confession would only make her stop what she was doing. There was no way in hell that he wanted her to stop touching him, especially when one very talented hand headed south.

"And the key?" she asked as her warm hand wrapped around the base of his cock.

"In my pants pocket," was his choked answer as she ran her hand along his cock, stroking him.

"The pair that I ripped apart?" she asked, her tone sensual as she pressed another kiss against his back and her other hand headed south, tracing lazy patterns down his torso as he struggled to take in his next breath.

"Yes."

"Tell me something, Christofer," she said as she continued to stroke him, the thumb of her other hand tracing lazy circles around the tip of his cock as he struggled not to flex his hips for more.

"What?" he asked, licking his lips hungrily as she ran her thumb over the drop of excitement that escaped him and coated the tip, heightening his pleasure.

"How long has it been?" she asked, pressing another kiss against his back as the hand stroking him paused long enough to squeeze a moan out of him.

"Been?" he asked, trying to make sense out of what she was asking.

"Mmmhmm," she said distractedly, pressing another kiss against his back before she dropped the hand that had been teasing the tip of his erection away and she slowly moved around him, the hard points of her nipples dragging across his back and over his arm until she was standing in front of him. She gave his erection another squeeze before she slowly stroked him. "How long has it been?" she asked, tilting her head slightly to the side as she studied him, waiting for an answer that he wasn't sure that he could give her.

Needing to distract her almost as much as he was dying to kiss her, he leaned down and took her mouth in a hungry kiss that had his breaths coming a little too quickly and his hips helplessly thrusting against her hand. He jerked his hands against his cuffs, desperate to touch her, but the damn things wouldn't give so he settled for devouring her mouth.

The sweet smell of her sex had him tilting his head and deepening the kiss. The kiss became aggressive as he slowly thrust against her fist, loving the way her soft hand glided over his cock and hating it at the same time. He wasn't going to last very much longer and he was helpless to stop.

"That long, huh?" Cloe whispered hoarsely against his lips with a breathless chuckle as she released her hold on his cock, but before he could complain or beg her to touch him again, she was pushing him back on the bed and straddling his lap.

"Ah, fuck!" he groaned long and loud as her wet slit came to rest against the underside of his cock.

She wrapped her arms around his neck, her fingers digging into his hair, her breasts pressed against his chest as she took his mouth in another hungry kiss as she pressed down against him, tracing his cock with her wet slit and coating him in her arousal. He met her stroke for stroke, swallowing every little sweet moan and groan that escaped her lips as she ground her wet sex down against him.

"How long has it been?" she asked, threading her fingers through his hair, holding his head captive. She suckled his tongue in one long caress before she suddenly abandoned his mouth and began kissing her way down to his throat.

"How long has what been?" he repeated, licking his lips hungrily when he felt the tip of one of her fangs tease his skin when Cloe pressed an open mouthed kiss against his neck.

"How," she started to ask in a sultry voice only to pause to press a kiss against his Adam's apple as he dropped his head back, giving her plenty of room to drive him out of his fucking mind, "long has it been since you were with a woman?"

He groaned, letting out the curse in German that he'd learned from his father when he was five and tried to "improve" some of the priceless artwork in his father's study. It wasn't a question that he'd expected, but really, given the woman currently driving him out of his fucking mind, he really should have expected it.

"Does it matter?" he asked, wondering why he hadn't used the lie that he'd prepared years ago when a woman demanded to know why he wouldn't fuck her, but he couldn't force the words out of his mouth, not with Cloe.

"No, not really," she said, brushing her lips over his pulse as one of her hands dropped to his lap and wrapped around his over sensitized cock. "I'm just wondering if we should get the first one out of the way or," she paused, her voice catching as she used her hold on his cock to tease her core with the tip, "if we can finally stop playing around and work this out of our systems before I lose my damn mind, Christofer."

Trembling from the effort not to come then and there as she began to settle down on his cock, he struggled to stay in control, to stop himself from coming, to stop himself from-

"*Oh, thank fucking God,*" he groaned, panting hard as Cloe slid down his cock, her nails digging into his shoulders as every muscle in his body clenched tightly. He forced himself to hold back as he felt Cloe clamp down around him, barely halfway down his shaft.

"*Oh God!*" Cloe cried out as her body throbbed around his shaft, sending intense pleasure like he'd never experienced before through his shaft, down to his balls, up his spine until finally every cell in his body seemed to explode with intense pleasure. The pleasure blinded him to everything but the way that Cloe's body wrapped around his, which was probably why he didn't realize that he'd lost control until it was too late.

—

Well, that was a first, she thought with a weak chuckle as she clung to Christofer while the last tremors of the most powerful orgasm that she'd ever experienced worked their way through her.

She'd never lost control like that before, that quickly. She should be embarrassed, but she was too sated to care. Sighing with pleasure she turned her head slightly so that she could press an apologetic kiss against Christofer's neck, hopefully conveying the silent promise that she would take care of him just as soon as she found the strength to move. Until then, she was more than happy to sit on his lap still intimately joined, snuggling up against him as he whispered what sounded like German in her ears while he ran his hands up and down her back, pressing kisses against her forehead as-

She froze, her lips pressed against his neck as her mind quickly caught up with what was going on and by the time that she figured it out.....

It was too late.

————

"*Mine*!"

"Christofer, wait!"

"*Mine*!"

"No, wait a-" she rushed out, trying to push away from him, but she wasn't fast enough.

Before she could get off his lap and put some space between them long enough for him to calm down, she found herself pushed back onto the bed. Christofer hovered over her. A scream tore past her lips as Christofer shoved forward, burying himself to the hilt inside her. A surge of pain accompanied the sudden invasion, earning a choked cry from her as her body tried to accommodate the large erection that had forced its way inside her.

"Mein Schatz," Christofer whispered hoarsely, lowering his body down on hers until his face hovered right above hers. "Meine Frau," he said with such a tender smile that she immediately forgot all about the pain and focused on the man above her.

"You are so damn beautiful, Cloe," he said, caressing her cheek as he leaned down and pressed a kiss against her forehead. "And you feel so fucking good," he said, sounding pained as he leaned down and took her mouth in a hungry kiss that had her wrapping her arms around his shoulders and legs opening wider, hoping to bring him closer, needing him closer.

He swallowed her gasp of surprise when he pulled his hips back and pushed back in, stretching her a little more, but this time there was no pain. No, this time it felt good, really good. She arched her back, desperate for more as she returned the kiss. God, could the man kiss.....

He thoroughly devoured her mouth as he thrust inside her, slow and deliberate as though he was savoring the sensation of moving inside her. She'd never had a man take her like this before. She normally liked sex hard and fast, making it impossible to think, but with Christofer she found herself enjoying the feel of him sliding slowly inside her, craved it even as she felt like screaming in frustration.

"Christofer," she found herself sobbing his name as she clung to him, her back arching as her hips shifted to meet his excruciatingly slow thrusts.

"Shhhh, I don't want to hurt you," he whispered against her lips as his thrusts slowed down even more, leaving her frustrated. Her body trembled, her breaths quickened to an unsteady cadence. She felt her fangs slide down and a slight tingle as her eyes shifted to red as he continued to torture her, drawing out every scrap of pleasure that he could while turning her into a quivering mass of nerves, ready to explode.

A scream of frustration tore from her lips when his thrusts slowed to a halt, leaving her ready to kill the bastard for toying with her. She enjoyed a little bed play just as much as the next girl, but this was too much. A few times over the years she'd ended up in bed with some asshole that thought he had something to prove by trying to turn her into a quivering mass of need by drawing out her pleasure until she was forced to beg, but she never begged.

No, not her. She couldn't stand guys who thought that they were God's gift to women and were hell-bent on proving it. It was a huge turnoff and it only managed to annoy her enough to push the guy off her and go find something else to do to kill a few hours, kind of like now.

Muttering a curse to cover her disappointment and the fact that she felt like crying, she opened her eyes, more than ready to tell the jerk to stop playing games, and found herself staring up into glimmering red eyes of a man who looked like he was in hell.

It was also when she realized that she wasn't the one trembling.

THIRTY-SEVEN

"I can't do this," he said in a strangled whisper, averting his eyes in shame as he moved to climb off her.

He forced himself to ignore the way her core gripped him tightly, refusing to let him go and the way that it felt to glide out of her, her warm juices coating every last inch of him, tempting him to slide back in for more, but he couldn't, not without scaring her. He'd fucked up. Christ, had he fucked up. He should have known better, did know better, but his brain didn't seem to work, not around Cloe.

She made him want things that he couldn't have, shouldn't want. He'd spent his entire life watching over his sister, protecting her and agonizing over her happiness. He would always love her and miss her, but after ninety years of playing protector, he should want his freedom and be willing to do anything to have it. Instead he was here, in bed with this beautiful woman that drove him out of his fucking mind, pretending that he could be something that she needed. He was obviously delusional and he would be paying for this mistake for the rest of his life.

Great, just what he needed, he mused, shaking his head in disgust, another fucking Kodak moment.

"Why not?" Cloe asked, reaching out to stop him, but he moved out of her reach, refusing to prolong this torture for another second longer.

"Sex doesn't work for me," he said, a fucking understatement.

He should have learned his lesson years ago in that cage, but obviously he hadn't. He always let his dick convince him that he could handle it now that he was older, more in control, but it was always a bullshit lie that he told himself so that he could take what he wanted. He thought he'd learned his lesson forty years ago, but that first glimpse of Cloe in the pharmacy had him forgetting what he was capable of and had him panting after her like a teenage boy with his first hard on.

"Because......?" she asked, stretching out the word as she sat up, following his retreat.

"Just because," he said, shaking his head in disgust at himself for being so fucking stupid.

He'd enjoyed touching her, loved it and would gladly give up his soul to do it again, but now he knew what he was missing. His cock ached so badly, every movement sending sharp pain up his shaft and quickly making breathing a thing of the past. A cold shower wouldn't help, he realized with a wince as he slowly made his way off the bed. The only thing that would help would be taking himself in hand, and with Cloe cursed with his condition, she'd know what he was doing. It was no doubt going to piss her off to know that he'd rather take himself in hand than finish with her, but right now he didn't have a choice if he-

A grunt escaped him as he suddenly found himself shoved back down on the bed and Cloe on top of him, pinning him down.

"Get off," he said, his hands clenching into fists as he forced his arms to remain where they were, afraid that if he touched her again that he'd lose control and fuck the life out of her. Not that Cloe could die, but he'd do enough damage to make the night he'd attacked her seem like a fun-filled day at Disneyworld.

He couldn't do that to her, no matter how badly his body ached to be back inside her.

She cocked her head to the side as she looked down, studying him with open curiosity before she shook her head. "No," she said, sighing heavily as she leaned forward, entwined their hands together and leaned back down until the tip of his cock, desperate to get back inside of her, was brushing up against her stomach just above where the hair that protected her sex began, "I don't think I will. At least not until you explain why you keep playing with me."

"I'm not playing with you," he bit out, moving to pull his hands away from her and risk touching her when she shook her head and gave his hands a gentle squeeze in warning.

"Yeah, you really are and I'd like to know why," she said, shifting over him so that the underside of the tip of his cock brushed up harder against the smooth warm skin of her stomach, driving him out of his fucking mind.

"No," he said through clenched teeth, deciding to put an end to this bullshit, "I'm not."

"Really?" she asked, cocking a challenging brow as she abruptly released his hands, sat up and then-

"*Oh, shit!*"

Sat down on his lap, her wet warm pussy landing right on top of the base of his cock. Locking eyes with him, she reached down and wrapped her hand around his cock, giving it a squeeze. When she stroked him, he reached up, the broken links of his handcuffs *clinking* lightly against the cuffs as he reached out to stop her, but a warning squeeze around his cock had him groaning long and loud and his hands dropping helplessly by his sides.

"So, then what are you doing?" she asked, stroking him as she pressed down, forcing the length of his cock between her wet folds.

"Nothing," he managed hoarsely, his eyes glued to the small tan hand wrapped around him.

"Nothing?" she murmured, watching him as she moved to grip him just beneath the head of his cock.

"Changed my mind," he lied, licking his lips as he watched her tilt her hips, the move pressing her core and swollen clit right against him.

"You just changed your mind?" she repeated, sounding amused as she looked pointedly down at the large erection in her hands.

"Yes!" he hissed out when she rocked her hips, rubbing her wet slit over him.

"I see," she said softly, her attention fixed on his cock as her grip tightened around him. She slowly canted her hips back and forth, riding the length of his cock as she moaned softly.

His fangs shot down before he could stop them. Glad that her attention was elsewhere, he ran his tongue over the tips of his fangs and willed them to retreat, but they wouldn't listen, not with Cloe coating his cock in her juices. His breaths came short and choppy as he desperately tried sending his fangs back, praying that he was able to do it before she saw them and started screaming. He felt the tingle of his eyes just before their surroundings took on shades of red again, but with a thought he had them shifting back to blue.

"So, you'd be okay if I stopped?" she asked, continuing to play with his cock as she shot him a questioning look.

Clamping his jaw tightly shut, he nodded, his cock jerking in her hands in protest.

Cloe sighed, long and loud as she reluctantly nodded. "If that's what you want."

It wasn't what he wanted, but he didn't have a choice. Never had. He could handle fingering a woman, licking her out and kissing her without losing control, but every time he slid inside a woman his grip on his control faltered, leaving him struggling to hide what he was. The few times that he'd allowed himself to take a chance he'd ended up scrambling for the door and running off like a coward, but the last time.....

That last time should have been enough.

He could still hear her screams for help....

It sure as hell wasn't something that he wanted to go through with Cloe. She made him lose control with a smile. He was a fucking moron for thinking that he had a chance of retaining control with her because of a pair of handcuffs. He should have……..

"Fucking hell!" he roared as Cloe took him by surprise.

"Much better," Cloe said, sounding pleased with herself as she slowly slid down his cock until he was buried inside her to the hilt. "Now, where were we?"

He opened his mouth to beg her to have mercy on him, but the sensation of his fangs shooting down had him clamping his mouth shut. His control over his eyes was tenuous, but for the moment he had them under his control. He used his eyes to convey the message that she needed to get off him, now. When she ignored his glare, he reached up to remove her with trembling hands only to have her intercept his hands and place them on her breasts.

"I believe you were explaining to me the reason why you've been screwing with my head," she said, covering his hands with hers and forcing them to squeeze her large pouty breasts as she shifted on his lap, drawing a strangled groan from him.

"Haven't been screwing with your head," he managed to bite out between clenched teeth, praying that she didn't see his fangs and realize just how close he was to losing it.

"Really?" she asked in a disbelieving tone as she slowly rode him, her wet core hugging his shaft tightly and stroking it with every motion.

"Yes!"

"I see," she said, releasing her hold over his hands.

The second that her hands dropped to her sides, he forced himself to drop his hands as well, ignoring the impulse to squeeze them, run his hands over them, play with the pretty nipples begging for his attention and...

And.....

And.....

Lick his lips hungrily as he watched Cloe reach between her legs and trace her wet slit with the tips of her fingers. Enthralled, he watched as she rode him, his cock disappearing inside her with increasing urgency as she played with her swollen clit for his viewing pleasure. Everything took on shades of red, but he was too lost to care or realize what that meant. A small moan dragged his attention north to find a similar pair of shimmering red eyes watching him.

He felt his body go still and swore that his heart stopped beating as he waited for her to scream, to yell at him, call him a monster, hit him, to look at him with terror and disgust as she realized that the man that was making love to her was the same man that had attacked her and destroyed her life. It was what he deserved, what he expected, but this was Cloe that he was dealing with here. Why he still expected her to act like a normal woman would was beyond him.

"You feel so good," she said, licking her lips hungrily as she continued to ride him.

For a moment he watched her, looking for any signs that she was frightened, but he could only sense her arousal. He hadn't lied to her when he'd told her that he'd never lost control when he was with a woman. He'd never wanted one badly enough to lose the kind of control that would put a woman's life in danger, not since the lab. He'd always had a problem with hiding what he was, which was why he usually settled for pleasuring a woman to get what he wanted.

"You're really not scared?" he found himself asking, curious about her reaction.

"Is that what was bothering you?" she asked, sounding just as curious.

"Yes."

"Afraid that I'd see the real you and make a run for it?" she teased, her lips twitching with amusement as her hand suddenly stilled between her legs.

"Something like that," he admitted, slowly sitting up and wrapping his arms loosely around her as she continued to slowly ride him. "You have more than enough reason to," he admitted as she wrapped her arms around his shoulders.

"Yes," she easily agreed as she leaned in and brushed her lips against his, "I do."

"Then why don't you?"

"Because," she said with a shy smile and a blush that took him by surprise, "I know that it wasn't you. You'd never hurt me, Christofer."

"No," he said, shaking his head as his hold on her tightened, "I wouldn't."

"Because you live in fear of my new mighty skills," she teased as she leaned in and playfully nipped at his lower lip, surprising a chuckle out of him.

"Yes, I do," he said, terrified of the power that she had over him, but craving it more than anything.

"Since we have that little matter straightened out........." she said huskily, letting her words trail off as her hips rolled with a little more force, reminding him that he was inside the woman that drove him out of his fucking mind and he was wasting time, something that he would never be able to forgive himself for.

He took her mouth roughly, careful not to nick her tongue with his fangs, uncaring if he cut his tongue on hers. She kissed him, meeting him stroke for stroke as he turned with her in his arms and laid her back on the bed. Before her back hit the bed he was thrusting inside her. There was no finesse or skill to his movements, something that he prayed that she wouldn't notice. He took her with everything that he had, opening his senses and focusing on the way that her nipples were pressed against his chest, the feel of her warm skin against his, the feel of her beautiful mouth, the way her hot sheath gripped him tightly with every stroke and the desperate way that she pulled at his ass, demanding that he fuck her harder.

Immense pleasure rode up his shaft and this time he didn't try fighting it, because he knew that he was beyond stopping with the way that she whimpered his name against his lips, dug her nails in his ass and worked her hips so that she could meet every one of his strokes. When the need to bite her took hold of him, he thrust against her harder, driving his cock into her wet core over and over again until it become too much.

Pressing one last desperate kiss against her lips, he turned his head and offered his neck, giving Cloe the pleasure that he could never allow himself.

"Cloe...mein Schatz.........*fuck!*" he growled incoherently as Cloe struck, burying her fangs inside his neck as her sheath clamped down around him, her walls pulsing uncontrollably as she ripped the orgasm from him, giving him what no other woman could.

Peace.

THIRTY-EIGHT

"What's our plan?" she asked, trying to focus on what they needed to do instead of the fact that she'd just had the most amazing sex of her life with a man that she refused to allow herself to fall for.

She didn't fall in love, she reminded herself as she barely resisted the urge to reach out and run her hand over his bare shoulder. It would only send the wrong message and right now she needed to remember that this wasn't permanent. While it was true that she would never have to worry about Christofer dying one day, she wasn't foolish enough to believe that this was going to last for eternity.

One day he'd grow tired of her or find someone new and then it would be over and she would be on her own. So, for now she was going to just enjoy the time they had together, have more of that amazing sex and learn as much as she could from Christofer before he walked away.

"I don't have a plan," Christofer admitted as he finished tying his shoe.

"You don't have a plan?" she repeated back slowly, sure that she'd misheard him.

"No," he answered as he stood up and pulled a grey tee shirt on, covering that incredible chest and torso that she hadn't fully appreciated yet, giving her a chance to stay focused on the fact that the man that she was trusting her ass with just admitted that he planned on escaping what came down to a military compound without a plan.

Yeah..........

"Then how exactly did you plan on escaping without getting caught?" she demanded, for the first time regretting turning down her social worker when he'd strongly suggested that joining the military was the best way for someone like her to pay for college.

"I figured we'd just wing it," he said with a shrug that she really didn't appreciate, not one bit.

"You figured we'd just *wing it*?" she repeated, truly at a loss for words.

Wow, just....wow.......

"Unless you have a better plan," he offered, moving over to her backpack and double-checking that they hadn't forgotten anything.

"We could give it another day," she suggested, sounding hopeful and for good reason.

She was not looking forward to this. Not at all. They had no weapons and apparently they didn't even have a plan. She really didn't see this working, but she didn't say anything, mostly because she didn't feel like putting up with him scowling at her for the next ten minutes.

He shook his head as he picked up the bag and headed for the door. "We can't wait another day," he said tightly, making her frown as she hurried after him.

"Why not?" she asked, catching up to him by the time he made it to the living room. "What difference will one more day make?"

He didn't look at her as he answered, "A world of difference."

"And why exactly is that?" she asked, struggling to keep up.

He paused at the penthouse door with his hand on the handle, his back to her as he gave her the answer that she'd really wished he'd kept to himself.

"Because I'm having a hell of a time keeping my hands off you right now. All I can think about is taking you back to bed, licking you clean, sliding my fingers deep inside you, taking you against every surface until you squeeze my cock dry, but I know that if I touch you right now that I won't be able to stop myself from sliding my fangs inside you and draining you dry the next time I hear you scream my name."

"Oh," was her lame reply as she tried to think about anything other than the visual that he'd just created in her mind and failed, a few times.

Was it wrong that she was actually thinking about saying the hell with it and tackling him?

Probably, she thought, absently frowning as she heard something like a motor and-

"The elevator," Christofer growled out viciously as he tore open the door and stormed out of the penthouse, leaving her standing there, debating her options.

After only a few seconds she came to the depressing realization that she really didn't have any other options.

—

Orlando, Florida

"We found her," came the announcement that he'd been waiting for.

"Where is she?" he asked his Beta, not bothering with any pleasantries as he abruptly hung up the phone on one of his suppliers.

His beta stood in front of his desk, his hands clenched tightly by his sides, his gaze downcast in submission as he admitted, "She's gone."

"Gone?" Aidan repeated with disgust.

Brock opened his mouth to explain further only to abruptly shut his mouth, nod and tense up as he risked a quick glance at his Alpha.

"How can she be gone if you found her?" Aidan asked, leaning back in his chair as he studied his beta, waiting for an answer that would satisfy him.

Licking his lips, his beta rushed to explain, "We were able to convince a human working at the agency that employed her to help us. She gave us an address in Massachusetts. I sent a team to retrieve her this morning."

"Then why isn't she here now?" he wondered out loud, his fingers drumming against his desk as he waited, patiently in his opinion, for his Beta to explain why his property wasn't at this moment quivering at his feet and begging for his forgiveness.

He saw his Beta hesitate for a moment and knew that he wasn't going to like what was coming. His Beta apparently sensed that as well since he started to take a step back only to remember how Aidan felt about cowards.

"Sentinels," his Beta said, keeping his gaze locked on the floor.

"Sentinels?" he repeated, the word leaving a sour taste in his mouth.

Brock nodded firmly, once. "It appears as though they're cleaning out the house."

"She was working at a Sentinel home?" he asked, wondering what kind of Sentinel would be stupid enough to harbor a bitch.

She was clearly marked and even though the Sentinels did everything they could to stop the practice of marking humans as property, once a human was marked, they couldn't do shit about it. That is, unless the human asked for help, but even then most Sentinels were forbidden to interfere, because of the potential for war. Knowing the Sentinels were involved, he couldn't help but wonder if she knew what he was and what that made her.

He'd rather keep her in the dark until he could claim her as his. He wanted to see the terror on her face when she realized what he was, her master. If the Sentinels had let that particular secret slip he may have to pay a visit to this Sentinel home in Massachusetts.

"I don't think it was a Sentinel home before," Brock said, his jaw clenched tightly as he forced himself to stand there.

"And now?"

A muscle ticked in Brock's jaw as he nodded, igniting his curiosity even further.

"And the family that lived there?" he asked in a deceptively calm tone as he waited for the bad news that he knew was coming. He could smell the spike of adrenaline coursing through his Beta's body, demanding that his beta make an escape or defend himself, but Brock would do neither. Not if he wanted to live.

"They're gone. No one in town has seen them in over a week," Brock rushed to explain.

"Does anyone know where they've gone?" he asked, relishing in the feel of his fingernails shifting to claws as he continued to drum his fingers against the desk, waiting for an answer that would lead him to his property.

"No," Brock reluctantly said as he continued to force himself to stand there, averting his gaze as Aidan digested his answer and when he did.....

"*You lost my property*?" he snarled in his Beta's face seconds later as he wrapped his hand around his Beta's neck, allowing his claws to dig into the vulnerable skin protecting his throat.

"It's complicated," Brock said, swallowing hard.

"I asked you to retrieve my property. What's so difficult about that?" he demanded, his voice deepening as he allowed his beast to come to the surface.

"The people that she was working for weren't human," Brock gasped out, forcing himself to keep his hands by his sides.

"*Another shifter touched my bitch?*" he snarled, his teeth shifting to fangs.

"No," Brock said, shaking his head adamantly. "The man that owned the house that she'd worked at was rumored to drink animal blood."

"Demon?" he asked, running possibilities through his head.

"We're not sure," Brock admitted, gasping for air when Aidan abruptly released his hold and began pacing the office.

"Tell me about him," he demanded, flexing his hands, trying to shake off the need to rip his Beta apart.

"He looks like he's in his late twenties, but the people in town swear that he's been living with his sister for over forty years. He never ages, can go out during the day and is rumored to drink animal blood," Brock explained as he rubbed his neck.

"And the sister?" he asked, wondering why the couple stayed in one area for so long.

"Human as far as we can tell," Brock said, piquing his curiosity.

"Human?"

"She was well into her eighties."

"Hmmm," Aidan said, tracing his claws over his desk as he walked past it, running several possibilities through his mind. "Any chance that they were only posing as siblings?" he asked, wondering if it was just a case of a demon falling for a human that he couldn't change.

Eyes locked on the floor, Brock shook his head, wincing when the action obviously pained him. "No, it was pretty clear to everyone in town that they were siblings. They somewhat welcomed the sister into the community, but it was pretty clear that they feared him."

Nodding absently, he drummed his claws against the desk as he digested the information. It was possible that this "brother" was a demon and that the mother had fucked around. Possible, but he didn't think so.

He wasn't a hundred percent sure, but he had a suspicion that his Beta had just stumbled across a way to make his old dream into a reality.

THIRTY-NINE

"Wow, I didn't know your son was a pussy," Caine said conversationally as he watched the large Sentinel struggle to get out of the obviously pissed off Pyte's hold.

Ephraim sighed heavily as he shook his head, watching as Chris continued to struggle while the Pyte stood there, looking bored. "I didn't know either."

"Mother fucker!" Chris roared as the sound of a bone popping out of place echoed throughout the large elevator.

Caine pinched the bridge of his nose, letting out a sigh of disgust as he muttered, "Fucking pathetic."

"Bring us to the ground floor.....now," Christofer said, keeping his gaze locked with Ephraim's as he gave Chris' dislocated arm a slight pull, earning a pained groan from Chris as his son finally went still in the Pyte's arms.

Ephraim ground his jaw firmly shut as he looked from the pissed off Pyte holding his son hostage to his son, who looked absolutely furious and a touch embarrassed at having been taken so easily. It had happened so fast that he hadn't had time to react. The funny thing about it was, they'd all expected an attack and had been ready for it, but Christofer had taken them all by surprise.

Before the elevator doors opened, Ephraim heard the other Pyte approaching the elevator at the same time as Caine. Without a word, they'd signaled to Chris to expect an attack. They'd shifted to the sides of the elevator, drew their weapons and-

Blinked in surprise to find the Pyte standing in the far corner with Chris pulled in front of him like a shield, a hand wrapped around his son's throat and the other twisting Chris' hand behind his back. No one seemed more surprised than Chris. It was a move that Chris normally would have seen coming a mile away, one he could easily avoid, but he hadn't seen it coming.

None of them had.

Christofer had moved faster than a Pyte should have been able to, his brute strength alone was amazing. It made him wonder what would happen if Christofer learned how to control that strength. It also made him wonder how Christofer had learned to harness the strength and speed that Ephraim could only touch when he'd slipped into bloodlust. He wanted to learn that kind of control for himself and judging by the calculating expression on Caine's face, he wasn't the only one.

But first, he needed to get this situation back under control. His gaze shifted to the woman standing by Christofer's side and for a brief moment he considered grabbing her to ensure his son's safety, but he knew that would only make things worse. Right now Christofer was in control, but if either one of them laid so much as a finger on the Pyte's mate, that control would snap and Chris would pay the price.

"We came to get you," he said, moving his attention back to the Pyte as he slowly reached over and flicked open the elevator button and scanned his fingerprint.

"You're about five days late for that," Cloe said, shifting her attention from him to Caine and then back again.

"And I apologize for that, but the situation was out of my control," he explained calmly as he pressed the button for the ground floor, cursing the Sentinel leader and his fucked up plans to hell and back again. "I'd like a chance to explain things to you before-"

"You had your chance," Christofer said, his hold around Chris' throat tightening just enough to keep him from doing anything stupid.

"You can't leave," Chris bit out, wincing when the Pyte's hold around his neck tightened even more.

"Watch me," Christofer said, the threat softly spoken, but it was enough to send Ephraim's heart racing, because he knew that this Pyte had been pushed too far.

It also let him know that the time for diplomacy and finesse was long gone. If he was going to get his son out of this safely and keep this Pyte couple out of the hands out of a Master, and the girl from the horrible fate that awaited her, he was going to have to be blunt.

"The moment that she steps out of this compound, every shifter within a hundred mile radius will be after her."

"What did you just say?" Christofer asked after a slight pause as the force of Ephraim's words nearly knocked him on his ass.

"They won't have a choice," Chris bit out.

"Bullshit," he said, praying that Ephraim was lying his ass off to manipulate them into doing what he wanted.

"She's marked," Ephraim explained in a hard tone. "You've not only fed from her without permission, but you've changed her and claimed her."

"You've stolen a shifter's property," Caine added as he sent Cloe a pitying look.

"What the hell are you talking about?" Cloe demanded, shifting the tension in the elevator as every man noticeably went still, even the man he held by the throat.

Two pairs of red eyes suddenly locked on him as Ephraim demanded, "Why the hell didn't you tell her?"

He shoved the Sentinel away so that he could get in the other Pyte's face. "That was your job," he snarled.

"Someone want to fill me in?" Cloe demanded, but his focus was locked on Ephraim.

"She's your mate!" Ephraim snapped, shoving him back.

"Ah, no I'm not," Cloe said with a snort of annoyance that he chose to ignore, mostly because this wasn't the time or place to explain that she did in fact belong to him. Besides, she'd eventually realize it on her own.

"We came here for the information that *you* promised," Christofer said, shoving Ephraim back and getting back in his face. "You're the one that fucked up when you didn't give us the answers that you promised us."

Ephraim shoved him back, getting right in his face. "We didn't have a fucking choice. As soon as we left you so that you could calm your mate down, our access to your floor was taken away. For the last week we've been stuck here, dealing with bullshit and trying to get our access reinstated so that we could keep our word to *you*."

Breathing hard, Christofer held the other man's murderous glare as he reached over and took Cloe's trembling hand into his. "You have an hour to explain what's going on and then we're leaving."

"One hour," Ephraim agreed with a firm nod.

"Fucking bastard," Chris muttered as he turned around and slammed his shoulder into the elevator wall in an attempt to put the bone back in its socket.

Caine sighed heavily as he reached out, grabbed Chris by the shoulder with one hand while he placed the other against his back. With a slight push, he had the bone shoved back in place with a sickening *pop* that had Chris grunting in pain.

"Thanks a lot, you fucking-*oh, shit!*" Chris snapped as he slammed back against the elevator wall, reached out, grabbed Caine by the arm and yanked the large Pyte in front of him.

Caine opened his mouth, then shut it as his eyes went wide and he noticeably swallowed, making Christofer frown as he muttered, "Oh, shit."

It wasn't until Ephraim muttered an, "Oh, fucking hell," and stepped back to block Chris from view that he realized something rather important.

Cloe's hand wasn't trembling because she was upset.

She was trembling because she had slipped into bloodlust....

While they were stuck in an elevator.........

Yeah, this wasn't going to end well, he thought dryly as he dropped her hand and rubbed his hands roughly down his face.

A small, vicious growl to his right had him reaching out and grabbing Cloe as she moved to attack the two men guarding Chris. There was no doubt in his mind that she was after Chris. The normally overly sweet scent that the Sentinel gave off was saturating the air of the enclosed space. He'd found the aroma a little distracting, but nothing that he couldn't ignore.

Cloe on the other hand.......

Had been turned only a week ago, hadn't learned self-control, was apparently seriously pissed and had slipped into what the other men had dubbed, "blood-lust." The scent of Chris' blood would be too much for her to ignore, especially right now.

"Mein Schatz," he said, turning around as he grabbed her by the shoulders and pushed her into the corner away from the trio behind him.

One look at her beautiful red eyes and he knew that there was no point in trying to talk any sense into her. Cloe wasn't in charge right now, which meant that there was nothing that he could say or do that would convince her that tearing Chris' throat open was a bad idea. Not that he really gave a fuck if the little bastard got his throat ripped open, especially since no one had given a damn that they'd risked her throat being ripped open when they'd locked her up with him.

He should let her do it, but he knew that she would hate herself later when she realized what she'd done. As tough as Cloe came off, he really didn't think that she was the type of person that could shrug off killing someone even if it had been out of her control. The other reason that he was stopping her from crossing that line was currently pulling his weapon free from its holster and cocking the weapon.

There was no question that she'd survive a gunshot wound, but the idea of her getting hurt was enough to make his stomach drop. He wouldn't allow anyone to hurt her, but if she got past him he might not have a choice. Ephraim would protect his son, Cloe would be hurt and that was all it would take to make him lose control of the monster inside him, something that he hadn't worried about since his days in the lab.

Not until she came into his life.

She drove him out of his fucking mind and made it difficult to think straight. Sometimes he didn't know whether he wanted to throttle her or kiss her. Definitely kiss her, he thought dazedly as he stared down at that beautiful mouth that had felt so good on his-

"Shit!" he snapped as that beautiful mouth struck, obviously deciding that if she couldn't have the Sentinel's blood, that his would do.

She latched onto his neck with a vicious bite, tearing into his throat and greedily swallowing his blood as it filled her mouth. He bit back a grunt of pain as she dug her fangs deeper into his throat.

"Get her off him!" Ephraim snapped, grabbing hold of his arm.

"No!" Christofer snarled, shaking off his hold, careful not to dislodge her bite. "It's the only way to snap her out of it," he added, gritting his teeth as he was forced to slap his hands against the wall above her and brace himself to endure her attack.

"If you don't stop her, you'll slip into bloodlust next," Ephraim warned.

He shifted his gaze from the elevator wall to the lit screen above the double doors, watching the countdown as the elevator made its slow descent to the ground floor. His hands balled into fists as he slowly exhaled, ignoring the black spots dancing along his sight and stood there, giving his woman what she needed. When he felt her mouth gentle against his neck and her arms wrap around his shoulders as she pressed up against him, he closed his eyes and released a heavy sigh, relieved that her loss of control was short lived.

"C-Christofer?" she murmured, her voice shaky as she pressed her forehead against his chest, her hands fisted in his shirt. "What just happened?'

"Shhh," he said, forcing his eyes open only to shut them again as the move made his head spin. He'd lost too much blood over the course of the day to have any hopes of fighting this. "Everything is fine," he said, his voice sounding hollow and far away as he pressed an unsteady kiss to the top of Cloe's head.

"Christofer-" Cloe started to speak, but he didn't have the luxury of comforting her right now.

"Take her," he said, dropping his hands to her shoulders and using the last of his energy to gently shove her towards the elevator doors just as they opened with a chime.

"What the hell is going on?" Cloe demanded as he forced his eyes open just as his legs gave out and he dropped to the ground.

"Get her the hell out of here," he tried to shout, but his words came out as a slurred whisper.

"Let me go!" Cloe screamed as he was forced to sit there while Chris shoved past his father who stood in front of him, stopping Cloe from going to him. Without a word, he grabbed Cloe and threw her over his shoulder and dragged her off the elevator with Caine right behind him.

Ephraim stared down at him for a moment longer before he nodded, turned around and walked off the elevator, pressing the "Close Doors" button on his way out.

Before the doors closed tightly shut behind Ephraim, everything went black as he felt himself falling, the sounds of Cloe's screams rushing him towards oblivion.

FORTY

"Get your hands off me!"

"Hold her back!" Ephraim shouted as he withdrew his weapon and took aim at the closed elevator doors.

"Let me go!" she snapped, pulling against Danni's hold as another roar shook the lobby.

"You're giving off the scent of fear," Danni explained calmly as she yanked Cloe back behind the men lined up with their weapons aimed at the quaking double doors of the elevator where Christofer was going crazy from the sounds of it. "It's making him nuts."

"Then let go of me," she snapped, struggling to get free and to…..to……

Oh hell, she didn't know what she was going to do if she managed to get free. She just felt like she needed to do something to fix this. It was her fault that poor Christofer had lost control.

She still didn't know how it happened. One minute she'd been trying to ignore the overwhelming sweet scent of Chris' blood, seriously pissed off to discover that she'd been kept in the dark about something that affected her, and the next she'd felt like she was drowning. She couldn't seem to think straight. Everything had been fuzzy and muddled. She'd been aware of what was going on, to a point, but helpless to do anything about it.

It was similar to the moment just before you pass out. Everything starts to get hazy, you feel your self-control start to slip and no matter how hard you try to fight it, you can't. It takes you over, knocks you on your ass and leaves you helpless. It was something that she never wanted to experience again. She also knew that if it weren't for Christofer, she would still be trapped in that hazy mess, helpless to stop herself from doing something that she'd regret.

"Get her out of here," Chris yelled over his shoulder.

"They're not really going to shoot him, are they?" she asked numbly, swallowing nervously as she watched the men and women forming a line.

"It won't kill him," Danni explained, pausing to watch as Caine moved over to the elevator doors and placed his hand over the small key that would unlock the elevator doors and allow them to open.

"Why can't they leave him in there until he passes out or the bloodlust passes?" she asked, desperate to find another way to handle this. She didn't want him shot or hurt in any way.

"Because there's no guarantee that he won't find a way out of there and if he does......," Danni started to explain as she was once again pulling her towards a set of double doors only to let her words trail off meaningfully.

Not that Cloe needed her to explain. She didn't. She'd been on the receiving end of the last time Christofer went into bloodlust and really didn't need a refresher course on the subject. She wouldn't wish that on anyone, but it still didn't make her feel right about this.

"Isn't there anything that we can do?" she asked, running what little information she knew about their kind through her head, trying to figure out a way to knock Christofer out of this without having to shoot him or risk anyone else getting hurt.

"Blood and time," Danni answered absently as she suddenly shoved Cloe behind her and pulled out her gun.

"Okay, so why don't we try that?" she suggested, sighing in relief. "We could drop a cooler full of bagged blood through the opening in the elevator and-"

"Not going to work," Danni said, using her body to push Cloe back against the wall.

"Why not?" she asked as the first tendrils of panic shot through her as her body registered the fact that someone had her cornered. Apparently she still had a problem with space, she thought numbly as her heart pounded against her chest and her breaths came out choppy.

She didn't have a problem when Christofer invaded her space, but for everyone else? Yeah, it was definitely a problem, she thought as her vision went red.

"Oh…….shit," Danni groaned, sniffing the air and shooting her a look over her shoulder before her attention shot back to the elevator.

"What?" she demanded, hyperventilating just a tad bit as she tried desperately to step away, but her trembling legs wouldn't work for her.

"You're giving off a shit load of fear," Danni said in an accusing tone.

"If that's a problem for you then get the hell out of my space!" she snapped defensively, barely noticing when Danni stepped away from her.

"Yeah," Danni said, cocking her gun. "I don't think that's going to be a problem."

"What are you........oh, shit......."

"You could say that again," Danni said, just as the elevator doors exploded.

"No," Cloe said, shaking her head as she moved away from the other woman, "I think I'll just run instead."

"That's probably for the best," Danni agreed as reached behind her, pressed her thumb to a scanner, opened one of the double doors, grabbed Cloe by the arm and shoved her into what turned out to be a very long hallway.

—

"Oh shit, oh shit, oh shit, oh shit," Cloe mumbled incoherently to herself as she blindly grabbed hold of another doorknob, tried to turn it only to be met with resistance. "Shit!" she groaned, dropping her hand away from the door and returning to her mad dash down the long hallway while the sounds of gunshots, fighting and screams of pain echoed throughout the long hallway, letting her know that the battle was still on.

Somehow she resisted the urge to look over her shoulder to see if the double doors were still standing, knowing instinctively that if she did that, it would be all over. So instead, she continued running down the long hallway, blindly testing doors every ten feet and wondering when her newfound abilities would kick in. Because right now as she ran down the hallway, telling herself that this didn't make her a coward, she couldn't help but feel that the ability to move her ass like the Road Runner would really come in handy at a moment like this.

"MINE!" came the monstrous roar just as she moved to test another door.

Deciding that perhaps putting a little more space between her and the blood thirsty bastard behind her was in order, she quickly changed plans from hiding under a bed to finding a stairway. Reasoning that there had to be a set of stairs at the end of the hall, she moved her ass and released a high-pitched scream, that she was going to pretend never happened, just as double doors burst open behind her.

"Oh, the hell with this," she groaned, knowing that she didn't have a chance in hell of outrunning him down a clear path. So, she went back to plan A and grabbed the handle of the next door that she came across.

Hands shaking violently to match her nerves, she grabbed hold of the doorknob of a gray door, not caring where it led and twisted it as hard as she could and kept going until it fell off with a loud *snap* and the door swung open just as another roar sounded behind her. Swallowing hard, she risked one look over her shoulder and wished that she hadn't.

There he was, covered in blood and looking every ounce the monster that she'd originally thought him to be. He wasn't running after her, she realized, which should have given her a little comfort, but instead it only scared the shit out of her even more. The way those red eyes locked on her as he moved at a predatory gait as he stalked her said it all.

Sooner or later he would have her.

It was only a matter of time.

———

"*Any casualties?*" she heard Ephraim ask as she stood there, frozen in fear as she watched Christofer make his way to her, his intent clear.

"*No,*" Chris groaned, "*we just got our asses handed to us.*"

It was then that she realized that she could hear the sounds and conversations from the lobby and nearly sagged with relief. She opened her mouth to ask for help, but Chris' next words stopped her.

"*We can't leave her to handle him,*" he said, sounding like he was in a great deal of pain. "*He'll tear her apart.*"

"*I wasn't planning on it,*" Ephraim said, sounding winded. "*But you're not going. Keep your ass here.*"

"*I'm fine,*" she heard Chris grit out.

"*You won't survive another round with him.*"

"*I said I'm fine!*"

"*You can barely walk, asshole,*" Caine snapped.

"*We need to seal the corridor off and I'm not doing it with her still in there!*" Chris shouted, sounding truly worried for her. In that instant he'd earned her forgiveness and respect. She also knew that she couldn't risk any of them coming to her rescue.

Closing her eyes in resignation. "I've got this. Don't worry, guys. Just....just have some extra blood ready afterwards," she said, knowing that she was going to need it.

She didn't wait around to make sure that they'd heard her since she needed to move her ass and quickly. So, she opened her eyes, turned around and swore as she found herself facing another long hallway. The only difference between this hallway and the one that she was escaping was the scent of chlorine and the sharp white tiles that lined the walls and floor.

An idea came to her, one that she prayed would work. It was something that she remembered from her early days in the Girl Scouts. Even though she knew that it probably wouldn't help, she slammed the door shut behind her, hoping the scent of chlorine would confuse him. She ran down the corridor, ignoring the doors that didn't look promising and followed the heavy scent of chlorine and the sounds of what she hoped was a filter.

"MINE!"

"Oh, shit!" she squeaked, wondering how she'd got herself into this.

Oh, that's right, she'd gone psycho on him first and payback was a bitch.

"*Shit, shit, shit, shit, shit, shit!*" she said, risking a look back and finding the hallway behind her still empty.

Another idea came to her, one that she hoped would confuse him and give her a chance to test out one of the new skills that Christofer promised that she could do now. She wasn't a hundred percent sure that she would be able to pull it off or that it would work, but she was definitely willing to try it if it meant saving her throat from another shredding.

With that in mind, she grabbed the next doorknob that she came across, twisted the knob until it broke off, shoved the door open, tore her shirt off and threw it inside and ran. A few seconds later she was doing the same thing with one of her shoes and kept doing it until she found herself in just her panties and in front of a double door that clearly led to the pool.

She yanked the door open, praying that the pool was empty and ran inside. When she spotted the large Olympic size pool, she spared a second to make sure that she was alone. A few seconds later she was running straight for the pool and diving in, praying that her old Troop leader was right about water hiding scents otherwise she was going to be sending the old bitch a strongly worded letter after this.

FORTY-ONE

"Lying bastard," she sputtered as she came to the surface and grabbed blindly for the edge of the pool.

When Christofer had explained that she didn't really need to breathe, he'd forgotten to mention that she could still drown. That tidbit of information would have come in handy, especially before she'd tried to hide from him at the bottom of an Olympic sized pool. If she'd known just how painful it was to hold your breath for, she looked at her watch, five minutes, she would have come up with a plan B. Now she needed to-

Scream her head off as she was suddenly grabbed by the arms and abruptly pulled out of the pool.

"Quiet," the glaring bastard that she didn't like said softly as he set her on her unsteady feet and shoved her behind him.

"What are you doing here?" she demanded, hastily crossing her arms over her bare breasts as she risked a peek past him and immediately wished that she hadn't. "Oh, shit," she muttered, locking eyes with Christofer, who stood directly across from them on the other side of the pool. He watched them through glowing red eyes that looked a hell of a lot more intense than they had when he'd made love to her earlier.

"Collecting another fee," Kale said, shoving her back with his body as he took a step back from the edge of the pool and drew his weapon out of its holster.

"Another fee?" she asked, frowning as she took another step back all while keeping her eyes locked on Christofer, terrified that if she looked away from him even for a second that she'd find herself pinned beneath him with her throat ripped out again.

"A mover's fee," Kale said, shoving her back again.

"A mover's fee?"

"Are you going to repeat everything I say?" Kale snapped, shoving her back again.

"Probably," she murmured absently as she watched in utter amazement as Christofer took a step forward and-

Didn't fall in the pool like she'd expected.

"Pytes can walk on water?" she murmured, watching as Christofer walked towards them.

"No," Kale croaked, sounding just as surprised as she was. "And he sure as hell shouldn't be able to do it while in bloodlust."

"*Mine*," Christofer growled, the sound low and sexy and instantly making her think of a hundred naughty things that she wouldn't mind doing with him as he whispered all the dirty things that he'd like to do to her while using that voice.

"Or talk," Kale added while she was busy letting her mind wander off a bit.

Now was not the time to be thinking of him bending her over, ripping her panties off with his teeth and sinking that wickedly talented tongue in-

A vicious growl and a muttered curse broke through her rather inappropriate thoughts. She bit her bottom lip as she watched Christofer's beautiful red eyes take in every single inch of her as he hungrily licked his lips. Her body shivered in response, which earned another muttered curse from Kale as the bastard, who seemed to be in love with glaring, shot a glare over his shoulder.

"Are you fucking kidding me?" he demanded, shaking his head in disgust.

Ignoring the heat spreading up her neck and pretending that the realization that they could scent her arousal didn't make her want to die of mortification, she glared right back at him. "Don't you have a job to do?" she reminded him, hoping that it was enough to distract him.

Still shaking his head in disgust, he returned his attention to the man now standing less than ten feet away from them. "Just as soon as he steps onto the tile."

"What happens when he steps on the tile?" she asked distractedly, her attention focused on the man watching her every move.

God, he was so damn sexy......

And he smelled incredible. Her vision went red as she licked her lips, running her eyes over his body and pausing at all the good spots. What was it about his scent that made her desperate to get him inside her? She should still be freaking out and trying to get away from him before he could attack her instead of standing here fantasizing about dropping to her knees and-

"I'm going to shoot him," Kale announced, quickly killing the mood and drawing her attention to the bastard now aiming his weapon at Christofer's chest.

"What the hell are you talking about?" she asked, licking her suddenly dry lips, sure that she'd misheard him.

"The Compound leader is no longer interested in keeping him," Kale said evenly, forcing her to step back once again.

"Is that why they kept us locked up?" she asked, hoping to distract him long enough so that she could figure out a way to get Christofer out of this without the glaring bastard putting a bullet between his eyes.

"That would be my guess," Kale said, stepping back again, his focus locked on the Pyte standing less than three feet from the edge of the pool, watching their every move.

"And now?" she asked, risking a quick glance over her shoulder to see that there was still a good ten feet between them and the tiled wall behind them.

"And now they're not happy," Kale said as he once again stepped back, forcing her to go with him.

She glanced back quickly and nearly sighed with relief when she saw that Christofer hadn't moved any closer. They still had time, not much, but she was hoping that it was enough.

"So, now what?" she asked, sending Christofer an imploring look to keep his ass right where it was. If he understood, it didn't show.

"So now I need to transfer you to a Compound that can handle you and take the asshole here to the Williams' mansion where the pain in the ass that's mated to my Izzy can train him," Kale explained, taking her by surprise not only because he usually ignored her questions and settled for glaring at her, but because he actually bothered to tell her his plans, which meant.......

She swallowed nervously. "You're planning on shooting me afterwards, aren't you?" she asked, this time stepping back on her own.

"Smart girl," Kale said, nodding approvingly as he took another step back.

"Why not keep us together?" she asked, her mouth going dry at the thought of being shot.

It didn't matter that they'd promised her that she couldn't die, she still didn't want to get shot. She also didn't want to be separated from Christofer and right now, she was terrified that the thought of being taken away from him scared her more than being shot.

"You're not going anywhere near my godchildren," he said, forcing her back another foot. "Come on, asshole, take the bait," he snapped in aggravation when Christofer still didn't move.

"I would never hurt a child," she said hollowly, truly offended that he thought that she was capable of harming a child.

Kale snorted in disgust. "Don't take it personally, cupcake."

"How the hell else am I supposed to take it?" she snapped, moving to step away from him, but he simply reached back, grabbed her by the arm and forced her to stay right where she was.

"You're marked," he said as if that would explain everything.

It didn't.

"And?"

"You're another shifter's property."

"I'm really not," she said with a snort of disgust as she yanked her arm free from his hold.

"You really are," he said dryly, shooting her a warning glare over his shoulder to keep her ass right where it was. For now she planned on doing just that, but there was no way that she was going to stand there and allow him to shoot Christofer, not when he wasn't even-

"Wait a minute," she said, frowning as she looked at Christofer, really looked at him. "He's not out of control."

"No," Kale said, forcing her back another step, "he's not."

"So, he's not in bloodlust?" she asked, her relief obvious. If he wasn't out of control, then-

"He's learned to stay in control even while in bloodlust," Kale said, sounding pissed when she would have thought that would make him happy. It certainly made her happy since he wasn't acting like a feral animal going for her throat.

"So, he's not going to attack anyone," she pointed out, relieved that this was over. All she wanted to do was to go to him. She wanted to wrap her arms around him and make him promise that he wasn't going to let anyone separate them. When she moved to do just that, she found herself once again being shoved back.

"Oh, I wouldn't say that, sweetheart," Kale said, nodding towards Christofer, who was practically eating her up with his eyes. The expression on his face had her swallowing nervously as she took an unsteady step back.

"He still hasn't done anything to deserve being shot," she mumbled, tightening her arms around herself as she started to shiver, from the cold or the way that Christofer was watching her, she wasn't exactly sure.

"Tell that to the shitload of Sentinels that he tore through to get to you."

"They locked us up!" she snapped, deciding not to mention her attack since it was one of those things that was better off left unsaid.

"True," he agreed, not sounding like he really cared.

"Look," she said, licking her lips nervously as she hesitantly took a step to the side and when he didn't move to stop her, she took another one until she was standing several feet away from him, her arms still wrapped tightly around her chest, "he didn't mean to hurt anyone. It was an accident. Let me try calming him down and we'll go-"

"You're not going anywhere," Kale said, pulling a second weapon free and aiming it at her before she could blink. Suddenly, she realized why he hadn't tried to stop her.

"You're really going to shoot me?" she asked, her voice cracking as she took another step back.

"In a heartbeat," he said without hesitation as Christofer released a vicious growl that actually comforted her instead of scaring the living hell out of her for once.

"Then what's the hold up?" she asked, scanning the large room, looking for a weapon or a way to get her and Christofer out of this.

"Him first," he said coldly as he watched Christofer, obviously waiting for him to do something.

"If you were really going to shoot him, you would have done it by now," she lamely pointed out, hoping that he wouldn't take it as a challenge and pull the damn trigger.

Kale shook his head. "I'm not in the mood to retrieve the body from the bottom of the pool."

"I see,......" she said in understanding, shifting as a plan quickly formed. It wasn't a perfect plan, but it would save them from-

"I'm glad that you do," Kale murmured, shifting his attention from Christofer to her as the sound of a gunshot suddenly rang out, echoing in the large room. A scream of agony tore through her lips as she felt something explode in her chest, burst through bone, shredding it upon impact and slice through her heart and muscle until it finally burst through more bone.

By the time she realized that she'd been shot, she found herself floating in a sea of pain, wrapped in darkness, the sounds of a violent roar the only comfort she had as she felt herself sink deeper into nothing.

FORTY-TWO

"You.....fucking.......asshole...," Chris choked out while he took in the scene before him as he hugged an obviously broken arm against his chest.

"Grab my bag," Kale said, nodding towards the bleachers as he quickly moved over to Cloe's body and rolled her onto her stomach.

"Who the fuck do you think you are?" Ephraim demanded coldly, coming to a stop next to his son, who was still standing there and being fucking useless.

"Get my bag or get the fuck out," he said, wiping the sweat off his brow with the back of his arm as he took in the damage from the bullet and cursed.

It was already starting to heal.

"Get away from her, you sick fuck!" Chris said, dropping unsteadily to his knees in front of him just as he was grabbed from behind and yanked back.

"I should tear your fucking throat out!" Caine shouted, grabbing him by the throat and pulling him to his feet so that he found himself staring into glimmering red eyes.

He didn't have fucking time for these games.

Sighing in annoyance, he allowed his eyes to shift, felt his fangs slide through his gums and with barely a thought, denied his body the shift that it so desperately craved, careful to retain his hold on his body. As soon as he felt the rush of energy flow through him, he reached up with one hand and laid it over Caine's hand at his throat. Before the Pyte could react, he pulled the hand at his throat away with a slight twist as he slammed the flat of his palm into the Pyte's chest and shoved him away with a loud *crack*.

"Fucking hell!" Caine gasped, pressing a hand to his chest as he stumbled back

He sent Caine a glare of warning, the only one that he would get if he tried to come between him and his work again. He might have taken it easy on the Pyte in the past, but not now, not when he had a job to do.

"Why the hell did you do this?" Ephraim demanded, looking from Cloe's blood soaked body to Christofer's and shaking his head in disgust like Kale really cared if he was pissed or not.

"Make yourself useful and feed the male. We're going to need him," was all he said as he made his way over to where he'd stashed his bag.

"You really are an asshole, aren't you?" Danni asked tightly as she took in the scene.

Since he'd never denied it and he really didn't give a fuck if another Pyte was pissed at him, he ignored her and made his way back to Cloe. The bullet wound was still healing, which meant that he had some time to get this job done.

"What are you doing?" Chris asked, watching as he pulled a large bottle of water out of his bag and poured it over Cloe's back so that he could see what he had to work with.

"Fucking hell," he said hollowly, seeing the extent of her marking.

Whoever had marked her was a fucking sick bastard. While most Shifters settled for a single swipe of their claws down their human's back to mark their property, this sick prick had sliced up every inch of her back. The message was clear, the shifter that had marked her wanted to make sure that everyone knew that she was someone's bitch.

This Pyte had seriously fucked up by touching her. Any hope that the shifter had forgotten about her over the years evaporated when he saw the extent of her mark. You didn't mark a human like this unless you had plans for her. He had no idea who'd marked her, but he knew one thing.

He was going to tear the sick fuck's throat out for this.

"I'm not going to be able to destroy the mark like this," he muttered to himself as he ran his fingers over the scars slashed all over her back and the large angry pink scar that ran across her side, confirming his fears for the woman.

The sick fuck definitely had long term plans for her, otherwise he wouldn't have bothered to rip Cloe's uterus out.

"You're removing the mark?" Chris asked, shooting him a questioning look that he would normally ignore, but since he actually needed the bastard's help, he decided to play along.

"Yes," he said, pouring more water over her back so that he could see the full extent of the damage that needed to be fixed.

"I didn't think that was possible," Ephraim said, getting up to grab a small stack of clean towels from one of the shelves lining the wall behind them.

"It's not," he said, shaking his head as he shot the male lying only a few feet away another glance. If this was going to work, he was going to need the big bastard. "We need him awake."

"Then maybe you shouldn't have shot him, asshole," Chris said with a snort of disgust as he released his hold on his broken arm and pulled his phone out of his pocket with a grimace of pain.

"He was in bloodlust and useless to me. I need him focused," he said, getting back to business.

"And you couldn't have waited until he snapped out of it?" Chris demanded as he sent a text message.

"No," he simply said as he mentally evaluated his choices. After a minute, he had to admit that they weren't very good.

"And why's that?" Caine asked, sounding pissed as he knelt by the prone male as he bit into his own wrist.

"Because," Kale said, reaching into his pack and pulling out the bottle of lighter fluid that he'd swiped from one of the weapons rooms, "word has spread about the theft and every shifter in the state is coming for her."

———

"About fucking time," was the warm welcome that Christofer received when he finally managed to crack open his eyes.

"What the hell happened?" he asked groggily as he reached up and attempted to the rub the sleep out of his eyes while he tried to make sense of the images racing through his mind. Most of the images were confusing, but between what he remembered in the elevator and the tenderness he felt in his chest, he knew that they'd been forced to put him down, again.

Shit!

He hoped like hell that Cloe hadn't seen any of it. He didn't like the idea of her having to see something like that, but he really hated the idea of her seeing him lose control. The last thing that she needed was to be reminded of what he really was and what he'd done to her. He wanted her to.......to......

To know why he could scent burnt human flesh.

Memories of his time in the lab tried to force their way in, but he ignored them, knowing that they wouldn't help as he opened his other senses and took in his surroundings. The scent of chlorine, blood, adrenaline, lighter fluid, smoke and the unforgettable odor of burning human flesh and the fact that he was in the back of a van registered.

As did the fact that another man had Cloe in his arms.

"Relax," Chris said calmly from where he sat across from him, but Christofer barely spared him a glance as he sat up and glared at the shifter who had absolutely no right to look at Cloe, never mind hold her.

"Slip into bloodlust while we're in this van and I'll blow your fucking head off," Kale threatened even as he shifted with Cloe in his arms and moved forward so that he could abruptly deposit her in Christofer's arms.

He caught her and hugged her tightly against him as he looked her over. She was pale, her beautiful brown hair was a tangled wet mess, she was wrapped in a damp white sheet and the scent of chlorine, lighter fluid and burnt flesh poured off her.

"What happened?" he demanded as he struggled not to lose control, but it was damn near impossible with Cloe lying limply in his arms like this.

"Why don't you tell us?" Caine suggested, drawing his attention to the man sitting by the doors with Danni sitting between his legs, a bag of blood pressed against her mouth, looking pale and exhausted.

A terrifying thought occurred to him as he took in the rest of the van's occupants. He took in the blisters and burns on Kale's neck and hands, the blood soaked bandages wrapped around his arms and the charred remains of his clothes before shifting his attention to Chris who sat beside him, holding a splinted arm against his chest and finally down at the woman in his arms. He swallowed back bile as he asked, "Did I hurt her?"

"Not from a lack of trying, but you did manage to tear through about six dozen Sentinels, demons and shifters if it makes you feel any better," Chris mused, shifting with a cringe as the move jostled his arm.

"Did I kill anyone?" he asked, not really caring, not after they'd locked Cloe up with him without making sure that they had enough blood so that he could keep her safe.

"No," Chris answered, his tone curious.

"And we'd love to know how you managed that," Caine said, regarding him with interest.

"What happened to her?" he asked, not giving a damn about anything else but how she ended up like this.

A heavy pause followed, drawing his attention away from the woman lying helplessly in his arms to the shifter glaring defiantly at him while Chris, Caine and Danni all looked torn between disgust and pity. Without a single word it told him everything that he needed to know.

The shifter needed to die.

"What did you do to her?" he demanded, welcoming the burn as his eyes shifted and his fangs descended.

"This shit can wait until we get home!" Ephraim pointed out firmly from the front of the van, no doubt hoping that he'd let it go for now.

"What needed to be done," Kale said evenly, meeting his red-eyed glare with a silver-eyed glare of his own.

"Don't start that shit in here. You'll hurt her," Chris warned, closing his eyes and letting his head drop back, looking exhausted.

"And what exactly needed to be done?" he demanded.

"He removed the mark," Danni explained as she removed the bag of blood from her lips and handed the half empty bag to her mate with a reluctant shake of her head that had her mate's expression shutting down, but not before Christofer caught the flash of fear in the man's eyes.

"And how exactly did he do that?" he drawled, shifting his attention back to the shifter who was starting to look bored with the conversation.

"By setting her on fire," Kale admitted with a shrug that had the other three occupants of the van cursing before he added, "But don't worry, I shot her in the heart first," with a wink that had Christofer carefully placing Cloe on the floor.

"I see," he said, the last coherent words that would leave his mouth for an hour as it turned out.

FORTY-THREE

"You don't want to do this," Danni said, licking her lips nervously as she shot another glance down at her unconscious mate.

Instead of arguing with her, he gestured with the handcuffs in his hand for her to sit back down next to her mate. "I've never hurt a woman and I have no plans to start now," he patiently explained as he waited for her to comply.

"I'm going to tear your fucking head off for this!" the shifter that he'd allowed to live for the moment, growled as he once again yanked at his handcuffs.

Since Christofer knew just how much it would piss the shifter off, he ignored him as he knelt in front of Danni, who looked paler, and handcuffed her right hand to her mate's. He knew that he was probably going to regret it later, but he left her other hand free.

"We're trying to help you," Ephraim said, trying to raise his head, but the effort proved to be too much so he just laid there on a bed of pine needles and groaned.

"Yeah, it feels it," he said dryly, shooting Cloe a quick glance to make sure that she was still curled up safely a few feet away from what was left of the van.

"We fucked up. I'll give you that, but we really are trying to help you," Chris said, releasing a groan of his own as he tried to sit up, but just like his father, he gave up after the first try and settled for falling back on the ground next to his father.

"We don't need your kind of help," Christofer said, stepping back to admire his work.

"You need our help more than you know," Ephraim explained as he tried to roll over onto his side, but since Christofer had cuffed his arms and legs to the men lying helplessly on either side of him, the move proved impossible.

"And why is that?" he absently asked as he walked back to the van lying in a tangled mess on its side and reached in and grabbed one of the coolers that had survived the crash.

He walked back over to the ragtag group of misfits sprawled out on the forest floor in various stages of unconsciousness and placed the cooler down. He grabbed two bags of blood before he sat down on top of the cooler, deciding that it was probably for the best if he overfed before he tried to hike out of here with Cloe in his arms.

"You have no idea what you're up against," Danni said, looking pained as she closed her eyes and dropped her head back against the tree.

"Why don't you explain it to me?" he suggested, glancing down at the bagged blood in his hand with a frown. He was definitely going to regret this later, he told himself as he tossed one of the bags to her.

She didn't even open her eyes as she said, "I can't drink that."

"Why not?" he asked, wondering if the female Pytes had some sort of defect or disorder that he was going to have to watch out for in Cloe.

"I can't consume human blood anymore," she said, shifting slightly as she gestured lazily towards her mate. "I need his blood along with demon blood."

"Then I suggest you feed him," he said, his upbringing too well ingrained in him to ignore. His father believed that it was a man's responsibility to take care of the women and children in his care and he'd made damn sure that Christofer believed that as well.

Danni's eyes flicked open and after a slight hesitation, she reached for the bagged blood with a trembling hand and a murmured, "Thank you."

"Do all females have this problem?" he asked, standing up so that he could grab another bag and toss it to her.

"No," Ephraim said with obvious difficulty as he sat up, forcing a whimpering Chris to sit up as well so that he could reach over Caine's prone body and pick up the other bag of blood.

Before Christofer could tell the asshole to give the blood back to Danni, Ephraim dropped the bag on Caine's chest and moved to tilt Caine's head back and force his mouth open while Danni bit into the first bag and then carefully positioned the bag at her mate's mouth. The move surprised him, as did the fact that this group of misfits genuinely cared about each other. He'd never really belonged anywhere, he thought with just enough self-pity to make him shake his head with disgust as he stuck the bag in his hand to his teeth.

"Danni was turned when she was dying of cancer. Caine didn't know about the cancer, not that it would have made a difference since he didn't have enough blood on hand to kill the cancer," Chris explained for his father as he shifted, careful of his broken arm and leaned back against the tree that Kale was currently attached to. The shifter's murderous gaze was focused solely on him, so of course he had to make a big show of enjoying the last sip of blood.

"Tear. Your. Fucking. Head. Off," Kale bit out, emphasizing every word with a vicious growl.

"Good luck with that," Christofer said with a chuckle, already knowing that he'd come back from that particular injury without a problem.

"You'll be putting her at risk if you try to do this on your own," Ephraim said, returning to that broken record that he just wasn't buying any more.

"The asshole removed her mark," he reminded them as he toyed with the second bag in his hands, wondering what bullshit they were going to spin for him now.

"Yes," Ephraim snapped angrily as he shifted his gaze to Kale, who was still glaring his way, "he did."

"Then she's all set," Christofer said, tossing the bag in the air as he looked over his shoulder at the deserted country road behind him, wondering just how long he had before someone showed up.

"The shifter that owned her will be looking for her, now more than ever since word has spread about a shifter's property being stolen by a Pyte," Chris explained.

"You never know, he might have lost interest over the years," Christofer said, knowing damn well that he would never lose interest in the woman that was currently pretending to be asleep.

"The shifter didn't lose interest," Kale said, his gaze shifting to Cloe. "He'll be coming for her sooner or later."

"I see," Christofer murmured absently as he studied the bag in his hands, wondering if it would be best to move Cloe up to Canada for a while until this blew over.

"No, you really don't," Kale explained coldly. "With or without that mark, the shifter that claimed her will find her. He will move heaven and hell to get to her and now that every fucking shifter, demon and vampire knows that a marked bitch was stolen, they'll be after her as well."

"Then I guess I should make sure that they don't find us," he said, having had more than enough of this bullshit.

———

"Are you," Cloe cleared her throat awkwardly as she struggled to free her hands from the blankets that he'd cocooned her in, "going to put me down anytime soon?" she asked, wrapping her arms around his shoulders with the hopes that it would help stop the jostling motion that was wreaking havoc on her stomach.

"No," Christofer said, not even bothering to spare her a glance as he jumped onto a boulder, causing her to suck in a surprised breath at the motion only to expel it with a stomach turning grunt a second later when he jumped down and continued running through the woods at a neck breaking speed.

"I'm perfectly capable of running," she pointed out, not mentioning that she could probably handle running a half mile before she was forced to take a break or pass out.

"No," he said firmly, forcing her to bite her tongue before she said something that she would regret later.

And right now she had plenty that she wanted to say and do, but she knew that if she opened her mouth right now that she would definitely regret it later. Maybe not in a day, a week, or month, or probably even in a year, but someday she would feel really bad about kicking the shit out of his balls.

Maybe.

"Can we take a break?" she asked, needing a moment to pull herself together so that she could digest what she'd learned.

"No," he said, not even sparing her a glance as he continued to run at full speed through the densely wooded forest, leaving her to cringe into herself and pull her legs in closer to her body out of fear that they would be snapped off at any second.

"Just for a minute," she suggested tightly between clenched teeth as her vision went red, from the breakneck speed or the fact that she'd just learned that the monster that had killed her family and attacked her, leaving her for dead, had marked her as his bitch.

Just the thought of that monster out there believing that he owned her made her sick to her stomach. It felt like she was relieving the horror of waking up in the hospital bed days later all over again when the social workers and doctors unloaded everything on her all at once. It was too much to take in and she just.....she just...

"Please put me down, Christofer," she said softly, her head spinning right along with her stomach.

"No," he said, somehow managing to pick up speed as he cut through a thick copse of trees.

She closed her eyes and exhaled slowly, so close to losing it, but fighting it every inch of the way with everything that she had. She'd cried enough tears because of the monster that had destroyed her life and she refused to shed one more tear because of him. She needed a minute, just one goddamn minute to pull herself together.

"*Please*," she said, putting everything that she had into that one word.

"I need to get you somewhere safe," he said harshly, but he did slow down.

"And how exactly are you planning on keeping me safe?" she asked, feeling hopeless and once again wishing that she could take her medication just so that she could stop feeling this terror and absolute dread that was slowly taking over and leaving her feeling helpless, a feeling that she hated almost as much as the knowledge that she was about to relive the worst nightmare of her life.

She was apparently being hunted down by all the monsters that humans liked to pretend were made up by some Hollywood suit looking to make a buck and she had no idea how to stop them. She didn't know anything about this world except for the things that she'd picked up in horror movies over the years. How exactly was she supposed to fight off demons, shifters and vampires all hellbent on getting their hands on her?

It wasn't possible.

They were going to find her and do whatever they had to in order to kidnap her and then....

Then they would hand her over to the bastard that had killed her family. The part of her that had prayed for vengeance over the years and wished that a hundred different things had gone differently that day should be ecstatic that she was finally going to get the chance to pay the bastard back for everything that he'd done to her and her family, but instead she was terrified.

She was afraid of seeing that monster again, of hearing the growls, howls, grunts and the sound of her own flesh being torn apart. She was terrified of experiencing a single second of that kind of pain and terror again, but what scared her most of all, she realized, was being forced to listen as someone else that she cared about was torn apart while she was forced to watch.

She was terrified that they would hurt Christofer.

"Just put me down, Christofer," she whispered, and this time, he listened.

"What's wrong?" he asked, sounding concerned as he reluctantly, and carefully, placed her down on her bare feet.

"I'm not going anywhere with you," she said, shaking her head as if the move would give her strength as she stepped away from him.

Christofer sighed heavily as he reached for her, but she refused to let him touch her, because she knew that it would break her. She needed to do this not only for him, but for herself, because there was no doubt in her mind that watching those monsters hurt him would completely destroy her. She would rather go through that hell by herself for eternity than to see them harm one hair on his head, because....

Because she'd done the one thing that she'd promised herself that she would never do, she realized as she struggled to take her next breath.

She'd fallen in love with the bastard.

FORTY-FOUR

"We need to get going," he said, fighting for patience that he didn't have as he looked up and noted that the sun was setting.

They needed to move their asses and put as much space between them and the pissed off group that he'd left chained up as they could before morning. Sooner or later that ragtag group was going to get loose and when they did, they were going to call for reinforcement and weapons. He'd already taken them by surprise once and he doubted that he'd get a second chance.

This time when they came after them, he doubted they'd bother wasting their breath trying to convince them to agree to their bullshit plan. They'd probably just shoot them, chain them up and drag them off somewhere where they wouldn't have a chance in hell of escaping. He couldn't let that happen.

They had enough shit on their plates at the moment without having to worry about this group hellbent on "helping" them. He needed to get Cloe somewhere safe and fast. He needed to-

"Get out of here, Christofer," Cloe said, folding her arms over the blanket wrapped around her chest as she backed away from him and turned her back on him.

"That's what I'm trying to do," he pointed out as he reached for her only to have her dart out of his reach and leave him standing there, flexing his hands with the urge to grab her and spank her beautiful ass.

"No," she said, shaking her head and causing her tangled locks to sway with the movement, "I don't think you understand."

"Then make me understand," he said through gritted teeth, forcing himself to stand there when they should be moving their asses.

"I'm not going anywhere with you," she said, her spine rigid as she walked away from him. He watched as she stopped by a large oak tree and leaned against it, keeping her back to him as she picked up a leaf and played with it.

"Oh?" he said in a deceptively calm tone as he walked over to where she stood and leaned against the tree next to her. Grinding his jaw, he focused all his attention on the foliage that she apparently found fascinating. "And why is that?"

"It's time to move on," she said, sounding bored and a little irritated at having to explain this to him.

"From what exactly?" he asked, reaching down and grabbing a leaf of his own to toy with.

"From everything," she said with a heavy sigh.

He chuckled without humor as the real meaning of her words sank in. "You mean from me."

"Yes," she said after the slightest hesitation as though she was trying to spare his feelings. He appreciated the sentiment, he really did, but he knew that she was lying her beautiful ass off.

If her scent hadn't clued him in to what she was really up to, then the fact that he'd tried the same bullshit with Marta after their escape definitely did. When they'd reached England he'd tried to leave her at an orphanage, telling her that it was for the best. When that hadn't worked, he'd told her that he was sick of her and that he didn't want to be tied down with a little kid.

Marta had listened with her little arms folded over her chest. When he'd finished lying his ass off she'd nodded, picked up a stick that she'd found on the ground and proceeded to chase him around the dimly lit street cursing him out as she left welts on his arms, back and legs until he'd finally had enough. He'd promised never to try to leave her again, threw the stick away and gave her a swat on the bottom for hitting before he'd thrown her over his shoulder and carried her away from the orphanage.

"So, this is your way of telling me that you're not interested?" he asked, biting back a pleased smile, because he'd seen this little scenario play out a hundred different times in those corny made-for-TV movies that Marta used to make him watch. God, how he'd hated those damn movies, but Marta had always insisted on making him watch them with her. Most of them shared the same plot, the same one that Cloe was currently trying to feed him.

She wanted to push him away, probably for his own good and while he appreciated the concern, he wasn't going anywhere. Especially now that he knew that she cared for him.

"I don't do relationships, Christofer. I'm sorry if you thought this was leading somewhere," she said, absently staring off as her fingers continued to toy with the leaf in her hands.

"I see," he said, letting the pieces of leaf fall from his hand before he grabbed another leaf and began toying with it while he enjoyed himself.

"Good," she said, nodding slowly as she looked off.

Biting back a smile, he sighed heavily. "I understand."

"Good," she murmured after a slight hesitation and a nod. "That's good."

"Well," he said, absently scratching his chest as dropped the leaf and pushed away from the tree. "I guess that's it then," he said with a shrug as he walked away.

She absently nodded as his words registered and when they did...

"Wait, what?" she asked as he walked away. "What do you mean that's it?" she demanded, annoyed and more than a little confused that he could walk away so easily after everything that they'd gone through. She hadn't expected or wanted begging, but a word or two to try to convince her to reconsider would have been appreciated. Her anger had her walking after him.

With every step that she took over the rock and twig laden ground, her annoyance and confusion morphed into irritation and anger. While she'd been trying to send him away as gently as possible to keep him safe because she loved him, he'd taken her words as an excuse to ditch her ass.

"I appreciate you letting me down gently," he said with a shrug and a barely-there glance over his shoulder as he continued to walk away.

"Yeah, I can tell," she said dryly, wincing when a twig snapped beneath her foot and bit into her skin.

He pointed to his right. "If you're looking for the main road, you'll want to head that way."

"And where are you going?" she demanded, rushing to catch up with him, but just as soon as she did, his long strides quickly put space between them once again.

"Oh, I don't know," he mused as she struggled to catch up with him again, tempted to kick his ass as another twig broke beneath her foot. "I was thinking that it might be time to take a vacation."

"A vacation?" she repeated back, sure that she'd misheard him.

"Yeah," he said, letting out a sigh as he reached back and rubbed his neck, "I could really use a vacation. Somewhere tropical."

"A tropical vacation," she repeated back suspiciously as a thought occurred to her.

Christofer would never abandon a woman that needed him. His sense of duty was too well ingrained too ignore. He'd move heaven and hell to take care of a woman that he felt responsible for and she knew damn well that he felt responsible for her. It wasn't flattering to be considered a responsibility, but to him, she was one. He would never just walk away like this, not this easily and certainly not to go on a vacation, which meant.......

The bastard was toying with her.

She hitched her blanket up higher, narrowed her eyes on the bastard and quickened her pace until she'd caught up with him and then she kept going, deciding that she had way too much shit on her mind to play this game. If he wanted to be an asshole then that was more than fine with her. Here she was trying to give him an out to keep him safe and he was toying with her? Seriously?

Oh, he could go fuck him-

"In a rush to get away from me, mein Schatz?" the bastard asked teasingly as he easily caught up with her.

"Fuck off, asshole," she snapped, quickening her pace yet again, but it was pointless since the bastard's long legs made it easy for him to keep up with her.

"*Ouch,*" he said with a mock wince, further pissing her off. "What happened to the gentle let down?"

"It went on vacation!" she snapped, wondering how she'd ended up falling in love with the big jerk.

Out of all the men that she'd known in her life she had to fall for the one that drove her insane and pissed her off. Then again, this could just be a side effect of Stockholm syndrome, which at this point she was ninety-nine percent positive that she was suffering from. How else could she explain the fact that she hadn't kicked his ass yet? Not only that, but she'd actually slept with him!

God, she was pathetic.

Maybe the bastard was onto something with his asinine vacation plans. Since she apparently had some deranged shifter, leagues of vampires, demons and shift-ers after her, she might as well go away and hide out on some tropical island until this whole thing blew over.

She'd never been on a real vacation before. At least, she hadn't been on one since she was a kid.

There sure as hell wasn't anything stopping her from going now. She had plenty of money in the bank, no responsibilities, and no job to worry about. Granted, she'd been saving her money to buy a house when she'd finally had enough of the life of a live-in nurse, but since that was obviously never going to happen...

Why not?

Why shouldn't she go hide out on a tropical island, lounging on the beach while hot cabana boys served her fruity drinks with umbrellas all day? She'd more than earned it. With every step she took towards God only knew where, the idea of running off to hide on a tropical island and getting over the jerk behind her sounded better and better.

Granted, she didn't have her ID, credit cards, bankcard, cash or clothes for that matter, but those were all minor problems that could easily be taken care of with a quick call to the agency. They wouldn't be happy that she was taking a vacation, but she really didn't care since her career as a home care nurse was probably over now. Since she doubted that there was a high demand for home care nurses that lived off blood and had an army of monsters after her, she was probably going to have to quit.

She hated quitting, but she really didn't have much of a choice in the matter. She wouldn't put anyone else at risk, not even the jackass walking next to her, who wasn't even trying to hide that cocky grin of his.

"So, you're in love with me, huh?" he suddenly announced, taking her off guard so that she didn't see the branch lying across her path until it was too late.

Without missing a step, Christofer reached out, caught her elbow and steadied her while she tried to figure out an appropriate response that wouldn't include the words, "fuck" and "off." Since she couldn't seem to make her frustrated brain work, she settled for just pretending that he hadn't called her out on the stupidest thing that she'd ever done.

"Nope," she said, lying her frustrated ass off.

"Really?" he asked, still sounding smug.

The bastard.

"Really."

"I see," he murmured, sounding thoughtful as she distracted herself with everything that she was going to have to do in order to get some semblance of a life back.

She was going to have to find some clothes, get her hands on a computer and have some money wired to her. Then she was going to have to hole up in a hotel for a few days while she waited for the agency to ship her emergency pack to her. It was something that the agency required of every employee that lived out of a suitcase. The pack held duplicates of her ID, bankcards, credit cards, passport and birth certificate. It was a safeguard just in case things got lost or stolen, or you were assigned to a patient with dementia who liked to set things on fire, which happened to her, twice.

"Where are you headed off to?" Christofer asked conversationally as he reached out and pushed a branch out of her way.

"To find a good travel agent," she said, storming off.

"Running away from our love?" he asked, making her lips twitch despite the fact that she wanted to kick him in the balls.

"Something like that," she said, trying to keep a straight face, but that damn boyish grin of his had her heart skipping a beat.

"So, isn't this the part of the story where you start sobbing hysterically as you profess your undying love for me and start worshipping my body with your mouth?" he asked, sounding so damn hopeful that she couldn't help but laugh.

Damn him!

She was supposed to be pushing him away for his own good, not finding him irresistibly charming and sweet. Normally she didn't have a problem getting a guy to split, but with Christofer she couldn't seem to make the stubborn bastard let her go. Granted, she hadn't tried the direct route, something that she normally saved as a last resort when a guy just didn't seem to comprehend that she'd grown bored and moved on.

It wasn't something that she wanted to do, not with Christofer, but if it meant keeping him safe then-

"Or, maybe this is the part of the story where I confess that I am head over heels in love with you and can't imagine living a single day of the rest of my life without you," he confessed, all signs of humor gone from his tone as he took her by surprise, sent her heart skipping and her brain turned to mush, which was probably how she missed the fact that the trail that she was following veered off to the right of a steep incline.

FORTY-FIVE

"**Y**ou're an asshole," Cloe declared as she shoved away from him and awkwardly climbed to her feet so that she could continue to storm away from him as though they hadn't just fallen fifty feet down the hill that he hadn't seen coming until the last second.

"You're welcome," he said dryly as he pushed off the ground and sat up.

"*I'm welcome?*" she repeated in disgust as she whirled around and stormed back over to him so that she could glare down at him through beautiful red eyes. "I wouldn't have fallen down that hill if it wasn't for you!"

"How is it my fault that you tripped over your own two feet?" he asked innocently, loving the scent of anger rolling off her. Not because he was a sick bastard, but because beneath the scent of anger was arousal.

God, she smelled fucking fantastic.

Okay, maybe he was a sick bastard, because he couldn't help but smile as the scent of her anger intensified right along with the scent of her arousal. He shifted back a bit until he felt his back come in contact with the large boulder behind him. He sighed with satisfaction as she glared down at him. He could smell the blood rushing to swell her breasts and harden her nipples and wondered if she'd consider letting him feed from her there one day. Probably not, but just the thought of feeding from her as he suckled her nipple had his cock hardening painfully.

"You bastard!" she hissed, as he relaxed back against the boulder, licking his lips as he smelled her sex swell.

She opened her mouth to say something else, but abruptly shut it, narrowed her eyes on him and then with a snort of disgust, demanded, "Are you fucking kidding me?"

"Hmmm?" he murmured, barely registering her reaction or the fact that she'd moved closer to him so that she could glare down at him.

"You're getting turned on? Now?" she demanded, the sound of disgust in her voice should have been enough to knock some sense into him, but sadly, it wasn't.

"Yes," he answered with absolutely no shame as he ran his eyes over her, devouring every last detail from her hair tangled with tiny sticks and leaves down to her dirt smudged face, the torn blanket covered in dirt and grass stains that she had wrapped around her body all the way down to her beautiful dirt smudged feet.

"Seriously?" she snapped, looking down at herself in disgust. "I look like I was dragged through a tornado and this is turning you on?"

He reached up and grabbed her hand, giving it a gentle pull before she could react. He yanked her down on top of him, giving her the choice to straddle him or fall over. "You always turn me on," he admitted, reaching up and cupping the back of her neck. He pulled her down for a kiss as she settled on his lap, the blanket bunching up around her hips to accommodate the move.

"You are a deeply disturbed individual," she whispered against his lips as she wrapped her arms around his shoulders and threaded her fingers through his hair as she returned his kiss.

"Yes, I am," he said, dropping his hands to her bare legs where the blanket bunched and running his hands up her smooth legs, forcing the blanket up even higher until he came in contact with her cotton panties.

She ended the kiss with a sigh as she sat back on his thighs, putting some space between them, which was probably for the best given the situation. "We should get going."

"Yes, we should," he said, sighing heavily because he knew that she was right.

They should be moving their asses, finding a car and getting as far away from here as possible, but the problem was, he had no idea where they should go. For the first time in his life he had the freedom to go and do whatever he wanted, but all he wanted to do was to find someplace to keep Cloe safe and he had no clue where that was.

"Do you think they've gotten loose yet?" she asked quietly, dropping her arms from his shoulders so that she could toy with his shirt.

He focused on the forest around them, listening for any signs that they were being hunted, but after a minute he shook his head and murmured, "No."

"They're probably going to be pissed when they get free," she said, all of her attention zeroed in on her fingers as they toyed with the hem of the tee shirt that someone had dressed him in when he'd been knocked out.

"Probably," he agreed, thinking about everything that they'd told him and now that they'd escaped, a sense of unease settled over him, making him wonder if he'd fucked up by taking Cloe away.

"Do you think it's true?"

"What's true?" he asked, reaching up and pushing a strand of her tangled hair behind her ear.

"About what they said about a shifter marking me," she said, swallowing nervously as she shifted her gaze up to meet his.

He bit back a sigh as he reluctantly nodded and moved his hands to her shoulders, moving them down her back as far as the blanket would allow, needing to offer her some comfort for the pain she'd gone through. He didn't think they were lying. He wasn't foolish enough to think that their group was above bullshitting them to get what they wanted, but because of what Seth had explained to him. Seth, shit! He hadn't thought of the vampire since this whole thing started. He owed it to the vampire after all these years of helping him keep his sanity to make sure that he was okay.

Just as soon as they were settled, he would……..

"What the hell?" he muttered as his hands moved over smooth skin. Heart pounding in his chest, he leaned forward, jerked the blanket away from her and turned her just enough so that he could get a good look at her back. What he saw there had him swallowing back a curse as he traced her back with trembling fingers.

"What?" Cloe asked, shifting anxiously on his lap. "What the hell is going on?"

"Your back," he choked out.

"What about it?"

"The scars.....," he said, shaking his head in an attempt to make sense of what he was seeing. "They're gone."

"Gone?" she asked, her tone disbelieving as she reached back and ran her fingers over her back, looking for scars that were no longer there.

"Oh, my God," she said, her voice breaking with emotion. "How did they do that?" she asked, wrapping her arms around her bare breasts as she sat back down on his thighs, but she wouldn't look at him, probably afraid that he'd see her eyes tearing up.

When he hesitated, she looked up at him through watery eyes. "How?" she demanded through clenched teeth.

"They had to burn them off," he said, forcing himself to look at her when all he wanted to do was to drive his fist through something at the idea of someone hurting her, no matter the reason.

She stilled even as her beautiful grey eyes shifted to a glimmering red, her fangs dropped and her eyes narrowed on him. "That bastard set me on fire?"

Shit, he thought, trying not to wince when he realized that she'd still been passed out when Kale made that revelation. "It was the only way to remove the mark," he said, praying like hell that was true otherwise the woman leaning forward as she released one of the sexiest growls that he'd ever heard was going to rip his balls off.

"Then why are we running?" she demanded, eyeing him suspiciously.

"Because," he said, sighing as he leaned forward so that he could brush his lips quickly over hers in a way of apology for not taking better care of her, before he sat back, "there are other ways of finding you."

She scrunched up her face adorably in thought as she thought it over before she slumped in defeat with a pout. "My identification and bank cards," she said with a slight whine that he would find annoying in any other woman, but when she did it he couldn't help but smile.

"Yes," he said, nodding in agreement as he reached over and entwined their hands together. "If they're looking for you now, there's a good chance that they're watching your bank activities," he explained, wondering if whoever was looking for her had tracked her to his house.

"Do you think they know that we're together?" she asked quietly, sounding worried.

He shook his head as he leaned in for another kiss. "It doesn't matter."

"And why doesn't it matter?" she asked, sounding a little distracted as she wrapped her arms around him and followed him as he leaned back, nibbling on his bottom lip as though she couldn't quite help herself.

"Because," he said, releasing her hands so that he could wrap his arms around her, "I'm not going anywhere."

He moved to deepen the kiss only to find Cloe pushing away from him and once again sitting back on his thighs, averting her gaze. "Don't make promises that you can't keep."

"I'm not going anywhere, Cloe," he said firmly, in no mood to argue with this woman over something that should be painfully obvious by now.

"You don't know that, Christofer," she said, looking up to meet his gaze. "Things happen, people change."

"That's true, Cloe," he agreed as he looked into her beautiful grey eyes that were so full of pain that his heart actually ached for her. "But, nothing's going to change the way that I feel about you."

She shook her head. "You don't know that, Christofer. It might not happen in a day or even a week, but at some point you're going to get bored, or get sick of me and you're going to move on," she explained before adding with a shrug, "It happens."

He wasn't going anywhere, ever, but in that moment he realized something very important. Words didn't mean shit to Cloe. A lot of people probably made her promises, promises that they'd probably had every intention of keeping, but hadn't. Cloe obviously learned that a person's actions meant more than their words, so instead of arguing with her or making her promises that would only push her away, he was going to show her. He would show her how much he loved her, how much he cared about her and wanted her so that she would never have reason to doubt him again.

He would show her just how much he loved her.

"Then let's just focus on today," he said as he cupped her beautiful dirt smudged face in one hand, his thumb gently caressing her cheek.

"Just today," she said, sounding relieved as she allowed herself to lean into his touch. "And what exactly is the plan?"

"That's a damn good question," he said, leaning in so that he could brush his lips against hers, paying special attention to the plump bottom lip that drove him crazy.

"As much fun as it is to run around the woods wrapped in a dirty blanket, I think that we need to find some new clothes and a safe place to figure out a few things," she suggested.

"Well," he said, pulling back so that he could gaze down at her pretty breasts that were just begging for his attention, "since I always manage to think better when I'm inside you......" He grinned, letting his words trail off as he pushed the blanket away from her.

"How exactly do you always think better inside me when you've only been inside me once?" she asked, her eyes flashing red as her nipples hardened with renewed interest.

"It's hard to explain, but," he said with a drawn out sigh as though what he was about to suggest pained him, "I'd be willing to show you."

"That's very generous of you," Cloe murmured as she reached for the hem of his shirt and yanked it up and over his head until it was flying in the air and landing somewhere behind her.

"I do what I can," he said, hooking his thumbs in the waist of her panties and with a flick of his wrists, tore them clean from her body to join his shirt.

"And being inside me....?" she prompted, letting her words trail off as she reached down and flicked his pants button open.

"Is important to the planning process," he explained, cupping her bare hips as he leaned back against the rock and watched as the little tease took her time pulling his zipper down.

She sighed heavily as she exposed the large bulge hidden behind his boxers. "Then I guess we should do a thorough job."

FORTY-SIX

Now this, she thought as she pulled down his pants as he arched up to make it easier for her, was more like it. This was a temporary distraction and exactly what she needed right now.

Well, that wasn't entirely true since what she really needed was to find a way out of the woods and out of this horrible situation. For right now though, she'd settle for slowly pulling his pants down to expose the large erection that was going to give her a momentary reprieve from this nightmare. She'd deal with trying to get her life back later. Right now, she just wanted this, wanted to be with Christofer, lose herself in his touch and the pleasure that he gave her.

Right now nothing else mattered but the two of them.

"Are you planning on teasing me the entire time?" he asked, but he didn't sound mad. He sounded intrigued and that turned her on a hell of a lot more than she thought it would.

She'd never been one to play around in bed or to draw out pleasure since she usually used sex to forget the past, her life and pretend that her future didn't matter. Sex had always been a fun way to work off some excess energy and get off. She'd never taken her time to be playful, not even with Aidan.

He'd been great in bed, but he'd been focused on getting inside her and getting her off. Aidan had taken sex seriously and until last night, so had she. But now, she wanted to be playful, to take her time and to enjoy every second that led up to what she hoped would be another earth shattering orgasm and it was because of the man watching her every move through shimmering red eyes.

"Yes," she said, loving the power she had over him and she knew without question that she had him wrapped around her little finger.

She couldn't exactly call him whipped, and didn't want to because that term didn't fit Christofer. She hated guys that were whipped, because it was a huge turnoff to be with a guy missing his spine, but with Christofer......

There was no question that he was letting her call the shots because he enjoyed it. He liked letting her take the lead, to tease and torment him, but only as long as she was doing it because she enjoyed it. She had no doubt that if she turned into a controlling bitch that was teasing him for shits and giggles that he would quickly turn the tables on her, bend her over, fuck her and be done with it.

"Keep in mind that the next time," he said, leaning forward as he dropped his hips back down so that he could kiss her hard, "I'll be calling the shots."

"Is that a threat?" she asked, smiling as he leaned back.

He shook his head as he placed his hands on her bare thighs. "More like a challenge," he promised, locking his gaze with hers as he slowly ran his hands over her thighs, his thumbs coming so close to the spot that craved his attention before slowly moving away.

"I see," she murmured, biting back a smile as she looked down at what she'd revealed. "Then I probably should make it worth it," she said absently as she licked her lips.

"Probably," he whispered, his deep voice nearly a growl that had her shifting on his lap.

As she stared down at the large cock straining to get to her, she couldn't decide what she wanted more, to take it in her hand and caress it and the heavy sack below it, or to lean over and run her tongue around the head before she took it in her mouth. Other than releasing a very sexy growl, Christofer didn't say anything as he allowed her to choose. After a minute of debating just how good it would feel in her hand or in her mouth she settled on a compromise.

"*Fucking hell!*" he growled as she scooted back so that she could lean over him as she gripped the base with one hand, barely able to fit her hand around it, while the other held her up. She used the first stroke of his cock to bring the large tip to her waiting mouth.

Wanting to see his reaction, she tilted her head to the side so that her eyes were locked on his as she brought the large head to her mouth and swiped the underside with her tongue. His jaw clenched tightly as every muscle in his body went rigid, his sexy red eyes locked on her as he watched her.

"Do you like this?" she asked, running the very tip of her tongue over the tiny slit of his cock where his excitement was already beading.

"Yes," he gritted out between his teeth, forcing himself to stay still when they both knew that he could take over at any minute and probably make her enjoy it.

The fact that he was still letting her call the shots turned her on even more. It also had her falling harder for him, which wasn't something that she wanted. She already cared too much about him and when the day came that he finally had enough and walked away......

God, she couldn't even think about it, it hurt so much. This was quickly turning into the biggest mistake of her life, but at the moment she just couldn't seem to make herself care.

"Like this?" she asked, making a show of moving his cock forward so that her tongue was forced to rub against the underside of the tip, earning a full body shiver from him.

He groaned loudly as she ran her tongue right back up and then let it slide right back down, hoping for another one of those sexy shivers. He didn't disappoint.

So she did it again.

For several minutes she contented herself with just teasing the tip as her hand slowly stroked him, bringing him close to the edge, but not close enough. His entire body was strung tight, his jaw was still locked tightly, his breathing was a little unsteady and those sexy eyes of his remained focused on her. Loving his responses, she decided to be a little more adventurous.

"Tell me what you want," she commanded softly as she pulled back and lightly blew over the tip of his cock, earning a ragged moan that had her nipples tightening painfully and her ass shifting impatiently, desperate to have something fill her. She ran her tongue over his cock again, thinking of the perfect response for when he told her that he wanted her to suck his cock, but he took her by surprise.

"I want to trace your breasts with my tongue, licking and suckling your nipples while I run my hands over your body," he said, sounding pained as she swallowed back a groan of her own. Her eyes slid shut as she imagined just how good his hands would feel on her, especially now that her scars were gone.

"I'd run my hands through your beautiful brown hair, running my fingers along your jaw, down your neck, between your breasts and over the slight slope of your stomach before I moved onto your hands, your fingers and then down your back," he said, continuing without having to be asked.

"And then?" she asked, licking her lips as she continued to imagine the feel of his hands learning her body.

"I'd wrap my arms around you while I kissed you," he said, just as she registered the feel of his fingers gently threading through her hair.

"And then?" she asked, her voice barely louder than a whisper.

"Then I'd lay you down on your stomach and kiss every inch of your back while my hands caressed your sides, down to your legs and then finally I'd run my hands over your ass," he continued, earning a surprised laugh from her that gave her the willpower to open her eyes and join him in this little game.

"And what would you do then?" she asked, cocking her brow in challenge as she leaned forward and took the tip of his cock in her mouth.

A surprised groan escaped him as his cock jerked in her mouth and for a moment she thought that was the end of the game, but he proved her wrong.

"I'd kiss my way down to your bottom, kissing and worshipping each cheek as I cupped your thighs and pushed them apart.

"Would you fuck me?" she demanded as she let the tip of his cock leave her mouth with a wet *pop*.

"Not yet," he said, abandoning her hair to caress her cheek.

"Then what would you do?" she asked, watching him as she took his cock back in her mouth, this time taking more than just the tip.

"I'd tease your pussy with the tips of my fingers until you were soaking wet for me," he said tightly, groaning when her hand and mouth met around his cock.

Before she could remove her mouth to ask, he continued, probably out of desperation to keep her mouth wrapped firmly around his cock. Whatever the reason, she was glad that he did.

"When you were wet enough for me, mein Schatz, I'd roll you onto your back and tease your wet pussy a little more."

"Mmmmm," she moaned around his cock as her sex clenched almost painfully, demanding some attention.

"While I teased your pussy I would trace your nipple with the tip of my cock until even that wasn't enough," he whispered reverently as she felt her hand slide down her stomach and between her legs to find herself soaking wet. She needed his tongue, fingers, and cock inside her, but she didn't want him to stop.

Would die if he stopped talking.

"Soon I'd need that talented mouth of yours sucking my cock while I spread your pussy so that I could see just how wet you were for me. I'd trace my finger through your slit," he said just as she ran the tip of her finger through her wet slit, imagining that it was his. "Then I'd find your pretty little clit and run my finger around it once.....twice......three times before I shifted my attention to your pouty little pussy."

When her fingers met her clit, she didn't tease, but began gently rubbing it, barely aware that her hips were moving along with every trace of her clit. She sucked harder on his cock as her grip tightened, the images that his words created driving her on. This was so damn good. She could only imagine how good he was at phone sex, or better yet, sexting, something that she was going to try with him, and soon.

Really soon.

"I'd trace your entrance with my finger while you sucked my cock, just like that, mein Schatz," he groaned. "While you sucked my cock, getting it nice and wet, I'd slide my finger inside of you to see how tightly you were going to wrap around my cock," he said just as she slid a finger inside of herself with a loud moan.

"I'd fuck you with my fingers until I felt you swell around them. Then I'd pull them out and replace them with my tongue, sliding deep inside of you, licking you out and sliding back inside of you, mimicking what I wanted to do with my cock."

"Oh, God," she whimpered around the tip of his cock as her fingers worked her sex.

"And just when you were about to come………," he said, letting his words trail off and sending her to the edge. "I'd stop."

"What?" she practically snarled as she let the tip fall out of her mouth.

He cupped her face in his hands and with barely any pressure had her moving forward as he leaned in and gently kissed her. "I'd stop because I'd be dying to feel you wrapped around my cock when you let go."

She returned his kiss hungrily, almost desperately, barely aware that she'd released her hold on his cock or sat up so that she was once again straddling his lap. Her fingers continued to work between her legs as she wrapped her arm around his shoulder, threaded her fingers through his hair. She gripped his hair, holding him still as she ran her tongue against his before he suckled it.

"You wanna fuck me?" she asked, so turned on that she knew that if she didn't have him within the next minute she'd scream.

"God, yes," he said against her mouth as she felt his cock slide against her ass.

After one last thrust of her fingers, she removed her hand and reached back. She gripped his cock, loving the way his breath hitched as he felt the evidence of what she'd been doing coat his cock. It took a little effort, but she managed to stroke his cock as it eagerly pressed against her ass.

"How badly do you want to fuck me?" she asked, getting lost in the feel of his erection in her hand.

His answer was a vicious growl. He dropped his hands away from her face so that he could grip her ass in one hand, careful not to interrupt what she was doing and slid a finger inside her. She used her grip in his hair to steady herself as she pulled back so that she could watch him. His red eyes glimmered in the fading sunlight as she moved her hand back to the tip and wrapped her hand around it, holding it tightly as she spread her legs further apart. It wasn't much, but it was enough for what she wanted to do.

"Oh, fuck," he groaned, a choked sound leaving his lips as she shifted back and pushed back until the length of him was pressed against the crease of her ass. She used her hold on his hair and the one that she had on the tip of his cock and slowly rode his fingers, the movement rubbing his cock between her cheeks and caressing him in a way that she was willing to bet he'd never experienced before.

"Do you like that?" she asked, moving down to take his fingers deeper inside her, and as a result, caressing his cock harder.

"Yes," he said hoarsely as he licked his lips hungrily.

"Have you ever fucked a woman here?" she asked as she pressed her bottom more firmly against his cock.

"No," he admitted with a groan.

Smiling, she leaned forward until their mouths were almost touching, but not quite. "Do you want to fuck me here?"

"*Yes!*" he snarled.

"How badly?" she asked, knowing that she was playing with fire and not really caring. Her nipples brushed against his chest with every movement. His thick fingers filled her nicely as his cock teased her ass, making her want something that she'd only tried once and hated, but with him, she was more than willing to give it another shot.

"Badly," he admitted through clenched teeth, and with a triumphant smile, she leaned back, releasing her hold on his hair and on his cock. She kept leaning back, loving the confused expression on his face. She kept moving back until she found herself lying on the ground between his spread legs, her arm folded behind her head and her free hand gliding absently over her stomach as she bent her legs and spread them wide.

"Well, that's too bad, because tonight you need to focus on somewhere else," she practically purred as she moved her fingers lower, deciding that perhaps he needed a visual aide.

Once again, she was wrong.

FORTY-SEVEN

Fucking little tease, he thought with a growl as the thoughts of sliding his cock in her ass evaporated and he was presented with an unobstructed view of her wet pussy.

She was soaking wet.

Praying for control, he licked his lips and shifted until he was on his hands and knees. He watched while Cloe moaned, licking her lips as she slid a finger inside herself. She was so beautiful, he thought as he leaned down and pressed a kiss against her stomach before he shifted back just far enough so that he could press a kiss to the back of her hand working between her legs.

"My turn," he managed to get out as he waited for her to remove her hand.

With a soft moan and one last slide of her fingers, she pulled her hand free and allowed him to lick her fingers clean. She tasted so damn sweet, he thought, forced to reach down and grip his cock to stop himself from spontaneously coming. She'd worked him up to the point that his control had almost snapped several times, but he wasn't complaining. Not when he had the woman that he loved driving him out of his mind.

She pulled her fingers away from his mouth and cupped his cheek as he lowered his mouth between her legs. He didn't waste time teasing her, not when she was this wet. Instead, he slid his tongue inside of her without any hesitation and fucked her with it. He slid his tongue in and out of her, squeezing his eyes shut tightly as he struggled not to come. Even with his hand wrapped tightly around his cock, squeezing it as he tried to think of anything else but fucking her, it was difficult while he had his tongue buried inside her.

"Christofer," she moaned his name, rocking her hips against his mouth as she rode his tongue. "Don't stop. Please don't stop!"

Fresh arousal coated his mouth as he felt her core tighten around his tongue, holding it hostage. Cloe rocked against his mouth, moaning his name incoherently as she begged him not to stop. He wouldn't, not even if it meant spilling his seed on the ground instead of inside her. He'd do anything for her.

He moved his tongue in and out of her, flicking the tip of his tongue up so that it would catch her in just the right spot. The scent of Cloe's arousal enveloped him as he continued to fuck her with his mouth.

"Oh, God," Cloe moaned as she continued to ride his tongue. "More! Please!"

Putting all of his weight on his knees, he reached around with his hand and placed it flatly against her stomach so that his thumb could reach her sweet spot. As soon as his thumb touched her clit, she detonated, flexing her hips up so suddenly that he damn near lost his tongue and fingers in the process.

When he felt her tremors start to slow down around his tongue, he pulled his tongue and fingers away and moved up her body, pressing quick, desperate kisses against her stomach and breasts as he went. The hand suddenly gripping his hair and yanking him away from her nipple brought him all the way up and suddenly he found himself kissing her harder than he'd ever kissed a woman before. Their tongues battled, desperate for contact as he lowered himself over her and with a quick thrust, sheathed himself inside her.

He pulled back and fucked her with quick, hard thrusts, too desperate to draw it out. She'd kept him on edge too long and the feel of her wrapped around him was driving him out of his fucking mind.

"You feel so good," she moaned against his mouth as he reached between them and palmed one of her breasts, wrapping his hand around it as he pinched her nipple gently between his fingers.

"You feel better than good," he groaned against her lips as he was forced to pull his mouth away, the need to bite her too intense to ignore.

But, he couldn't do that. So instead he closed his eyes and licked his lips as he concentrated on the feel of his cock pushing inside her. She felt fucking fantastic.

"Christofer, I-I need to…to…oh, God!" she screamed, coming so hard that he was the one left seeing stars as he continued to push past her quivering walls.

He didn't need to ask to know what she needed since he was battling that need himself. He simply turned his head, exposing his throat to her and said, "Take what you need, mein Schatz."

A hungry groan escaped her as she struck, a little gentler this time, but it was enough. The first pull on his neck had him bucking inside her, the second had him fucking her hard and fast and the third had him roaring her name as his cock swelled and his balls pulling up tight as he exploded. The words, I love you, almost followed, but somehow he managed to hold them back, but just barely.

Manhattan, New York

"He's positive?" Aidan asked, looking past the Alpha, that he was forced to play nice with, to the fucking traitor standing by the boardroom doors.

"Yes," Thomas said, gesturing for the mutt to come forward.

With a shake of his head, the mutt reached for the doorknob. "I did my part. He can find his own fucking property."

Aidan returned his attention to Thomas, confident that his men would grab the mutt before he had a chance to return to the Sentinel compound. Working against his own kind, Aidan thought in disgust as he focused his attention on the man that better have more answers for him.

Thomas sighed heavily as rubbed the back of his neck. "My Pack is against marking humans," he began to explain as though Aidan fucking cared.

"My Pack isn't," he said evenly, in absolutely no fucking mood to discuss morals and all the bullshit. They were human concerns and rules, and he refused to live by them.

Humans were beneath them in every way possible and if pricks like this one didn't see that, then that was his problem. He wasn't here to get into a debate. He was here to get his fucking property and bring her and his prize back. Once he brought her home, he would fuck her into submission and use his prize to tip the odds in his favor.

"Obviously," Thomas said, shooting him a look of disgust as he shifted his attention to the large grid map of Manhattan.

Perhaps he'd bring his Pack back up here when they were ready and tear this piece of shit and his fucked up excuse of a Pack apart, he thought idly as he followed Thomas' finger to a starred section on the map. It would certainly put a smile on his face, he mused as he caught the hostile scent coming off the Alpha and the men that were leaning against the walls, watching his every move.

"This is the Sentinel compound," Thomas explained. "My men have been stationed around it since word spread."

"Any sightings?" he asked, wondering if Cloe was going to be happy to see him, or if she was going to be pissed.

Pissed, definitely pissed, he thought with a smirk. That would be more than fine with him since it would make fucking her into submission more pleasurable.

"No one has seen her or the Pyte," Thomas said, confirming his suspicions, but just in case.....

"How do you know it's a Pyte?" he asked, turning his attention to look around the large office where the pussy to his right and his Pack practiced law during the day so that they could blend in with humans.

Fucking traitors, he thought once again with disgust.

"They were brought in by a team from upstate. The shifters in the compound scented them before they'd stepped foot inside."

"Them?" he asked, his mind locking in on that one word.

Thomas sighed, not looking at all happy about answering his questions. Not that he had a choice. Aidan's marked property had been taken into his territory and as Alpha of the controlling Pack, it was his duty to get Aidan's property back no matter the cost. The Alpha wasn't happy about it and no doubt would love nothing more than to separate Aidan's head from his body, but as long as his property was in this territory, he was untouchable.

"A group made up of Sentinels, shifters and Pytes delivered them to the compound," Thomas said, sounding pissed with himself for answering.

His brows shot up with surprise. "More Pytes?"

"Apparently the Sentinels have several working for them," Thomas said, shifting his attention to a stack of files on the long boardroom table that took up more than half the room.

"Interesting," he murmured, as he considered trying to grab more than one, but after only a few seconds he decided against it.

He only needed one for what he had planned. Besides, there was no way that his Pack would be able to capture more than one Pyte. At least, not yet. Maybe in a few months, if his plans worked, he'd be able to work a few more Pytes into his plan. If not, he'd just have to make sure that he found a way to take them out permanently.

"The last we'd heard, they were being held on the secure floor before they broke free. The male lost it to bloodlust and they had to bring Kale Quinn in to handle the situation," Thomas recited absently as he looked over a file.

Aidan couldn't quite hide his surprise. "Kale Quinn is helping the Sentinels?" he asked, sure that he'd misheard.

Kale Quinn might be a mutt, but last he knew, the Alpha wasn't a traitor. He was a ruthless piece of shit that would fuck over his own kind for a buck however.

Thomas nodded as he picked up the file and gestured for the man standing across from him to take it. "He's been doing freelance work for the Council."

"I see," Aidan said, mentally adding the traitor to his list.

He normally didn't bother dealing with traitors, but for Kale Quinn, he would make an exception. The man was too powerful, if all the rumors were to be believed, to be allowed to work with the enemy. But, it was going to have to be dealt with another day, because right now he had other things that needed to be handled.

"Where is she now?" he asked, making sure not to give away his interest in the male.

"The last anyone saw of her, she was being transferred back to the secured floor with extra security," Thomas explained, his attention back on the large pile of folders in front of him, but there was something in the way that he'd shifted ever so slightly that told him that there was something the Alpha wasn't telling him.

"And?" Aidan said softly, because he didn't need to yell, the threat was clear.

He watched as the man shifting through files stilled. There was a heartbeat of charged silence before Thomas sighed, dropped the file he'd picked up and turned around to face him.

"They removed your *mark*," Thomas growled, his eyes shifting silver as he snarled the last word.

"That's impossible," he snarled back, because he'd made damn sure when he'd marked her that no one and nothing could remove it.

She was *his*.

Thomas' disgusted expression shifted to downright smug as he announced, "It's very possible, especially since a Pyte made her his mate."

He felt his stomach drop as his heart skipped a beat, knowing what the Alpha just announced was impossible.

"*She's mine!*" he snarled viciously.

The other man didn't cower or cringe as he gestured for him to get his ass out of his building. "Her mate may have a thing or two to say about that and now that I've done my duty, you can get the fuck out of my offices and go handle this bullshit on your own, you sick fuck."

"You owe me aid in recovering my property!" he snarled, his rage keeping his feet locked in place.

"No," Thomas said coolly with a shake of his head as he turned his back on him and returned his attention back to his files, "I owed you information and now you've got it."

"I want my property back!"

"Then I suggest you think of something quickly before the vampires get their hands on her, because from what I've heard, they just put out a reward for her...........and her mate."

FORTY-EIGHT

"Shut. The. Fuck. Up," Kale snarled, clearly unhappy with Chris' choice of entertainment to pass the time.

Chris sighed dramatically. "I've lost my place," he said with a shake of his head. "I guess there's nothing to do but to start over again." He pointedly cleared his throat, preparing himself for another round of "A thousand bottles of beer on the wall," but before he had the chance to utter another syllable of torture, Ephraim was slapping a hand over his son's mouth and ending his son's reign of terror.

"Thank fucking God," Caine said weakly from where he sat with Danni curled up in his arms and somehow fast asleep.

Ephraim wasn't sure how she'd managed to block out Chris' bullshit, but he had to admit, he was impressed. Over the last couple of hours he'd been forced to remind himself that he loved his son and would regret killing him, but a few times he found himself reaching out to strangle the little bastard. While his son normally loved nothing more than to aggravate the shit out of the shifter straining against his chains so that he could wrap his hands around Chris' throat, he'd gone overboard this time.

Then again, Chris hated being restrained almost as much as he did, but what made matters worse was the fact that Chris couldn't get to his mate. He could tolerate being away from her for a few days only because he knew that he could drop everything and go to her or at the very least, call her. This time, there was nothing. He hadn't spoken to his mate in over twenty-four hours and it was killing him.

So, of course he was taking it out on the rest of them.

"Is anyone else here curious how one Pyte not only managed to take us all by surprise, but also survived the car crash without so much as a scratch and managed to chain us all up together like ragdolls?" Danni asked from the safety of her mate's arms as she continued to lie there with her eyes closed.

He shared a look with Caine. Oh, they were more than a little curious and judging by the way that Kale's eyes went all silver at the reminder of his recent ass whooping, he was also curious.

"I'd love to know how he did it, especially just coming out of bloodlust," Chris said against Ephraim's hand.

"You and me both," he muttered, dropping his hand away from Chris' mouth even as he shot his son a warning glare not to start the bullshit back up again.

"She didn't have a mark on her either," Caine added, looking thoughtful.

"That's because he wrapped his body around her and protected her," Chris pointed out, wincing as he shifted his broken arm. It was already halfway healed, but the process hurt like hell. Not that Chris would let anyone know just how much pain he was in. He hated being fussed over by anyone but his mate.

"He didn't grab her until after the van had already rolled over once," Kale said, looking equally thoughtful. "She should have had a few bruises or cuts from that crash, but she didn't. Not a single one."

"She was wrapped up in a blanket so for all you know, she could have had a few injuries," Chris said, giving up on trying to sit up and just laid there, staring up at the early morning sky.

Caine shook his head right along with him as he answered, "We would have smelled the blood pooling beneath her skin. She wasn't injured."

"Now that I think of it," Caine said, looking a little confused, "her back healed a hell of a lot faster than it should have."

"That's because we kept a line down her throat, pumping blood inside her the whole time," Chris added, but the expression on his face told him that even he realized that she'd healed a little too fast.

"The cut on her hand didn't heal quickly," Danni pointed out, reminding them of Ephraim's fuck up.

"No, it didn't," Ephraim said, frowning as he tried to make sense of everything.

"But she also didn't slip into bloodlust," Kale announced, drawing everyone's attention.

"How do you know?" Caine asked before Ephraim or anyone else for that matter, got the chance.

"Because I slipped back up to their floor and listened," Kale admitted with a careless shrug.

"He probably fed her," Danni pointed out around a yawn as she settled more deeply in her mate's arms.

"Not for a few hours," Kale said, leveling a pointed look on Ephraim, making sure that he got the message.

He definitely got it.

There was something different about Christofer's blood, something that allowed the woman he'd turned to put off bloodlust a hell of a lot longer than she should have been able to after being freshly turned and losing blood. If what Kale said was true, and he had no reason not to believe it, something had changed since the last time that they saw the couple and when they returned for them and he had a feeling he knew what that something was.

"He's fed her his blood," Caine murmured, a pained expression on his face as he looked down at Danni, who was looking worse as the morning progressed.

"Maybe he's part demon," Chris suggested, raising his broken arm and resting it across his stomach, taking Ephraim's arm right along with it. The bones had fused back together so that the arm was no longer hanging at an odd angle, but it was still broken. He could smell the marrow slowly seeping out.

Kale shook his head as he pulled his leg up, which of course dragged Chris' good arm up along with it since it was handcuffed to the shifter's ankle. "We would have smelled demon blood on him."

"Then-"

"Oh my God!" a woman's shriek drew their attention to a man and woman stumbling out of the woods to their left.

"What the hell happened?" the man, who appeared to be around fifty, demanded as he pushed past the gawking woman and rushed over to help them.

"Oh, this?" Chris asked, all innocence as he raised his head to give the man his most charming smile. "Just a simple misunderstanding."

"A misunderstanding?" the man repeated back, sounding horrified as he looked at what was left of the van.

"What should I do, Alfie?" the woman asked, shifting nervously where she stood, gawking at them.

"Call 911," Alfie said, moving to help them, but came up short when he saw that they were all handcuffed to one another. "Why are you handcuffed?"

"Our friend has a sick sense of humor," Chris claimed with a straight face as the rest of them were forced to look away so that the couple didn't see them all roll their eyes.

Ephraim would have said something, but since the scent of the human blood had caused a rather unpleasant reaction, he decided, along with Caine and Danni as it turned out, that it was probably for the best if they just went ahead and pretended to pass out while Chris used a mixture of charm and bullshit to get them out of this without the humans finding out that they'd stumbled upon a group of ravenous Pytes and an asshole.

———

"She bit me!"

"Great," he sighed, wondering why he'd let Cloe talk him into this.

Oh, that's right, because she'd woken him up just in time for him to watch as his cock disappeared inside her tight pussy and had taken advantage of his distracted state. While he'd been sleeping, she'd been thinking, and at some point she'd come to the conclusion that they needed this group's help.

When he'd pointed out that he could damn well take care of her and that he didn't need any help, Cloe had given him what he could only describe as evil smile as she ground down on him, shifting her hips in a circular motion that had made it impossible for him to talk, never mind argue. So, now he was here, hauling ass through the woods and trying to figure out the best way to accept their offer without having to grovel.

Or apologize.

"Call the police, Mary!" a guy screamed just as Christofer picked up the scent of freshly spilled human blood.

"I can't!" a woman, whom he was guessing was Mary, screamed. "I don't have a signal!"

"Run!" Ephraim roared just as Christofer stepped out of the woods and into the small clearing by the road.

Yup, he definitely regretted leaving Danni's hand free, he mused as he reached out and grabbed Cloe by the arm to steady her as she stumbled out of the woods.

"Thanks," Cloe murmured absently, her attention on the large pair of boxers that she was once again forced to yank up or risk giving little woodland creatures a show. Once she had the boxers yanked up and the large tee shirt that he'd given her pulled down, she looked up and frowned.

"What.....," she paused to lick her lips and give her head a little shake as though that would somehow help her make sense of the scene before them, "Why is Danni playing tug of war with that man?"

"Because she apparently went into bloodlust," he said, sighing heavily as he watched Danni try to drag the human male kicking and screaming back while Caine tried to pull her away. The fact that his left arm was cuffed to her and his right arm was cuffed to Ephraim, who had positioned himself in front of Chris, was making things a bit awkward.

"That's what I look like when I go into bloodlust?" Cloe asked with a frown as she watched Danni trying to drag the human back with one hand, but from the looks of things, the human was winning.

"No," he said, pausing to press a small kiss against her lips before he headed over to the group screaming for Danni to let go, "you would have torn that poor bastard apart by now."

"Well, that's comforting," Cloe said dryly as she followed after him.

"I'm sure it is," he returned as he walked around the group struggling to get Danni under control and protect Chris. Without pausing, he grabbed the screaming male by the arm, yanked him out of Danni's grip and dragged him over to the screaming female by the woods.

"Go," he simply said as he released his hold on the male and sent the couple running for their lives.

"Oh, shit!" Chris yelped, dragging his attention back to the group and to the woman now trying to climb over her mate and Ephraim to get to Chris, who was now pressed back against the pain in the ass shifter. Kale struggled against his chains as he yelled at Danni to stop.

That was interesting....

But something that he was going to have to worry about at another time since Cloe had taken it upon herself to help out. With a muttered curse, he walked over to the group, grabbed Cloe just as Danni snarled a warning to get the hell out of her way. With a sigh, he threw Cloe over his shoulder and carried her over to the van and put her down with another swift kiss, simply because he couldn't help himself.

"See if any of the blood is still cold," he said abruptly as he turned to-

"Mother fucker!" Chris shouted as Danni somehow managed to squirm her way between Ephraim and Caine and sank her teeth in Chris' broken arm.

Sighing, he walked back to the group, leaned over Chris and pinched Danni's nose closed. He ignored everything around him and just focused on the stubborn woman refusing to release her hold on the Sentinel reciting every swear imaginable. Shimmering red eyes shifted to him and narrowed as she released what she probably thought was a vicious growl, but really, it was just too damn cute to be taken seriously.

She didn't need air to live, but without it, swallowing that sweet blood that was now permeating the air became damn near impossible. It took her a good minute to realize that she had to let go and when she did, he was ready. With a snarl, she released her hold on Chris and went for him. Before anyone could react, he had her on her stomach and was pinning her down with his knee.

"Don't fucking hurt her!" Caine roared, reaching for him, but Ephraim grabbed him by the arm and held him back before he could do anything to make Christofer lose his hold on Danni.

"Relax," he said to no one in particular as he reached down, grabbed Danni and Caine by their wrists and yanked, breaking the small chain connecting their handcuffs. As soon as her hand was free she began thrashing beneath him, desperate to get free, desperate for blood.

"Any of that blood cold, mein Schatz?" he asked, keeping just enough pressure on Danni's back to keep her down.

She really was a weak little thing, he thought with a frown as he reached over and broke Caine's other cuff, deciding that it would probably keep the other man from going into bloodlust if he could hold his mate. The second that Caine's chain broke he was by Danni's side, holding her hand and calmly promising to put her over his knee and spanking her ass until it was black and blue for scaring the shit out of him.

"This cooler is still cold," Cloe said, dragging the large cooler over to him. He opened his mouth to tell her that she could probably lift that thing with one hand, but decided against it since it would probably lead to more of her "experimenting."

He shifted his attention from his mate's long, tanned legs to Caine. "Think you can get her to eat if I flip her over?"

"Yes," Caine answered hoarsely, reluctantly releasing his mate's hand.

Within seconds, he had the growling, snarling woman on her back, her hands pinned to her stomach with one arm and was reaching with the other for Ephraim's chain, deciding that an extra set of hands couldn't hurt. With a flick of his fingers he broke the chain. Ephraim didn't waste any time. He moved until he was sitting behind Danni and then just as quickly, propped the pissed off woman's head on his lap so that Caine could feed her. He watched as the Pyte bit into his wrist and placed it against Danni's mouth as he released her hand so that he could stick a bag of blood against his teeth.

"How did you do that?" Ephraim asked, looking truly confused.

He opened his mouth to answer, but he never got the chance as Kale made an announcement that he fully supported.

"I'm a fucking idiot," the shifter said with a humorless chuckle. "He's ion."

"He's what?" Chris asked, cringing in pain as he shifted his bleeding arm against his chest.

"He's a pure Pyte," Kale said as though that made any sense to them.

"What the hell are you saying?" Christofer demanded, looking up from the struggling woman.

"He's saying," Ephraim said, drawing his attention to find the other Pyte looking at him curiously, "that your father is really fucking old."

FORTY-NINE

Williams' Mansion

"Chris!"

The excited squeal drew Cloe's attention to a short woman standing at the top of the grand staircase with beautiful long blonde hair, a huge smile and an even bigger stomach. When the woman took an unsteady step down, Chris and Ephraim tried to go to her, but since Ephraim was still supporting most of Chris' weight, he'd barely stumbled two feet before Kale shoved past him and raced up the stairs to stop her from taking another step.

She watched as Kale swooped the smiling woman off her feet and proceeded to carry her down the stairs. About halfway down the stairs her smile faltered and her expression of pure joy quickly turned to dread.

"Ummm, maybe you should bring me back upstairs?" the woman suggested, keeping her eyes locked on the foyer as she nudged Kale several times to turn around.

"Don't you want to see your mate?" Kale asked, his tone mocking as he glared down at the woman in his arms.

"Ummm no, that's okay," she said, licking her lips anxiously as she shot another nervous look down at the foyer where they all waited.

Curious, Cloe followed the other woman's gaze and found herself taking a step closer to Christofer and thanking God that the murderous look on Chris' face wasn't directed at her. Since the woman wasn't screaming for help, Cloe stayed where she was, watching the scene unfold with morbid curiosity.

"You haven't seen him in two weeks, no doubt you're eager for a reunion," Kale said casually as he walked down the stairs, bringing the panic stricken woman closer and closer to her doom. Cloe listened as the woman's heartbeat quickened with every passing second.

"I'm more tired than anything," the woman said, adding a really loud, and really fake yawn at the end that for some reason, she couldn't explain, had Cloe biting back a smile.

"You can take a nap afterwards," Kale said, taking that final step down.

"But I would *really* like one now," the woman insisted, swallowing nervously as she grabbed onto Kale's shirt and held on.

"And I would *really* like to know why you were trying to use the stairs," Chris said, pushing away from his father to go to the woman that Cloe was assuming was his wife or mate, or whatever the hell they called each other.

"Ummm," the anxious woman said, obviously searching for the right words as she gave Chris a tentative smile, "because it was the quickest way to run into your arms?"

"You're supposed to use the elevator," Chris growled, reaching out and taking one of her hands away from Kale's shirt so that he could press a tender kiss against her palm before he entwined their fingers.

"But I really missed you," she said with a sniffle.

Chris muttered something as he leaned in, ignoring the shifter's scowl and kissed her. "Little liar," he said, chuckling as he shifted his backpack forward and carefully reached in with his still-healing arm and withdrew a small white confectioners box.

The woman gasped. "Is that-"

Chris cut her off with a frown. "It's empty."

Immediately her gaze shifted to Kale, who merely shrugged as he moved forward and handed her off to Ephraim. "Didn't see your name on it," he said, turning away and heading back up the stairs.

"You bastard!" she hissed in outrage.

"I'll have more fudge delivered, Izzy," Chris promised, stuffing the empty box back in the bag as leaned over and pressed a kiss to her pouting lips.

"It won't be the same," she muttered with a slight wince as she shifted in Ephraim's arms.

"Hip acting up?" Chris asked, his expression and tone tender as he carefully laid his hand just above her left hip.

"It's fine," Izzy mumbled, not quite meeting Chris' gaze and making the nurse in Cloe wonder just how bad her hip was.

"Izzy," Caine said softly as he stepped up beside the small group with Danni in his arms, who was looking paler and weaker than before, "did they deliver Danni's blood?"

"I'm fine," Danni muttered weakly as she lay limply in Caine's arms.

"Blood was delivered this morning. I'm not sure about the demon blood though," Izzy said, her expression full of worry as she looked at Danni.

"What's the demon blood for?" Cloe found herself asking without thinking and just like that, everyone's attention was back on them.

Well, it had been nice while it lasted, she mused with an inward sigh. For the past six hours their little "rescue" group had been eying them curiously, except for Kale that is. If anything, Kale seemed to hate them even more now. She still wasn't sure why. She also didn't know why they kept looking at her and Christofer like they had two heads. Christofer on the other hand hadn't seemed at all interested or looked like he cared. Once they'd told him the truth about his father, he'd shut down and hadn't talked to anyone since.

Not even her.

When she'd tried to talk to him, he'd simply shook his head and turned his back on her. If it had been anyone else, she wouldn't have cared, but it wasn't anyone else and she did care, a lot more than she wanted to. As she'd watched him walk away she'd felt like he was taking a chunk of her heart along with him. It hurt more than anything she'd ever experienced before, more than she'd ever imagined it could, but it hadn't hurt for long.

Not even a minute later, Christofer cursed, turned right back around and stalked back to her. Before she could rail at him for brushing her off, he'd had her in his arms and was giving her the sweetest kiss as he whispered to her how sorry he was. Much to her shame, she'd melted, instantly forgiving him. She'd never given a guy that pissed her off or hurt her in any way a second chance before, but with him, she hadn't hesitated for a second before she was wrapping her arms around him and letting him know that everything was going to be fine.

However, she did make him carry her on his back during that ten-mile hike to the next town as punishment. He hadn't said another word since and she hadn't pushed him for anything and neither had anyone else. They seemed to understand that he was dealing with some personal issues and had left him alone for the most part. The only time they'd bothered him was to make sure that coming with them was what he wanted. Other than a nod, he hadn't acknowledged them at all. Now, thanks to her big mouth, they were once again the focus of attention and judging by the way that Christofer had stilled behind her, he wasn't happy about it.

"You must be Cloe," Izzy said with a sweet smile. "I'm Izzy, Chris' mate."

"And the biggest sugar addict that you'll ever meet," Ephraim said with a fond smile as he looked down at the small woman in his arms.

"It's nice to meet you," she said quickly, barely paying attention to the woman as her attention locked back on Danni, who was now gripping Caine's shirt tightly as she buried her face against his chest. "Do you want me to take a look at her?" she asked, moving forward.

Caine arms tightened around Danni as he glanced at Ephraim, who explained, "She's a nurse."

"Nurse practitioner, actually," at Ephraim's confused expression she added, "I work at the RN level so that I can work as a live-in," with a shrug as she moved forward, but she'd barely taken two steps before she found herself shoved back behind Christofer.

"She's not going anywhere near her," Christofer growled, and wasn't that sweet? He was worried about her.

It really was nice to have someone care about her safety, she thought as she stepped past him, pinching the back of his hand when he went to grab her again. "Ow!"

"I'm fine," Danni said, looking anything but fine. "I just need to lie down for a bit that's all."

"Are you sure?" Cloe asked hesitantly, not entirely sure that she should take no for an answer, but after a minute she reminded herself that this wasn't one of her patients. If they wanted her help, they'd ask.

"I'm sure," Danni mumbled sleepily as she closed her eyes.

"I'm going to take her upstairs," Caine said softly, pressing a kiss against the tip of Danni's nose, which earned him a tired smile from his mate as he carried her up the stairs.

"Are you mates?" Izzy suddenly asked, startling her.

"I'm sorry, what?" she asked, not a hundred percent sure that she'd heard correctly or even how to respond.

Izzy frowned, looking adorably confused as she asked, "You're mated, right?"

When Cloe didn't answer right away, because she couldn't seem to find the right words, Izzy quickly explained, "It's just that there are children in the house and we don't want them to get the wrong idea. If you're not mated, then I planned to set you both up in different rooms. If you are-"

"We're mated," she blurted out before Izzy had the chance to suggest that they stay in separate rooms.

She didn't know anyone here, didn't trust anyone and until she-

Okay, fine. She just didn't want to be away from Christofer. She'd grown addicted to sleeping in his arms over the past week and she wasn't ready to give that up yet. She felt safe in his arms. Besides, if she was going to end up getting her heart broken she should at least be able to enjoy herself before she ended up hating him.

FIFTY

*D*emon.
His father was a fucking demon, he thought with a bitter laugh at the irony as he dropped his head forward, allowing the hot water to rain down on him.

Of all the rumors that he'd heard over the years, it figured that the one that he'd never believed would turn out to be the truth. His father was a demon, one of the first that Satan supposedly set loose on earth in an attempt to gain the upper hand in this fucked up game he played against God. He didn't want to believe it, would give anything for it not to be true and as Ephraim had delivered the bad news to him, he'd known that there was no denying it.

He truly was a monster among monsters.

"Are you okay?" Cloe asked, pressing a kiss against his back as her arms wrapped around him.

"Yes," he said automatically, the habit well ingrained in him after too many years of trying to protect Marta from his personal bullshit.

"Liar," Cloe said, chuckling as she pressed another kiss against his back.

Lips twitching in amusement despite the fact that he felt like putting his fist through a wall, he placed one of his hands over hers where it laid against his stomach. "I'll be fine," he promised, wondering how it was possible for one woman to bring him so much peace.

"That's better," she said, turning her head so that she could rest her cheek against his back as she held him.

"How are you holding up?" he asked, wondering how she was taking the news.

"Oh," she said, wrapping her fingers around his hand as she allowed her other hand to trail over his stomach, "I think I'll be okay."

"Even after what Ephraim just told us?" he asked, not really sure that he would be.

"You mean that you're really part demon?" she asked in a seductively teasing tone as she trailed her fingers down his stomach until she was tracing the trail of hair that led from his navel to his groin with the tip of her finger and making it damn near impossible to stay focused on anything other than just how good it would feel if she would lower her hand and wrap it around-

A loud groan escaped him as she did just that. He licked his lips as he watched her stroke his hardening cock. The sight of her running her hand over his cock was enough to have his balls pull up tight, greedy for her touch.

"You done pouting now?" she asked, giving his cock a hard pull.

"*Yes,*" he growled, finding it difficult to care about anything, even his fucked up existence, when he had the woman he loved stroking his cock.

"It doesn't change anything, Christofer," she said, punctuating her words with another kiss to his back.

"It changes everything," he told her, slapping his hands against the tiled wall when he felt his legs begin to tremble.

"And how exactly does it change anything?"

"It-"

"-doesn't change anything," she finished for him, giving the head of his cock a squeeze that had him moaning. "But......," she said, letting her words trail off as she suddenly dropped his cock and stepped away, taking her warmth and his peace away. "If you would rather pout, I could-"

Her words ended on a pleased sigh as she suddenly found herself in his arms. "I'm done pouting," he promised, leaning down to kiss her.

"Are you sure?" she asked against his lips.

"Yes," he swore, willing to promise her anything as long she stayed in his arms.

"Then you're willing to give this a try?" she asked, pulling back just far enough so that she could meet his gaze as she wrapped her arms around him.

"Will it make you happy?" he asked, because he refused to argue with her and risk making her unhappy.

He'd done that with Marta, taking her from place to place, constantly on the run, always looking over his shoulder, terrified that if they didn't run fast enough, far enough that he'd fail her, but in the end, he'd failed her anyway. Too many years on the run had drained Marta and he couldn't stomach the idea of doing that to Cloe. He should have listened to Marta the first time she'd asked him to stop running. It was a mistake that he was going to have to live with for the rest of his too long life, and one that he had no plans of repeating.

If Cloe needed to stay in order to feel safe, then that's what they would do, because there was nothing on this earth that he wouldn't do for her.

God, help him if she ever figured that out.

———

One week later.....

"I tagged her!" Ephraim frantically pointed out as Christofer grabbed him by the back of his neck and pulled him away from the adorable giggling baby girl rolling over on the mat.

Danni sighed contently from the sidelines where she sat between Caine's legs. "Karma's the best."

"It really is," Caine said, wrapping his arms around his mate and pulling her back as they settled in to watch the daily show.

"Chris is getting away!" Ephraim shouted, struggling to get free, but after two straight hours of getting his ass handed to him, he was too exhausted to put up much of a fight.

"You bastard!" Chris gasped from where he lay bone-less on the floor, breaking his own heavily enforced rule about not swearing in front of the children. "I'm your son!"

"You're also a Sentinel trainer so man up!" Ephraim groaned as he was yanked to his feet.

"Baby on the mat!" Chris called out, sounding almost relieved.

Christofer looked down to see baby Jessica crawling towards her daddy. With a bored sigh, he dropped Ephraim, who hit the ground with a weak grunt, and picked up the adorable baby girl who was quickly staking a claim on his heart. All the children living in the mansion had him thinking about something that he'd once refused to even consider.

But now......

Things were different.

At first he hadn't been happy about staying here, but after seeing the others with their mates and their families he'd quickly changed his mind. He'd never thought that a future with a wife and children was in the cards for him, but now he couldn't help but hope for more. He wanted it all, a wife, children, and a purpose in his life and now he could have it all. There was only one thing standing in his way.

The past.

He couldn't risk a future with Cloe, not until he took care of the monsters from her past. He'd already lived a life on the run. He didn't want that for Cloe, or God help them, their children if they were ever lucky enough to have them. He wanted to see the world with her, to live their lives without fear, but until he took care of the bastard that had marked her, they couldn't do anything. They were stuck here, and even though he was enjoying himself more than he thought he would, they were still trapped.

"You think maybe it's time to stop '*Assessing*'," Danni said, making air-quotes around the word assessing, "his skills and actually move on to training him."

"I hate you," Chris said, trying to sit up, but only managed to fall back on the mat with a pained groan.

"Such a big baby," Christofer said softly, smiling down at the grinning baby in his arms. "You want a chance to beat up your daddy?"

Deciding to take her excited giggle as a yes, he carried the little girl over to Chris and placed her by his side. The little girl immediately attacked, going for her daddy's nose. No doubt she was getting a little revenge for all those games of "I've got your nose" where Chris stole her nose and refused to give it back. Chris took his beating like a man, properly whimpering and pleading for mercy as she continued her attack.

"I think I'm dying," Ephraim said from his spot on the floor.

"Wimp," Madison playfully teased as she walked in the large training room with her two baby boys in her arms and her oldest son bringing up the rear with baby CJ in his arms.

As soon as little Jessica spotted Marc, she released her hold on Chris' nose and went for the little boy. With a patient smile, he handed CJ over to Christofer and picked up the little girl who was known to throw screaming tantrums in order to gain Marc's attention. Sighing, Marc carried the little girl, who now had a firm grip on his nose, over to the section Chris had set up for the babies and sat down with her in his lap.

"I thought I'd go into town tonight. Does anyone want to come?" Madison asked, walking over to Danni and handed one of the babies to her.

"I think we're going to stay in tonight," Danni said, smiling down at the baby in her arms, which didn't exactly surprise him since she didn't seem to be able to do much more than sit on the sidelines when she wasn't sleeping the day away. The woman was sick and getting sicker each day. He wondered just how long it would be before even coming downstairs to sit became too much.

"I need to patrol, but after that I can take you out if you want," Ephraim offered, rolling over onto his side with a pained grunt.

"Will you be able to walk by then?" Madison asked, sounding thoughtful as she looked her husband over.

"Probably not," he said, chuckling as rolled over onto his back.

"I promised Izzy that I'd watch an *X-File* marathon with her," Chris said with a pained sigh that probably had more to do with the night Izzy had planned for him than the actual damage that Christofer had done to him.

"What about you, Christofer?" Madison asked as the baby boy in his arms smiled sleepily as he nodded off.

"We'll probably just stay in," he said, carrying the sleeping baby boy to one of the bassinets lined up against the wall and placed the baby carefully on the small bed.

"Are you sure?" Madison asked, sounding like she wanted to say more, but thankfully she kept the questions to a minimum.

That was one thing that he liked about this group, they didn't ask too many questions. They didn't harp on him or demand answers. They left him alone to do whatever he wanted. He could train, draw, walk the grounds or sit in the nursery with a baby in each arm in peace and enjoy the quiet-

Screams for help.

FIFTY-ONE

"Stop!" Izzy screamed as she tried to slap Cloe's hands away, but she'd been doing this long enough now to know that stopping was the last thing that she should do.

"She's trying to kill me!" Izzy yelled, continuing to slap at her hands until she finally accepted the fact that Cloe wasn't going to stop and decided that it was time to make her escape. Unfortunately for Izzy, that large belly of hers and the agonizing pain that had twisted her muscles and forced her to drop to the floor stopped her from moving more than a few inches.

"What the hell is going on?" Christofer demanded, dropping to his knees across from them.

"What the hell are you doing to her?" Chris snapped as he dropped by Christofer's side on the foyer floor and moved to pull Izzy into his arms, but Cloe took him by surprise by taking a firm grip of his hand and placing it on Izzy's ruined hip.

"Keep your hand here while I work the tension out of her muscles," Cloe ordered, returning her focus to the tense muscles cramping up in the smaller woman's back, hip and leg.

"What are you doing?" Christofer asked, watching them with a frown.

"What does it look like she's doing?" Izzy snapped, once again trying to shove Cloe's hands away. "She's trying to-*ooohhhhhh, oh God, yes!*" she ended on loud moan as her eyes slid shut and she smiled.

"What exactly are we doing?" Chris asked, looking amused as Izzy let out another small sigh of pleasure while Cloe continued to work the knots out of her muscles.

"We're helping to stretch Izzy's muscles so that she can function without pain," she explained, carefully massaging Izzy's back and hip, knowing that the wrong amount of pressure could trigger a muscle spasm.

She honestly didn't know how Izzy had managed to go all these months like this. It was crazy. She'd understood, after she'd made them explain everything to her a few times to make sure that she understood correctly, that medication didn't work on Sentinels. She also knew that they hadn't wanted to risk surgery, but that didn't necessarily mean that the situation was hopeless. There was absolutely no reason for this woman to be in constant pain and while she was here, she was going to do what she could to help her.

"Please don't stop," Izzy moaned, a smile of pure bliss lighting up her face as her body finally relaxed.

"I won't," Cloe promised, happy to see a real smile on Izzy's face instead of that fake smile that she wore in the hopes of making everyone around her believe that she was fine.

She wasn't sure if anyone else had bought it, but she certainly hadn't. A few times over the past week she'd offered to look at Izzy's injury and see if there was anything that she could do to help her, but every time she'd asked, Izzy would simply give her another one of those aggravating smiles, thank her and lie her adorable little ass off and tell her that she was fine. Even though she'd wanted to argue with the stubborn woman, Cloe had bitten her tongue.

She didn't want to ruin things by offending anyone. She liked being here, liked living here, learning how to control her abilities, liked learning how to fight, and even though she felt like she was dying a little inside each time she saw Christofer holding one of the babies, she liked being around the Williams family. She probably should have kept her mouth shut and pretended that she didn't notice how much pain Izzy was in and if she hadn't walked in the foyer just as Izzy had stumbled and dropped unsteadily to the floor, obviously holding back a scream, she would have continued to feign ignorance.

Before Izzy could move, Cloe had her lying on her side, her shirt pulled up and her skirt pushed down. As soon as she'd placed her hands on Izzy's hip and back she'd realized just how tight her muscles were. Working the muscles wouldn't take all of her pain and discomfort away, but over time it should loosen the muscles and allow her to walk without much difficulty. She would need physical therapy every day for a while. Eventually she should be able to function with just a rubdown every day, which was something that her mate could learn to do for her.

"*Get your hands off her,*" the bastard that never stopped seething, growled, earning a collective sigh from their little group and a growl of warning from Izzy as she slapped her hand over Cloe's to keep her hand right where it was.

"She's helping her," Chris said, a look of deep concentration on his face as he slowly moved his hand over Izzy's damaged hip.

Refusing to listen, big surprise there, Kale moved closer and reached down, but she'd moved before he could remove her hand. She grabbed his and placed it just below Izzy's ribcage.

"Gently rub," she ordered absently as she focused on working the tension out of Izzy's back.

"What?" Kale asked after a slight hesitation, sounding confused as he knelt there, his hand remaining still on Izzy's side.

"She said rub!" Izzy snapped, sending the bastard a murderous glare that had Cloe biting back a smile as the large man hurried to do just that. Izzy released a drawn out sigh as she relaxed back on the floor, her arm folded beneath her head, her eyes closed and a small smile tilting her lips up as they worked her muscles.

"Where did you learn that?" Christofer asked as she used her thumbs to work out a particularly nasty knot in Izzy's back.

"I took a few extra courses when I was in school," she said, following the direction of the knot until it hit the scar tissue decorating Izzy's hip.

"Is this going to help her?" Chris asked, gently rubbing his mate's hip.

She hated making promises, but one look at the expression on his face told her that he needed to hear something, anything that would give him some semblance of hope. "It should help relieve some of her pain," she promised, praying that she was right.

"Can I help?" Marc asked as he walked into the large foyer.

She opened her mouth to say no, but something in Marc's expression told her that Chris wasn't the only one punishing himself over Izzy's injury. "Actually, I could use some help. I was thinking of walking into town and picking up some oils that might help her. You can be my escort as long as it's fine with your parents."

"It's fine. Just make sure you're back before dark," Ephraim said, walking into the foyer with a baby in each arm.

"When are we going?" Marc asked, standing tall and looking like he was ready to take on the world.

He really was such a sweet kid. He was also too serious for a kid his age. In the last week here, she hadn't seen him playing any video games, watching television, playing outside or having a friend over. He was always looking after Izzy and Jessica, making sure they were taken care of. He did so much, too much for a kid.

"Give me an hour?" she asked, shooting Marc a smile.

"One hour," he agreed solemnly, appearing as though he carried the weight of the world on his shoulders.

"Chris, could you make sure that Izzy soaks in a hot tub for at least thirty minutes?" she asked, moving to stand up when Izzy made a desperate grab to stop her. "The hot water will help your muscles relax," she promised Izzy as she gently pried the woman's fingers off her arm.

"Fine," Izzy grumbled as she released her hold on Cloe and allowed Chris to pick her up. "You may carry me to my room and draw my bath for me," she said on a bored sigh as though she were somehow doing Chris a favor.

"Little slave driver," Chris said, chuckling as he leaned down and kissed Izzy on the forehead.

"I don't believe I gave you leave to kiss me, good sir," Izzy sniffed haughtily, folding her arms over her ample breasts as she looked away, making everyone in the foyer smile, but not for the reason that Cloe thought. It had been long time since Izzy was able to tease her mate and smile about having to be carried around. They took it as a good sign of things to come.

———

"Do you want me to go with you?" Christofer asked as he followed Cloe into their room. Not that she really had a choice in the matter. He was going no matter what, but he liked to make her think that she had a choice.

"Do you want to go with me?" she asked, eying him curiously as she picked up her backpack.

"Of course," he said, lying his ass off.

He wanted to spend time with her. He just didn't want to do it in another small-minded town. It had been close to three weeks since he was last forced to spend time with humans and he would have been more than fine with turning that three weeks into an eternity, but it seemed that Cloe had other plans.

"Hmm, you don't sound very excited," she noted as she searched through her bag.

"I'm ecstatic," he said dryly as he watched her bend over.

"You could check out the art supply store," she suggested, shooting him a quick glance over her shoulder.

"I could," he said absently as he eyed the pile of drawings he'd done since this whole thing started, still wondering if his new life was going to have room in it for his first love.

He needed to protect Cloe, to make this world safe for her and that was going to take a great deal of training and time to accomplish. His desire to spend every waking moment escaping through his art had started to diminish over the past few weeks. He still loved to draw, took great pleasure from it, but that overwhelming need to lose himself in his art just wasn't the same anymore.

Not since Cloe became the center of his world.

"We have forty-five minutes to kill," Cloe suddenly announced with a coy little smile that he knew too well.

"What do you have in mind?" he asked just as casually as he shifted to make room for his growing erection.

"Well," she began, kicking off her shoes, "we could go for a walk."

"We're walking to town in forty-five minutes," he said, kicking off his shoes.

"True," she said with a slight nod as she reached for the hem of her shirt. "We could go for a swim," she suggested, pulling her shirt off and revealing a very sexy baby pink bra.

"We probably wouldn't have enough time to change," he pointed out, removing his shirt and tossing it aside.

"True," she sighed, nodding in agreement as she pulled her socks off. "I guess we could watch some television."

"There's nothing good on television," he said, having absolutely no idea if that was true or not as he pulled his socks off and tossed them aside.

"That's true," Cloe nodded, looking thoughtful as she undid her jeans and shimmied out of them, giving him a view of her matching panties. "We could go train for a while, I guess," she said, crawling onto the bed and leaning back against the pillows.

"We could," he murmured as he unsnapped his jeans, "but then we'd probably lose track of time."

"This is true," she said, bending a knee as she spread her legs apart so that he had a good view of her dampening panties. "Well, I'm out of ideas," she said as she absently traced her fingertips between her breasts, down to her belly, back and forth she moved her fingers while she made a show of trying to figure out just what they should do for the next forty minutes.

"I have an idea," he said, pulling down his zipper.

"Oh, and what's that?" she asked, sounding breathless as she watched his every move.

He reached into his pants and pulled himself out. "You could peel those pretty little panties off and show me how wet you are."

"I could……," she said, looking thoughtful even as she started to do just that. "But, I'm really not sure how that would help us kill forty minutes."

"Cause while you're sliding a finger inside your sweet little pussy, I'm going to tell you just how badly I want to fuck you."

FIFTY-TWO

Oh, God……..

He was going to make her spontaneously combust.

She felt herself become wetter as his words registered. Her eyes were locked on that large cock standing at attention, begging for her mouth and God help her, but she wanted to crawl over to him and worship it.

"Show me how wet you are, mein Schatz."

Everything shifted red as she moved her gaze away from the erection that had brought her so much pleasure over the past week, up to the incredible torso that she loved running her tongue over and up to his handsome face to find his eyes were just as red as hers. Keeping her eyes locked with his, she spread her legs wider, making sure to give him an unobstructed view as she reached between her legs and spread herself so that he could see just how wet he'd made her. He growled in approval as he licked his lips, making her wonder if he was imagining licking her.

"What should we do now?" she asked, somehow resisting the urge to slide her fingers inside herself and find the relief that her body was starting to demand.

"Take your bra off so I can see just how hard your nipples are," he said, leaning back on the loveseat, looking completely relaxed and acting as though having his cock freed and curving into his stomach was the most natural thing in the world.

"And what will you be doing while I take my bra off?" she asked, seconds away from saying the hell with it and ending this game. She was so turned on, but then again, he always seemed to have this effect on her. Morning, noon and night he made her crazy for him. She'd lost count of how many times she'd woken in the middle of the night to find his tongue sliding deep inside her or the tip of his cock waiting patiently for her to open her mouth and suck him dry.

No matter how many times he took her, she could never seem to get enough and judging by the way that he went out of his way to find her and bend her over most days, neither could he. He was an incredibly gifted lover and somehow he seemed to be getting better each time. She would never forget yesterday when he'd taken her by surprise, pushed her up against the wall and ground himself against her ass as he whispered everything that he wanted to do with her, starting with sliding his fingers deep inside of her to pulling his cock out of her wet pussy and letting her finish him off with her mouth. He'd had her biting back a scream as she came hard just from his words and the way he'd rubbed against her. It had never happened to her before and she couldn't wait to do it again.

"Imagining my mouth on them while you suck my cock," he said, raising the temperature of the room by a good ten degrees.

"So in your dreams I'm a contortionist?" she asked teasingly as she removed her bra and dropped it on the floor.

His lips twitched with amusement even as his eyes ate her up. "You'd have to be pretty flexible to do all the things I've been imagining doing to you."

"Oh?" she asked, licking her lips as she reached up and traced one of her nipples with her fingertips while she placed her hand between her legs and traced her slit for him. "And what kind of things have I done in these fantasies of yours?"

"Things that you should be ashamed off," he growled, watching her, his eyes shifting from her breasts to her fingers playing for his enjoyment as he reached down ran his palm down the underside of his cock.

"And what have you done in these fantasies?" she asked around a soft moan as she watched him tease his cock.

"Everything," he rasped as she made a show of spreading her swollen lips apart for him again.

"Everything? That's a little vague for me, Christofer. Why don't you tell me one of these little fantasies of yours," she suggested, tracing the tip of her clit as she gave her breast a squeeze, loving the way that he licked his lips as he took it all in.

"I've fucked your pretty little ass," he said, making her breath catch and just like that, she wanted him to do just that.

"And did I love it?"

"You fucking adored it. Begged me to slide my cock in your ass again and again," he said, moaning as he cupped the tip of his cock and squeezed.

"And did you?" she asked, her hips shifting restlessly as she imagined just how good it would feel.

"No," he said, shaking his head as he wrapped his hand around his large cock and stroked himself, slowly, "I missed your pussy too much."

A gasp escaped her as she rubbed her clit. This man was so good at this. They needed those phones that Ephraim promised them, immediately. She'd probably never get anything done with him sexting her all day. Then again, she probably wouldn't care, not as long as he kept driving her out of her mind.

"It makes me wonder," Christofer said, continuing to stroke his cock while he watched her.

"Makes you wonder what?" she asked, struggling to stay focused.

"If your pussy misses me right now."

"There's only one way to find out," she said, resisting the urge to slide a finger inside herself and end this torture.

"True," he said, getting to his feet, his hand never stilling on his cock as he walked over to her, but instead of crawling between her legs like she'd expected, hoped, he stood by her head, placed a hand against the wall, a knee on the bed and brought the tip of his cock to her mouth. "I need it wet."

"That's funny," she said, taking his hand away from his erection and bringing it between her legs, "so do I."

———

I will break you the fuck off if you come too soon, Christofer promised his cock as his fingers traced between Cloe's wet slit. He wasn't sure how much more he could take. He loved playing these games with her, loved driving her out of mind until he was intoxicated on the scent of her arousal, but sometimes he was afraid he'd lose his god-damn mind if he couldn't just slide home like now. She'd never smelled so damn good before. Normally the scent of her made him crazy, but today it was driving him out of his fucking mind until all he could think about was fucking her.

A strangled groan escaped him as Cloe wrapped her lips around his cock and took him in her hot, wet mouth. *Don't even think about it,* he inwardly snarled at his poor defenseless cock when he felt his balls pull up tight. As he slid a finger inside Cloe to find her ready, he tried to think of something, anything that would keep him from-

Shit!

Too late, she had him ready to come the second she traced the slit of his cock with her tongue. Refusing to come anywhere but between her legs, he pulled his cock free, removed his hand and moved between her legs, slammed his cock home, pulled back and......

Froze.

"You're fertile," he blurted out as realization slammed into him.

The reason why he hadn't been able to keep his hands off her, more than usual, was because she was ripe. *Shit!* They'd never talked about a future, never mind children. His focus right now was to protect her and keep her safe, happy and crying out his name when he made love to her. They weren't ready for kids.

Not yet.

They were being hunted, didn't have a home of their own, but the main reason that he didn't want children yet was because he hadn't won her heart yet. He didn't want to force her to stay with him because they had a child and he sure as hell didn't want to risk losing her and their child if she ever decided to walk away.

"It's okay," she said, her expression guarded as she wrapped her arms around him to stop him from pulling out.

"We need to talk about this, mein Schatz," he said, reaching up to gently take her hand away, but the stubborn woman simply shook her head and tightened her hold around him.

"You're not going to get me pregnant," she said, threading her fingers through his hair in that way she knew drove him out of his mind and pulled him down for a slow, passionate kiss that had him groaning in defeat.

"Are you sure?" he asked as realization dawned on him. She probably had an IUD or something to keep her from getting pregnant.

"Yes," she answered against his lips, and with that he gave in and slid back inside her until his balls rubbed against her ass.

After that he stopped thinking altogether. He wrapped his arms around her, holding her tightly against him as he thrust inside her, loving the way that she suckled his tongue while her body tightened around his, refusing to let him go.

As he rolled his hips, he stared into her beautiful red eyes and realized that he couldn't go another minute without telling her that he loved her.

"Ich liebe dich, mein Schatz" he said hoarsely, wishing like hell that he could tell her so that she would understand what he was saying, but it was too soon.

"What-"

He cut her question off with a kiss as he quickened his pace, doing his best to distract her so that he wasn't forced to lie to her. He didn't want to scare her off so for now he would keep his mouth shut and hope that she didn't get her hands on a German dictionary, because-

"I love you, too," Cloe blurted out against his lips, making his hips still in mid-thrust.

"What?" he asked, sounding like an idiot, but he didn't care.

"If you stop I'm going to have to kill you," she groaned, rolling her hips to force him back inside her.

"That's not what you said," he said, struggling to focus as she found a way to ride him by simply rolling her hips, back and forth.

"Well, I'm not going to say it again so you might as well get back to doing that thing you were doing with your hips," she explained, riding his cock no doubt to distract him.

"I see," he said softly as he took over again, trying his best not to grin, but after a few seconds he gave up trying to hide it and grinned hugely, earning a murderous glare from the woman that he loved.

"It was a slip of the tongue!" she snapped, sounding adorably irritated.

"I see," he said, grinning hugely simply because he just couldn't stop.

"I hate you," she muttered, looking disgruntled.

"Would it make you feel better if I told you that I loved you more?"

"No."

"Would it make you feel better if we both pretended that it never happened?" he suggested, doing his best to stop smiling.

"Yes!" she hissed, wrapping her legs around his waist, no doubt thinking that he was going to forget the sweetest words that were ever spoken to him.

"Sorry," he said, shaking his head as he leaned down and kissed her, "I can't do that."

"Bastard," she mumbled against his lips.

"Would it make you feel better if I pulled out and used my tongue to help you forgot that little slip of yours?" he suggested innocently as he stilled inside her.

She licked her lips hungrily as his words sank in and then, once they did, she was shoving him off and sighing heavily, sounding put out as she said, "Fine, I guess we could give it a try."

Smiling once again, he kissed his way down, pausing at her breasts to lick and suckle her nipples in his mouth while he enjoyed the sweet scent she was giving off before moving south. She smelled so damn good, he thought as he licked and kissed her skin, wondering how he was going to stop from coming at the first swipe of his tongue through her delicate folds. Once he came to her navel an unexpected scent hit him. It was weak, barely noticeable, but while he inhaled, his smile disappeared as he caught the scent of something he'd never expected.

She was pregnant.

FIFTY-THREE

"If you stop," Danni said, panting heavily as she pulled her mouth away from his cock, "I will kill you!"

"Ditto," Caine growled against her slit as he reached between them, wrapped his hand around his aching cock and brought the tip back to her mouth. The little tease flicked the ring with her tongue, making him growl against her pussy as he stroked his cock.

He speared her with his tongue as he continued to stroke himself, moaning with pleasure as Danni licked and teased the tip of his cock. She loved to tease him, driving him out of his goddamn mind. Her favorite thing was to reduce him to a snarling animal that only cared about mounting her and fucking her until neither of them could barely move, which he was about five seconds from doing.

"More," she moaned, rocking her hips so that she was riding his tongue, sliding her core up and down his tongue while she took the tip of his cock in his mouth and-

"Fuck!" he growled as she scraped her teeth over the sensitive tip.

"What did I tell you about stopping?" she asked with a long, drawn out sigh that she'd learned from that bastard

Chris, as she released her hold on his needy cock and moved to climb off him.

"The same thing I told you, little tease," he growled, grabbing her as she moved to climb off him, his control snapping as he shoved her face first on the bed.

The little tease laughed as she folded her arms beneath her head, spread her legs just enough and sighed as he covered her with his body. He kissed the back of her neck as he positioned himself between her legs and pushed in, his cock slid inside her tight wet hold, loving the resistance this position created. They moaned in unison once he was in as far as he could go, her beautiful bottom pressed against his stomach.

"That feels so good," Danni moaned as he gently rocked inside her, making sure that his piercing hit her in just the right spot as he reached over her, entwined their fingers and held her hands above her head as he slowly rode her.

As he pushed inside her, his balls rubbed against the comforter, adding immense pleasure to what he was doing to her. She was so wet, so tight, and still hiding something from him, he thought as he spotted that white gauze bandage that she'd been wearing for over a month now. He'd asked her a few times about it, but each time she managed to change the subject, mostly by dropping to her knees and making it impossible for him to focus on anything other than just how good her mouth felt wrapped around his cock.

But now......

He released her left arm, continuing to thrust, but mostly now just to distract her. Keeping a firm grip on her right hand, he reached over and-

Danni squealed as she tried to pull her hand away, but he held tight, keeping a firm hold on that hand as he reached over and tore the bandage off. "No! Stop!" Danni cried, desperately trying to wiggle free, but there was nowhere to go, not with him on top of her and buried inside her. The only thing that she managed to do was to ride his cock harder, which he was more than fine with.

As soon as he had the gauze off, he turned her hand and-

"A tattoo?" he asked with a frown, because he hadn't smelled the ink when she'd first started wearing the bandage, but he had a feeling that he knew the reason why.

The cancer had hidden it from him.

It was getting stronger and becoming more aggressive, something that terrified and frustrated him, but right now his focus was on the tattoo that his mate had kept hidden from him.

"I hate you," Danni groaned pathetically as she buried her face in the comforter.

He frowned down at the large Celtic cross with the small crescent moon. It took him a minute to realize that he was looking at the Sentinel mark, only in reverse. Each Sentinel was born with a crescent moon with a small cross marked right below their navel. This was……

"Why do you have the Sentinel mark tattooed on your arm?" he asked, wondering how to tell her that the tattoo artist had seriously fucked up and switched the positions of the cross and moon.

"It's not the Sentinel mark," she mumbled against the comforter only to add after a pause, "well, not really anyway."

"Then what is it?" he asked, tracing his fingertip over the black tattoo.

She sighed heavily as she said, "It's something I designed when I was a kid."

"For......?"

She grumbled something inaudible into the comforter.

"What was that?" he asked, pulling his cock out until only his piercing touched her core, knowing that she'd get him back for this and not really caring, not when she was hiding things from him.

"I wanted my own Sentinel design," she muttered stubbornly as she tried to push back and force his cock back inside her.

"I see," he said, pressing a kiss against the back of her nape, because he knew his mate well.

The Sentinels had been her life. She'd worked her ass off, training, fighting and doing whatever she could to prove her worth. While most humans born to Sentinels liked to bitch about the unfairness of their situation, Danni had accepted her fate as a mere human with grace and dignity. She'd never used the fact that she was human as an excuse, never hid behind it, because she considered herself a part of the Sentinel world.

"Why didn't you get this sooner?" he asked, sliding back in, her wet walls making the move easy.

"You know why," she answered with a disgruntled snort.

"Because they would have mocked you?" he asked, chuckling when she tried to throw him off.

Human children that got the Sentinel mark tattoo were usually mocked and ridiculed and for good reason. They usually believed they were just as good as or better than Sentinels and had the attitudes to match, which was mostly why they were mocked. They were cocky little bastards.

"Yes!"

"And the reason that you hid it here?" he asked, feeling like an idiot because the answer was pretty obvious.

"Chris."

He chuckled as he pulled her hand closer so that he could press a kiss against her tattoo. "Is that why Chris and Ephraim have been wearing matching bandages?"

"They're mocking me, because I've been wearing this thing for so long," she mumbled pathetically. "Just imagine what they would do if they knew what I've been hiding."

They would make fun of her day and night, because they viewed her as a little sister and saw it as their responsibility, and right, to torment her. Even he'd admit that they did a great job. They took their job seriously, very seriously.

"Do you want me to kick their asses?" he asked, linking their fingers back together as he adjusted the angle of penetration.

"No," she muttered, sounding pathetic and making him glad that she couldn't see him smile. "They'd just make fun of me more. I'll deal with it, I guess," she decided, finishing it off with another drawn out sigh that had him biting back a chuckle that would probably end with him taking a very cold shower.

"Do you want me to distract you?" he asked, punctuating each word with a slow roll of his hips.

"I suppose," she said, sounding put out.

"I could stop," he offered, releasing her hands so that he could slide his hands between Danni and the bed. He cupped her breasts, making sure that her firm nipples peeked through his fingers so that they rubbed against the comforter as he pushed back inside her.

"And I could kill you," she reminded him, earning a chuckle, because he knew that if he stopped right now, she'd kick his ass, make him finish her off with his mouth and then leave him to either relieve himself or deal with blue balls, neither prospect sounding pleasant at the moment.

FIFTY-FOUR

"Wait. Where are you going?" she managed to ask, panting heavily as she struggled to push herself up on trembling arms.

"Shit!" Christofer said, rushing across the room towards the door, shoving his hand through his hair, his pants unbuttoned and his-

"You may want to put that thing away," she said, trembling as she watched him, torn between amusement and frustration as he grabbed his erection, forced it back into his pants and-

"God damn it!" he shouted, stumbling into the wall, wincing as he reached down and cleared the zipper.

"Christofer?" she said, trying to get his attention as he continued towards the door.

"Be right back," and with that, he was gone.

"Okay.........," she said, watching as the door closed behind him, leaving her to wonder what the hell just happened.

One minute he'd been driving her out of her mind as he'd kissed his way down to where she *really* needed him and the next he was falling off the bed, stumbling to his feet and racing for the door. She'd still been able to scent his lust, but there had been another scent coming off him, one that she couldn't quite figure out.

As she sat there, struggling to catch her breath, she thought over what had happened over the last few minutes, trying to figure out what she'd missed. Maybe-

"Go sniff her," Christofer suddenly demanded just as the bedroom door flew open and Ephraim and Caine came stumbling into the room, struggling to zip up their pants.

"Ummm," was her only response, because really, what else could she say when the man that she loved left her naked, trembling and alone in bed only to return a few minutes later, shoving two half naked men into their room and demanding that they sniff her.

"Bossy bastard," Ephraim muttered as he finished buttoning his pants.

"You could have at least waited until I was done!" Caine snapped.

"Sniff!" Christofer bit out, pointing at her.

It took a few seconds for what he was asking them to do to really sink in and when it did, her jaw dropped. He didn't just seriously ask them to-

With a muttered curse, Ephraim walked over to her, leaned over and inhaled, but before she could die of mortification, Caine followed suit, swearing more vividly as he leaned over, inhaled, frowned, inhaled and muttered a whole new genre of curses.

"Is she?" Christofer demanded, staying where he was by the door.

"Yeah," Caine said, rubbing his hands roughly down his face.

"It's fresh. Probably by just a few hours," Ephraim explained, doing a wonderful job of keeping her in the dark.

"It shouldn't be possible," Caine said, dropping his hands by his sides as he shared a look with Ephraim.

"She was fully marked."

"It must have grown back during the change," Caine said, shooting her a curious look that had her pulling her sheet up higher as she tried to make sense of their words.

"We overfed her," Ephraim explained. "It was probably enough blood to fix everything and restore her body."

"What grew back?" Christofer asked, and at that moment she could have kissed him, because she was wondering the same damn thing.

"Her uterus," Caine said gravely, his expression full of pity as he looked at her. At least she thought he'd said her uterus, but that was impossible.

"What the hell are you talking about?" Christofer demanded. "What does her uterus have to do with her being marked?"

And just like that, she lost the ability to breathe.

They knew.

"When a shifter marks a human," Ephraim explained, looking disgusted, "they make it impossible for their property to have a child. They want their property sterile. They might tolerate their property having sex with someone else, but they refuse to allow anyone else to set any type of claim."

And just like that, her stomach dropped with the realization of why tearing her back apart hadn't been enough for the beast that attacked her. He'd wanted to make sure that she could never have a child, because he'd seen her as nothing more than a thing to do with whatever he'd wished, even making sure that she was never able to live a full life and to-

"She's definitely pregnant," Caine announced. "It's a Pyte," he added, sounding relieved and making her wonder what else he'd expected it to be when his announcement registered.

"I'm sorry, but what did you just say?" she asked, absolutely positive that she'd misunderstood him.

Caine opened his mouth only to quickly close it and shoot Ephraim a panicked look. Ephraim simply rubbed the back of his neck as he muttered, "We fucking suck at this."

"There's no way that I could be pregnant," she said, expecting all three men to quickly agree, but they didn't.

"Can we have a minute?" Christofer asked, suddenly looking exhausted.

"Congratulations, Cloe," Ephraim said with a warm smile as he headed for the door. Caine said something, probably congratulating her also, but she couldn't hear him over the loud buzzing going off in her head as she struggled with the news.

"Are they sure?" she found herself asking as she sat there, feeling numb.

Christofer walked back over to the bed and sat down next to her, he took her hand into his, entwining their fingers and nodded, slowly, looking shell shocked. She expected him to say something, to explain how this happened, to reassure her, to tell her that everything was going to be okay and that this wasn't some sick joke, but he just sat there, staring off at nothing. She didn't know what to say or do at this moment. It wasn't something that she'd ever expected to hear and it sure as hell didn't feel real by having three men sniffing her.

A small knock sounded at the door, followed by a hesitant, "Cloe?"

Damn it, she'd forgotten all about Marc, but as much as she wanted to stay here and let everything sink in, she couldn't ditch Marc. The poor kid needed a distraction and as she looked up at Christofer, sitting there looking like he'd just been kicked in the balls, she decided that perhaps she did too.

———

"That looks like a fun game," Cloe said, picking up another copy from the shelf.

"Izzy would love it," he said, calculating how much money he had in his pocket and how much he had in his sock drawer at home. He quickly realized that he was about ten dollars short. He'd have to wait until next week when he got his allowance to buy it, he decided as he reluctantly put the game back.

"What about you?" Cloe asked, looking at the game.

"What about me?" he asked, looking around the large game section, hoping to find a game that he could afford for Izzy.

"Wouldn't you like this game?" Cloe asked as she turned the game over.

He shrugged. "I don't have time for games anymore."

"Why not?" Cloe asked, putting the game into the hand basket that he was carrying for her.

"I just don't," he said, shrugging as he moved down the aisle only to stop when he'd spotted the game that he'd asked his father to reserve for him last year. He'd forgotten all about it. His fingers shifted anxiously by his sides, anxious to pick up the game and buy it, but he forced himself to look away and move on.

"That's a shame," Cloe said with a shrug as she picked up the game that he'd forced himself to walk away from and dropped it in the basket.

"Why's that?" he asked, looking towards the toy section, wondering if he should just buy Jessica and the babies something to keep them occupied so that Izzy could rest when he spotted Christofer.

He didn't know Christofer that well, but he liked him. He especially liked the way that Christofer was able to tap into his bloodlust strength without losing control, something that he was hoping the Pyte would show him how to do once he went through the change. Marc was about to turn his attention to the toy section when he realized what section Christofer was standing in.

The baby section.

He felt his stomach drop as he caught a glimpse of the expression on Christofer's face, the same one that his brother Chris had worn after he'd found out that Izzy was pregnant the first time. He looked miserable and terrified as he picked up a pink baby blanket and stared at it as though he wasn't quite sure what he was looking at.

"Because I was going to ask Mr. Grumpy pants over there to take us to-"

"You're pregnant," he blurted out, hoping that he was wrong.

Cloe sighed as she dropped another video game in the basket. "Please tell me that you didn't scent it," she said, cringing slightly.

"No," he said, his stomach turning as he swallowed back bile.

This couldn't be happening. There were already four babies at home with two more on the way. Six babies to watch over and protect was going to be hard enough, but seven? He couldn't protect them all, Izzy and his mother. It was too much. It was-

"Hey," Cloe said, sliding her arm around his small shoulders as she pulled him into her side, "relax, kiddo."

"I can't," he said, shaking his head as he struggled to take a breath, but it wouldn't come. He couldn't get enough air, the store wouldn't stop spinning and the image of Jessica's bleeding head and the sounds of Izzy screaming in pain because of him blared in his head, growing louder and louder with each passing second until-

"Shhh, relax," Christofer said soothingly as he suddenly found himself being held like a child in the large Pyte's arms.

"I'm fine," he tried to tell him, but the only thing that came out were choked sobs as he embarrassed himself by crying like some little kid.

He wasn't a little kid. He was a man now. He had responsibilities. His little brothers, his nephew, Jessica, his mother and Izzy were all counting on him to take care of them. He shouldn't be losing it like this. He should be manning up!

"Let it go," Christofer said, holding him tightly.

He stubbornly shook his head, desperately trying to get himself under control. He needed to stay in control, needed to keep a level head, especially with so many people counting on him. He needed to-

"Let go," Christofer whispered again and just like that, he did.

FIFTY-FIVE

"**P**lease don't tell anyone," Marc said, looking miserable as he sat across from them, absently playing with a French fry.

"There's nothing to tell," Christofer said, gesturing for Marc to eat. She was glad to see him so relaxed. He'd given her quite a scare earlier when he'd lost it. She'd been about to wrap him in her arms when Christofer had swooped in and taken over. She'd been amazed at how great he'd been with Marc. No matter how hard Marc cried or shook, Christofer had been patient with him, listening to him and reassuring him that everything was going to be okay. She'd never thought of Christofer as the fatherly type, but the way he'd handled Marc had warmed her heart.

Reluctantly, Marc took a large bite out of his French fry before dipping what was left in ketchup while she sat there, trying not to pout. She missed food, real food, right now more than ever as she was forced to sit there on the hard plastic bench in the diner filled with mouthwatering scents. What she wouldn't give for a double cheeseburger, fries and a triple chocolate milkshake with-

"Why aren't you eating?" Marc asked her, looking curious as he shoved the rest of the fry in his mouth.

"I can't eat food," she explained, almost positive that he'd been told that she was a Pyte.

"Except when you're pregnant," Marc said with a shrug as he grabbed another fry off his plate.

"She can eat real food?" Christofer asked, resting his arm along the top of the bench behind her.

"Mmmmmhmm," he answered around another fry. "It will help with the morning sickness, but she still needs," he paused to look around the diner and make sure that no one was listening, "blood."

"But I can eat?" she asked, trying not to get her hopes up.

"Yup."

As soon as the word was out of his mouth, she stole one of his fries, shoved it in her mouth and closed her eyes, grimacing at the memory of what had happened the last time she'd tried to eat food only to moan in pleasure. It tasted so good, so damn good. She opened her eyes to steal another fry, but Christofer beat her to it by placing a fry against her lips as Marc gestured for the waitress. As she sat there, savoring fry after fry, she decided that perhaps being pregnant wasn't going to be so bad after all.

"Kill me," she whimpered, holding her stomach as she leaned against the tree, her eyes closed as she tried not to lose the rest of her dinner.

"We should get going before it gets any darker," Marc said, shifting nervously by the road.

"Call your father or brother to come get you," Christofer said, standing beside her as he rubbed her back.

"Kill. Me," she stressed, wondering why he wasn't putting her out of her misery.

"She needs blood," Marc said, shifting the shopping bag that she'd asked him to carry for her to his other hand so that he could pull his phone out of his back pocket.

At the mention of drinking blood, her stomach rebelled. Just the thought of drinking or eating anything was too much to handle. She was starting to think that she may have overdone it a bit at the diner. She hadn't planned on eating so much, but the moment that she'd been able to swallow that fry without wanting to puke her guts up, she'd sort of lost it.

Not that it was her fault. It wasn't, at least not as far as she was concerned. It was Ephraim and Christofer's since they'd convinced her that she'd never be able to wash down a juicy cheeseburger with a thick chocolate milkshake again. Once she'd discovered the loophole, an unexpected pregnancy, she'd decided to indulge herself......just a bit.

Two double cheeseburgers, fries, onion rings, chicken tenders, three chocolate milkshakes, two large Pepsis, one ice cream sundae, and four different slices of pie later and she was regretting a few of her choices tonight. At the time, she'd been relieved that Christofer had been too lost in his own thoughts to comment on her dining choices, but now she really wished that he'd bitched about that second burger that was threatening to make another appearance.

"How far away is the house?" Christofer asked Marc as he rubbed her back.

"About a mile," Marc answered as he searched through his phone for a number. "Half a mile if we go through the woods."

"Do you know the way through the woods?" Christofer asked quietly, his hand stilling on her back as she registered an odd note to his tone.

"Why?" Marc asked, looking up from his phone the same time that she looked past Christofer towards the road, both of them spotting the large beast from her nightmares standing on its hind legs at the same time. Her heart skipped a beat as the beast turned its large, black head in their direction, its silver eyes narrowed on them as it bared its teeth.

"Because I think you're going to need to take that shortcut through the woods," Christofer said, keeping his eyes on the large black beast as he slowly moved forward, grabbed Marc by the back of his shirt and pulled him back just as the large beast released a howl that sent shivers down her spine.

"Run," Christofer ordered, keeping his eyes locked on the large beast as he shoved Marc towards her.

—

"I can't run," Cloe said, bending over and clutching her stomach as the sounds of snarling grew louder.

"You have to run, Cloe," Marc pleaded, throwing a frantic look over his shoulder as he grabbed her hand and tried to pull her to her feet, but the cramp tearing through her stomach had her pulling back and shaking her head.

"Go, Marc," she said, licking her lips as she struggled not to lose consciousness as another cramp tore through her stomach, followed by another one and another one. "Go home and get your father," she said, pulling her hand from his and blindly pushing him away as another cramp tore through her, dropping her to her knees with a muted cry.

"I can't leave you!" Marc hissed, dropping to his knees beside her and putting his small arm around her, the sounds of growls and snarling surrounding them.

"You have to," she said, forcing her eyes open, but the sharp pain shooting through her stomach had her quickly closing her eyes and trying to bite back a groan.

"I can't leave you here!" Marc urgently whispered, the small arm around her tightened as he tried to pull her to her feet, but she wasn't going anywhere, not with this pain ripping through her and certainly not with Christofer back at the road trying to stop that monster from finding them.

"We need help," she said, knowing that there was no other way to get Marc to leave her. She needed him to leave, to know that he was safe. The thought of that thing getting his hands on Marc and doing to him what had been done to her brothers terrified her more than the thought of that monster finding her.

"Help is already on its way," Marc whispered, dropping his arm from around her so that he could take her hand into his.

"How do you know?" she asked, giving his trembling hand a gentle squeeze.

"I sent the signal," was all he said before a man's bloodcurdling scream tore through the dense forest.

"Christofer!" she cried out as her eyes flew open.

"No!" Marc screamed, his hand tightening around hers as she tried to get to her feet. "Don't go!"

"I have to help Christofer," she said, ignoring the cramps playing tag in her stomach as she forced her legs to work. "He needs me."

"I need you!" Marc cried as she pulled her hand free and took a step towards the sound of another scream. "Please, Cloe! I need you!"

She stopped, her heart pounding in her chest as that scream tore through her. She needed to go to him, to make sure that he was okay, but she couldn't leave Marc, not when leaving him meant that she was abandoning him to the same fate that she'd endured.

She refused to make the same mistake that her mother had made.

"Let's go," she said, taking Marc's hand and stumbled forward, forcing her legs to move until she soon found herself running with Marc away from the screams, hating herself more than she'd ever thought possible.

———

"Let's go!" Chris yelled jumping into the back of the van behind Caine as Ephraim hit the gas.

"Where's the signal coming from?" Caine asked, as he double-checked his weapons.

"Baby, where's the signal coming from?" Chris asked, pressing the switch to the microphone attached to his collar.

"*A hundred yards ahead and two hundred yards in the woods to the north. They're on the move and heading towards the mansion,*" Izzy answered, trying to stay calm, but he knew that she was terrified and for good reason.

Marc.

His little brother wasn't the type to call for help unless the shit hit the fan. He'd been trained on how to protect himself, how to hide and how to get his ass to safety and wouldn't use the Sentinel system unless it was really fucking necessary.

"I shouldn't have fucking let them go!" his father repeated for probably the hundredth time since the signal came in two minutes ago.

"He's fine," Chris said, forcing himself to remain calm, knowing that if he didn't, it could cost his brother his life.

"Christofer wouldn't let anything happen to him," Caine said and heaven help him, but he wanted to believe him.

"He wouldn't," his father agreed, sounding more like a prayer than anything.

The alarm on his phone went off, signaling another emergency call. He ripped his phone free and looked down at the screen.

"Mother fucker!" Caine snarled, voicing the thought going through his head.

"*Chris, Marc's phone just sent a second emergency call,*" Izzy said over the radio, her beautiful voice cracking with fear.

"Where are they?" he asked, taking a knee by the open van door as his father sped down the road.

"*They've stopped about two hundred yards from where you are now.*"

"Send him a message that I'm on my way," he said, grabbing the side of the van door and jumped out, hitting the pavement at a dead run.

———

"Where's the bitch?"

"Don't call her that," Christofer growled, stumbling awkwardly as he kept his eyes on the man that not even a minute ago had been a raging beast trying to tear him apart.

He'd done a damn good job of it, he had to admit as he reached up and absently wiped blood out of his eye as his other arm hung uselessly by his side, blood dripping down his fingers to join the blood pooling by his feet. His breaths were raspy, his head filled with hazy thoughts as he struggled to stay focused. He couldn't lose control, not now.

The man standing in front of him grinned as he looked past Christofer towards the woods. "Went for a little run in woods?" he asked, chuckling as Christofer watched with dread as all the wounds that he'd inflicted on the bastard quickly disappeared.

If he'd only stayed in his beast form he'd be dead by now, Christofer thought in a daze, stumbling back a step as his legs threatened to buckle. He'd had the beast howling in pain, battered and broken. He'd been damaged as well, but not as badly as the werewolf lying on the ground gurgling blood. He'd been moving in for the kill when the bastard started to change, startling him. Stupidly, he'd stood there trying to make sense out of what he was seeing and by the time he'd realized that the werewolf had shifted to heal, it was too late.

"An unturned Pyte?" the shifter demanded around a growl, scenting the air as all signs of amusement left his face and his eyes flashed silver.

Christofer held himself still as he waited for the shifter to mention the baby, but he never did. Instead, the shifter shook his head menacingly, his focus on the woods. "Not fucking happening," the shifter growled as he took a step towards the woods.

"What's not happening?" Christofer asked, moving to block him and wincing as his broken ribs rubbed against his lungs, threatening to slice them open.

"The Pyte won't be reaching his immortality," the shifter sneered. "My Pack won't allow it."

The meaning behind the shifter's words hit him as he stumbled to the side, a breathless laugh leaving him as he felt the familiar stirring inside his head. He sent up a silent prayer for his mate and the boy, hoping like hell that they were back at the mansion and out of his reach as he let go.

FIFTY-SIX

"Shhhhh, stay calm," Cloe whispered, keeping her eyes locked on the bloody back of the man crouched down in front of them.

"I'm trying," Marc whispered as she reached back and took his hand in hers as she pushed back, making damn sure that he wasn't going to get another chance to push past her and put himself in front of her again. She swore that if he tried to do that again, that she'd put him over her knee and spank the shit out of him.

"He's going to hurt you," Marc said, trying to step past her again, but a firm squeeze had him keeping his butt where it belonged.

"No, he's not," she said as she debated telling Marc to keep running towards the mansion, but she wasn't sure if Christofer would chase after the boy or not.

Since he'd snarled at the boy when he'd stepped in front of her the last time, she couldn't be sure of anything at the moment. She knew that Christofer would rather die than hurt a child, but in this state….

She wasn't exactly sure what Christofer would do if Marc took off running and she didn't want to find out.

A vicious snarl drew her attention back to Christofer as he tensed, every blood coated muscle in his back bulging as he prepared himself to face whoever they heard running towards them. A few seconds later she nearly sagged with relief when she caught the sweet scent of Sentinel blood until she realized something very important, Christofer had also caught the scent. He growled viciously as he shifted his weight forward, preparing for an attack.

"Christofer," she said, licking her lips anxiously, praying that she could talk some sense into him before this turned into a bloodbath. "I think we're okay now."

"*Mine!*" he snarled, shifting as he searched for the new threat that was coming their way.

"I-I think that's my brother," Marc said, squeezing her hand as he shifted behind her and she knew, just knew, that if she gave him a chance that he'd try to make a run for it to stop Chris from coming too close, but she wasn't giving him that chance.

"Don't move, Marc," she whispered, moving back to make sure that Marc wasn't going anywhere. "Chris can take care of himself. He'll be fine."

"No! Please, just let me go to my brother!" Marc said, frantically trying to pull his hand free.

"Marc, he'll be-"

"You stay where you are, Marc," Chris suddenly said as he came into sight, about twenty feet away to their right. He immediately stilled when he caught sight of Christofer.

"Don't move," Ephraim said softly, coming into sight fifteen feet away and to their left.

"Shit," Caine said, stopping right beside Ephraim as he took in the scene before him. "What the hell happened?"

"Shifter.....attacked.....," Christofer answered, taking everyone by surprise. "Scented my mate, my child and the boy," he answered in a low growl that sent chills down her spine.

"A shifter attacked you?" Chris asked, looking as surprised as the other two men. "How the hell did he get in town?"

"It was black," Marc told them, once again trying to move past her, but she wasn't having that.

"Where?" Ephraim demanded, his eyes shifting red.

"It was waiting for us on the road," she said, swallowing nervously as she watched Caine's eyes shift as well and wondered if she was about to have two more Pytes going into bloodlust.

"Caine, can you hunt the shifter down and-"

"Dead," Christofer bit out in a guttural tone as he slowly stood up and faced the three men.

"Were there any others?" Chris asked, looking past Christofer to make sure that they were okay.

"Two men....armed......smelled like the beast," Christofer answered.

"An Alpha and two shifters," Caine surmised, looking thoughtful as he leaned back against the tree.

"I take it they're dead as well?" Chris asked, and after a slight pause, started walking in their direction.

When Christofer growled in warning, Chris continued towards them, "No worries, big guy, I just want to make sure that my brother is okay," and to her utter surprise, Christofer let him by.

"Are you okay, little man?" Ephraim asked his son, stepping past Christofer with a nod.

"I'm fine," Marc said firmly as she released his hand, but he refused to let hers go. "But Cloe is sick."

Before the last word was out of his mouth, Christofer was standing in front of her, cupping her face gently in his hands as he looked her over. His red eyes searched every inch of her, looking for an injury that wasn't there. When he dropped one of his hands away from her face and pressed it against her stomach, she fell a little more in love with him even as she struggled to not flinch away from him.

"The baby's fine," she said, her breath catching as it finally started to hit her.

She was pregnant.

"Oh my God," she whispered, her lips curling into a watery smile as her eyes teared up. "Oh my God!"

"Cloe?" Ephraim said, sounding worried as he moved to her side, but all she could say was, "Oh my God," as she placed her hand over Christofer's where a baby was growing, their baby, a baby that she was told would never be possible.

"Cloe, are you sure that you're okay?" Chris asked, sounding worried.

She opened her mouth to tell him that everything was fine, when she suddenly found herself racing for the nearest bush and cursing Christofer to hell and back for not stopping her from having that second burger.

———

"Where are you going?" Cloe asked sleepily as she tried to force her eyes open, but after the day that she'd had she was too exhausted to do much more than to give him a sleepy smile as he leaned down and kissed her softly.

"Go back to sleep, mein Schatz. I'll be back in a few minutes," he lied to her, indulging himself in one last kiss before he forced himself to step back when all he wanted to do was pull his clothes off, climb in bed beside her and make love to her one last time.

"Hurry back," Cloe said with that same smile that she'd been wearing since she'd realized that they were really having a baby, the same one that felt like a kick to his gut every time he saw it.

They were having a baby and he wasn't ready.

His father might not have expected him to have a family of his own one day, but he'd taught him what it meant to be a man nevertheless. His father had taught him that the first thing a man needed to do was to keep his family safe and that's exactly what he was about to do.

He'd planned on staying here, getting trained and learning as much as he could about the piece of shit hunting his mate, but now he didn't have time, not with a baby on the way and not after what happened this afternoon.

Not after they'd found her.

His first instinct had been to grab Cloe and get her the hell out of here, but then he'd caught Marc's fear and he knew that there would be no more running. Not for him. Leaving wouldn't change anything, they'd still be hunted and the Williams would still be in danger because they'd led the piece of shit to them. He needed to take care of this problem before it got any worse.

He started to head for the bedroom door, but the sound of the other men waiting in the hallway for him had him turning around and heading for the window. With one last look at Cloe, he opened the window, climbed out and dropped, landing on the ground forty feet below with a soft *whoosh.* He started to walk away when Chris stepped out from behind a tree with CJ in his arms, greedily suckling on a bottle.

"Going somewhere?" Chris drawled as he leaned down and kissed the tip of CJ's nose, earning a cute little giggle from the smiling baby.

Christofer stared at the little boy in Chris' arms as he nodded, more determined than ever to put an end to this nightmare. "I'll be back as soon as I can," he said, moving to walk away when Ephraim and Caine stepped in front of him, looking oddly determined.

"Do you really think that going off on your own to take care of this piece of shit is going to change anything?" Ephraim asked, getting in his face.

"It will put an end to this," he bit out, moving to step past him only to have Caine move in front of him, cutting him off.

"It will start a war," Caine promised.

"According to you, we're already at war," Christofer pointed out, in no mood for more of this bullshit, not with that piece of shit somewhere out there, still breathing.

"Yes, we are," Ephraim agreed firmly. "But if you go back there now and kill him, you will be starting another war, one where every shifter on earth will be honor-bound to hunt you and your family for eternity. They will go after your children, do unspeakable things to your mate, all because of some fucked up code that more than half of them disagree with."

"Every shifter will turn its back on us, demons will follow and soon the Sentinels will lose every ally that they have, turning this war into a massacre," Caine added.

"But before that happens, they'll wipe out that little town that you came from, attack the Sentinel compound that we hid you in, then come here to punish everyone that you've ever known and make sure that you don't have any allies left," Chris said, drawing his attention back to that baby in his arms.

He didn't give a flying fuck about anyone in their old town, but Marta had. She'd had many friends there, had loved that little town and would be devastated to find out that the only home that she'd ever known was destroyed. As for the rest of it, he couldn't stomach the idea of putting women and children in harm's way and they must have known that, which would explain why Chris was out here with CJ in his arms while they did their best to convince him to sit back like some coward and let the piece of shit that had ruined Cloe's life live.

"What are you suggesting?" he bit out, turning his attention back to Ephraim and Caine. "That we sit on our asses and wait for them? I've made that mistake before," he said, shaking his head as memories of the SS storming his childhood home replayed in his mind. "I won't make it again."

"We're not suggesting that," Caine said.

"Then what exactly are you suggesting?" he demanded again.

"We're not about to let anyone attack our home or hurt anyone in our family, Christofer, and that includes you and Cloe, but we can't do anything until he makes the first move," Ephraim started to explain.

"They attacked today!" he snarled, getting in the other man's face, but Ephraim didn't back down.

"That was just a shifter trying to gain leverage over whoever marked her, nothing more," Caine said, shaking his head as though the attempted attack today was no big deal when it had left him scared out of his mind.

"It's only a matter of time before her marker finds us and when he does, we'll be ready," Ephraim said, placing his hand on Christofer's shoulder. "All of us."

"This isn't your war," he reminded them, resisting the urge to shrug off the other man's hand.

"You're one of us, Christofer. That makes this our war."

"I can't ask you to put yourself at risk for us," he ground out, the need to take care of his own problems too well ingrained to ignore at this point.

"And we can't just stand by and let you handle this on your own, not with a child involved now," Ephraim said, giving his shoulder a reassuring squeeze before dropping his hand away, but not before Christofer caught sight of what he'd been hiding behind that gauze for the past few weeks.

Frowning, he looked over his shoulder and spotted the same tattoo on Chris' wrist. He opened his mouth to ask about the symbol when he realized that he'd truly fucked up.

"*You.....bastard!*" Cloe snarled, shoving Ephraim and Caine apart as she stepped past them, her red eyes locked on him as she pulled her fist back and let it fly seconds before she followed it up with a knee to his balls.

FIFTY-SEVEN

"We shouldn't be watching this," Izzy said, her eyes locked on the large flat screen monitor as she blindly reached into the bowl for another peanut butter cup.

"Then look away," he said, taking a large bite out of the fudge brownie that Chris had delivered earlier for Izzy to make up for the stolen fudge.

"I can't," she admitted whispering almost as though she was in a trance as they watched Cloe pull back her foot and-

Fuck, even he winced on the Pyte's behalf as she made contact with his balls before Ephraim and Caine could pull her away. Trying to sneak out on a pregnant Pyte while her hormones were out of control to do something stupid was a bad fucking move. He still cringed when he thought about the hormonal rages that Madison went through while she'd carried the twins.

"Maybe you should help them," Izzy suggested, grabbing another handful of peanut butter cups as he stole her glass of chocolate milk and finished it off.

"But then we'd miss all the good parts," he pointed out, looking around the large office for another drink.

"Chris re-stocked the fridge this morning," Izzy murmured, shoving another handful of peanut butter cups in her mouth even as she cringed when Cloe managed to break free and go for Christofer's balls once again.

He pushed his chair back and leaned down, opening the mini fridge that Chris had installed a few months ago when it became obvious that Izzy wasn't able to handle the short walk to the refrigerator by the door, and pulled out two bottles of water. He handed one to Izzy as he looked up just in time to see Christofer tackle his mate to the ground when she went for his balls again.

"How long do you think they'll hunt them?" Izzy asked just as his phone went off.

With a reluctant sigh, he looked away from the monitor and looked down at his phone. "Probably not for long," he said, replying to the text with a counteroffer that was quickly accepted.

"Where are you going?" Izzy asked, still watching the monitor as he stood up.

"I have to take this job," he said, leaning over to press a kiss against her head and place his hand over her stomach where his godchildren slept. "I'll be back before the babies start popping out."

"Bring me back fudge?" she asked, absently as she cringed at whatever was happening on the monitor.

He didn't bother making her any promises that he couldn't keep and they both knew that he wouldn't be able to keep a promise about fudge.

"You bastard!"

"Calm down, mein Schatz," he said, trying not to vomit when sharp pain shot through his balls, making him wish that he'd been born a eunuch.

"You don't get to call me that ever again!" she snarled, trying to get free so that she could go for his balls again.

"Can we talk about this?" he asked, the effort costing him as the pain shot through the tip of his cock and as much as he'd love to bitch about the abuse to his poor balls and cock, he couldn't. He'd more than had this one coming to him.

"Talk?" she repeated, laughing bitterly as she struggled to break free. "You want to talk? Now?"

"Yes!" he hissed, his stomach rolling as he struggled not to pass out.

"It's a little too late for that, asshole!"

"We're going to leave you two to handle this," Ephraim said, gesturing for the other men to leave.

"Cowards," he muttered, keeping his eyes locked on the furious woman beneath him as the other three men made their escape.

"Damn straight," Chris said, walking past them.

"Get off me, Christofer!"

"Are you going to take another shot at my balls?" he asked, even as he loosened his hold on her.

"No," she bit out, shaking her head firmly and as much as he wanted to believe her, he didn't, but he still rolled off her anyway, terrified that he was hurting the baby by keeping her pinned to the ground.

As soon as he rolled off her, he expected her to go for his balls or to storm off, but she didn't do either of those things. When he looked over at her, he realized that she was crying. The realization that he'd made her cry hurt a hell of a lot more than his balls at the moment and had him reaching for her.

"Leave me alone," she whispered, absently wiping at her face as she got to her feet.

"I can't do that," he said hoarsely, coming to his feet.

She shook her head, laughing without humor as she said, "That's kind of funny since you were about to do just that."

"Mein Schatz-" he said, reaching for her, but she pulled her arm away as she stepped away from him.

"It's over, Christofer. I'm sick and tired of your secretive bullshit!" she said, delivering the final blow that knocked him on his ass before she turned around and walked away.

———

"Cloe, please-"

"Just leave me alone, Christofer," she said, too exhausted to play this game with him.

Falling in love with him had been a mistake, something that she'd tried to stop herself from doing, but clearly she was an idiot because-

"They came for us in 1941," he announced as he closed the bedroom door behind them.

"What?" she asked, turning around to face him only to find him by the window, bathed in moonlight as he stared off into the distance.

"It was a cool night, much like tonight when they came for us. My father thought, hoped really that we had a few more weeks, but someone must have tipped off the SS because they'd showed up at our door, armed and looking for me."

"Why were they looking for you?" she asked, her anger pushed aside as her curiosity got the better of her and she found herself sitting on the edge of the bed, waiting to hear the rest of his story.

"Because I was an oddity," he said with a sad smile. "I was sixteen years old, on the cusp of manhood, but trapped in the body of a child. Someone in the village had talked, someone that my father had helped, had kept safe, had decided that a few dollars was worth betraying my father's kindness. They came with orders to find the boy that wouldn't age and bring him to one of the labs that the Nazis were so fond of."

"My father refused to let them take me. He screamed for me to take Marta and run, but I couldn't force my legs to listen. I stood there like a fool while a soldier pulled out a gun and placed it against my father's temple as he struggled to get to us. I remember screaming his name as his body fell to the ground, but nothing much after that."

"A few days later I woke up in a cage being held in a large white lab. I had no idea how I got there or where I was. I just remember being hungry, really hungry, which was odd since my appetite had waned over the last few years."

"What happened after you woke up?" she found herself asking once he'd grown quiet.

"The guards told the doctors that I was awake. They started asking me a million questions, but once they'd realized that I wouldn't talk they brought Marta out, fresh from surgery."

"What did they do to her?" she asked, immediately wishing that she hadn't.

"They performed an autopsy of sorts on her, the first of many," he said, folding his arms over his chest as he leaned back against the wall. "When I fought to get to her, one of the doctors placed the sharp edge of a scalpel to her throat and just like that they owned us. I couldn't do anything without risking Marta's life."

"W-what did they do to you?"

"Everything," he simply said, looking as though he wasn't going to continue, but much to her horror, he did. "They started off with trying drugs out on me, then gases, looking for better ways to kill. When nothing worked on me they turned to weapons, fire, acids. They systemically cut off every body part, watching in fascination as it grew back."

"Oh, my God," she whispered, horrified.

"When they realized that I couldn't die, they decided to try and make an army of monsters. They stole my blood and would give it to volunteers, prisoners, anyone that they could get their hands on and when that didn't work, they started to shove women in my cage."

"Women?"

He nodded as he shifted closer to the window. "They were brainwashed, led to believe that they were doing their part for the Aryan race. At first, I'd attack the women, half-starved and desperate for blood, but soon the scientists running the lab learned to overfeed me before placing a woman in my cage."

Her stomach dropped as she imagined all the women being shoved in his cage. "Did you......," she started to ask, but she couldn't make the words come out of her mouth.

"Did I fuck them?" he asked, looking at her for the first time since he'd started. He shook his head as he dropped his head back against the wall. "No, I didn't. No matter what they did to entice me, I refused to touch them. I refused to let them get their hands on my child. I've touched women after that, but I've never risked a child, not until you," he added with a shrug as she struggled to accept what he was saying. He'd been a virgin? Impossible. Before she could ask him, he continued distracting her.

His eyes locked on hers as he said, "And I refuse to let it happen now, Cloe. I wasn't leaving you behind to be an asshole. I was trying to put an end to this and keep our child safe. To keep you safe."

"By leaving me here to wonder if you were okay, Christofer?" she demanded, angry with herself and with him for feeling like this, like she'd die if anything happened to him.

"You don't understand, Cloe," he said, shaking his head as he pushed away from the wall and headed for the door.

"Then make me understand," she said, coming to her feet and grabbing his arm to keep him from leaving.

"It's my job to protect you and to keep you safe," he said firmly, his muscles tensing beneath her touch.

"Who says?" she asked softly, moving to stand in front of him.

"My father," he said with a sad smile as he looked her in the eye. He ran his fingertips along her jaw, his touch tender and sweet.

"And what exactly did your father tell you?" she asked, reaching up and covering his hand with hers.

"To always guard my heart," he said as he leaned down and kissed her. "And that's you."

FIFTY-EIGHT

Manhattan, New York

"What the fuck?"

"Good morning, sunshine," Kale said as he popped open a fresh can of Coke and took a long, satisfying sip of the sweet, life-giving nectar that allowed him to function without killing everyone in sight.

Well, almost everyone in sight, he amended a moment later when he opened his eyes and spotted the man that he'd knocked out and chained to a chair only an hour ago. He would have killed him immediately, but there were two parts to the contract that he needed to fulfill before he could collect his pay. Granted, he would have done this job for free, planned to the moment he saw those marks on Cloe's back.

Since the asshole had stirred up a bee's nest that had ended with shifters sneaking into his territory and coming within a mile of his godchildren, he'd decided to pay this piece of shit a visit sooner than later. The job offer had only given him the excuse that he needed to leave.

"I'm under protection," the piece of shit snarled with a cocky grin. "You can't touch me until my property is returned to me."

"Yes, I can," he said, taking another sip as he glanced down at his watch, noting that his contact was two and a half minutes late.

"You work for the Sentinels, don't you?" his mark asked, sounding disgusted. "You're a fucking traitor, aren't you, *mutt?*"

"Occasionally," Kale said unconcerned, looking down at his phone when it chimed and shaking his head when he read the message that waited for him.

She really was a greedy little thing, he thought as he texted Izzy back and agreed to pick up three boxes of fudge. Not that she'd see any of it, but that fudge had been pretty good and he wouldn't mind having a little extra for the trip back to the mansion.

"You have no idea what you're doing," Aidan snarled.

"I'm collecting a bounty for killing a sick fuck who likes to tear apart little girls for fun," Kale said, meeting Aidan's cocky glare with one of his own, knowing just how much it would piss the piece of shit off.

Aidan chuckled, as he tried to shift in his chair, but the silver infused titanium chains that Kale had used to secure him to the chair wouldn't allow him so much as a centimeter of space. "This is over a human? A bitch?" Aidan asked, chuckling darkly. "Oh, you dumb fuck," he said, shaking his head in wonder, "you're going to start a war over a bitch."

"There's not going to be a war," he said absently as he picked up his backpack and riffled through it only to curse vividly when he realized that the little sugar addict had stolen his bag of little white powdered donuts that he'd been craving all morning. "There's definitely going to be a spanking," he muttered darkly when he realized that she'd also stolen his bag of Hershey Kisses.

"If you don't release me right now there will definitely be a war, mutt!"

"Only if someone bitches," Kale pointed out, making a mental note to raid Izzy's stash once he got back to the mansion.

"They will," Aidan said firmly, which was sad.

Kale didn't bother looking up from his backpack as he chuckled. "And who do you think hired me?"

"They can't do that!"

"No," Kale said, grabbing a pack of Twinkies and sitting back, not wanting to miss a single moment, "they can't touch you, but they can arrange to have you wiped from the face of the earth."

"They'd have to face my Pack!" Aidan snarled with that same cocky grin that Kale was really going to enjoy wiping off his face.

"No, they wouldn't," Kale's contact said as he walked into the room with his Pack filing in after him.

"Brock," Aidan bit out, his eyes shifting silver as he spotted his Beta and his Pack.

"Aidan," Brock said, tilting his head in acknowledgement to his former Alpha as he approached Kale and handed him a duffle bag.

"You little son of a bitch!" Aidan snarled, struggling to get free of his chains, but he wasn't going anywhere anytime soon.

"Before we begin," Kale said, bringing back the Alpha's attention to him as he pulled out a serrated knife. "I'd like to clear a few things up."

"Such as?" Brock asked, gesturing to the rest of his Pack to form a circle around them.

"The search for Cloe ends now. She's under my protection," he began, sending the Beta a look that promised all sorts of pain if he was ever crossed.

Brock nodded. "We have no plans on continuing the claim on behalf of the Pack."

"She's mine!" Aidan snarled viciously, his eyes flashing silver.

"Her child is also under my protection," he said, shifting his gaze back to Aidan.

Aidan laughed cruelly. "She can't have children."

Kale smiled, a cold smile. "Her mate changed her. She's a Pyte now and with her change, her ability to have children returned. She is now expecting her first son."

"I'll kill him!" Aidan shouted, snarling as he struggled to shift, but the silver in the chains wouldn't allow it.

"No," Kale simply said as he reached over and slit Aidan's throat from ear to ear, "you won't."

It wouldn't kill him, but it would release enough blood for Brock to steal the Alpha position away from Aidan. "You need to release the claim on the girl," he reminded Brock as he grabbed his bags and headed for the door.

"Consider it done," Brock said, dropping to his knees in front of Aidan, who couldn't do much more than gurgle and glare as his Beta leaned in and stole his birthright.

FIFTY-NINE

Two Weeks Later........

"Shouldn't you be in the infirmary?" Christofer asked, glancing up in time to see Izzy, pale with a pinched expression, sit down on the couch next to him as she swiped the video game controller out of Caine's hands.

"Shouldn't you be groveling to your mate?" Izzy snapped back, the contractions that she'd been hiding from Chris obviously making her a tad bit bitchy.

"You're not going to be able to hide this from him for much longer," he decided to point out as he returned his attention back to his sketchpad since he wasn't in the mood to discuss his hormonal mate or the fact that he'd ended up spending three hours comforting Cloe this morning after she'd watched a Huggies commercial.

"You're only going to make this worse by hiding it from him," Caine pointed out, sounding bored, but he knew that the Pyte was miserable.

About a week ago Danni had gone to her room to lie down and she hadn't gotten up since. She kept giving her mate bullshit excuses, that she was tired, reading or just getting some much needed R & R, but they all knew the truth, could scent it now that it had reached her skin.

The cancer was kicking her ass.

The Council was going nuts looking for a cure, but so far, nothing was working. The demon blood stopped helping and so had Caine's blood. Nothing was helping her, absolutely nothing. Caine hadn't left the house since his mate took to their bed. He spent most of his time glowering at everyone and everything when he wasn't trying to convince Danni to eat or try to get up.

She refused to do anything but lie there and soon she probably wouldn't even be able to do that without crying. The cancer was already making her weak, frail and from what he'd heard from the woman muttering at the video game next to him, she was losing weight. They were quickly running out of options to save her and it probably wouldn't be long before waking her up would be impossible.

"Hey, little man, give me your controller," Caine said, drawing his attention to the boy lounging on the couch, his attention focused on the large flat screen television as he battled it out against Izzy's character.

"*Nope*," Marc said, letting the word pop out of his mouth as he blindly reached for the bowl of caramel popcorn by his side.

Instead of snatching the controller out of the boy's hand, Caine smiled fondly at the boy before he returned his attention to Izzy and reached for the-

"Ow!"

"Don't interrupt me when I'm in the zone," Izzy said, her forehead glistening with sweat as she bit her bottom lip, her muscles tensed as she kept her focus locked on the game.

Christofer sighed heavily as he looked back down at the drawing that he was working on. "Another one?"

"I don't know what you're talking about," Izzy said, lying her little ass off.

"Uh huh," he said, adding some shading to the drawing, knowing that it wouldn't be long until Chris came looking for his mate and realized that she was in labor.

"You really should be in the infirmary," Marc pointed out around a large handful of popcorn.

"You're just trying to get me to stop playing!" Izzy snapped.

"Well, you are holding back the mission," Marc said, earning a chuckle from him and Caine and a pleased smile from Izzy as she focused her attention back on the game. He'd come a long way in the last two weeks, which probably had something to do with his father stringing him up and hanging him in the foyer until he'd promised to cut the shit and start acting like a kid again.

"How did you hide it from Cloe?" Caine asked, making another grab for the remote control only to pull back his hand with a curse and a scowl.

"Chocolate," Izzy announced proudly, making his lips twitch even as he wondered if he was going to have to make another run into town to get her takeout from the diner tonight.

"You really should be in the infirmary," Caine said, eying the game controller in Izzy's hands.

"And get stuck lying on an uncomfortable stretcher for the next twenty hours with nothing to do?" Izzy asked, shaking her head. "Not going to happen. Not again."

"Hey, who's that?" Marc suddenly asked, popping more popcorn in his mouth as he leaned over to look at the drawing pad on Christofer's lap.

"She's beautiful," Izzy murmured, leaning over him to study the picture.

"Is that one of your jobs?" Caine asked, carefully leaning over Izzy to get a look as he-

"My game!" Izzy snarled, slapping Caine's hands away.

"I was playing first," Caine grumbled as he sat back, pouting.

"And now you're not," Izzy said, her focus still on the drawing. "Who is she?"

"Jessica," he said, smiling fondly down at the beautiful woman that the little girl that liked to steal his nose would one day turn into.

"My Jessica?" Izzy asked with a watery smile.

"Yes," Christofer said, carefully removing the paper from the pad and handed it over to her.

"She's beautiful," she said, carefully tracing the picture with her fingers.

"That's my baby girl?" Chris asked as he walked into the room and leaned over the couch to get a better look just as a contraction tore through Izzy, one that she had no hopes of hiding.

"Uh oh," Marc said, his hand pausing mid-grab as he reached for another handful of popcorn. His eyes darted from Izzy, who was even now trying to pretend nothing was wrong. She blindly reached out and grabbed

Christofer and Caine's hands as she attempted to give Chris one of her sweet smiles.

Unfortunately for her, the bloodcurdling scream that escaped her lips ruined it for her. In an instant, Chris' adoring expression for the image of what his precious baby girl would one day turn into was gone and in its place was a stone cold killer who sensed his mate's distress. He considered saying something, but he knew that if he opened his mouth right now that he'd embarrass himself with a pained moan or a whimper.

For such a small little thing, Izzy had one hell of a grip!

"Tell me," Chris said coolly, "that you're not in labor."

Izzy opened her mouth, no doubt to lie her adorable little ass off to buy herself more time out of the infirmary, but instead she ended up crying, "Daddy!"

Within seconds, Ephraim was there, kneeling in front of Izzy as Christofer was forced to grind his jaw shut as another contraction tore through Izzy's small body.

"So soon, baby girl?" Ephraim asked, reaching up and gently cupping Izzy's face as she nodded with a broken sob.

"Is there anything that I can do?" Marc asked, falling back into his old role as Izzy's protector.

"Go get Cloe," his father said, getting him out of the room, which was for the best since it probably wouldn't do for the boy to see two grown men cry.

Holy shit, she had a strong grip!

"What the hell is going on here?" Kale demanded, dropping his backpack to floor as he walked over and knelt beside Ephraim and took Izzy's hand away from Caine.

Caine sighed heavily as pulled his hand away, and fell back against the couch, hugging his abused hand to his chest while Christofer was forced to sit there and suffer through another contraction. When he felt the first bone in his hand snap, he held his breath, forcing himself to take it as Izzy screamed her way through another contraction. He couldn't help but sag in relief when Chris suddenly reached over and scooped Izzy up. He carried her out of the room with Ephraim and Kale hot on his heels.

"She break your hand?" Caine asked, shaking his hand to work out the pain.

"Yeah," he said, wincing as he felt his bones in his hand snap back in place with an audible *crack*.

"She's a violent little thing," Caine said with a fond smile as he continued to shake out his hand.

"That she is," Christofer agreed, nodding slowly as he turned his head to study the Pyte. After a moment, he decided that it was time to end this game and get to the point.

"What do you want?"

———

"That's my precious baby girl!"

"She's my godchild!" Kale snarled, his eyes shifting silver as he leaned down, keeping his eyes locked on Chris as he planted baby kisses on the newborn's forehead.

Eyes narrowing to slits, Chris snuggled his newborn son in his arms. "Fine, but you're not holding my precious baby boy."

"Oh," Kale said, pausing to press another kiss to the sleeping baby's head, "I'll be holding him next. You can count on that."

"We'll see," Chris said, making a show of kissing his son's head.

"Yes," another kiss to the baby girl's forehead, "we will."

"Can I hold one of the babies?" Izzy asked, sounding exhausted with a hopeful smile only to end up dropping her arms by her sides, muttering about the "big babies" and curling up onto her side as both men snapped, "No!"

Cloe bit back a smile as she stepped past the men caught up in a glaring match and checked on Izzy who'd already fallen asleep almost instantly. Poor thing, she thought, pulling the blanket up and tucking Izzy in as she shot Ephraim a smile. "How's the hand?"

"Healing," he said with a wince, cradling his hand against his chest as he stood up. "Since I'm probably not going to get a chance to hold one of my new grandchildren until later," he said, sounding amused as he got to his feet, "I think I'll go help Madison with the children."

Cloe glanced at the clock and noted the late hour. It had taken Izzy ten hours to deliver the twins and now Cloe was exhausted. She wanted nothing more than to stumble her way to her room and fall asleep in Christofer's arms, but she had to check on Danni first.

She hadn't seen Danni all day, hadn't had the chance to check up on her to make sure that she was okay. In the last of couple weeks she'd watched as the woman slowly wasted away and knew that it was only a matter of time until she slipped into a coma. It was a process that she was too familiar with and one that she didn't want to see Danni fall victim to, especially since there would be no escape for her.

She wished there was more that she could do for her, but there wasn't. Medicine was like poison to them, blood transfusions seemed to make her sicker. They couldn't use normal cancer treatments to treat her. Cloe couldn't help but wonder if-

"Get her off of me!" she heard Christofer's pain filled roar as she climbed the steps to the living quarters.

"Stop moving and I will!" Caine shouted.

"Grab her before she-*fucking hell!*"

She was up the stairs and down the hall before she realized that she was running. She skidded to a halt in front of Caine and Danni's room. She raised her fist to knock, but then shook her head, calling herself an idiot as the sounds of a struggle became louder. She grabbed the knob and threw the door open and then....

Stood there.

She just stood there, trying to take in everything that she was seeing. Christofer lying on the floor, his clothes ripped to shreds, Danni's arms wrapped around his bicep, holding his arm tightly so that he couldn't pull his wrist away from her bite while Caine had his arms wrapped around Danni, trying to pull her off Christofer, pleading with her to let him go.

"All right then," she muttered, around a yawn.

After noting that Danni's color had improved, she turned around, shut the door behind her and headed down the hall towards her room where she planned on spending the next hour lounging in a hot bath and enjoying the box of fudge that she'd swiped from the glowering bastard's bag.

SIXTY

"How's Danni?" Cloe asked, not bothering to open her eyes as she raised one leg out of the water and laid it across the top of the tub. The white bubbles sliding down her smooth tan leg drew an appreciative smile from him.

"Hungry," he said, wincing as the torn skin marring his wrist quickly knitted together. He reached back, grabbed a handful of his ripped shirt and pulled it off, letting it drop to the floor to join Cloe's small pile of clothes.

"I take it that your blood worked?" she asked, bringing that beautiful long leg of hers back into the water so that she could sink lower in the deep tub.

"Like a charm," he murmured, kicking off his shoes as he unzipped his pants.

"I was wondering when Caine was going to get around to asking you for some of your blood," she admitted on a sigh as she sank even lower in the tub.

"Me too," he said, surprised that Caine had been able to hold off this long.

Then again, he'd also been terrified that Christofer's blood was Danni's last hope. Caine hadn't been in a rush to find out that even that wouldn't help her. He'd wanted to hold onto any hope that he could for as long as possible, but after refusing to eat for the fifth day in a row, Caine had lost the luxury of time. Christofer had considered offering his blood to Danni several times over the last couple of weeks, but like Caine, he hadn't been ready to find out that his blood was useless, which as it turned out, it was.

The first attempt to feed Danni his blood had failed miserably. She'd barely managed to swallow the first mouthful of his blood when she'd reacted violently, leaning over the bed and spitting it up in a trashcan just as she had done after every other attempt. Caine, looking like his whole world had been destroyed, had been willing to accept defeat.

Christofer hadn't.

He refused to let another woman in his life down. He'd be damned if he was going to be forced to sit back and watch as another woman suffered. He hadn't been able to save Marta and he would have to live with that for the rest of his very long life.

Caine shouldn't have to.

"How long did it take for your blood to work?" she asked as he shoved his boxers down and stepped out of them.

"A couple of hours," he said, pressing a hand to his upset stomach at the reminder of what he'd had to do to make his blood work.

He paused by the tub, wondering if he should go downstairs and binge on a few bags of bagged blood to work the rest of the demon blood out of his system. His stomach took the decision out of his hands. Placing a hand over his increasingly upset stomach, he leaned back over to pull his clothes back on when Cloe's hand covered his, stopping him.

"What's wrong?" she asked, releasing his hand to reach over and run her wet fingers through his hair.

His first instinct was to lie to her and tell her that everything was okay. He didn't want to burden her with his problems, but he couldn't lie to her. He knew that lying to her, even a small lie, would hurt her and he'd rather spend an eternity in the lab than to cause her anymore pain. She would find out that he'd lied of that he had no doubt. By morning everyone would know about the miracle cure that had helped Danni get better.

"Demon blood," he groaned, wincing when sharp pain shot through his stomach.

"Demon blood?" Cloe asked, moving to her knees so that she could reach over with her other hand and gently run her fingers over his lightly whiskered jaw as she ran an assessing eye over him.

"Yeah," he said, pressing his hand tightly against his stomach. "My blood alone didn't work. So, we decided to see what would happen if we mixed my blood with the demon blood the Council had originally given her to help keep the cancer at bay."

"How much did you drink?" she asked softly, gently cupping his jaw.

"Twenty bags," he admitted, closing his eyes when his stomach rebelled at the reminder of all that acidic blood that he'd forced himself to consume.

Drinking the blood had been time consuming. It had taken him a lot longer to drink the bagged demon blood than the cold human blood that he normally consumed. The taste and the texture was not only different, but it had filled him up a lot faster. He'd managed two bags an hour, force-fed Danni his blood and then started the process all over again. They'd been prepared to do it all night, but by the third feeding Danni was with it enough to be able to feed herself. By the fifth feeding.......

She'd been ravenous.

Thank God she'd decided that she preferred Caine's blood to his, he thought wincing as more pain shot through his stomach, reminding him that he needed to dilute the demon blood in his system. It shouldn't take much since Danni had nearly cleaned him out with the last feeding.

"Baby, you're in pain," Cloe said, sounding worried as she continued to fuss over him.

"It will be fine," he said, opening his eyes as he reached up and covered her hand against his jaw. He forced himself not to smile, knowing that she'd just fumble for an excuse for the endearment. So instead of letting her know just how much the endearment meant to him, he leaned forward and brushed his lips against hers. "A bag of blood should take care of it," he promised her as he pulled back so that he could quickly get dressed. He wanted to be back in time to join her before she-

"Why don't you drink from me?" she suggested, knocking him on his ass.

———

"Danni," Caine said, groaning long and loud as Danni moaned against his skin, her arms wrapping around him as she pulled herself onto his lap.

With a little sigh that had his lips twitching, Danni gently removed her teeth from his neck, pressing a soft kiss against the tender skin as it started to heal. "Did I take too much?" she asked, resting her forehead against his shoulder.

"No," he said, shaking his head, ignoring the black spots dancing along his vision as he turned his head so that he could kiss his mate.

Danni chuckled, moving to sit up so that she could look him in the eye as she said, "Liar."

"I'm a little hungry," he admitted, returning her grin as he leaned in to kiss her, unable to help himself.

She looked so.........

Beautiful.

Her hair was fuller, silkier. Her face flushed beautifully against her tanned skin. Her body had filled out in the last few hours and smooth muscle once again shaped her body. Her breasts were fuller, larger than he'd remembered. Her hips were curvier than he'd remembered them ever being. But, the thing that had him sighing with relief was the sound of her heartbeat.

It was beating strongly against her chest.

"Thank God," he murmured, brushing his lips against hers.

"Can you smell the cancer?" she reluctantly asked as she pulled away just far enough so that he could see her nervously nibbling on her bottom lip.

He met her frightened gaze and held it, along with his breath, terrified that Christofer's blood had strengthened the cancer right along with Danni's body. Realizing that he couldn't put this off, he slowly exhaled and then, keeping his eyes locked with hers, he inhaled, scenting the air around her.

"Well?" she asked, holding her breath as she waited for an answer.

His lips pulled into a grin as he leaned forward and kissed her.

"Gone."

"Gone?"

"Gone," he repeated, grinning against her lips. "Be sure," she said, pulling back so that she could search his expression, looking for any sign that he was only saying what she wanted to hear.

He reached up and threaded his fingers through her hair. "I can take you to the Boston Compound right now, sweetheart. We can probably get the test results within a day or two," he offered, moving to get up and set her aside when Danni pushed him back down with a firm shake of her head.

"That would take too long," she said, reaching up and moving her hair back away from her neck.

"What are you suggesting?" he asked, not sure that he wanted to be the one to tell her if the cancer was starting to spread again.

She sighed as reached down and took his hands into hers. "You know what I'm suggesting."

He opened his mouth, but nodded. "No matter what I find, remember that Christofer promised to supply you with blood everyday if you need it."

"I know," she said, giving him a small smile.

"And remember," he said, leaning in to kiss her again, "that I love you."

"I love you, too," she said, her smile genuine this time.

He kissed her one more time before he pulled back, tilted his head to the side and leaned in so that he could press a kiss against her neck. "Ready?" he asked her, though he was preparing himself for the acidic taste of her blood.

"Yes," she whispered, threading her fingers through his hair, holding him close.

He pressed one last kiss to her neck as he allowed his fangs to slide down. Sending up a prayer, he opened his mouth and struck.

———

A low growl shook her out of her thoughts.

Caine's arms tightened around her as he released another sexy growl that had her licking her lips. When he suddenly stood, bringing her with him, and turned around, slamming her against the wall, she may have let out an embarrassing squeal. A gasp escaped her when he tore her shorts and panties clean from her body, but it was quickly forgotten as a scream of pleasure tore from her lips as he suddenly filled her with a hard thrust that had them slamming back into the wall.

She chuckled breathlessly as she asked, "I guess it's good?"

His answering moan had her smiling and closing her eyes in relief and thanking God for stubborn Pytes like Christofer.

SIXTY-ONE

W hat the hell was wrong with her? she couldn't help but wonder as she found herself shifting forward to let a reluctant Christofer step into the tub behind her and sit down.

"You don't have to do this," he said as he adjusted his legs on either side of her and wrapped his arms around her, bringing her flush against his body.

"I want to," she said, embarrassed by just how badly she wanted to be the one to feed him.

After what he'd done to her, not to mention the attack that she'd endured as a child, she shouldn't want to experience his bite again, but she did. Call it morbid curiosity, momentary insanity, but she wanted to experience the kind of pleasure that she saw on his face when she bit him while they made love and replace her nightmares. She wanted to know if Madison was right, if being bitten by a Pyte while making love was the most erotic experience of her life. But, most of all, she wanted Christofer to experience the pleasure that he denied himself every time they made love.

She also wanted to change the past.

"Why?" he asked, pressing a kiss just below her ear as she wrapped her arms around his as they held her tightly against him.

"Does it matter?" she asked, shifting so that her legs were touching his.

"Yes," he said hoarsely.

"Do you want to bite me?" she asked, wishing that he would just go ahead and bite her before she lost her damn nerve.

He pressed another kiss to her neck as he released a low, sexy growl that had her toes curling. "More than anything."

"Then do it," she said, tilting her head to the side to expose the base of her neck to him.

When she felt his warm breath tickle her neck, she squeezed her eyes tightly shut, her entire body going tense as she waited for those razor sharp teeth to slice through her skin and-

"No," he said, pressing a kiss against her neck.

"But-" she started to argue even as her body remained tense, ready for his attack.

"No," he said, cutting her off with another kiss as he moved his arms out from beneath hers.

"But-"

"Shhhh," he whispered soothingly as he pressed another kiss against her neck. "Just let me hold you for a few minutes."

She nodded numbly as she lay in his arms. There was no point in pushing him. He'd made up his mind and nothing she could say would change anything.

Which of course meant that she was just going to have to go ahead and take the choice out of his hands, because there was no way that she was going to put this off for another day.

———

"Can I have some of that, please?" Marc asked, yanking him out of his thoughts as he sat at the large kitchen island, staring down at the large glass of lukewarm blood in front of him.

He looked down at the counter and frowned until Marc gestured to his glass of blood. "You drink blood?"

"Yup," Marc said with a careless shrug as he reached for the cookie jar and pulled it closer so he could grab a handful of Oreos.

"Why?" he asked, handing the glass of blood over to the boy, his own bullshit momentarily forgotten as he watched the young boy stuff an Oreo in his mouth and follow it with half the blood.

Marc popped another cookie in his mouth before he answered. "So I can grow normally," he explained, grabbing another cookie as Christofer digested the information.

"So, when you're sixteen you'll actually look-"

"Sixteen," Marc finished for him around another cookie.

"Of course," Christofer said, chuckling as he shook his head in wonder. Of course his embarrassingly slow growth rate could have been fixed with something as simple as drinking blood, he thought as he grabbed the bag of warmed blood from the bowl and another cup from the cabinet.

As Marc polished off the contents of the cookie jar and two more glasses of blood, he sat there sipping blood and thinking about all the things that his child was going to need. Christ, they weren't ready, but that didn't matter. He had a baby on the way and responsibilities to deal with. The first of course was to find a home of their own.

He liked the Williams family, liked living here, but they were just starting out and needed some time alone before the baby came. He wanted to spoil Cloe, learn everything that he could about her, and make sure that she knew that he wanted to spend the rest of his very long life with her. He wanted to have the freedom to make love to her wherever he wanted, whenever he wanted and he couldn't do that in a mansion filled with children and five other people who could hear every single thing they did.

He would have liked to take Cloe away on a trip first. He wanted to explore the world with her by his side, but that wasn't an option. He had a family now and that meant that he had to put his wishes aside and take care of them. They came first and always would.

Everything else came second.

"Do you think that-"

"What the hell?" he rasped, cutting Marc off as he came to his feet, the scent of Cloe's blood and an unknown shifter pushing all of his worries aside as terror struck.

———

"Real smart," Cloe grumbled, shaking her head in disgust as she opened another window, grimacing when the cut she'd stupidly made across her palm stung as she gripped the window and pushed it up.

There really was nothing sexier than a gushing hand wound, she thought dryly as she opened the last window, hoping to air out the room before Christofer returned. Sighing, she walked to the bathroom for a quick shower. This really hadn't been her best idea.

God, what the hell had she been thinking?

She wanted to experience his bite, to see if it was pleasurable and for some asinine reason she thought cutting herself was the best way to make that happen. For about thirty seconds after she'd cut herself, she'd stood there, prepped and ready to get it over with. She'd been determined to get rid of this fear, to overcome her past so that she could honestly say that she wasn't still afraid of him, but then she started to remember what it felt like that night of his attack and all her bravado had quickly fled.

She hated this, hated the way she tensed up when he went too close to her neck, hated the way she forgot to breathe when his fangs dropped while they made love. She loved him so much, but this fear that she felt every time she saw his fangs was killing her. She didn't want to live the rest of her life like this. She didn't want to feel like she had to watch her back or worry when he didn't feed every couple of hours, terrified that he would lose control and mistake her or their child for a late night snack.

She wanted……..

She just wanted him, but she knew that she wouldn't be able to have him until she got over this innate fear of him. They were having a baby together, something that she'd known would never happen for her and now that it had, she would greedily protect it, even from its father.

God, she hated feeling this way.

She-

Gasped as a strong hand grabbed onto her arm and yanked her out of the shower. Before she could scream, she found herself pushed back against the wall and staring into glimmering red eyes as trembling hands moved over her, searching for something. Her heart pounded against her chest as her gaze locked on the long, white fangs that looked ready to tear into her throat. When her mind raced to catch up with her erratically beating heart and she realized who was standing in front of her, her fear spiked.

"Where are you hurt?" Christofer demanded as she took a deep breath to calm her frayed nerves. "I smelled your blood."

"I'm fine," she said, pushing his hands aside as she stepped away from him, needing a moment to compose herself before he realized-

"You're terrified," he said hollowly.

She tried to shake it off as she grabbed a towel, forcing herself to appear casual as she headed for the bedroom, needing to put a little space between them so that she could calm down just enough to hide her reaction from him, something that she normally could do, but tonight, he wasn't going to give her that chance.

"Look at me," he said, grabbing her arm more gently this time to pull her to a stop when all she wanted to do was to walk away from him and pretend that he hadn't just scared the hell out of her, and probably always would.

Swallowing back her fear, she forced herself to look up and immediately wished that she hadn't, especially when her breath caught and her stomach dropped when she realized that his fangs were still down. This time when she tried to step away from him, he refused to let her go.

"You're terrified of me," he rasped, noticeably swallowing as he waited for her to deny it, but she couldn't.

So with a shake of her head, she closed her eyes in surrender and admitted, "Your fangs."

"My fangs?" he repeated as though he wasn't quite sure that he'd heard her correctly. "You haven't reacted negatively to my fangs since-"

"I started to accept what I'd been changed into," she finished for him, opening her eyes so that she could look at him as she admitted, "You scare me when you lose control."

"Then why did you want me to bite you?" he asked, looking as confused as she felt.

She sighed, looking away from him, having absolutely no idea how to explain to him that she wanted to replace her fear with pleasure, to erase the memories of what he'd done to her, what she feared that he would one day do.

"Look at me," he said, reaching out and cupping her face as she tried to step away from him.

"I would never hurt you," he swore, gazing down at her with adoring eyes making it difficult to believe that he was capable of hurting anyone.

But she knew the truth.

"*Never*," he stressed, giving her the courage she needed to find out.

"Then prove it."

SIXTY-TWO

"What?" he asked, unable to hide his confusion as he watched Cloe's expression turn from wary to calculating in a matter of seconds.

"You're going to prove it," she said with a determined glint in her eye as she reached up and pushed him back.

"How exactly am I supposed to prove that?" he asked, more than willing to do anything to make sure that she knew that he would never hurt her.

"You're going to bite me," she announced as she shoved him back again.

Well, almost anything.

"No," he said with a hard shake of his head as he moved to step around her, but she wasn't having that.

With one last push he found himself stumbling back and falling on the couch. Before he could get up, Cloe, naked and still wet from her shower, was climbing on his lap and straddling him.

"Yes," she said, placing her hands on his chest and pushing him back when he tried to stand up.

"No," he said, placing his hands on her hips to move her aside.

She sighed as she settled more comfortably on top of him as she dropped her hands away from his chest and reached down to grab the hem of his shirt. "Yes."

"Not gonna happen, mein Schatz," he said, moving to stop her, but she simply used the move to pull his shirt up until he was left with no other choice but to lean forward so that she could pull the shirt off the rest of the way. It was either that or allow her to rip the shirt clean from his body and judging by her expression, she'd been seconds away from doing just that.

"You don't want to bite me?" she asked casually as she pulled her long beautiful chestnut hair up and twisted it into a loose bun, drawing his attention to her neck where her pulse beat at a hypnotizing tempo.

"No," he lied, swallowing hard as he forced himself to look back up and meet her determined grey eyes, "I don't."

Smiling coyly, she leaned in and brushed her lips against his. "Liar," she said, pulling back before he could savor the feel of her lips on his.

"I'm not going to bite you," he said firmly, leaning in to kiss her to distract her from this asinine plan of hers.

She leaned back and with a little sigh and a shake of her head. "I think you will."

"And why is that?" he asked, wishing like hell that she'd just drop it, because he wanted nothing more than to slide his fangs inside of her while he slid himself between her legs.

"Because you owe me a redo," she simply said, as she ran her fingers through his hair.

"A redo?" he repeated dumbly, trying not to groan at the feel of her fingers going through his hair.

"Mmmmhmm," she said, leaning in and kissing him again. "A redo."

"And what exactly are we redoing?" he asked, placing his hands on her hips to pick her up and end this.

"The night that you bit me," she explained calmly, threading her fingers through his hair, "I want a redo."

He didn't want to think about that night, never mind relive it.

"Why?" he asked, reaching up to trace the back of his knuckles along her jaw, wondering why this was so important to her.

"Does it matter?" she asked, not quite meeting his gaze.

"Yes."

For a moment, she didn't say anything. She just sat there, running her fingers through his hair. Just when he was about to press her again for an answer, he smelled it.

"What is that?" Cloe asked, sounding nervous. Frowning, she quickly folded her arms over her breasts to cover them as she caught the scent that had sent him running in the first place.

"The main reason that I was checking on you," he said, all his focus on the window where the scent of shifter was coming through stronger than ever.

"What is that?" Cloe asked, swallowing nervously as he helped her climb off his lap.

"Grab your clothes and go to the others," he said, moving past her towards the open window where the scent of shifter was becoming stronger with each passing second.

"But-"

"Go!"

"Christofer, I-"

"Goddamn it, run, Cloe!" he snapped, abruptly turning around, fully prepared to throw her out into the hall if that's what it took when he found himself stumbling off balance.

He felt hot liquid dripping down his stomach. Numbly, he looked down at the tip of the blade sticking out his chest. He looked up at Cloe just as she screamed.

"*Run,*" he said hoarsely as a second blade rammed through his chest, piercing his heart and sending him into oblivion.

—

"Christofer!"

"Shhhh, none of that now," the man that looked vaguely familiar said as he pulled one of the large hunting knives out of Christofer's back, making sure to keep his gaze locked on her.

Before she realized what she was doing, her fangs had shot down and she was going for his throat only to come to an abrupt halt when he pulled out a gun and aimed it at her stomach. Fear for their baby had her ignoring the need to rip his throat out, but just barely.

"I see it's true," the man remarked casually as he openly studied her. "I guess that means that everything else is true as well," he mumbled to himself, his expression turning worried. "He's not going to be happy about this."

"Who?" she demanded, risking a glance down at Christofer only to force herself to bite back a sob when she spotted the large, thick black handle of the knife sticking out of his now pale back as more blood pooled around him, soaking into the beige carpet.

"Your owner," the man said, drawing her attention back up in time to see him gesture towards the open windows with the gun. "He's waiting for you."

She started to shake her head in refusal when she heard the familiar, long suffering sigh that normally had her rolling her eyes and biting back a smile.

"Please tell me that you didn't really break into my family's home," Chris said, shaking his head in disgust as he swung inside the room through one of the open windows.

"Get back, Sentinel!" the man said, shifting slightly to the side so that he could keep them both in sight and the gun firmly aimed at her.

"No," Chris said firmly, his gaze locked on the man starting to shift towards her.

He cocked the gun in warning, making her breath catch as her hands shot to cover her stomach in a hopeless attempt to protect her baby. "*Please*," she whispered as her eyes watered, terrified of losing the precious gift that Christofer had given her.

"Put the gun down," Ephraim said as he stepped into the room.

"I can't," the man in front of her said, licking his lips nervously as Caine slowly climbed in through the window, his murderous red glare locked on the man holding the gun. "I have my orders."

"And what orders would those be?" Ephraim said, moving to step further into the room, but the intent expression the man in front of her had stopped him and every other man in the room as they realized that there was a chance that they wouldn't get to her in time.

"Retrieve the Alpha's property," he said, his expression resolved as he shifted his attention back on her.

"And when you fail to do that?" Chris demanded. "Because you have to know that you're not leaving this room alive if you hurt her or the baby."

He didn't answer, but then again, she didn't need him to. The way he looked at her said it all. They both knew that she wouldn't die, but the baby could. Her body would reject the fetus in order to repair itself and he knew that, had anticipated it and now, it seemed as though he was willing to sacrifice his own life to make that happen.

"Cloe," the man said softly, "I'm sorry."

She opened her mouth to scream, to beg him not to do it, anything, but the only thing that came out of her mouth was a choked gasp as he pulled the trigger. Out of the corner of her eyes, she saw all three men move, desperate to get between her and the bullet speeding towards her, but it was pointless. No matter how fast they were, the bullet was faster. She sent up a prayer for her unborn child as she waited for the impact from the bullet, but it never came.

At least, not for her.

With a roar, Christofer surged to his feet, jumping in front of the bullet meant for their child and stumbled back in time with the sound of the gunshot exploding in the large bedroom. Blindly, she reached out to grab Christofer as he started to fall, but she never got the chance as a large body from her right tackled her, bringing her to the floor only to shift midair to take the impact and protect her.

She barely had the chance to gasp when Ephraim snatched her out of Chris' arms, tucked her against his body and flashed them out of the room. She moved to close her eyes in attempt to fight the dizzying effect on her stomach, but before she did, she saw him, standing in the hallway, eyes turned liquid silver with fangs that looked deadlier than Christofer's.

It was then that she decided never to cross Kale Quinn.

SIXTY-THREE

"Just kill me!" the shifter demanded as he dropped to his knees, the gun falling from his hands. "Fucking do it!"

"*Cloe*," Christofer rasped, his unseeing eyes shifting desperately around the room for his mate as he struggled to get up, but one look at him and Caine knew the man wasn't getting up for a while.

At least, not unless he fell into bloodlust and then they'd really have their hands full.

"She's fine," Chris promised as he jumped to his feet, his gaze never leaving the shifter kneeling before them.

"What are we going to do with him?" Caine asked, gesturing towards the shifter as he kicked the gun away.

"He's *mine*," Kale announced as he walked into the room, looking every bit the deadly mercenary that he was rumored to be.

Kale had the shifter by the neck and slammed against the wall before Caine could blink. When he pulled the shifter back and slammed him back against the wall he destroyed it in the process.

"You fucking dared to play me?" Kale snarled, getting into the shifter's face.

The shifter didn't say anything, didn't fight, didn't struggle, just stood there waiting for Kale to tear his throat out. Caine couldn't help but frown at the sight before him. For someone hell-bent on kidnapping Cloe or the very least, killing her unborn child, he'd done a shitty job of it.

He'd snuck into a house filled with predators and gone after his prey with her overprotective mate in the room. If he'd been smart, he would have watched the house and waited for Cloe to leave unaccompanied before he made his move. He sure as hell wouldn't have stopped with just one bullet. He would have kept firing that gun until he'd ensured his duty was done. Instead, the shifter had fired once, dropped his arm by his side and waited for their retribution.

"What exactly was it about my fucking sunny disposition that made you think that I would overlook being fucked with?" Kale snarled, his voice guttural and the closest that Caine had ever seen the annoying shifter coming to losing control.

"Do it," the shifter gasped.

"I want to know who gave the order to go after my property," Kale demanded, making Caine frown with confusion. He shot Chris a look only to find the Sentinel looking equally confused. As far as they knew, Kale had no marked humans. He didn't bother with humans, most of the time acting as though they didn't exist.

"You know the answer," the shifter bit out, meeting Kale's silver-eyed glare with one of his own.

"Everything was a set up?" Kale demanded, looking seriously pissed.

"Yes!" the shifter hissed.

"Was it your Alpha's idea, Brock?" Kale asked, shoving the shifter back into the wall.

"Yes," Brock bit out, looking tortured. "*Now fucking do it!*'

Kale cocked his head to the side in an appraising manner as he studied the shifter. "Why the rush to die? Do you fear that your Alpha will do worse to you for failing?"

"He will do worse if I live," Brock bit out.

Frowning, Kale looked down. Caine followed the shifter's gaze and swore when he saw the mated mark on Brock's wrist.

"He threatened your mate?" Kale concluded, returning his attention to Brock.

Brock looked away as he answered, "Yes."

"Any children?" Caine found himself asking.

"No," Brock croaked, looking miserable. "We're not allowed to have children in our Pack."

Meaning that there was a good chance that this man's mate had been forced to endure an abortion at least once. Pack life could be seriously fucked up, especially with an Alpha sick enough to mark a fourteen-year-old girl, Caine thought with disgust.

"Either kill me or let me go so that I can go to her," he demanded, meeting Kale's glare once more.

"No," Kale said, shaking his head as he stepped back, keeping his hold on the shifter's neck until he was an arm's length away. He dropped his arm away only to swing the other one, hitting the shifter in the side of his head and knocking him out with a punch that sent him flying back, slamming him into what remained of the wall. He dropped to the ground without a sound.

"Lock him up," Kale said, turning his attention to Christofer.

"What's the plan?" Chris asked, pulling a pair of handcuffs out of his back pocket as he knelt down next to the shifter and secured his hands behind his back.

Kale leaned over and yanked the knife out of Christofer's back, a mistake that Caine had no doubt they would all pay for and soon, and looked up and met Chris' questioning look and simply said, "Revenge."

———

It's about fucking time.

He leaned back, preparing to savor the moment when his bitch was brought back to him. When he caught her scent breaking through the stale scents left over by the hotel room's many occupants over the years and the blood of the bitch who'd had the misfortune of being left with him, he closed his eyes and inhaled deeply. His cock began to stir, preparing for the night ahead when he caught another scent, one that had his eyes opening and a curse forming at the tip of his tongue.

"Hello," the bastard said with an amused smile just as Aidan registered the feel of cold steel pressing against his throat, a reminder of the bullshit that he'd been forced to go through to find his bitch.

Aidan chuckled, uncaring that the move caused the sharp edge of the knife to press into his skin and draw blood. "Figured it out, did you?" he asked in a bored tone as he reached back and scratched his head, wondering if this meant that his Beta was dead.

He looked past the shifter perched on the edge of a chair next to him and shrugged when he spotted the pale, bloody hand hanging over the side of the bed. At least he didn't have to worry about coming up with a half-assed excuse as to how he'd killed the stupid bitch. Not that he had worried about upsetting his Beta when he'd been fucking the bitch. He'd been trying to work off some of his excitement at having his property back with the willing bitch. When she'd started moaning his name as he sank his claws into her back he may have gotten a little carried away.

Kale followed his gaze and shook his head with disgust as he pressed the edge of the blade more firmly against his throat. "The Beta's mate?" he asked, returning his attention to him.

"Got carried away," he said, fighting back a yawn.

"You seem to have a problem with that," Kale mused, his attention focused on the knife at his throat.

"You mean the bitch?" Aidan asked with a dark chuckle. "Is that what this is about?"

Kale shook his head slowly. "No, this is about something entirely different than how a sick fuck gets off."

"Then tell me, Kale Quinn," he said mockingly, "what is this about?"

"Revenge," Kale said, stepping back and taking the knife with him.

"Revenge?" he asked, his lips twitching with amusement as he watched the notorious Kale Quinn sheath his knife and lean back against the wall.

"Mmmmhmm, revenge," Kale said, folding his arms over his chest, looking as though he was settling in for a show.

"And what exactly are you getting revenge for?" Aidan asked, leaning back in his chair, deciding that he could spare a few minutes and perhaps get a few answers before he ripped the bastard apart for interrupting his night.

"Where's my Beta?" he asked, drumming his fingers against the cracked armrests of his chair.

"Preparing to become the Council's bitch," Kale said in an offhanded tone.

"And my bitch?" he asked, chuckling at the murderous look the mutt shot him.

"You mean my mate?" the gravelly voice demanded, bringing his attention to the doorway where a man stood, his red eyes matching the blood staining his large body.

Slowly, he came to his feet as he faced the son of a bitch that had stolen his property. The one that had damaged his bitch and changed her. The one that he was going to use to make all his dreams come true, including getting his bitch back. He was going to-

"You son of a bitch," Cloe said, stepping around the red-eyed male. "It was you all this time."

"Cloe," he said, smiling as he watched the shocked expression on her face as she realized that the man that she'd allowed to fuck her had also been the one to rip her family apart.

"Aidan," she said, her eyes watering as she came to a stop in front of the large male who dared to call himself her mate.

"Miss me?" he asked, allowing his eyes to travel down her body, making note that his beta had failed in getting rid of the bastard in her womb.

He would have to rectify that and soon.

It wouldn't do to allow anything but his mark to wreck her delectable body after all, he thought as he prepared himself for her attack. He knew it was coming. He could see it in her face, the blind hatred that had sent her running most of her life, had terrified her so badly that she avoided the night, avoided everything and everyone.

It was coming.

He'd seen it a hundred times before when someone allowed their emotions to take over. She'd think about that night, about what he'd done to her family, what he'd done to her and all the ways that he'd made her scream his name before it became too much to hold back and she went for his throat. When she did, he would use it against her. He'd use her to get out of here and once they were far enough away, he'd get rid of that parasite in her womb and force her to submit. He would-

Never leave this room alive, he realized in horror as Cloe stepped aside as two more Pytes stepped inside the room, flanking the one that carried her scent.

If he hadn't been so focused on the Pytes watching his every move, he would have noticed the Sentinel sneaking inside the room behind him. By the time the silver plated knife was shoved through his spine, it was too late.

SIXTY-FOUR

"Shit!" Cloe hissed, fumbling to catch the bar of soap before she dropped it, but her shaky hands only managed to send the bar of soap flying across the large stall.

"God damn it!" she said, biting back another sob as she shoved her hands through her wet, tangled hair before she was dropping them away and reaching for the hot water nozzle.

Why wasn't it getting hotter?

She needed it hotter. She needed more water, more soap, she needed...she just needed.......

To feel clean.

That monster had destroyed her family. He'd torn them apart. Ate them! Then he'd held her down, pinning her with his claws while he'd meticulously shredded her back, finishing her torture by slicing her open and ripping out her womb. If that wasn't bad enough, he'd also stalked her, toyed with her, seduced her and then-

A broken sob broke free as she forced her trembling legs to work and carry her to the bar of soap forming suds on the tiled shower floor. She picked it up only to drop it again when it slipped out of her hand. She tried again and again with the same results until she couldn't take it anymore.

She covered her face with her hands and stopped fighting it.

The grief that she'd held in, tried to ignore, broke free. The tears that she'd refused to cry wouldn't stop. God, she missed her parents and her brothers. She'd give anything to see them one more time, to tell them that she loved them and hold them.

She just wanted her family back.

She'd do anything to have them back, to not be alone again. All these years, she'd been so lonely, so afraid and now she-

"Shhhh, mein Schatz," Christofer said softly, enveloping her trembling body with his as he pressed a kiss against the back of her neck. "You're not alone. Not anymore," he said, making her realize that she must have spoken out loud.

"P-please just leave me alone, C-Christofer," she said even as she grabbed onto the arms wrapped around her and held on as another sob rocked her.

"No," he said, pressing another kiss to the back of her neck, "I'm never leaving you, mein Schatz."

She shook her head, trying to stop crying so that she could call him a liar, to yell at him for making promises that he couldn't keep, but instead she felt herself relax in his arms and say, "Then make me forget. Make it all better, Christofer."

—

"Cloe, I don't know how to-"

"Please, Christofer," Cloe whispered, turning in his arms so that she could kiss him.

The kiss was desperate and angry, but he took it. For her, he took it. Her nails dug into his shoulders as her kiss became harder, punishing. Her body shook against his, her nails bit through skin as she sobbed against his mouth. He felt his heart break a little more with each sob.

What he wouldn't do to take this pain away from her. He'd do anything to free her from this pain, anything, but he knew there was nothing that he could do for her. She'd bottled up her pain for too long, and now, it was breaking free. When she tore her mouth away from his and buried her face against his neck as loud sobs rocked her body, he tightened his arms around her and sat back against the shower and held her.

As she finally mourned her family, he gently pried one hand away and moved it down, pressing it against her stomach. When she tried to pull her hand away, he gently pushed it back and covered it with his own. Closing his eyes, he pressed his lips against her hair and held her.

"You will never be alone again."

———

"Give. Me. A. Coke."

"No," Chris said, pressing a tiny kiss to the top of his newborn daughter's head. "Not while you're breastfeeding."

"Then we'll buy formula," Izzy bit out evenly, looking close to killing her mate.

Chris paused mid-kiss to glare at his mate. "You dare suggest giving my precious babies formula?" he demanded as though Izzy had suggested giving the babies crack cocaine.

Shaking his head with a sigh, Kale carefully placed Jessica on the bed beside her mother. Once the toddler was settled in next to Izzy, he sat down on the bed and laid back with CJ in his arms. The baby boy curled up against him in his sleep as he continued to dream of that 69' Mustang that Kale had promised him for his sixteenth birthday.

"Don't you have some place to be?" Chris snapped at him.

"No, not really," he said, kissing the top of the baby's fuzzy head.

"Well, get the hell out anyway," Chris snarled, apparently still pissed that he'd kept the whole New York episode to himself.

"It was none of your business so get over it," he said, turning his head to give Jessica a mock glare as the little girl reached for his nose, apparently still hellbent on getting revenge for the game they'd played earlier.

"You should have told us," Chris said, apparently deciding to take up where his father had left off, bitching him out about loyalty and all that other bullshit that he didn't owe any of them.

"But, I didn't," he pointed out with a shrug.

"You should have-"

"Oh, my God!" Izzy snapped, cutting off her mate. "He never tells us anything! Either get me a Coke or let it go! You know this was just a job to him!"

Kale didn't say anything, just continued to hold CJ in his arms. He didn't bother telling them that this was anything but a job to him, that after he saw what that piece of shit had done to Cloe that he'd decided to give her the one thing that he'd swore he'd never give to another woman.

His protection.

For the rest of his life, Cloe and her children would be his to protect and watch over. Her children, God help him, would make it to their immortality. As much as it pained him to protect more Pytes, he didn't have a choice. He couldn't protect the mother and not the children, couldn't let Cloe experience the pain of losing a child. As far as the rest of the shifter population was concerned, Cloe belonged to him.

"Is no one getting me a Coke?" Izzy demanded when the silence in the room thickened to the point of danger.

As one, both men turned their glares at the small woman breastfeeding her newborn baby daughter and snapped, "No!"

Izzy looked pointedly away with her little nose in the air. "Then I hate you both," she said with an uppity sniffle that had them both rolling their eyes and their lips twitching despite the tension in the room.

She was just so damn cute sometimes.

"If you want our help then you're going to start sharing," Chris announced, ruining his, semi, good mood.

"No," he said immediately, because he didn't need their help.

"How exactly do you plan on finding the other Pytes without our help?" Chris asked, sounding genuinely curious as he carefully sat down on the chair by the large bed.

"The same way that I handle any other job," he said, pressing a baby kiss against CJ's head before he carefully laid the sleeping baby on the bed as he stood up, making sure to put a pillow on either side of him to keep him safe.

"And how's that?"

"Sorry," he said, leaning over the babies and pressing a kiss against Izzy's head, ignoring the little grumble she muttered in response, "but that's a trade secret."

———

"How is she?"

Christofer looked up from his quickly cooling glass of blood and shrugged. "As good as can be expected I guess."

Which wasn't saying much.

For the past few hours he'd held her in his arms while she'd laid there, staring off into space, appearing lost to the world. She hadn't moved or spoken since she'd broken down. He'd dried her off, dressed her and tucked her into bed after he coaxed her into taking a little blood from him. Once she was done, she'd closed her eyes and drifted off, all the fight in her gone.

She was lost and he had no idea how to bring her back.

Ephraim nodded as he grabbed a glass and poured blood into it. He took a sip, cringing at the cold metallic taste as he sat down across from Christofer at the kitchen table.

"What's your plan now?" he asked, taking another sip before he pushed the glass away with a disgusted shake of his head.

"You mean now that my mate is no longer being hunted by some sick, psychotic piece of shit?" Christofer asked with a humorless laugh. "I have no idea what we're going to do now."

"You know that you're welcome to stay here as long as you want," Ephraim reminded him.

"I know and I appreciate that but-"

"But, you want a home of your own," Ephraim finished for him with an easy smile. "That's understandable."

"I just have no idea how we're going to manage that," he admitted, dropping his gaze back down to the cup of blood he'd been toying with for the past two hours.

"Because of the bounty?"

He sighed heavily as he sat back in his chair. "I'd actually forgotten about that."

"No matter where you go, Christofer, you need to be careful. They can't kill you, but they can bring you to your knees."

By hurting Cloe was left unsaid, but they both knew that she was his greatest weakness now. That is until their son came. Then there would be two people with the power to destroy him.

"Do you want to stay here until after the baby is born?" Ephraim offered and he knew that he should take him up on his offer, but he couldn't.

Staying here would just be a constant reminder of the world they lived in, the dangers and everything that had happened to Cloe. She deserved a home of her own, some peace. He owed her a chance to be happy, a chance to raise their child away from all of this.

"No," he said, shaking his head as he swirled the blood in his cup, "I think it would be better to get her out of here before the baby is born."

Ephraim opened his mouth, no doubt to argue, but in the end he simply nodded. "At least let me ask the Council to set you both up somewhere safe."

"Thank you," he said, looking up and meeting Ephraim's kind gaze. It went against what his father had taught him, leaving it up to someone else to take care of what was his, but he knew when he was over his head. He didn't have the first clue about finding a home that would be safe from demons, shifters and vampires. This man did and he'd be foolish to refuse his help.

Ephraim nodded as he got up to get a fresh glass of blood. "We'll find you something in the morning."

SIXTY-FIVE

One Week Later........

"How are you feeling?"

"Good," she mumbled, watching as the small town's busy road disappeared and was quickly replaced by a winding country road.

"Are you okay with this?" he asked, caressing the back of her hand with his thumb as he continued to drive towards what would be their home.

"Yes," she said, although she wasn't so sure that she was.

Only a few months ago she was on her own, living life on the go with no one and nothing holding her back and now.....

Now she no longer had a reason to run. Her nightmares were a thing of the past. She was in love, expecting a baby, heading towards her new future, one that had been chosen for her, would live forever and she felt oddly...disappointed. Everything had been decided for her. There had been no planning, no agonizing over the details, researching, getting excited about planning her future, nothing. The same could be said for her relationship with Christofer.

There'd been some excitement, but she'd found herself falling in love with him without him having to romance her. Not that she was a hopeless romantic or anything, but shouldn't they have experienced the anxiety of dating and falling in love? Of not knowing what the future held? The blood exchange had ruined all of that.

There would be no romance.

No chance of experiencing the ups and downs of falling in love, because it was simply impossible to love him anymore than she already did. He was her rock, her heart and soul and that should make her happy that she'd found the one person meant for her, and she was, it was just that....

She inwardly sighed as she admitted to herself that she wanted it all. She wanted him to sweep her off her feet, to bring her flowers, chocolate, to see really horrible romance movies, to go for walks on the beach, enjoy candlelit baths with him after a romantic dinner. She wanted the dream, her Prince Charming trying to win her hand. Instead, her Prince Charming had captured her heart by being everything that she needed. She loved him so much and couldn't imagine life without him. She had no problems with spending the rest of her life with him, she just wanted.......

More.

They were going to have a child in a few months and once that happened they'd most likely already be settled into their new life. There would be no chance to enjoy their time together for another eighteen years at least. She just wanted to-

"Where are we going?" she asked, her brows furrowing in confusion as she slapped her hands against

the dashboard in an attempt to keep herself upright as Christofer did a u-turn in the middle of the road.

"I can't do this," he said, shaking his head as he headed back the way they'd come.

"Do what?" she asked, already deciding that if he was having second thoughts about them after making her fall in love with him and knocking her up that she was going to go for his-

"This."

Yup, she was definitely going to have to rip his balls off just as soon as he pulled over and shut the engine off.

"It's a little too late for that, don't you think?" she pointed out through gritted teeth.

He shook his head, keeping his focus on the road. "No, it's not."

"You want to fill me in before I start having paranoid thoughts about being left by the side of the road with a kid in tow?" she suggested, dropping her hands and sitting back to-

Squeal as he suddenly veered off the road, slammed the brakes and threw the truck in park. Panting hard, she found herself sitting there, gripping her seatbelt tightly as she stared straight ahead, watching as the dust began to settle around the truck.

"Stop doing that!" she snapped, closing her eyes as she swallowed in an attempt to catch her breath.

For several minutes he didn't say anything and her pounding heart thanked him for that. While they sat there, him staring off into space and her trying to calm down, she studied him. He sat there, gripping the wheel, his jaw locked and pointedly not looking at her while dread filled her. He couldn't be doing this to her. Not now, not after she'd allowed herself to fall in love with him. He just......he couldn't.

"I love you, Cloe," he started off saying and just like that, she knew that it was over.

"You fucking bastard," she said, shaking her head in disgust as she reached down and struggled to release her seatbelt, but the damn thing refused to release her.

"Cloe-"

"I don't want to hear it," she snapped, struggling with the damn seatbelt. Why the hell wasn't it releasing her? She needed to get out of here before he could say another word. She didn't want to hear this.

God, she'd been so stupid to fall in love with him, she berated herself as her hands shook and her sight went red. She should have never-

"Shhhh," Christofer said, reaching over and releasing the seatbelt for her. Before she could make her escape he'd picked her up and pulled her onto his lap, forcing her to straddle him and sit there as he broke her heart.

"Let me go, Christofer!"

"Never," he whispered, leaning in to kiss her, but she turned her head, refusing to allow him to kiss her and make this worse.

When she tried to move off his lap, he reached up and cupped her face so that he could lean forward and rest his forehead against hers. "I can't do this, mein Schatz. I'm sorry. I love you so damn much, but I can't just meekly walk into this future and put my dreams on hold again. I can't do it."

"Maybe you should have thought about that before you got me pregnant," she bit out angrily as she attempted once more to get off his lap, but he refused to let her go.

He ignored her struggles as he tilted his head and brushed his lips against hers. "I want to see the world with you, mein Schatz," he whispered softly against her lips.

"W-what?" she asked, feeling herself soften in his arms.

He pulled back so that he could look in her eyes as he explained, "I've always wanted to see the world, visit historical sights, famous museums and to see what I could do with my art, but now," he smiled as his eyes devoured her, "now I want to take you with me. I want to take you to fancy French restaurants, to walk with you through the Highlands, to make love to you in some ridiculously expensive Italian villa, to hold you in my arms while we watch the sun set on a different continent, to go for midnight swims with you and to make love to you on a beach."

"There is just so much that I want to do with you," he admitted hoarsely. "I want to have a life with you, to raise a family with you, but first-"

"You want to see the world?" she guessed with a wobbly smile.

"Yes," he said, before rushing on to explain, "I want this life with you, the one where we plant some roots and watch our sons grow into men, but I need to do this with you now, because I don't think I'll be able to survive the next eighteen years without knowing how it feels to have salt water lapping at our toes while I make love to you on the beach."

"And if I say no?" she asked, having absolutely no plans on refusing this man.

"Then I'll turn this truck back around and we'll go start our lives."

"And you'd be okay with that?" she asked, watching him as he nodded.

"I'd do anything to make you happy, mein Schatz," he swore as he sat back, patiently waiting for her answer.

One look at the expression on his face and she knew that he would give up his dreams for her in a heartbeat. In that moment she knew that he truly loved her, which was a good thing since she was head over heels in love with the brooding bastard.

Smiling, she leaned in and asked, "So, where should we go first?"

"Where do you want to go?" he asked, his deep voice sending tremors through her body and making her toes curl with pleasure. Speaking of toes......

"How about the beach........."

EPILOGUE

Three months later.....
French Riviera

"I'm fat," Cloe said, pouting as she nibbled on some fancy French pastry that he wasn't even going to attempt to name out of fear that he would say the wrong name and spark her interest, resulting in him making another midnight run to the all the bakeries in the area.

"You're beautiful," he told her, leaning in to press a kiss against her forehead while he placed his hand over the very noticeable baby bump that she was now sporting.

"I'm fat," she muttered pathetically as she took another bite of the decadent dessert and adjusted the towel she'd wrapped around her after her bath.

"Beautiful," he corrected her, pulling away and picking up his pencil stub from the patio table as he returned his focus back to his sketchpad.

"You're just saying that out of fear that my hormones will make me homicidal again," she grumbled, making him chuckle.

"You are truly dangerous, mein Schatz," he admitted, only half teasing.

When she didn't say anything for several minutes, he became understandably worried, afraid that he'd somehow caused her to cry again. He looked up only to find the woman that he loved, *the very hormonal woman that he loved*, sending him the look that he was all too familiar with by now.

Knowing what was coming next, he placed his sketchpad and pencil down. He reached for her only to have her push his hands away as she stood up and dropped the towel, exposing her back to the moonlight as she leaned forward and placed her hands against the stone wall that surrounded their private villa. When she sent him a sultry smile over her shoulder, he found himself going to her.

"How?" he asked, not bothering to clarify his meaning since she knew exactly what he was asking.

"No waiting," she said, already panting as she spread her legs and arched her back, letting him know just how desperately she wanted him.

"No waiting?" he asked, pressing a kiss against her shoulders as he reached down and freed his eager erection.

"No waiting," she confirmed, pushing back against him in demand.

He moved the tip of his cock down until it was touching her wet slit and then with a groan, he pushed in, her velvety wet walls welcoming him home. He pressed another kiss against her shoulder as he pulled back until just the tip of his cock was inside her. "God, I love your hormones," he admitted, licking his lips as he placed his hands by hers on the stone wall and slid back in.

"Better enjoy it while it lasts," she said on a choked laugh as he pushed all the way in.

"I plan to," he admitted, spreading his legs just a little more so that he could take his mate, his wife now, on a slow ride.

She dropped her head back against his chest, moaning as he slowly fucked her. The sounds of the tide coming in mixing with her moans was like music to his ears. He would never tire of hearing her moan his name while her tight sheath gripped his cock, caressing it like a fist and robbing him of rational thought.

"I love you," he gasped against her neck as she reached back and threaded her fingers through his hair, holding him prisoner and no doubt hoping that he'd finally give in and give her what she'd been demanding for months now.

His bite.

Every time they made love, she tried to coax him into biting her, but he always refused, too afraid that he'd go too far, but not tonight. After he'd overheard the real reason why she was so desperate for his bite while she'd spoken with Madison over the phone tonight, he'd realized that she needed this. She needed to know that she was safe with him and even though she'd assured Madison that she'd never felt safer and more loved, he needed to show her that she would never have a reason to fear him.

"What do you want, mein Schatz?" he whispered near her ear.

"You know what I want," she moaned.

"Tell me anyway," he said, smiling when she let out a vicious little growl.

"You'll just say no again," she reasoned, tightening her grip on his hair as he continued to slowly thrust inside her.

"Try me," he whispered softly, pressing a kiss against her neck and nearly groaning when she released a little tremor that had her sheath tightening around his cock.

"Will you do it?" she asked, her voice trembling as she rewarded his cock with her juices.

"Yes," he said, mentally calculating the number of bags that he'd gorged on while she'd bathed to prepare himself and wondering if he should sneak back into the kitchen to down another bag when she took the decision out of his hands.

"Then do it," she said breathlessly, tilting her head to the side, exposing her neck for his bite.

He leaned down and pressed a kiss against the sun kissed skin and said, "Not there."

"What?" she asked, sounding confused as he slowly pulled out of her.

"Turn around and spread your legs," he ordered, already dropping to his knees in front of her.

Licking her lips nervously, she slowly turned around and leaned back against the wall and after a slight pause, she spread her legs for him.

He nearly came from the sight of the glistening pink lips between her legs. "Beautiful," he murmured reverently as he leaned in and pressed a kiss against her slit. "Absolutely beautiful," he whispered, as he cupped her thighs and gently pushed them apart.

"Christofer," she moaned, threading her fingers back through his hair as he decided to take a little taste of the sweet little pussy that he craved day and night.

He worked his tongue inside her, loving the way she struggled to keep still, but every few seconds she'd lose a little more control and rock her hips against his tongue. He hoped this would be enough to distract her and to give her some pleasure. He'd done this to a lot of women in his past, but never for a woman like Cloe, who knew what could happen if he lost control.

Knowing just how important this was, he withdrew his tongue and moved his mouth to her swollen nub. He took it in his mouth and gently suckled as he flicked the tip of his tongue over the tiny bud of nerves, but it was enough to get Cloe close. When she started to tremble and her breaths became choppy he made his move.

He moved his mouth away, making sure to replace his mouth with his fingers out of fear that she would tense up, preparing for his bite, something that could turn this into another nightmare. Careful not to disturb her pleasure, he gently suckled the pulse point near her sex as his fangs slowly descended in his mouth. With one last prayer that this wouldn't send her screaming, he bit down.

Cloe screamed as liquid ecstasy poured down his throat. He prepared himself for her attack, expected it, but instead she brushed his hand aside and replaced it with her own, working her clitoris in time with his mouth. The scent of her arousal intensified, nearly smothering him as he continued to feed from her. He could hear her fingers working her wet folds, the sound erotic and dangerous as it threatened to make him lose control.

Just when he didn't think that he could take any-more, he found his mouth suddenly dislodged and his back hitting the cold patio tiles and his cock once again sheathed in Cloe's body.

"I take it that you liked it," he said with a strained chuckle as he sat up and wrapped his arms around his mate.

"It was okay," she said, panting.

"Liar," he chuckled, as she wrapped her slim arms around his neck and used the move to ride him.

"Shut up, Hoodie," she said with a mock scowl as she leaned in and brushed her lips against his.

"Shutting up," he mumbled with a grin as he felt Cloe's lips curl up into a matching grin.

As she kissed him, he couldn't help but wonder what he'd ever done to deserve such a wonderful life.

———

He really needed a vacation, he decided as he slammed the silver tipped dagger into the heart of the werewolf, who'd been a heartbeat away from crashing through the woods and going after the couple making love on the patio, again. When the werewolf released a whimper that threatened to alert Christofer and Cloe of his presence, he twisted the dagger, making sure to cut the heart in two, instantly killing the large beast.

When he was sure that the beast was dead, he pulled the knife out of the body and shoved the beast into the pit he'd dug earlier when he'd spotted the shifter following the woman that he'd stupidly claimed as his. Every time he hunted the couple down to the check on them, he found them being hunted by demons, shifters and vampires. He shook his head in disgust as he heard the couple start up all over again.

This honeymoon was exhausting him as well as giving him another reason to hate Pytes. As he picked up the shovel and started burying the body, he decided that they damn well better name this child after him to make up for all the bullshit that they were putting him through.

Bastards.......

Williams Mansion............

Karma really was the best, Danni decided with a pleased little sigh as she sent Chris flying across the room.

He landed with a grunt and a loud groan that put a smile on her lips. She really couldn't help it. For too many months the big bastard and his father had taken great pleasure from "toughening her up" and now.......

Now, she was savoring the sweet revenge that came from a combination of powerful Pyte blood and years of Sentinel training. God, life was good. Could it get any better?

"Kill. Me," Ephraim mumbled a few feet away from her.

Smiling, she decided that yes, life could definitely get better. She moved to get in a few more minutes of sweet revenge before she had to meet Caine for patrol only to stop when she saw that Jessica was already heading towards her grandfather to finish him off with a few new nose grabs and giggles. She looked at Chris and considered going a few more rounds with him, but the fact that he could barely move kind of wrecked it for her.

"I'm going to kill that SOB for giving you his blood," Chris mumbled pathetically.

"Getting a good work out?" Caine asked as he walked into the training room, chuckling when both men flipped him off.

Ignoring them, she rushed over to Caine, only pausing for a split second to kick Chris, and wrapped her arms around her mate. He pulled her into his arms with a pleased smile. Three months later and it still felt like a dream.

Her cancer was gone. Completely gone. She had her blood tested every week and so far, nothing. She couldn't get over how good she felt, how strong and fast she was and she wasn't the only one. Caine had benefited from her blood as well. He was stronger and faster than ever. They both healed faster and needed less blood. They weren't sure if this was going to last forever so for right now, they were going to enjoy it and all its benefits, she thought with a smirk as she turned her head to shoot Chris a wink as the large Sentinel struggled to get to his feet, only to fall flat on his face with another groan.

"I think that we can safely say that she's toughened up now," Ephraim said weakly as Jessica attacked his nose.

"I can't believe that you would do this to your own family," Chris muttered with a pout as he raised his tattooed wrist as a pointed reminder that they'd marked themselves to show their support. It was sweet, very sweet and touched her deeply, but....

That still hadn't been enough to save them from a well-deserved ass whooping.

"You want to go upstairs before we have to head out?" Caine offered, brushing a kiss against her lips as he reached up and cupped her jaw. She caught a glimpse of his matching tattoo before she closed her eyes and savored his touch.

"We don't have time," she grumbled, wishing that that they'd taken Ephraim up on his offer to patrol for them tonight.

"We can switch with Ephraim," Caine suggested, nibbling on her bottom lip.

"I-I can't feel my legs," Ephraim muttered, earning a chuckle from Caine and an eye roll from her as they broke apart to glare at the big baby.

Before she got a chance to mock him, Madison walked into the large room, looking grim and close to tears. She swallowed nervously as she weakly held up a blood stained piece of paper.

"Madison?" Ephraim said, his paltry wounds instantly forgotten as he got to his feet and quickly limped over to his mate. "What's wrong?"

"He's got her," she said, choking back a sob.

"Who?" Ephraim asked, gently cupping his mate's face as he searched for answers.

"Jill! The bastard has my sister!"

54005423R10328

Made in the USA
Columbia, SC
24 March 2019